Welcome to the Fun House

By Jack Corbett

Nirvana Publishing
11/26/2011

Published by Nirvana Publishing Company

1st Edition

Front cover design and art work by Ludwig Johner,
http://www.oasislivingandcare.com

Back cover design—Jack Corbett

For information, address:
PO BOX 3181
Prescott, AZ 86302

http://www.alphapro.com
jack.corbett@gmail.com

Copyright   February 2011   by Jack Corbett

ISBN- 978-0-9647143-1-1

Table of Contents

Introduction

There is no place on earth like Pattaya, home to over 5000 bars and over 100 strip clubs called Go-go bars, with the widest open night life in the world. But there's another side of Pattaya that hardly gets a glance from the sex tourists who never venture far from their favorite water holes. And that's the Pattaya that offers outstanding sights and diversions that extend far beyond the commonly held image of Pattaya as a Sodom and Gomorrah that's fit only for the world's most dedicated reprobates. There's several world class zoos, the 600 acre Nong Nooch Tropical Garden, the Sanctuary of Truth, Buddha Hill, Koh Larn Island with its magnificent Beaches, the Elephant Village where one can enjoy hour long elephant rides through the jungle, Underwater World, the new Central Festival Shopping Mall which is billed as Asia's largest beach front department store along with a huge selection of ethnic restaurants from all over the world.

All of that is not the subject of this book, however. "Welcome to the Fun House" is all about the seamy side of Pattaya, about the men in search of endless sexual pleasure and the women supplying it. It's about the schemers, the misfits, the alcoholics living at the Fun House, and the Thai bar girls whose main goal in life is to separate their customers from as much cash in as short a time as possible.

I've been living in Pattaya for six years and when I started looking around at many of the people living around me I've noticed that I'm surrounded by a lot of men in their forties all the way into their seventies who behave as if they were living on a college campus in a party school where 40 % of the students flunk out during their first year. The only difference is the college students seem to be a lot more mature. One can only imagine how such college students would behave if they never had to study, had a lot more money to spend, and were surrounded by an almost infinite supply of beautiful sexy available women. I was reminded of the movie, "Animal House".

Although the college frat boys in "Animal House" resemble many college party animal types, such a concentration of misfits hardly exists in real life. And so it is with the "Fun House" in which nearly every resident in the book is each in his own way, more than a little demented, the police are all corrupt, and the Thai women are hardened to the point of being without redemption.

The characters in the book are all fictitious. And so is the basic plot line in which some of the characters react to a murder that never actually happened that I am personally aware of. I don't think that anyone could seriously believe that the police would try covering up such a crime--certainly not here in the Land of Smiles.

If after reading "Welcome to the Fun House" one might think that I have an overall negative impression of Thailand or of Thais in general, just keep in mind that I own a condo here and that I am still living in Thailand. If living in the U.S. was so terrific I'd back living there. As for Pattaya, one of my German friends kept pointing out to me how dirty and disorganized the place was and how there were so many idiot tourists running around compared to other places in Thailand where the air is so much cleaner and the ocean isn't polluted after telling me, "I don't think Pattaya is for me". He's right of course. Thailand has some of the most pristine beaches in the world while Chiang Mai, Thailand's second largest city, is much cleaner without having the same quick buck atmosphere or Pattaya's insane motorists. But Chiang Mai isn't just an hour away from one of the world's best international airports. And those unforgettably beautiful beach destinations do not begin to have Pattaya's excellent infrastructure with its world class hospitals, excellent bookstores, wide variety of cuisine, excellent shopping, and world class nearby attractions. And none of these other places can provide as much as a fraction of Pattaya's night life. For that matter not even Bangkok comes close. Warts and all, Pattaya has to be one of the most interesting places in the world to live.

Collision Course

Except for its concrete reinforced hull, the Ardatov was just another Russian fishing boat, but its altered hull had been transformed to deliver a message to Norwegian authorities in no uncertain terms to relax their restrictions on Russian fishing interests. To the captain of the Ardatov, the Norwegian vessel had no right to stop the Russian trawler, yet that was exactly what it was doing by boring down on the Russian fisherman to inspect the fish it had onboard, its registration papers, and its ship's log. Sergei ordered his helmsman to bring his bow around to intercept the rapidly closing Norwegian at full speed.

As the Gynt bore down on the Ardatov Mickel watched the trawler abruptly turning to face him. With the distance between the two vessels narrowing rapidly the bow of the much larger Russian trawler started to loom ominously above his cutter's low slung silhouette.

"Starboard. Move, move, move," Mickel screamed to his helmsman standing next to him on the bridge as the front of the Russian trawler towered over them.

Luckily his helmsman had already anticipated the order by starting evasive action on his own. Mickel braced himself as the Gynt started to break suddenly to the right as the bow of the Russian trawler bore down on them like a tidal wave of death that would disintegrate everything in its path. Ninety meters in length, the Ardatov was one of the largest fishing trawlers Mickel had ever encountered. Its sheer mass dwarfed the Gynt which had been built for speed and maneuverability. With its concrete reinforced bow the Ardatov would have easily crushed the Norwegian cutter, but Mickel's boat was a Hauk class vessel that had been designed to initiate and withstand the most violent turns.

The Russian ship thundered past his port side in a near miss and shot past them. Mickel breathed a sigh of relief, and then he calmly spoke into the intercom, "Arm the torpedo."

From this point on, his tactics would change. He'd no longer attempt to close in on the Russian trawler–not until it was dead in the water, incapable of moving. He'd need at least several hundred meters between the two vessels before he could initiate a successful torpedo launch. His mind focused upon a single imperative with no other thought intruding upon it–the destruction of his enemy. The words "Get ready to fire" were already on his mouth as he visualized the transformation of the Russian trawler into a burst of flame.

"No don't. Don't give the order," Lars yelled into his ear.

It had been Lars who had been piloting the Gynt who was still standing next to him looking massive in his greatcoat. Suddenly Mickel felt his helmsman's huge hands shaking his shoulders. "Stop it, Lars. I know what I am doing."

"No you don't. You torpedo those Russians and your career with the Coast Guard's finished. That Russian trawler's bound to be in radio contact with someone. Also it's now customary on such ships to carry a camera in a watertight container that's designed to float. It's got a homing device that emits a signal so it can easily be found in case of a ship wreck. If you unleash a torpedo at those Russians, the incident is bound to be filmed and sealed in that container so even if there's hardly anything left of that trawler the digital film is going to be easily found and then your career is going to be toast."

"You are right, Lars. I want to kill all those sons of bitches right now, but I cannot."

"So you will just have to revert to standard operating procedure. You will have to communicate to those Russians to prepare to be boarded. They will then dutifully stop their ship. We will go on board to inspect the ship and to have a good look at its log. If we find they are doing anything illegal we will force that trawler to follow us into one of our ports and if they are not we will have to just wish them all good luck while sending them on their way. And as far as their trying to ram us, they will simply deny the whole incident ever happened. They will claim they were training a new crewman how to pilot the ship or that they never saw us, or they had a mechanical problem with the ship's steering or whatever."

The whole incident had sent shivers up and down Mickel's spine. If it hadn't been for Lars standing next to him he would have been unable to control his ungovernable temper. Had he been alone on the bridge steering the patrol boat, the Ardatov would have been blown to pieces and his career would now be finished. Mickel had only two weeks left before he could retire. Just two more weeks and it was back to his home in Norway, back on land with no more chilly water cruises for him. He'd be finished putting in his twenty years and he could then start enjoying his pension. He had already paid for his plane ticket to Thailand so he could start enjoying the rest of his life.

Please–dear God please, let this next two weeks go without incident, so I can start calmly planning what I'm going to be doing with the rest of my life.

The Menace from the North

Mickel's concentration on the Japanese fishing trawler was absolute as he viewed it through his Nikon binoculars. To the untrained eye, the boat looked like most other fishing trawlers. One hundred-ninety feet long, with a cargo hauling capacity of six-hundred tons, constructed from white fiberglass, it was typical of thousands of factory trawlers used all over the world. At first Mickel would have passed it off as just another Russian fishing boat fishing in the Norwegian sea. But Mickel's eyes were excellent and his Nikon binoculars were the best that money could buy. He could pick out small inscriptions in Japanese across the bow of the small ship. The location of the head was in Japanese. His instincts told him, *something's wrong here. There are not many Japanese fishing boats in these waters, and this one I've seen before. Just two months ago to be exact.*

Mickel immediately called the helmsman on his ship's intercom, "Move in on that slant-eyed son of a bitch. I want a closer look."

The helmsman obeyed instantly, gunning the Norwegian patrol boat's twin diesel engines to the boat's top speed of 32 knots. When the cutter drew within four hundred meters of the Japanese trawler, Mickel spoke into the intercom a second time. "Stop all engines. I take a look now."

Raising his binoculars to his eyes, it took him only three seconds to make his decision. His crew was out on the deck, ready to take orders, each man recognizing that the time for action had arrived. They all watched Mickel still peering through his binoculars and waited.

"Men. Raise the flag and go get that yellow prick."

It had been standard operating procedure for the Norwegian cutter to fly the Norwegian flag while policing Norway's maritime sphere of influence that extended far out into the into the Barents Sea and Artic Ocean nearly all the way to the North pole. Technically Norway and all other sovereign nations can only claim a scant twelve miles from their coasts as their territorial waters, a distance that had been significantly expanded since the old days when it was just 2 miles—the distance of a cannon shot. But there's also an outer zone that begins where a nation's territorial waters end, which is called the exclusive economic zone. Norway, like most other coastal nations, claimed exclusive control of all economic resources as far out as two-hundred miles outside its territorial limits including all fishing, mining and the pollution of such resources. But Norway goes much farther than enforcing its jurisdiction in Norwegian waters, whether one chooses to call it a 12 mile territorial limit or 200 mile economic zone of interest. As a member of the European Union Norway collaborates with the other members giving all member nations the authority to enforce the EU's fishing laws wherever an offender's fishing boats are intercepted. Fishing vessels violating the common fishing policy of the EU including those that are improperly registered under the EU's maritime laws are recorded in a special blacklist which names the vessel, the country it is registered in, and the cause for its being on the blacklist. The blacklist and the common fishing policy that is observed by all EU nations gives each member nation's Coast Guard absolute police power over all noncompliant vessels regardless of nationality or where they are intercepted.

Mickel detested anyone who threatened Norway's vital resources. Enraged, he ordered "the flag" to be raised. It was obvious to everyone on board that he meant the infamous ship's flag, and not the flag of Norway. On the flag was a picture of an 11th century Viking warrior's head wearing a horned helmet and several lines of text in five different languages, Norwegian, English, Russian, Japanese, and German. The flag read "The Menace from the North" which was the unofficial name of Mickel's vessel. "The Menace from the North" was a name that was not easily forgotten, thanks to Mickel's obsessive zeal in making life miserable for anyone he suspected of over-fishing because according to Mickel's implacable logic the overexploitation of a steadily declining fish population would ultimately result in worldwide famine.

Once the Norwegian cutter had closed in on the Japanese trawler Mickel could see through his binoculars Japanese writing across the ship's stern in addition to what he had already seen on the bow. The painted inscriptions across the stern had long since faded whereas the paint across the bow had been freshly painted. The trawler's name, "Iatsu", had been recently painted on the hull of the boat for a reason, and that reason was two months ago the Iatsu had been the "Yamagatoe". Mickel was sure of it. His almost photographic memory and his strong powers of observation were two of the primary reasons for his being one of the most respected captains in the Norwegian Coast Guard.

Mickel concluded that two months ago the crew of the Yamagatoe had touched up the paint on the boat's bow by painting a white strip over the black lettering of the ship's name that would closely match the white color of the trawler. The crew had then painted "Iatsu" in black lettering across the freshly painted white strip, and that's how the Yamagatoe became the Iatsu.

As far as Mickel was concerned the fishing trawler was illegally fishing–case closed–"It is up to me to hang the bastards." But he still had to gather enough evidence to make it stand up in court once the Japanese captain was officially arraigned on the Norwegian mainland and charged with exceeding his limit of fish.

The Iatsu was a freezer trawler that had been designed to be a virtual factory of the seas. Large scale commercial fishing is a subject the average person never thinks about. But if doesn't take a mental giant to conclude that if a trawler scours several tons of fish off the ocean bottom with its large net, and then releases the net's contents onto the trawler's deck, something must be done with the dying fish before they start to decompose. The solution is as simple as the family freezer. Newly caught fish are cleaned and cut up to customers' specifications, packaged, frozen, and stored until the trawler docks and its cargo is transported to the customer's warehouse. Although a customer's specs might call for fillets of Cod between four and five inches long while another customer's order might call for one half kilo cans of tuna, nothing is left to waste with fish meal and other end products completing the onboard processing.

Large factory trawlers, some much larger than the Iatsu, that are capable of pulling in more than 35 tons of fish with a single tow of the net, had become a major threat to the world's supply of fish. Able to travel thousands of miles from their home ports for weeks on end, national territorial waters could be crossed with impunity as the new breeds of factory boats could simply move on to exploit new waters after depleting entire varieties of fish in those areas it was overfishing. The economic costs from the abrasion of huge fishing nets scouring ocean bottoms, coral and other ocean ecosystems had become incalculable. This caused widespread unemployment in fishing communities dependent on an abundant supply of fish, for unlike the large factory fishing boats, the small fishermen, families and dependent community couldn't simply up and moves to a better ocean.

Norway viewed all violations of the CFP as criminal activity becoming one of the most vigilant countries on the planet in its efforts to constantly monitor all fishing resources within its economic protective zone. Thorough and without compromise, monitoring included sending out inspection teams in specially equipped fishing trawlers to catch up to one-hundred tons in their nets. Scientists would then analyze the various fish species the inspection trawlers brought in to determine which species were increasing or decreasing, the overall health of each species and how much fishing of each variety of fish should be allowed.   All violators of quota limits, boat and company registrations, and sizes of fish they were permitted to catch were subject to immediate arrest by the Norwegian Coast Guard, imprisonment, and large fines.

Mickel's patrol boat was a Hauk, (Hawk) of which 14 had been built to defend Norway's jagged coast line.   120 feet long the Hauk sported twin diesel engines producing 6820 horsepower that were capable of propelling its 24 man crew 31 knots up to 440 miles.   Armed with two torpedo tubes, six Penguin anti-ship missiles, twin surface to air missles and a 40 mm Bofors L7 gun, his Hauk was easily up to just about anything Mickel expected to encounter.   As his Hauk drew up alongside the Japanese trawler, Mickel made several phone calls--one to a fellow chief inspector, a man who also was a great friend of his, who was known affectionately by his peers as Titanic.

"The Iatsu? Sure sure. I know it, said Titantic. "I boarded it just two month ago and inspected the boat's log book. It had nearly met its quota of Arctic Cod."

"Thanks my good friend. I cannot begin to thank you enough. Next time we are in Pattaya together, I will buy you a beer. In fact, many many beers I buy for you."

One of his crewmen brought a megaphone to Mickel whose voice carried loudly over to the Japanese: "We are boarding you now and do not fuck with me."

Turning to his crew he shouted: "Pull up alongside and use the grappling hooks. We are boarding that little Japanese shit, so help me God."

Once the crew of the Norwegian cutter had pulled alongside the Japanese trawler and latched the two vessels together with grappling hooks and ropes, six powerfully built Norwegians jumped out onto the Japanese vessel and headed straight to the cargo hold where all the fish were kept.   After briefly looking over the ships catch one of the crewman came out on deck and shouted across to the remaining crewman on the cutter.

"There's over ten tons of fresh Arctic Cod here."

Mickel yelled into the megaphone at the Japanese captain, "How come you almost catch your quota of Arctic Cod two months ago and here you have 10 tons of it now. And why do you change name on your ship?"

"Me no understand English," the Japanese captain called out. "Me Japan."

"Bullshit. Even I understand English," Mickel screamed back at the Japanese captain--"And I just a stupid Norwegian sailor."

"English no understand," the Japanese captain replied a second time.

"Well comprehend this or otherwise my men help you. Understand? Get your log book and come on my boat now. And I don't mean two minutes from now. I mean now. And don't be telling me I gotta wait while you have to take a shit because I really don't give a shit."

Then Mickel turned to one of his men standing next to him and said quietly to him, "Get out the oil. Let's give this little man a nice Norwegian reception."

It took the Japanese captain sixty seconds to have one of his men retrieve the vessel's log book from the pilot house and hand it to him on deck. By this time one of Mickel's crew members had poured oil on the cutter's deck in the exact spot everyone knew the Japanese captain would be jumping onto from his own boat. While several Norwegians held the two vessels tightly together to keep the gap between them from spreading in the ocean's swell the Japanese captain jumped into the middle of the oil slick on the cutter's deck. The captain's feet suddenly went out from under him as he sprawled headfirst onto the deck.

"Welcome to my little Norway, you little midget, Mickel said to the prostrate Japanese lying practically beneath him.

Mickel stared down at the scrawny Japanese captain from the full height of his more than six foot frame. His eyes were icy blue, like the hard cruel waters of the North Atlantic. Although he was now close to fifty, Mickel was still a trim two hundred pounds with large shoulder muscles and arm muscles of tempered steel.

"I have special place for you my little guest of honor." Mickel spoke down at the Japanese as the man struggled to his feet, his face a white sheet of embarrassment.

The Menace from the North spoke to his crew through clenched teeth. "Get this little Jappo's guest room ready." The Japanese captain's eyes suddenly changed from embarrassment to fear. Ever since the Norwegian patrol boat had hoisted its "Menace from the North flag" he expected the worse. He had heard the rumors about the Coast Guard patrol boat's unorthodox methods of enforcing Norway's strict fishing laws while Norwegian officials turned a blind eye to Mickel's unorthodox methods. Mickel and his superiors tacitly agreed that anyone using high volume factory trawlers to break the law were nothing more than pirates.

"We must always remember how they used to hang pirates," Mickel had kept reminding his crewmembers. The point was not lost on his men who never forgot that both Mickel and his superiors longed for the good old days.

Nonetheless, the Japanese captain had not quite believed the rumors considering them to be just so many modern fairy tales for the weak minded. He didn't understand one word of Norwegian but one look into Mickel's pitiless eyes as he listened to Mickel barking out orders in a guttural no-nonsense accent told him that there really was a Menace from the North, but it wasn't the Norwegian cutter. It was Mickel, the 21st century incarnation of the Viking warrior. The captain looked once again at Mickel's face seeing eyes that looked right through his skull, and saw a man who would have gladly raped all the women and killed all the men of any village in his path if only he had been born a thousand years earlier.

Two of his crew swung the cutter's 40 mm Bofors gun across the Iatsu's deck as four burly men brandished 7:62 millimeter automatic rifles. Two men came up from below the deck. One of them saluted Mickel and said, "The guest room is ready Sir."

Mickel shouted in English to the Japanese on the fishing vessel while patting the muzzle of the 40 mm Bofors gun: "You know what this gun will do. It will go right through your ship and it will go through your ship's bulkheads and make matchwood of your bridge. It will open big holes in your hull and you will all be swimming in the water while your boat sinks. So I take your captain with me and you will follow my orders or die."

Mickel followed two of his crew escorting the Japanese captain below the deck. The little storage room was ready for its new occupant. Just five feet in length it was too short for the Japanese to comfortably stretch out in. As one of the Norwegians opened the door to the storage room, the putrid odor of rotten fish poured out of the small confined area. The rotten fish were an entire two week's leftovers from the galley Mickel had ordered his crew to save for such "just in case situations".

The Japanese captain recoiled in horror when he saw the two pillows that had been laid out for him on the storage room's floor. At each end of the little cubbyhole was a single steel cage full of rotting fish. But the Norwegians had been kind enough to put a thick towel across the top of each cage so that he'd have something soft upon which he could rest his head. It would be up to him which cage he'd use for his pillow. Since it was less than three feet high, he couldn't sit up in the storage hold either-- which meant that he'd be forced to sleep with his head just inches above a few hundred pounds of rotting fish.

The Menace from the North had stopped the Japanese fishing trawler two hundred miles from the Arctic Circle. It would take the Norwegian cutter a day and a half to tow the Iatsu to the nearest port where the Japanese ship captain and his crew would be met by Norwegian authorities. The Iatsu would be impounded while its crew and captain would be arrested, thrown into jail, and only then would they be allowed to seek legal representation. But Norway was among one of the most civilized countries on earth so everything would be handed with the utmost diplomatic protocol. From then on everything would be handled in a proper court of law. And by the time the Norwegian cutter got to port, the Japanese ship captain would be let out of the stinking storage bin. He would be given a clean shower, the rotten fish would have been thrown overboard and the storage room given a thorough cleaning. Except for the cutter's Norwegian crew there would be no witnesses to back up the Japanese captain's stories, and other than a little bruise here and there from his falling on the deck when his feet had gone out from under him in the slippery oil, there would be no evidence of any physical abuse.

So the entire event never happened. It would just become one more chapter in the legend of the "Menace from the North."

Camelot

When Hermann the German finished building the Baht House he saw what he had done and he was proud. Its walls were thick, its foundation was deep and secure, and its frame was as strong as a Tiger tank. As he paced its seven floors he said to himself, "Well done Hermann." He had aged ten years building his masterpiece which had chronologically taken three years off his life. "The owners will never understand what I've gone through but I love them anyway. The owners don't know what's best for them so I'll just have to decide for them, even if there aren't any owners yet," Hermann said softly to himself.

Hermann the German had arrived in Pattaya just three years ago, full of hope and idealistic notions of what a paradise the place could become. But so had thousands of other Germans before him, who had seen the constantly twisting and curving shoreline with its many rock formations, coves and inlets, and recognized the place's vast potential. It was only 2 hours from Bangkok, which meant close proximity to one of the largest international airports in the world which created a vital link between the Fatherland and a little Germany set in a tropical paradise. But even before these fearless pathfinders came, the Americans had come for R & R during the Vietnam War when Thailand served as a major base for American servicemen. The Americans swiftly turned the former fishing village of Pattaya into what would soon become the world's largest whorehouse. Through the years, the little fishing village exploded in much the same manner that such boom towns of the American West as Dodge City, Abilene, Deadwood, Virginia City, and Tombstone had a hundred years earlier. Like mushrooms the boom towns had sprung up once gold, silver, or other riches were found close-by. And with them came hordes of highwaymen, murderers, thieves, gamblers, con artists, claim jumpers, rustlers, and whores all out for a quick buck while miners and cattlemen settled in to make their fortune. The boom towns started off as tent cities, which later gave way to more permanent communities of wooden or brick houses as dirt streets started to sprawl out in all directions without the slightest concession to urban planning.

And so it was with Pattaya. The whores came to service young American servicemen who had arrived from half way around the world to fight a war they never had any business being in. But for Pattaya it wasn't gold or silver or cattle that brought in the dregs of Thai society. It would be the constant flow of Westerners that had started with these young American soldiers looking for cheap sex that would soon turn the place into the fastest growing boom town in Southeast Asia.

Knowledgeable cognoscenti often joked that Pattaya's foundation is a solid bedrock of cum stains. And through the years as the numbers of whores and sex starved men increased, Pattaya became known as Fun City, a place that is still being called a Disneyland for adults except the rides are much longer and the lines are shorter.

The beaches started to fill up with litter and because of the torrent of men coming to Pattaya for cheap sex and the surge of women willing to supply it, the city started to grow helter-skelter in all directions. And never mind the legality of it all, for although the city major and his henchmen were theoretically responsible for curbing the huge growth of prostitution and keeping the beaches clean and in good repair, they found it to be far more profitable to turn a blind eye to what good government is supposed to be doing.

And so the Germans came, and when they saw how chaotic the place had become, they simply couldn't stand it, for the Germans are a very strange race of people. If it wasn't for all the good sex that was on sale practically everywhere, the English, Americans, and Australians would have simply run as fast as they could to find other promised lands. But the Germans saw how hopeless the place had become and instead of becoming filled with despair they rose up together and cried out in unison, "Something must be done about this mess and we are just the people to do it."

And the Germans tried and they tried, but no matter what Teutonic efficiency and great planning they put towards such a hopeless task, all their hard work came to nothing. The problem was that even though once upon a time Germans considered themselves to be the master race with considerable justification, the Thais have always considered Thailand to be the foremost country in the world. But although they've treated this conception as gospel for hundreds of years, the evidence indicated that Thailand is a number one contender only when it's being compared to Cambodia, Burma, and Lichtenstein. Thailand is an insular country that is controlled by a rich and educated elite with the bulk of its population being too uneducated to be able to point Cambodia out on a map even though Cambodia lies next to Thailand. So it is very easy to understand how these Germans, who had previously been successful at producing the first jet fighter and the first practical rocket for military use, could not make cream rise to the top in Thailand.

The Germans failed to add order and stability to Thailand in a defeat that can only be compared to their defeat at Stalingrad at the hands of the Russians. After all, it really didn't matter to the average Thai if the Germans could build great cars or if they were brilliant engineers, architects, or successful businessmen who are supremely gifted at making superb products at a decent price, because the average Thai kept thinking to himself, "Who are these square heads to teach us anything? We already know everything there is that's worth knowing."

And that was exactly the whole point, Herman kept repeating to himself day after day, night after sleepless night. *Here in Thailand I have an almost perfect climate, where I can swim or take comfortable walks nearly every day—a little too hot—well perhaps. But I can stay outdoors 365 days a year if I want. And the women—my God—this is the best place in the world to find beautiful women. Thousands of them so slender and cute and most of them are willing to go with men for the price of a lunch at McDonalds for two back in Germany. There's great shopping, excellent bookstores and terrific restaurants but these people are so unwilling to even consider that an entire world exists outside Thailand which has different ways of doing things. I really don't know how long I can tolerate such obliviousness.* Yet Hermann kept thinking how materialistic and "correct thinking" most Germans had become. He loved the carefreeness of most Thais he had met in Pattaya and their valuing the present over the future, but at the same time he despised their complete lack of accountability for their actions.

He had played his part well back in Germany, working hard all his life, of being logical and accountable so that all his decisions could have a good outcome. But now looking back on it, he found a strange emptiness welling up inside him. He had accumulated a sizeable fortune which was far more than enough for a comfortable retirement. *But for what?* He kept asking himself. Memories of a failed marriage continued to haunt him. He had bought a nice house in Hamburg and grown to liking it more with each passing year. He had particularly loved the den where he kept all his books in shelves that rose all the way from the floor to the ceiling—bookshelves that completely surrounded him when he sat in an exquisite leather couch far removed from the thoughts of his many successful businesses and what he had to do and keep on doing to ensure that they would remain successful. But, although he could keep his thoughts while at home far away from the demands of his work, his house was close to an underground train station just a few minutes away from his office. He could read his morning paper going to work while avoiding the rush hour traffic on his way home. But his marriage had changed all that.

His garage, which had only been large enough to accommodate a single car, wasn't big enough, his wife had told him. She needed her own car even though his BMW 325 XI remained garaged most of the time. And the yard, which measured just 20 by 40 meters, wasn't nearly large enough. Against his better judgment he wound up selling his house in order to buy a larger, more expensive home in the suburbs. The short walk to the underground train station had become a bus ride through heavy rush hour traffic. It was either that or driving his own car to work. And although he had kept his beloved BMW 325 XI, his wife had found reasons for buying something larger and more prestigious. A much more powerful 700 series BMW soon gave way to an even more potent Mercedes which could easily seat five in sumptuous leather appointed surroundings.

His yard was large enough to require the services of a part time gardener, which on reflection Hermann felt was just a small step above having to have a full time gardener. Many of his neighbors had even larger yards than his which irked his wife because she could not boast of having to employ someone full time.

When his wife asked him to buy an even larger house, Hermann had had enough. Thankfully the pair never had children so at least he didn't have to contend with that by the time the divorce was underway. He wound up selling his house just to make a down payment on his settlement to her. So when it came time to deciding where he would live next, once it was time to move out of his temporary quarters in a hotel close to his office, he started to look at other options.

He had been selfish and so had most of the people who had lived around him, Hermann decided. He had done well in his business dealings, but where had it gotten him? His wife had gotten fatter and fatter with each passing year while it seemed that the fatter she had gotten, the more voracious her demands had become for more material things. Above all, he still missed his den in the first house he had bought and all the carefree rides he had taken on his way to and from his office while reading his paper or observing his fellow passengers as he tried to discover what made each of them tick.

He found in most of them the same attitude of "I come first and to hell with everybody else." Meanwhile attending to the management of his businesses had started to bore him. So he had decided to take a long vacation trying to get away from it all.

He had found an article in a travel magazine extolling the wonderful scuba diving in Koh Tao and the Simian Islands, and after traveling to Thailand he had found the crystal clear turquoise waters in both places to be a refreshing change of pace from the rat race of Hamburg. But he wound up dismissing them as merely "nice places to visit." Bangkok he had found to be too much like Hamburg with its heavy traffic and bustling crowds. Then he had discovered Pattaya and found himself staying there for an entire month, but after returning to Germany he had gone back—two more times, staying the second time for three months before making a life altering decision.

Hermann had found the internet to be far better than he had expected. Pattaya had just started up broadband internet services. Hermann discovered that he could stay in touch with his company managers by email and by using a voice software program called Skype. But when he found out how well Skype worked with video, Hermann decided that he could easily manage all his businesses from Thailand and only have to go back to Germany one or two times a year. With online banking he could manage all his bank accounts and investments while drinking coffee in his hotel room as he conversed with his employees in full screen video on his laptop.

Yet Hermann found his new existence posed a dilemma. The thought of his old neighbors living in their big houses back in Germany not even being able to find the time to get to know each other made him unwilling to want to repeat the experience of having to live around such shallow minded people. But he didn't want to become part of the typical expat landscape of Pattaya either with its focus on drinking seven nights a week in a never ending cycle of aimless debauchery. He thought about the possibility of finding the "right girlfriend", settling down with her and living out a relaxed existence "Thai style" with its "Mai Pen Rai" attitude of "Never mind, it really doesn't matter" to be too mindless for his tastes. As for settling down with one girl, that would negate the entire point of why a man would want to move to Pattaya in the first place, which was to seize the opportunity of savoring the largest smorgasbord of delectable women in the world.

If I should move into an upscale neighborhood in Germany, I am going to get stuck with the same kind of narrow minded superficial status seeking assholes I had around me before, Hermann decided. *And if I move into an expensive beach front condominium in Thailand, it's going to be the same thing all over again. I'm going to be running out my front door and meeting one of my new neighbors out in the hallway, and the man will probably not even say good morning to me. Or if he does, he's likely to think, "I really wish I didn't have to run into this guy." And even if I move into a modestly priced less upscale neighborhood, most of the people living around me are going to turn out to be assholes too. They are just going to be a different type of asshole.*

I will be stuck with whatever is in store for me. Since I can't choose my neighbors, I will be stuck having to live around whatever dregs of humanity are chosen for me, Hermann concluded. Then suddenly an idea started to form in Hermann's mind. *I have money. In fact, I have lots of money. So why can't I create a world of my own choosing? Or at least my own castle? I can have it constructed exactly the way I want. And then I can populate it with only those people I want to have living around me. If a man seems to be too much concerned with money or status, I simply won't have to deal with him. If a man is stupid, I'll refuse to sell him one of my units. If a man is dishonest I'll tell him to go buy a condo from someone else. I will be free to sell not only to Germans but to people from any country I choose so long as "my people" can meet my very strict standards."*

Mickel goes Condo Hunting

With the exception of a single secretary and Hermann the German the Bahthaus sales office was empty when Mickel walked in. The secretary was a slender Thai woman just over thirty, but like many Thai women she looked much younger. Until now, Hermann the German had not sold a single condo. Although a handful of potential owners had come in who were anxious to hand over their deposits, Hermann had turned them down for reasons that he alone could understand. But all of this didn't matter to Hermann. Back in Germany his family owned several automobile parts factories, a cosmetics company that had plants in both Germany and Thailand, and a company in Thailand that produced electronic components for BMW, Mercedes and Volkswagen. Although he wouldn't admit it to anyone in Thailand, at this point in his life money really didn't mean all that much to Hermann. As for the condo building, so far, only several levels had been constructed.

"What is this Bahthaus all about?" Mickel asked in a loud voice.

Looking up from his paperwork, Hermann the German studied the tall burly Norwegian striding over to his desk. *Looks like he's the kind of man I need for a body guard*, thought Hermann. *Where'd they get this guy from, a professional wrestling ring? No. He looks too tough to be screwing around like those clowns.*

"You want to take a look at the building?" Hermann asked. "Come, I show you. It is just down the street."

"Okay. I follow you," Mickel replied.

The construction site was just two blocks from the sales office. One glance told Mickel that the place was being built as solidly as a Viking sword. Massive concrete columns supported the concrete floors; each one over twenty-four inches thick. But so far only the concrete columns of the bottom two floors had been filled in with the large concrete blocks that would become the walls of the building. Mickel noticed that the entire structure was completely unlike any condo building he had ever seen in Pattaya. What really struck Mickel was the curvature of one of the sides of the building. It was not linear, forming two curves instead of just one, each curve flowing outward away from the exact center of the outside wall. Mickel couldn't believe his eyes.

"My God--That looks like the prowl of a Viking ship!" he exclaimed.

"Exactly," Hermann replied. "I am from Hamburg and Hamburg's not that far South of Denmark and you know the Vikings all came from Denmark, Sweden and Norway. We Northern Germans are not all that different from people living in Scandinavia. And I have for a long time been an admirer of Scandinavian architecture."

"Oh my God--My God," Mickel shouted out loud. "It is. It really is like an old Viking long boat.."

"You are from Scandinavia then?" Hermann asked.

"Oh yes. I am from Norway. And all my friends are from Norway."

"If you move into this condo building, they won't be," Hermann replied with a broad grin.

"What do you mean?"

"They are going to come from everywhere-- from England, and Germany, from Australia and France, America and even from Russia. Well maybe from Russia. I am not sure yet if I want to allow Russians in. Do you want to see the display condominiums?

"Look, Hermann, I not come all this way to look at nothing. Show me. I want to take a look."

The display condominiums were on the first floor. As they entered the first one, Hermann explained, "This is one of our larger units. It's 145 square meters, but it faces the Gulf of Thailand so most of the time you are going to get a nice breeze off the sea which will cool you off--especially at night.

In Thailand the area of a condo or house is designated in square meters instead of square feet. There's 10.8 square feet to one square meter.

In the entryway, which was a short hallway entering the condo's living room, Mickel noticed a replica of a medieval crossbow hanging on the wall. Off this hallway Hermann showed him the guest bathroom.

"This particular unit has two bathrooms. In fact every one of our units has two bathrooms with the exception of the two Penthouse apartments up on the top floor. They are going to have three bathrooms and be about 200 square meters."

As they walked into the living room, Mickel noticed several paintings hanging on the walls. One portrayed a medieval jousting match with two mounted knights riding at each other that accentuated the first knight's long lance aimed at his adversary's shield only inches away from making contact while capturing his opponent leaning over his horse's neck as he thrust his lance through the first knight's helmet. In intricate detail, the painting revealed the splintering of the lance as blood spurted out of the knight's visor from the shattered head inside the helmet.

"Oh my God," Mickel exclaimed excitedly. "I like it. All that blood and violence.—it's so good for the soul.   You know, Hermann, men are such violent people. They are like beasts. But that is the truth, but nobody wants to hear the truth."

Two English broadswords from the 13th century adorned the opposite wall while a full suit of armor stood upright from the floor, and a mace and battle axe were fixed to the wall beneath the broadswords.   The final touch was the living room's deep red wallpaper which contrasted nicely with the medieval weapons of war.

Their next stop was the master bedroom. The bed frame and its headboard, the doors to the living room and the adjoining bathroom, the small end tables on both sides of the bed, and even the picture frames were all made of Teak, which gave the impression that the bedroom was the states room of an old clipper ship from the 1840's. One entire wall supported a 14 foot long wardrobe which was also made completely from Teak.   A large oval shaped picture frame displaying a picture of a tropical island completed the motif of an old sailing ship. Unless one looked very closely, the picture and its frame could have passed for a sea going vessel's porthole.

 "Where's that picture from?" asked Mickel.

"That picture is from an island somewhere near Krabi. I'm not sure exactly which one it is, but Krabi's very nice to visit," Hermann replied.   "It's not too crowded, the water there is very clean and there's lots of karsts close to the water there, which are perpendicular limestone formations so you can actually practice mountain climbing techniques on them and still go scuba diving the next day."

"How much is this condo?

"4,200,000 baht which is around 105,000 U.S. dollars," replied Hermann.

"I think I buy a condo here. I think I buy tomorrow.   The only question is which one I should buy. That is the question."

"If you want to buy, you will have to give me a 50,000 baht deposit to start off with," replied Hermann.   "But there's another thing too."

"What's that?"

"Well, you look like the kind of person we want living here, but please understand that not just everyone can get a condo at the Bahthaus. Three million baht is very cheap when you consider what you are getting."

"Why so cheap then? Hermann, I have to agree with you. Three million is very cheap. I have never heard of such a thing."

"I will be very honest with you, Mickel. I am building this condo to the highest level of European standards, and if you go out and see what other condos are bringing, you will see that this is the best deal you are going to find. And it's right next to the Gulf of Thailand, so no one can build in front of you to spoil your view. But there is a catch, and that catch is I will decide whether or not someone is the kind of person who's going to fit in here, so I want to take you somewhere right now and we will have a couple of drinks together to discuss this. Then you can decide if this place is for you and I will decide if you are the kind of person I want to have living here."

"What? Are you telling me that I might not be good enough to live in this place?"

"No, I am not saying that. I am only saying that we should go right now and have a few beers together so that we do not make an unwise decision and that each of us gets what he wants."

"Okay. That sounds reasonable, Hermann. Perhaps I think about retiring here while we go drink a lot of beer together."

The Menace from the North goes fishing

Thirty stories high, with its white Corinthian columns lining its large atrium through which the ocean breeze courses through from the Gulf of Thailand, the Park Beach Condominiums could easily make one forget the seediness of Pattaya just a mile and a half away. Upon entering the atrium one can look directly at the sky above. The upstairs architecture of the building can be compared to a funnel of air that is surrounded by small apartments on all four sides. The base of the funnel is the center of the atrium's ground level while the top is open to the stars at night just above the 30th floor. On ground level in the center of the atrium there is a fish pond meandering off to the left of this central area. On its right side there are several shops; a small convenience store, the condo management office, and the Noi Bar. Swimming lazily in the shallow marble lined fish pond are carp of many colors, gold, white, red and blue, with some of the multi-hued fish weighing as much as ten pounds.

As one passes through this atrium one comes to a large swimming pool extending out to the beach. The view across the swimming pool from inside the building to the Gulf of Thailand is magnificent. Because the atrium is open to both the East and the West the sea breeze coming off the Gulf travels into the building, then upwards through the air funnel between the condos to such an extraordinary degree that air conditioning becomes entirely unnecessary.

Hermann the German led Mickel into the Noi Bar while explaining, "Here you can get a lot of things you want including alcohol, pineapple, coconut, and banana shakes, soft drinks, coffee and you can even get a massage." Hermann pointed at several massage chairs off to his right, then pointed to a small winding staircase at the back of the room. "And up there is where you can get either a Thai Massage or Oil Massage."

The bartender was a Thai woman in her mid-thirties. Seated around her were several older women dressed in the orange uniforms massage girls often wear.

"I'm buying, so order anything you want," Hermann told Mickel. Then pointing out the bartender, Hermann continued, "And this is Manny, our bartender here and owner of this place. She also gives the best massages here or practically anywhere else also."

Mickel stared at Manny through eyes as harsh as the Norwegian Sea, paused for a moment, then his face softened. "So you are Manny. I am so pleased to meet you. I'm Mickel and I'm from Norway believe it or not and of course I want to have a drink. Give me a Singha. Then he laughed and said, "I think I will have many beers here, so help me God."

Mickel and Hermann were on their second beers as Manny studied the two men. Then she asked them: "Lady you want?"

"Do I want lady?" Mickel replied in a loud voice. "Of course I want lady. Who doesn't want a lady?"

"Me can do, have ladies come—you want?" Manny asked as she looked at Mickel while ignoring Hermann.

"Please, Please. By all means, bring on the ladies so we can all have a good time together," Mickel replied.

Hermann cringed as he watched Manny ring calling out on her cell phone. *She's actually doing it,* he thought. *Now that's all I need is having someone pick out my ladies for me. Damn that Mickel. I wish he hadn't opened up his mouth. Now how do I get out of this one without having one of the girls lose face?*

It took the two freelancers half an hour to arrive. One of them was pretty in the face but a little plump, too plump for Hermann's tastes, since Hermann preferred slender girls, but not for Mickel, who was already on his sixth beer. Although it was only his fourth beer since he got to the Noi Bar, he had already had two beers at his rented condo before meeting Hermann.

The other girl, who was tall for a Thai girl and slender, immediately went over to Mickel which left the plump one to prey on Hermann. Smiling, the girl approached Hermann as she took a bar stool next to him.

"My name me Ahm. Name you call yourself?" the girl asked him.

"I'm Hermann," Hermann replied abruptly as he tried to hide the fact that he was not at all pleased with how the evening was regressing.

"How old you?" the girl asked.

"Old enough to be your father."

"What you tell to me?"

"I'm forty-seven."

"How old?" the girl asked with a touch of impatience in her voice.

"Me siesip-geht", said Hermann.

"Okay, okay," the girl replied. "You young man. You handsome man."

Bullshit, thought Hermann. *She must have learned that working in a bar the same time she learned other famous bar girl lines like "Where do you come from?" And "How long you stay in Pattaya?" And "Hey sexy man," while yelling out onto the street at men walking past the bar to get the men's attention in the hopes of getting them to come into the bar.* Hermann knew from experience that a bar girl would slightly modify this last line to "You sexy man" once a man actually sat down with her. Bar girls used this slight modification to appeal to the ego of any man sitting near them hoping he'd buy her a drink and eventually bar fine her. *I mean who doesn't like to be called sexy? And then, this girl asks me how old I am so that she can better access how well I am going to perform in bed, so if she thinks I'm old, she can hopefully bang me just once and then roll over to fall asleep while hoping I'll do the same. She can also use it to appeal to my ego because if she thinks I'm old, she will say, "Me no like young man. Me like old man." But if she thinks I'm reasonably young, she will say, "I like only young man. Old man no good."*

Now how do I get rid of her? Hermann asked himself.

Hermann shot a quick glance at Mickel who already had his arm around the tall slender girl standing close to him, as she fondled his thigh.

"Name me Nang," the girl said to Mickel. "What your name?"

"I don't have a name," Mickel replied. "But you can just call me Prick."

"Pick," the girl replied unable to pronounce the R.

"Yes. That's me," said Mickel. "Pick. As in pick of the litter. And as far as it concerns you, I am the pick of the litter. But the reality is, I'm a prick."

"Me no unnerstand."

"I bet you have many many boyfriends," said Mickel as he raised his voice to an even louder level than it was before. "Too many to count, but that's okay because I like lady who boom-boom many times."

"I no boom-boom many times. I only boom-boom you."

"Then we have party tonight--in the condo I'm renting," said Mickel. Mickel looked over at Hermann who was starting to look uncomfortable from pondering how he was going to get rid of his girl, and added, his voice nearly shouting into his companion's ear, "Hermann. Let us have us a little party tonight. You are invited. We have fish dinner tonight, Norwegian style."

Suddenly realizing that he didn't have any fish left in his fridge, Mickel remembered the plump Carp he had seen on his way into the Noi Bar. He looked back at the fish pond and observed a row of flags planted along its bank--flags from the United States, the United Kingdom, Germany, Canada, Australia, the Netherlands, Switzerland, France, Japan, Thailand, Korea and China. Once Mickel concluded that the flags represented the home countries of condo owners living in the building, an idea started to form in his alcohol addled mind.

"Perfect. One of those flags will be perfect", Mickel announced while looking at Hermann. "They have to have points on them or they cannot go into the ground very easily and they don't have barbs on them so it will be hard for me to hook the fish securely. I will just have to stab and drive my spear through the fish and thrust it up into the air so the fish cannot wiggle off the point. Watch me, Hermann. When I was a teenager, I used to harpoon small whales. That was so much fun."

Mickel's mind went back to when he was a young teenage boy and how hard he and his whole family had to work just to survive the harsh Norwegian winters. He remembered how his mother used to plant and tend a large garden, and how she used to can all the produce so they would have enough to eat in the winter. The family also had a few milk cows which his father milked twice a day, after getting up as early as 5 a.m. They had an ancient used John Deere model A tractor, which they used to till the fields before planting wheat on them and from some of the harvested wheat his mother would make bread. The family had several farm implements which they pulled behind the tractor. One was a harrow they used to open up the ground to make a seed bed they planted the wheat in with a grain drill. But harvest was a different matter. They couldn't harvest wheat by hand so the family had to wait for another farmer to come to their field with his combine, which he used with its flail header to harvest the wheat. The farmer who owned the combine was the only one in the village to have one since combines were very expensive to buy. When it was harvest time he'd go from one farmer's field to the next and collect a harvesting fee from each family for doing the work.

Mickel's family had a half a dozen beef cows and steers, which was just enough to keep replenishing the small herd and still allow them to slaughter two animals a year. But most of the family's meat came from the sea. It was Mickel's job to go out in a small boat to tend to the fishing nets he and his father had set in the water. There would often be hundreds of pounds of fish in the nets, which Mickel had to haul back to the family's house, oftentimes by hand.

It was backbreaking hard work. And it was a life Mickel never wanted to go back to again. He had left the farm at 16 to work on a fishing boat while sending most of his wages back home. Two years later he enlisted in the Norwegian Coast Guard.

"I get us some fish for dinner," Mickel shouted at Hermann and the women in the bar. Mickel's girl, Hermann's girl, the bartender and the massage girls watched Mickel through gaping mouths, as he ran out to the fish pond, snatched one of the flags out of the ground, and started harpooning the largest fish he could find.

It was all a joke. Mickel really didn't intend to harpoon the fish at the Park Beach condo so all his thrusts with his makeshift harpoon were misses--as he intended them to be. Hermann looked on the madcap scene with horror thinking Mickel really was killing the fish. The condo's security guards rushed up, as one of the two Thai men tried to wrench the flag from Mickel's grasp while the other man tried to restrain the boisterous Norwegian. Then they called the police.

"Get the fuck away from me, you little men!" Mickel shouted at the two Thai security guards. "Do you really think you can stop me, you little weak pieces of shit."

Two Thai policemen arrived onto the scene on their motorcycles five minutes later. But they had almost arrived too late because Mickel had already thrown one of the security guards onto the atrium's floor and was starting to press his foot into the top of the man's head as the other man retreated.

"Yeah Yeah, Yeah, just try and get up. You can't because I am too strong for you," Mickel shouted down at the man whose head was firmly pressed into the tiled floor.

Finally with Hermann's help the two policemen and the remaining security guard were able to pull Mickel off the helpless security guard lying on the floor.

"I am so sorry," Hermann said to the policemen. "He mal. Mal mok mok." Then Hermann pulled out his wallet and handed one of the police officers five thousand baht.

"Just leave. I can handle him. I take care Norway man. He not do again."

The policemen left, for after all, five thousand baht was almost an entire month's salary for an ordinary policeman. Hermann then turned to Mickel and said, "I take you back in the car to your condo. It is best for us to leave."

Mickel followed Hermann to the condo's parking lot laughing his guts out. "I pay you back Hermann. As soon as we get back to my lodging I'll get the money out of my safe." Then he looked back at the bar and added, "There's one thing we forgot, Hermann."

"And what's that?"

"The women. After I pay you back let's you and me go out and pick us up two women. Make that four women", Mickel added as an afterthought.

On the way to Mickel's studio, Hermann contemplated what it would be like having Mickel living at the Bahthaus once the building was completed. *He's a wild man*, Hermann said to himself as he considered the assets and liabilities of the Norwegian as a full time resident at the Bahthaus. *He's about as hard to handle as a half- starved piranha in a goldfish aquarium, but he's strong and he's tough. And he's fun and interesting. I can sure use someone like him when I need some muscle to back up my security once the building is occupied.*

"Tell you what," Hermann said to Mickel. "You come into my office tomorrow with a 50,000 baht deposit and I'll knock 200,000 baht off your price for that condo you said you are interested in buying." Hermann knew he was making Mickel an offer that the Norwegian could not refuse.

Do Germans allow Englishmen in the Bahthaus?

Hermann studied the Englishman sitting across the table from him in his Bahthaus office. Hermann had rented a medium sized room several blocks down the street from the condo construction project in which he had put a temporary partition to subdivide the room into two smaller rooms. He kept his computer, filing cabinets and desk in the back room while he handled potential customers in the front room. The Englishman had confessed to being 65 years old although he looked ten years younger thanks to his having a wiry body along with the alert glint in his eyes of a much younger man.

"Your prices are well under market," the Englishman told Hermann skeptically. "How can you make such an offer? It all sounds too pie in the sky to me."

"I'm doing this for fun more than profit," said Hermann. "But rest assured, I will make a small profit on this project. I'm just not looking for those 40 and 50 % profit margins most developers are asking. My businesses in Germany are doing well while this project allows me to diversify into future projects in Thailand and if all goes well it gives me a better place to live. But the main thing is to do something that's new and interesting."

"So you will hold that condo for me if I put down 50,000 baht?" the Englishman asked.

"That's all I need from you for now, although in one month you will have to sign a contract with me and put 20 % down on your purchase less the 50,000 baht you have already deposited."

"So when do I have to give you the rest of your money?"

"We are looking at another ten months until completion. So each month you will be putting up 5 % of the total purchase price and at the end of this period, assuming the project is complete and ready for you to move in, you will pay the last 30 % of the contracted price."

"Which is just 2.8 million baht for 110 square meters?" asked the Englishman.

"That's pretty inexpensive, don't you think so?" asked Hermann. That's just 25,000 baht a square meter. As you have seen, they are now asking at least 35,000 baht per square meter for buildings of this quality and that's far away from the beach whereas you are going to be within 30 meters of the ocean. I don't think you can go wrong on that, do you?"

"I've looked everywhere and I haven't found anything this solid at anything near that price," the Englishman replied. "Let me sleep on it, and if I want to buy the condo, I'll come in and bring you your 50,000 baht tomorrow."

"There is one catch, however," Hermann added mischievously.

"And what's that?"

"You must qualify."

"Qualify? I am giving you your deposit, aren't I?

"You have to pass some personal tests that I set for all of our future owners," said Hermann. "I look at this as being a very special community that is similar to an American fraternity on a college campus. I went to a university in America--the University of Wisconsin, and I truly enjoyed the fraternity system where each fraternity decides what kind of members it wants to have and then it pledges those freshmen students who meet the fraternity's qualifications. But it works both ways with the students choosing which Fraternity is right for them as well. So I'd like to ask you a few personal questions."

"Go right ahead," said Lawrence. "I have nothing to hide."

"Do you have any women in your life?"

"No. I'm done with English women now."

"You mean you used to have a wife or girlfriend?"

"I had a wife, but we got divorced and she cost me a bloody fortune?"

"So what do you think of marriage?" asked Hermann.

"I think it's a bloody nuisance. English women want to get married. It's all about money so they convince some sucker into sticking his head in the noose and from that moment she's got her entitlement. Then she's got half his pension, half the house, the car, half his money and for what?"

"I agree with you," said Hermann, "It's the same in Germany. The reason I'm asking you about marriage is because I'm not going to allow any married couples in the Bahthaus and only because they are far too dull to have around here." Then Hermann asked almost as an afterthought, "What do you think of the Thai women around Pattaya?"

"Fuck them."

"What do you mean?"

"I mean fuck them all. Fuck all you can because given enough time they are going to be fucking you over. A lot of guys don't really realize it, but they can have sex with practically any woman they want, and not just with the bar girls. They can get it from the girls who clean their houses, to the girls working at the local Seven Eleven, the waitress in the restaurant and even the teller at the bank or the girl who's fitting you with your latest pair of glasses because all of them have one thing in common."

"Are you sure of that?" asked Hermann. "I happen to disagree with you. I don't think you are going to be having sex with the teller at the bank or the girl fitting you with your eyeglasses simply because Thai society would reject her for going with foreigners. To most Thais, you being a foreigner are inferior since they see you as being one step above a monkey on the evolutionary scale, but they aren't going to tell you that. They are going to smile at you and then go about their daily business as soon as you leave. But that's just my opinion. Now keep on telling me more about yours."

"Well, they all want to send money home to the family--to mother and papa and to their brothers and sisters. So if the brother wants a new motorbike, a girl is going to want to buy one for him and she doesn't mind having to fuck big fat smelly falangs to do it. You see, women have been kept down for so long in Thai society and kept so subservient to men that they actually get a lot of self-satisfaction out of doing all of that. But whereas we Westerners like to think of the brother who expects his sister to buy him the motorbike as being lazy and demanding, the women here think it's the brother's divine right to get everything that he wants. And let's face it, Hermann, where are they going to get this kind of money in this country where the average wage is only 5000 baht a month? That's just $125.00 in U.S. dollars. You aren't going to get it at Seven-Eleven and you aren't going to get it cleaning floors. Even if you have a highly paid skilled job such as being a nurse, you are still getting only 15 to 20,000 baht a month and that's just not going to cut it when dear old dad wants a new roof on his house and a new car."

"So what you are telling me, Lawrence, is that practically any woman here in Pattaya's going to want to sell her body just so that she can buy as much as she can for her family back in the village?"

"You're damn right," Lawrence replied. You can sleep with anybody you want in this place just as long as you don't fall in love with them."

"Why shouldn't you?" Hermann asked.

"Because they will never fall in love with you. All they care about is money and sending as much of it as they can back to their family. And to their family all you are is an ATM. They don't care about you. They don't even respect you half as much as the family dog. You aren't even worthy of the buffalo they use to plow their fields with. That's because if the buffalo dies, they must replace it immediately and buffaloes are expensive. But you--you're just another sex hungry falang, who's overweight, who smells funny and who's got far more money than brains. The family will never accept you as being even a human being. So you never want to get involved with these families who are only interested in sucking you dry. Believe me, if you go out with a Thai woman often enough she's going to start trying to get you to start giving to the family."

"And how long does that take--for the Thai woman to start working on you to give to her family?"

"After about the first four or five dates. Then she wants to move in with you, and that's when it all starts. The first time or two you see her, you are giving her 1000 baht a night for long time which is only about $25.00 U.S., but when you take that times 30 it's really costing you $750 a month. So the girl will often propose that you contract with her on a monthly basis for say 10,000 baht a month which is just $250 U.S. to have a woman at your beck and call for an entire month. It sounds too good to be true."

"And it is, because first you have to feed her," Lawrence continued. "Then she's going to be drinking a lot of coca cola's every day and if she's a drinker it's going to be beer, wine or Bacardi Breezers. You have to pay for any of her medical problems that come up and eventually you will probably wind up buying her a motorbike. And once she's comfortably living at your place there will be all these things coming up back home that she's going to be asking you to pay for. Like I said, little brother needs a motorbike--Papa just fell off the roof of his house while working on it and his hospital bill needs to be taken care of. And the list goes on and on and most of the time it's complete and utter bollocks and that is why we call them Buffalo stories. Oh yeah, I forgot to mention, the buffalo fell down in the rice paddy while working and broke its leg so now the family needs a new buffalo." Believe me, a man's much better off never having a girlfriend here in Pattaya. They are nothing but trouble, and all of them, without exception, are lying, cheating whores."

"Okay Lawrence, you make yourself pretty clear about Thai women in Pattaya and I think you are completely right. Other owners are going to need someone like you to confide in and to give them advice. Welcome to our little community. If you want to join us and have your own condo here, please bring in your deposit tomorrow." Hermann stood up, smiled and extended his hand. It was both a handshake and a sign of dismissal. The interview was over.

"I will," promised Lawrence, "but first let's have dinner together to celebrate my becoming your next condo owner resident."

Driving in Pattaya

It wasn't easy keeping up with Lawrence on their way to one of Lawrence's favorite South Pattaya bars.   Hermann the German was driving his Honda Airblade--the latest and greatest of Thailand's current crop of urban transit people movers. Fully automatic, the Airblade was a magic carpet for getting around in Pattaya traffic.   One only had to fire the little machine up, twist the throttle, and whoosh--you were off and running. A superb handler in traffic, the Airblade was so narrow that it could squeeze in anywhere--between cars, other motorbikes, buses, food carts, drunken pedestrians or anything else Pattaya could throw at a motorist. And it was so small, one could park it anywhere.

Hermann usually drove his car, a small Honda, certain that it was far safer than any bike.   But for short distances he'd simply jump on his Air Blade which was perfect for the short hops to the local Seven Eleven or neighborhood restaurants.

Following Lawrence was a different matter because it didn't take Hermann more than five minutes to realize the magnitude of his error.   Lawrence's motorbike was a 135 c.c. Yamaha Spark, a manual transmission model, but a manual that produced a lot of horsepower for those 135 cc's, boasted liquid cooling and dual disk brakes that could easily out accelerate most of the 125 c.c. Honda Waves that had dominated the small motorbike market for so many years.

Lawrence could have chosen a Soi that intersected Naklua Road where there was a stop light. Instead he chose Soi 18 where there wasn't one.

> A Soi is a short street oftentimes only a block or two in length but which can extend upwards to 1 or more kilometers.

Hermann watched Lawrence smoothly ease out into the first lane of traffic, then the second where he pulled up to a stop while watching the Southbound traffic in the last two lanes as he looked for his opening.   Hermann nervously followed Lawrence as he held his breath, hoping that no one would hit him as he sat on his motorbike idling at a standstill between the Southbound and Northbound traffic lanes. For a moment or two one or two bikes nearly did since both Hermann and Lawrence were now blocking one lane of traffic coming from the South.   Then Lawrence saw his opening and made his move out into the southbound lanes. Hermann anxiously nudged his motorbike forward. Both Lawrence and Hermann sped out into the far lane as fast as possible to avoid being tailgated by the much faster moving cars and motorbikes coming up behind them.

Suddenly Hermann saw the Thai man with the sun baked brain immediately in front of him, driving the wrong way. It was bad enough having to concentrate on what four lanes of traffic were doing while following Lawrence without having to put up with all the miserable drivers, who either were too ignorant of the rules of the road or too lazy to follow them in the first place. But suddenly having to face one of Thailand's finest citizens, who suddenly pops up in front of you because he's driving the wrong way, was just too much.

The man's eyes stared blankly ahead, his brain sun-drenched and undernourished, as his motorbike loomed twenty feet in front of Hermann heading right at the suddenly pissed off German. Hermann immediately veered to his right, just a couple of feet, to avoid hitting the other motorbike just enough for a miss and hopefully not enough to cause whoever was behind him to hit his bike from the rear. There was no time to crane his neck to the rear, to see if someone was right behind him and no time to check his mirrors either. The little man with the slow brain was coming right at him forcing Hermann to suddenly change course to his right.

Fifteen seconds later, Hermann spotted another lazy minded Thai heading towards him driving the wrong way. Fortunately Hermann had time to check his mirrors, and then seeing no one was immediately behind him, he was able to veer over into the next lane to avoid the mindless Thai motorbike taxi driver driving in the wrong traffic lane.

Finally, with no more drivers in sight driving in the wrong lane, Hermann started to relaxed. But one look in his right mirror made him focus once more on the simple fact that driving a motorbike in Thailand is a deadly serious business. A boy between twelve and fourteen drove his motorbike a scant foot from Hermann's back wheel and just six inches to Hermann's right. Had Hermann braked the slightest amount while drifting right, the little boy would have rammed his bike right into the back end of Hermann's Air Blade.

If there would have been an accident, Hermann would have wound up buying the little boy a new motorbike and only because in Thailand it's always the Westerner's fault whenever there's any accident. Hermann remembered the time he was driving his motor bike back to the condo he had rented and how he had driven over a speed bump very slowly because he had just bought a set of kitchen glasses at the market. Suddenly he felt the impact of his motorbike being struck from the rear. He remembered only going one mile an hour over the speed bump and how he had lightly applied his brakes and waited. He saw the Thai woman who had been tail gating him sprawled out next to her motorbike on the concrete behind him. *The bike has to be damaged*, Hermann thought, as he watched the woman slowly get up. *If I were in Germany I'd go over and help her. I'd help her get her bike off the pavement and see if she's hurt, offer to take her to the hospital, but not here. If I go over to her, a crowd of Thais will suddenly appear and they will all be yelling at me to pay her and then the police are going to arrive and the police will demand money from somebody to pay for the repair of her motorbike and any injuries she's suffered. But they aren't going to be asking her to pay–they are going to be asking me. It's my fault. They will all see me as being rich and as the stupid falang who can be made to pay for everything.*

It must not have been easy for her, but the woman somehow managed to pull her wrecked motorbike off the concrete. Hermann didn't wait to see if she had a broken arm or leg. He immediately restarted his Air Blade and accelerated away until he drove several hundred meters down the street where he suddenly made a left turn onto another street. He didn't stop until he had gotten several kilometers from the accident and only then did he stop at a restaurant to get a little something to eat and to calmly reflect on what had happened and what could have happened had he been a nice guy and stuck around. *The woman must have been tail gating me when I crossed the speed bump. Perhaps she was even on her cell phone gossiping with one of her girlfriends. Now, perhaps, she will be a better driver*, Hermann reasoned.

Hermann couldn't keep the incident out of his mind as he followed Lawrence up to the light at North Pattaya Road. The light didn't just suddenly change from red to green. Instead a series of numbers appeared indicating the number of seconds that were left before it would turn green. "40 (seconds), 35, 30, then finally 20, 10, 5 and zero." In all there must have been ten motorcyclists besides Lawrence and Hermann. But when the number got down to five, several of the Thai guys started moving across the intersection before the light turned green. "What! Is time that valuable to these guys that they have to run this red light?" Hermann asked Lawrence.

"They must know more than we do about traffic laws," Lawrence replied sarcastically.

Lawrence waited until the light changed to green before accelerating out into the intersection. The pair was now on Third Road heading south. Carre Four would be on Central Pattaya Road except they were not going to Carre Four, the large shopping center the French had built. Instead they were going to Soi Buakhao to a favorite bar of Lawrence's. Hermann would have driven to Central Pattaya Road, turned right on it at the light, and then continued on until they reached Soi Buakhao where he would have made a left turn-- but not Lawrence.

This was Lawrence's territory. It was where he hung out almost every night. Two hundred meters before Hermann and Lawrence got to Central Pattaya Road, Lawrence turned right and Hermann followed. Here the street was only two lanes wide. There were hundreds of pedestrians but there was hardly a sidewalk to be seen which drove the pedestrians to using the street which they had to share with all the motorcyclists, cars and tuk tuks. But the two lanes of traffic were both one way. Not once, but twice Hermann saw a Thai man driving his motorbike on the sidewalk as several men and women scurried to get out of his way.

That's just like a lot of these Thais, thought Hermann. *Instead of going around the block to get back on the street so that they can be going in the right direction, they will make use of the sidewalk instead. Either that or they will simply drive the wrong way up the street. The men especially have got to be some of the laziest people on earth.*

Plunged deep into his thoughts Hermann suddenly was jolted into the here and now. A Thai man had suddenly pulled out in front of him from the sidewalk and stopped his motorbike right in Hermann's path. The man then calmly reached down onto the street to pick up a sandal that had fallen off his foot a few moments earlier. He had been driving his motorbike two hundred meters in front of Hermann before deciding to double back on the sidewalk to retrieve his sandals. Hermann had to suddenly veer to his right to avoid hitting the man and got nearly creamed by a baht bus that was driving far too fast in the lane to his right. The baht taxi missed Hermann's motorbike by just six inches.

Totally shaken, Hermann watched the Englishman weave adroitly between all the vehicles and pedestrians that stood in his way. By this time Lawrence was barely in sight after gaining two-hundred meters on Hermann. Finally Lawrence pulled his motorbike to the side of the street so that Hermann could catch up.

"What did you say you used to do in England before retiring?" Herman asked.

"I worked for the Bank of England foreclosing on mortgages."

They were just a couple of minutes from the bar Lawrence was taking Hermann to when Hermann decided that Lawrence was just the sort of man he wanted living at the Bahthaus.

The man's tough, thought Herman—*very tough. I need people like him.*

Spicy Girl

The waitress had just taken Hermann the German's order of spicy chicken curry in coconut milk over to him when he noticed the tall Russian plunking himself down at the last remaining table, smashed out of his gourd. One of the Thai women, sitting across from the Russian, rolled up her eyes in disgust. A pretty girl in her late twenties, she had dyed her hair blonde. Hermann hated it when Thai women dyed their hair blonde feeling they just didn't look right and that it made them look cheap and tawdry. But not this girl, who looked just as becoming as a blonde as she would have had she left her hair Oriental black. She was the owner of the beauty salon across the street from the Pink Grasshopper Restaurant where she and her little coterie of friends were now sitting. Never mind that it was her French boyfriend who had paid for the beauty salon and everything in it. She had title to the place so if push came to shove the French boyfriend would just have to go, and she'd wind up with the place and all the money it could generate for years to come.

The beauty salon was in a prime location right across from the four-star Diamond Star Hotel where the clientele was primarily Russian. Since the recent resurgence of the Russian economy that came with the explosion in oil and natural gas prices, Pattaya had been getting annual increases of Russian tourists of 30 to 50 percent. Compared to the number of visitors from Russia, the number of Americans visiting Pattaya each year had become only a dribble in comparison. For one thing, much of Russia was much closer to Thailand than the U.S. Another reason for the huge influx of Russians is most of Russia is cold whereas much of the U.S. has a much more moderate climate. To the average Russian, who has to endure most of the year with little sun, Thailand, where the sun shines nearly every day, is paradise on earth. But the biggest reason for the huge influx of Russians into Thailand over the past couple of years was all that recently acquired gas and oil money had made many Russians wealthy. And when such people come to Pattaya, they aren't too particular about how much money they spend or what they spend it on.

Although some of the Russian tourists are well educated cultured people, the vast majority are the rudest, most ignorant arrogant people in Thailand. Hermann had seen Russian men sitting by one of the Diamond Star Hotel's two swimming pools take their shoes off and wash them right there in the water. He had seen fifty year old fat Russian women lounging around the pools, topless-- their breasts sagging masses of wrinkles. He had seen them flip their cigarette butts and empty beer bottles out onto the sand down on the beach with repetitious regularity. Most of them didn't speak English, and ninety-nine percent of the time he had never heard a single Russian even try to speak one word of Thai to the Thais–not even as much as a sawadi krap or a Kap Kun Kap –which are short phrases for Hello, goodbye and thank you.

Hermann decided that not all the Russians are crude hard spending spendthrifts, just most of them. *Even so, for all their boorish manners, the Russians are not half as bad as many of the English although there are none better than the older generation of Englishmen. It's the younger generation that needs to be rooted out of here and sent packing.* Hermann was thinking about the soccer hooligan types-- the forty-five year old and younger cockroaches with shaved heads and tattoos. *Most, thankfully don't hang out in North Pattaya or Naklua, preferring the more boisterous bars of Sois Seven and Eight, Soi Six and the Soi Buckow area.* Herman had noticed the overshadowing air of menace hanging over the bars wherever such English riffraff congregated, and had concluded that the soccer hooligan types live to fight and when they do, it's often three or four of them against one.

Hermann remembered how he had recently joined several friends in a Soi Seven Bar when he saw a man going down just inside the bar. For a moment it had appeared that the guy was having a heart attack. At first Hermann couldn't tell if the man was collapsing just outside the bar on the street or if he was falling down inside the bar itself. It was one of the many open fronted beer bars, dotting not just the more infamous short streets such as Soi Six, Soi Thirteen, Soi Seven and Soi Eight, which provided much of the landscape for so many of Pattaya's streets. The man had collapsed on the floor a few feet away from where Hermann and his friends had been sitting. Hermann had then watched several men carry the prostrate man over to where he and his friends had been sitting where they put him on the floor next to their table.

It had taken the man more than five minutes to come to as one of the bar girls scurried by their table muttering, "He not do anything wrong. He good. He just outside dancing and then this falang hit him."

It had turned out to be another Englishman. Whether he had a grudge against the man or not, Hermann would never know. All anyone seemed to know is that the second man had either been with the first Englishman or had just encountered him outside the bar, punched him in the face and then quickly walked away while his victim collapsed. Neither Hermann nor his friends had seen the punch or even recalled the second man being there in the first place.

What was remarkable is that no one even tried to follow the second man down the street, to call out to him or to try and find a policeman. No one cared. This was Pattaya where there was no police protection for anyone. Meanwhile the owner of the bar, another Englishman, was fast asleep in a small bedroom right inside his bar, obvious of the assault and battery that had just taken place at his place of business, an offence that might have required some jail time in the United Kingdom, Germany or the U.S.

Hermann continued to watch the group at the table next to him. A slender Westerner sat across from the beauty shop owner and next to him sat a woman who was obviously his girlfriend, a Thai woman around thirty, holding his hand. But one of the largest people present was the ladyboy waiter who kept bringing beers back to the table. Both the Westerner and his girlfriend were doing their share of the drinking, but surprisingly the pretty owner of the beauty shop was matching them glass for glass.

> Often referred to as Thailand's Third Sex ladyboys are males who decide at an early stage to become Kathoey. Wearing their hair long, dressing as women and wearing makeup Kathoey's often look the part so well that they are mistaken as women. Many get artificial breasts from plastic surgeons while a few have sex change operations. In general Thais are very tolerant of Kathoeys who are readily accepted both culturally and in the workplace. A large percentage of Thailand's sex workers are Kathoeys. It is often said that the best looking women in many bars aren't women.

The ladyboy kept bringing back large bottles of Heineken and Singha, and each time he did he'd pour beer from one of the bottles into his own glass. He had worked at the same beauty shop where the pretty beauty shop owner used to earn tips giving manicures and pedicures. Both of them had worked for Nit, an older Thai woman, who had a great gift of gab with her customers. But whereas the pretty blonde stayed in the business long enough to get her own shop, the ladyboy had decided to become a waiter instead.

The ladyboy was almost as tall as the Westerner and just as broad in the shoulders which made him taller and stockier than most ladyboys. He or she also smiled more often than most ladyboys, for Ae liked most people, and it didn't seem to matter whether they were male or female, Westerner or Thai.

No one paid much attention to the Russian, who already had a few too many before deciding he needed some company. Both the ladyboy and the pretty beauty shop owner knew the Russian, and neither of them liked him.

The Westerner sitting with his girlfriend introduced himself to the Russian. "My name is Frank. I'm American. Are you Russian?"

"Me Russia," the Russian replied. "Me smoke too much," the man continued as he pulled out a cigarette and lit it with a cheap lighter. "But I don't care."

Hermann noticed that the Thai woman seated next to the American had a nice shapely ass, *but then again, a lot of them have beautifully shaped asses,* thought Hermann. The Thai woman's face suddenly broke out into a smile.

"What your name?" she asked the Russian. "Me Spicy."

"Your name Spicy?" asked the Russian. "What kind of name is that?"

"Me no understand," replied the girl. "Name I Olm." She pointed at her American boyfriend and said, "Tilak call me Spicy. Frank think I Spicy lady."

"He know nothing because he's American. He and President Bush are bullshit," the Russian said.

Until then the American had been pretty quiet, but the American president's name being mentioned jolted him to the edge of his seat.

"Screw Bush," the American replied. "He's no good, and I'll drink to that", Frank added as he clinked his beer glass against the Russian's bottle of Heineken.

"I never wanted Bush who is a stupid man so say what you want. You're not hurting my feelings."

He would fit right in, Hermann said to himself, as he listened in on the conversation. *I will probably have more Europeans living in my condo building than Americans and they all have to get along together. This American isn't one of these flag waving idiots who believe the United States can do no wrong.*

Suddenly Spicy spoke up, in a seething voice hot with anger. "You Russia man," she blurted out. "You no like America. You fucking idgit." Then she turned to the American and said, "I want tequila. I want drink too much." Then she hissed: "Russia man stupid."

"What? Call me stupid?" the Russian shouted. "You are nothing. Nothing. You are lazy Thai whore."

"Fuck you," Spicy spat back at the man.

"I want you out this place. Now!" the pretty beauty shop owner shouted at the Russian.

"Come on. You go now," the ladyboy said to the Russian as he walked behind the Russian's chair. "You big problem. We no need big problem in restaurant."

"Go now", the beauty shop owner repeated to the Russian as a waitress came over to the table and glared at the man.

Confronted by the pretty beauty shop owner, the waitress, Spicy and the ladyboy, the Russian suddenly realized that he'd soon have a fight on his hands. If he had learned one thing in Thailand, it was that if a foreigner ever fought a Thai, every Thai within shouting distance would immediately join in, oftentimes carrying steel pipes or heavy wooden objects. The foreigner would be beaten senseless and if the police ever arrived, they'd arrive too late. And if they arrived on time, the police would more often than not sit with the locals watching the spectacle. Sometimes the foreigner would be carted off to the local monkey house, which was Thai slang for jail. The Russian got up from the table on wobbly legs. And then he left, muttering "Fuck America. Fuck this crazy place."

Hermann continued to study the American, impressed that the man had kept his cool after being provoked by the drunken Russian. He's the kind of man I need for my little community, Hermann thought. The man's cool and he keeps his temper but he's no chicken.

Hermann got up from his table and walked over to the group. He smiled and introduced himself. "Sawadi Kap," Hermann said in Thai. Then he said in English, "Excuse me for intruding, but I'm having a condo building built near here, and I want you to know about it. My name is Hermann."

The American stood up and extended his hand. "Hi. My name is Frank."

"Why hello Frank," Hermann replied. "Are you new here?"

"I've been living here in Pattaya for a few months. And this is my girlfriend, Spicy."

"You seem Angry," Hermann told Spicy.

"No like Russia man," Spicy spat out. "He no good."

"I'm sure he will not bother you again," Hermann said kindly. Then he turned to Frank. "I am having a building constructed- -a condo with sixty units right here close to the beach. Have you bought a place yet?"

"No. But I've been looking," said Frank. "I found a place down in Jomtien near the beach that looks good but the units there are a little high."

"You might want to check what I'm offering," said Hermann. "The prices are quite reasonable. I represent a German company and we are building our condo building to European standards."

"Continue on," said Frank. "You Germans always build great stuff. My last two motorcycles I had in the U.S. were BMW's and I have also owned four German cars. "

"Then you know what I mean."

"Yes. I really liked my BMW's," said Frank.

"Our units go from 100 to 200 square meters. We expect to be finished eight months from now. You can meet me soon and take a look," Hermann said as he smiled at Frank.

I like the look of him, thought Frank. *His blue eyes are clear and they look a man square in the face without a hint of deviousness.* "When can we meet? Frank asked Hermann.

"Tomorrow will be fine. Say tomorrow afternoon? Or is that inconvenient for you?"

"That will be fine. Do you have a card?"

Hermann reached into his back pocket and pulled out a business card from his wallet. "Call me tomorrow so we can get together.

"You got it. I'll be there."

Frank buys his condo

Hermann had just finished taking Frank to the display condos where he had explained the benefits and drawbacks of each type of unit he had to sell even though he had only three display units to show. Then he took him back to his office where he could hopefully nail down the sale.

"So Frank, what brings you to Thailand?"

"I liked the climate, the food, and the women," the American replied.

"Most of us enjoy all those things, but what is your story, Frank? It often takes a lot more than warm weather, good looking women and good restaurants to make a man want to leave his country. For me, I had just gotten divorced in Germany. It seemed my whole life was falling apart and that is was time to do something new."

"You really want to know?"

"Yes. Why not?"

"My marriage was falling apart. I suppose a lot of guys come here when that happens. Life starts to feel so empty back home—the girls are pretty and so loveable here in Thailand so the guy becomes seduced and wants to start a new life, but for me there was a little more to it."

"Please continue," Herman replied.

"The problem with marriage in the United States, and I suppose it's pretty much the same in Europe, is as soon as a woman gets married to a man she gotten her entitlement which is her pension in advance. From that point on she doesn't have to do anything. She can get fat and stop cleaning the house. She can start hitting up the credit card for huge amounts, and there's no stopping her. She can stop providing sex. And if her husband doesn't like it, there's bound to be a divorce and she's probably going to get the house, and she's going to get custody of the kids and she's going to wind up getting half the marital property which is all the money and property, plus the increased value of the business and so on since the marriage began. In my case, my business flourished during our marriage so during the divorce proceedings I would have had to produce years upon years of financial records for my company along with all my bank and credit card statements. The court would have set a value upon all my net worth at the time our marriage started and then it would have set a value on its value at the time of my divorce.

49

It would then have divided this total value of everything I owned which the court would have interpreted as "we owned" by half and made me pay her 50 %. So, I made it my business to make sure that my company would be a complete failure."

"So what did you do then?" Herman asked.

"I was in the construction business, Herman. So I made sure I paid too much for practically everything, and I did a lot of work for cash, which of course never made it into any of my bank accounts. It took me over five years to run my flourishing business down to the point that it was barely making enough for us to survive."

"So what did your wife do?"

"It didn't take long for her lawyer to discover that we were practically bankrupt so he decided that since there wasn't much money in it for him that he'd try to get her to agree to an early settlement for very little money. He urged her to take what she could get instead of my having to declare bankruptcy and have everything liquidated by the bankruptcy court. Meanwhile I had salted a lot of money away and figured it would be better not to have it ever appear in any U.S. bank account or investment."

"So what did you do? Did you bring it all over here in large suitcases? I imagine Thai customs would have had a lot of fun with you then."

"You got the suitcases part of it right," Frank replied. Except I took it over the Canadian border. I'd tell everyone I was driving to Las Vegas except I'd be heading north instead of south. But I didn't put the money in a Canadian bank right away. I put it in storage but now I've got a lot of it in a Canadian account. I want to move it right away but if I transfer all of it into a Thai account, I'm not going to get clear title on a condo here."

"That's right," said Herman. "You will need to prove that the source of any money you have paid for a condo came from a foreign bank account. If you use money from a Thai bank account to buy any real estate here, the Thais are going to assume that you made the money here and that you probably did that through doing something illegal. That means if and when you should decide to sell your property here in Thailand the authorities are not going to allow you to take your money out of the country."

"Exactly. So I will want to transfer the money from my Canadian bank accounts directly to whoever I buy a condo from. That way if I should ever want to leave Thailand I can sell the condo and take my money with me."

"I have an idea for you," Herman suggested.

"What is it?"

"You might want to consider buying your condo in a company name. You probably already know that only 49 % of all condos sold by any developer can be sold to falangs. The other 51 % must be sold to Thais. So we do the same thing most other developers do by setting up "Thai companies" which are controlled by the real buyer but which nominally are Thai owned. One ends up with a bunch of Thai names on the deed, but none of the Thais have any say over the property."

"So what's the advantage of buying in a company name?" Frank asked.

"For one thing you must pay a transfer fee to the government. When you buy your condo from me, I will pay half the transfer fee and you will pay the other half. Normally the seller pays the entire transfer fee. But if you later on decide to sell your unit, you would have to pay the transfer fee so it winds up being paid each time the property is sold. If you buy your condo in a company name, you don't sell the condo, you end up selling the company instead so there are no more transfer fees."

"Is that all there's to it?"

"You must have your company audited each year by a Thai lawyer. That costs about $300.00. Buying in a company name is considered by many to be illegal but now everybody's doing it. And your condo might not be worth quite as much when you sell it because of that black cloud of possible illegality hanging over it. But I would give you a nice discount if you should happen to buy in a company name. But one thing you might want to think about is this. Your ex-wife might somehow decide to come after you. And you might have some problems with the American tax authorities considering what you have just admitted to me. I doubt if you will have a problem but one never knows. If you buy in a company name it just makes you a little more difficult to trace."

"I am not worried about that at all. That's because I'm really not me."

"You really aren't you? Who are you then?"

"I was somebody else. I went to school as that person, conducted my business affairs as that person and I got married as that person but soon after I started to move all that money to Canada I created my new identity. I had a friend who had once spent some time in the penitentiary for armed robbery help me do it. I started out getting a new social security number."

"Now how in the world did you manage that?" Herman asked incredulously.

"One starts out looking for a baby that died just a few days after its birth whose birthdate is similar to yours. Then you apply for a social security number from Social Security. You give Social Security the dead baby's name, where he was born and if anyone asks why you are asking for the baby's social security number you claim it's been lost or that you never got one. Since the dead baby's never used his social security number on account of his having been dead for so many years there are no records pertaining to that social security number. Usually no one's going to ask too many questions on account of this sort of thing happening all the time."

"Somehow I doubt that."

"Then you haven't been to Arkansas then."

"Arkansas?"

"Yes. But I'm only using Arkansas as an example. A lot of people grow up in rural areas and they really don't get out of their local communities much. A lot of people have no use for a social security card. A lot of people don't even use banks and there are some places where a lot of people don't even bother to get driver's licenses. So if someone asks, you just say you grew up down in a swamp somewhere and never needed your social security card and if someone asks for your driver's license you just tell them that you are visually impaired and that you never drove a car in your life."

"Okay. So what happens next?"

"You need to get a copy of your birth certificate which is of course the birth certificate of the dead baby. But now you have your social security card and with that you can go down to the state where the dead baby had been born and request a copy of the birth certificate so long as you have one other proof of identity. That can be a bank statement or a copy of a bill sent to you at your present address, an insurance policy, and so on. "

'And then what?"

"Now you have two valid IDs. With those you can now get a driver's license. And now you are set to establish new bank accounts, to take out new credit cards, and so on."

"So what's the entire point of taking hard cash across the border into Canada. It seems to me that all you would have had to do was to set up a new bank account in another city and then you could have transferred your money to a Thai account."

"That is exactly what I eventually ended up doing. I only started out by taking money in a suitcase into Canada. I was moving money around from what could be traced to what couldn't be so easily traced a long time before I actually got divorced. I hadn't met John yet either."

"Who's John?"

"John is the friend I have already mentioned who spent time for armed robbery."

"So he masterminded your acquiring a new identity? What caused you to believe in this John in the first place?"

"Because seeing is believing. John had at least five different identities. He spent time in the pen as John Mint but when I met him he was working for the Ford Motor credit department as Ralph Laruzo. I actually saw all his IDs or at least some of them. I saw at least five driver's licenses and each one of them had his picture on it. He also showed me several of his social security cards."

"This means I cannot convince you to buy a condo from me in a company name I take it?"

"Absolutely not. There's no way my ex-wife or anybody else is ever going to be able to trace me to buying a condo here. So my buying under my new identity is sufficient. However, even if my ex-wife knew I had put a lot of money into my Thai bank account and bought a condo here, there's no way she could ever get at that money because American courts have no jurisdiction here.

"Would you want to buy a condo with a sea view or is that not so important to you?" Herman asked.

"What do you think Hermann?" asked Frank. "Is it really worth paying all that extra money for a sea view?"

"It's a lot cheaper getting a condo from us on the other side where you cannot see the ocean," Hermann replied. "And if you want a view of the ocean, all you have to do is take a short walk so I really don't think it's worth it."

"And you Hermann, will you be living in one of the condos?"

"You mean, will I be one of your neighbors? Not to worry. I'll be living in the building also."

"Do you plan on getting a sea view?"

"Well for me, it's not so important where I live so long as I'm living in the building," Hermann replied.

"So on which side of the building do you plan on being?"

"I think it will be a small unit facing the West."

"Which has a sea view," Frank replied pointedly.

He's a sharp guy, thought Hermann. *He's asking the right questions and he caught me on that one. Here I've shown him several units, both of them display condos. I have explained how the sun will come in from the West and make the ocean view condominiums hot during the hottest part of the afternoons. And I have shown him a nice corner unit facing the other direction without the sea view. But the time period when the sun starts to really come in from the West only lasts for an hour or so while the sea view condominiums catch the sea breeze which keeps them cooler most of the time. But he's neatly maneuvered me into telling him where I want to be. So now he knows. He's certainly no fool.*

"Of course there's the money," Hermann added. If the money's all that important to you."

"Yes. Your units with the ocean view cost $25,000 more-- at least that much more," replied Frank. "But I think they will be quieter since they don't face the road. Someday that road might become very busy whereas your sea view condominiums don't have a road in front of them and it is unlikely there will ever be one. So okay, I want to buy one of your units facing the sea--one of your smaller units."

"When?" Hermann asked. "When do you want to buy?"

"Why today," Frank replied. "What do you have left facing the sea?"

"Well, most of them remain unsold."

"What did you say the deposit was to hold one of your condominiums?"

"50,000 baht."

"Which is $1250 U.S, " Frank added.

The overall structure of the building had really impressed Frank. Although so far only three of the buildings 7 floors had been built, the size of the concrete pillars on which the whole structure rested were twice the size they needed to be, which is typically German. Frank already knew a lot about building construction since he had been a builder in the U.S. for most of his adult life, having started out as a carpenter. After serving his apprenticeship he had quickly branched out on his own, specializing in building homes during the course of which he became skilled at all aspects of home construction including the electrical, plumbing, and concrete work. He had developed a reputation for being a perfectionist and oftentimes he was only able to complete one house in an entire year. But people lined up to get him and he often had a two year waiting list. And although it would cost them more in addition to their having to put up with the wait, there were more than enough people who would be satisfied with only the best.

"Correct," Hermann replied.

"I want a unit up on the sixth floor. I know it's pretty high priced, but this is going to be my only home. So I'm not worried about whether or not it's going to be the best investment. This is where I plan to wake up every morning for the rest of my life, so for me, it's worth it."

Frank knew from experience that the high rises sprouting up in the area were not for him. In those thirty to fifty story buildings one would oftentimes have to wait too long for an elevator, and if the elevator would break down--then what? Up on the sixth floor he could still use the steps whenever he wanted, get a little exercise coming up those steps, and the view was good enough to suit him. He could see the ocean, and that was all that mattered. He knew just by looking at the man that the German felt likewise. Frank had liked the German immediately after meeting him at the restaurant and now that he was talking to him in the man's office he had begun to like him even more. The German's crystal blue eyes never wavered from looking at him square in the face. That alone spoke volumes for the entire project, and whether or not it would be completed as well as its overall quality and most importantly, the honesty of the company he would be dealing with. Frank also appreciated how the German never hesitated to answer his questions, replying in a matter of fact simple manner even if his answer might jeopardize the possibility of a sale.

Hermann took Frank back into the building one more time, and Frank chose a unit in the middle of the condominiums facing West. The unit was 118 square meters. Of course they never actually looked at the unit itself since it had not been built yet, but there was a display unit just like it on the 2nd floor. Then the pair returned to the office.

"Just give me one hour," said Frank. "I'll just go to my bank and get the 50,000 baht, so consider this a done deal.

Ted Buffalo

Hermann didn't like the man seated in front of him from the first moment the man had walked into his office. It was not just that he was overweight--it was those flabby pinkish hands of his that showed that the man had never done one ounce of physical labor in his life. He had also told Hermann that back in the U.S. he had been a lawyer. In general Hermann despised lawyers and for the same reasons most people hated lawyers. Of course Hermann often had to hire lawyers and had considered many of them to be a necessary nuisance. But this one was quite obviously soft and irritating.

"How did you find us?" Hermann asked the lawyer.

"On the internet. I looked at your web site and liked what I saw."

"What did you say your name was again?" Hermann asked the lawyer.

"Ted Buffalo."

Of course Hermann had remembered the name. But he was doing everything possible to put the man off and the slight of forgetting his name was just one little thing, a minor insult, that would hopefully discourage the lawyer from wanting to buy a condo from him. But the man's name was simply too much. Up country in the rice paddies the Thais employed water buffaloes to do a lot of their plowing and other heavy work, and although the Thais revered the buffalo for their ability to get a lot of work done and respected the fact that they were expensive for the average family living on the farm to buy in the first place, they also regarded the buffalo as a stupid animal. And to the Thais, especially the Thais living in Pattaya the name had been transferred to the Westerner, who most Thais considered to be naive.

"Well let me ask you a question," Hermann asked. "As I've already told you, we are looking for a special kind of person to live in our little community we are creating here. My question is, considering there are so many beautiful women here, exactly what is it you are looking for in the many attractive women of Pattaya?"

Ted Buffalo brightened, his gaze suddenly reminding Hermann of so many true believers who never failed to piss him off. "I know a lot of guys come here to see how many women they can have intercourse with," Ted replied, "but for me, what I really want is the girlfriend experience. I want a girl to stay with me for many months, a lifetime even, and I want to make her happy."

Hermann was shocked. He had heard the same line so many times in boring repetitively, from more Western visitors than he could count, but never so directly. *Sure, sure, the perfect woman who's going to appreciate me so much for what I'm doing for her.* Hermann wanted to throw up knowing all too well that one girl could never do it for him. It would take many girls, especially in Pattaya. Hermann knew from years of experience never to enjoy a Pattaya woman just for her conversation. *It wasn"t just the language barrier, but the inescapable fact that Thais, especially Pattaya Thais already know everything there is to know. They have nothing to learn from Westerners. So there is no reason to get to know a man or to even contemplate what makes him tick. To most Thais the concept of the human mind as a highly developed instrument in which Western logic had been instilled at an early age is of no value. To Thais as to most Asians, face means everything and it is face that allows everyone to get along. One does not criticize others because doing so will cause the other to lose face and to create friction. To Thais Westerners are always creating problems arguing with each other, arguing with Thais and causing the other person to lose face or losing face themselves by getting angry in the first place which means a loss of self-control. Thais are much smarter than that, living in a better world of Sanuck, of feel good fun where critical thinking and open disagreement with others can not be allowed.* Hermann's mind drifted as it considered 201 reasons why any Western man who took any woman he was likely to find in Pattaya to be completely out of his mind.

"I like the idea of, what is it you Americans call it?" Hermann interrupted—"To love the one you are with."

"There is no meaning to that," Ted Buffalo continued. "That's just meaningless sex which does nothing for the human spirit."

"I don't think so," said the German.   "I feel much relieved every time I have sex. My mind suddenly is at ease and I then feel I can truly relax. I can now enjoy conversation with intelligent men around me, or I can lay back and watch a movie, not wanting anything, existing only to keep the mind alive."

"A man can only have real meaning by becoming one with a woman," Ted Buffalo replied pathetically. "When two people can fuse their goals and desires to form a unity--now that is something that is very powerful."

That will never exist, with a woman, thought Hermann, *and especially with a Thai woman. While Mr. Buffalo here thinks he's realizing goals that are mutual between him and his girlfriend, his girlfriend is only thinking about how much money she can get out of him to send to her family and how much she can get to buy herself new clothes, makeup, snacks down at the Seven-Eleven, money she can lend to her friends, a new motorbike, a car, a new house for her parents, and finally a house for her and her Thai boyfriend once he's out of the picture.*

"You need to change your name," Hermann suddenly suggested.

"What?"

"Buffalo is very bad name here in Thailand. You see, Ted, in Thailand they use buffalos as beasts of burden. They are slow and they plow fields, so Thais call anyone who they think is slow in the head a buffalo–especially Westerners who they call falang. To call a man a buffalo is the greatest insult."

"I will never change my name."

"You don't have to. You can still sign your checks and have on your passport your name Ted Buffalo, but you can be like a writer and use other name. You can choose any name you like." Hermann had started to revert to a kind of English he used with Thais, who never used or understood articles such as "a, or the". When talking with Thais he nearly always used the present tense because Thais never understood the difference between "I went to the beach last week," and "I go to beach." Thais especially did not understand the subjunctive tense. Hermann had learned to avoid the "if phrases", especially with Thai women such as "If you don't keep my apartment cleaner, I will have to get another girlfriend." All the girlfriend hears is, "You no good. I want new lady." And it's all because of the difference between Thai and Western logic. To the Westerner "If A happens, we will get result B, and from B we can choose either C or D. whereas to the Thai, "we can choose C or D, up to me (you).

"I'm not going to change my name. I will always be Ted Buffalo," Ted Buffalo replied, his voice rising in anger. I went to Yale back in the U.S. My father went to Yale. The family name has always been Buffalo. My father and I even use the same cuff links and tie clips which are all shaped like buffalos-- the Cape buffalo, the fiercest animal in Africa. We use it on our letter heads and I even have its image etched into some of my custom made boots and belts. My family takes great pride in the buffalo."

"All of this makes no difference. You will be living in Thailand--not America. And to Thais the buffalo is a symbol of stupidity," Hermann replied impatiently.

"Well I don't care what a lot of people think," Ted Buffalo said. "Those who get to know me respect me for my intellect. Do you know much about the Cape Buffalo, Hermann?"

"A little. In Africa it's one of the Big Five or most highly rated Big Game Animals.   I think they are the Lion, the Elephant, the Cape buffalo, the Rhinoceros, and the Leopard. Every one of these animals is considered to be dangerous and that is why they make the top five list."

"And out of the five, the Cape buffalo is the most dangerous of them all, "Ted Buffalo continued. "The Cape buffalo causes the most deaths among those who hunt the Big Five. In a charge he is very difficult to stop and if you don't stop him in his tracks he will keep going until he kills you. But that is not all. His hatred is so great that he isn't content just to kill you. He continues to gore his enemy with his horns and trample it with his hooves until his adversary is nothing more than a twisted remnant of bones, blood and gore. I read a story once about how a Cape buffalo charged a hunter who had wounded him with his rifle, and when the buffalo got done with the man all that was left of him were a pair of boots with two stumps protruding out of them."

"And since you are American, "I'm sure that you are acquainted with the Bison or American Buffalo and how American Indians stampeded whole herds of them until they all jumped off a cliff together. One after the other they all follow their leader. They are sheep. Complete idiots. You can even shoot one with a bow and arrow or sometimes even with a rifle and you can hit it three or four times and it will just stand there wondering what has happened."

"I choose to think of the buffalo as the Cape buffalo which is intelligent, fast, overpowering, and completely relentless in battle."

"Think what you want then. It's not going to matter because the Thais will think you are completely stupid. After all, you are the one who will have to live here, so what other Americans think of you isn't going to change the minds of the Thais. I've lived here a long time, so I know.   If you not believe me, I cannot help you and you will learn a very huge lesson. This I can assure you."

"I'm not changing my name. My family takes great pride in it."

All these newcomers think they know everything, thought Hermann.   *And expatriates such as me have learned nothing. They will never listen.   They are so boring and they are complete idiots.   They all think they are so special and so smart and they have everything figured out. I'm tired of these people. I have no time for them.*

"Okay then", said Hermann changing the subject.   Let's go over your application to purchase a condo here at The

Bahthaus. I see you want something high up such as on the sixth floor overlooking the Gulf of Thailand. I also notice that you are currently staying at The Shady Inn and that you have been there for one month. I will need to do a little background check on all of this." Hermann's eyes widened with surprise when he suddenly discovered that he knew the man who owned The Shady Inn and had drunk beer with him several times. The man's name was Gunther Schmidt.

"Will you excuse me for a few minutes," Hermann continued. "I have an important phone call to make."

"No problem. Take your time, Hermann."

Hermann fumbled with his cell phone as he left the room already dialing the number.

A voice answered on the other end. "Gunther speaking."

"This is Hermann. Do you have time for me?"

"Why sure, Hermann. So how are things in Little Germany?"

'As you know, I am looking for candidates to buy condos from me, and I have here in my office at this very moment a man who is staying with you. His name is Ted Buffalo. What do you know about him?"

"He always pays his bills on time. He even pays a week ahead of time if that's what you mean." Gunther replied.

"I didn't mean that. What I mean is, "What kind of man is he?"

"You want to know my honest opinion, Hermann?"

"I want to know your true feeling."

"He's a complete idiot.--especially with women."

"How do you know that?"

"Well, for one thing he's got a girlfriend who has a Thai husband."

"So what's so new about that?" Hermann asked.

"I told him the woman was married but he didn't believe me."

"Tell me the story."

"Ted Buffalo met the woman when she was working at Hooty's Go-Go Club and let me tell you she's a hoot alright. He started paying her 4,000 baht to spend the night with him. As you know only too well, Hermann, he could have found a sweet young thing at a beer bar and been paying her just 1,000 baht a night or a girl who has a regular job, but not Ted Buffalo. I told him I thought he was foolish to do his hunting in a go-go bar on account of the girls charging so much more than he should be paying, but Ted persisted. He didn't like the heat. He told me he needed the air conditioning so the beer bars were not for him. And he's one fat mother fucker. So who knows, maybe when your body and mine are at 98.6 degrees Fahrenheit, his is running at 106 degrees, while he's sitting there sweating. I mean, for him, sweating must be awfully hard work."

> In 2006 the rate of exchange was approximately 40 baht to the dollar. By 2011 the American dollar plummeted to 30 baht to the dollar. In 2006 most go-go dancers were asking 1000 baht for short time and 1500 to 2000 baht long time. In spite of the plummeting exchange rates of the American and European currencies to the baht in 2011 most go-go dancers are now asking 1500 baht for short time, 3000 baht long-time.

"He's a fat American alright," Hermann agreed.

"So you know the ritual. He's got this go-go girl lined up every day for the whole two weeks he's staying here. But she keeps leaving my guest house every night by 1 a.m., 2 a.m. in the morning. Well, you know as well as I do if the girl leaves without spending the entire night with you, it's a short time arrangement so he should be paying her only 1500 baht. But she keeps leaving here early in the morning."

"Do you know the reason for that?"

"She's got a husband, that's why."

"So I see this picture of this girlfriend leaving your guesthouse every night. How does she go home?"

"She gets picked up by her husband."

"You must be joking, Gunther."

"No, I'm not joking. It's always the same Thai man who picks her up and he's always driving the same motorbike. The reason I know it's the go-go girl's husband is the girl who works night shift tells me he is."

"How does she know?" Hermann asked.

"It's the same old story," Gunther continued. "The girl has this Thai man hanging around with her. So she tells her Western boyfriend it's her brother. My night girl is picking up on all these little things, such as how the man picking her up on the motorbike looks at her, how she treats him, and so on and she would know that the motorbike driver is not the girl's brother."

"Let me get this straight then. You actually told Ted Buffalo that his girlfriend was being picked up by her Thai husband and he asked you why you knew and you told him that your night shift girl told you it was the husband and he still didn't believe you."

"Yes. That is exactly correct."

"Why didn't he believe you?"

"He told me I didn't have any evidence that it was the Thai husband picking her up, and when I explained that my night girl had informed me it was her husband, he told me he wanted to interrogate her. But my word should be good enough for him and when I told him my girl was not lying, he should have left it at that. So I had to inform him that if he asked my night shift girl anything about the subject I would have to throw him out of my guest house."

"Why?"

"Because it would cause nothing but problems between me and the girl," Gunther replied. Not to mention between her and the go-go dancer. As it is, he's already told his go-go dancing girlfriend that my night shift girl has told him her husband is picking her up despite my telling him not to tell his girlfriend. My girl has told me all of this so whenever Miss go-go walks through my lobby she now ignores my night girl because she has broken the code of silence governing Thai-falang relationships. If I now allow Mr. Buffalo to ask my girl a lot of questions, that's going to cause problems between us. She might even quit her job here."

"Did you try and explain all of this to Ted Buffalo?" Hermann asked.

"I did, but he immediately dismissed everything I was telling him. He said to me, "Why she won't ever quit her job with you if I question her. I must question her or everything she says is completely false. I even think your night girl is jealous of my go-go dancer girlfriend," Ted had the balls to tell me. Ted then told me that whereas my night girl was probably making just 8000 baht a month, his girlfriend was making more than that amount in just one week. He even told me he had discussed all of this with his girlfriend and that she explained to him that my night girl didn't like her, that she was jealous of her much better looks, and that she hated her because she was making a lot more money working at a go-go than she was."

"I think I got the picture," said Hermann.

"It gets even better than that."

"Surely not."

I once went out with him to the movies. I took my girlfriend along and he was supposed to bring his girlfriend with him. So here he's paying her 4000 baht a day, right?

"That's what you told me."

"And she's supposed to be with him, taking care of him, and fucking him, okay?"

"Well sure. If he's paying her 4000 baht a day, that's an awful lot of money for a Pattaya girl."

"But she's not with him. My girlfriend, Ted Buffalo, and I took a baht taxi straight down to the new Central Festival Shopping Center to watch the 7:00 p.m. show. She's supposed to be there waiting for us, except she's not there."

"And?"

"We have already purchased the tickets. I went down there early afternoon and picked them up. Ted Buffalo did the same thing, so here he's got two tickets for the movie but no girlfriend. We wait about five minutes for her, then he calls her and she tells him she's not left her room yet because she's feeding the dog."

"Dog! Feeding the dog? That is ridiculous."

"Exactly. And then she doesn't show up for another two hours. Somehow I convinced Ted Buffalo not to wait for her and that he should see the movie with me and my girlfriend so we went in the theater and took our seats."

"Then what happened?"

"After the movie, we went to dinner at a restaurant close to the cinema. Meanwhile Ted has called his girlfriend at least two more times to see where she's at, and when she's coming. She tells him she's gotten stuck in traffic."

"I suppose her room is close to the cinema," Hermann suggested.

"Close enough. The room is down on Pattaya Tai and from there you'd drive to 2nd Road and after that it's a straight shot down 2nd Road which takes only about ten minutes. That's the thing about so many of these girls. There's no logic to them whatsoever. If the go-go girl dancer was smart she would have realized that Ted could figure that out. She should have known that he knew that her getting caught in heavy traffic was a complete impossibility and that she was completely full of bullshit. But guys like Ted Buffalo turn off their brains as soon as they arrive at the airport."

"So how long did it take her to finally show up?"

"We had already ordered our food. She came into the restaurant about ten minutes after we arrived, so considering that the show takes about two hours, that makes her over two hours late."

"What do you think she was doing?"

"I think she was doing something with her Thai boyfriend or with another customer."

"That is very possible. But even if she wasn't, Ted allowed her to simply run over him. He wasted that ticket on her when she never made it to the show and she kept lying to him about feeding the dog and getting stuck in traffic."

"Is he still with her."

"Yes. Absolutely. I would have finished her without question if she would have pulled that on me. Obviously the man has no self-respect and she knows it."

"I don't want him buying a condo from me. Many thanks for the information, Gunther. I will buy you a beer the next time I see you."

Reentering the room, Hermann announced. "I'm sorry about the interruption. Let's take a look at what condos are still available." Hermann re-seated himself at his desk in front of Ted Buffalo and pulled out a list of condos that had not been built yet.

"What size are you interested in, and do you want an ocean or town view?" Hermann asked.

"How high up do your condos go?"

"We will have seven floors when we are finished. We are constructing a low rise and we will be offering sixty units altogether. The reason we have chosen a low rise is there are many laws governing high rises. There are annual building inspections for example, and then there are all the additional rules and regulations one has to follow. I have decided it's much better to keep things simple."

"You are offering two types of condos, those having a sea view and those with a city view. If there a difference in price?"

Of course the condos facing the Gulf of Thailand will be the most expensive, and that is because they offer a view of the sea and that side is quieter. The other units, what we call having the city view, are all on the road, so as Naklua gets busier it's going to get noisier when you sit out on your balcony."

"I'd like a large two bedroom on the Gulf of Thailand up on the sixth or seventh floor where I can get a good view."

"Let me see what we have available," Hermann replied as he started to leaf through a computer printout describing all the units, their size in square meters, and each unit's gross sales price.   After studying the printout for a brief moment, Hermann continued, "We have a penthouse up on floor seven for 15 million baht.   Until now I would have recommended to you a 143 square meter unit on floors 5, 6 and 7.   But these are already taken.   We also have 100 square meter units on floors 2, 3, and 4 but none of them have a sea view."

"You must be joking!" Ted Buffalo replied.   "Do you mean to tell me that you have just started your building, and all those units are already sold out?"

"I'm afraid so," Hermann lied considering that he still had most of the units available, but he wanted to keep Ted Buffalo out of his community at all costs knowing only too well that such idiots are nothing but trouble.

"Then tell me about what you do have," Ted Buffalo replied.

"These units are still around 118 square meters so they are not small.   They face North so they don't have a sea view, but after a while when you have a sea view, you will take it for granted and not even notice the sea view.   And these units are much cheaper.   As you know the higher you go when buying a condo, the more money you must pay per square meter and if you get a sea view you must pay even more money."

"How much are the 100 square meter units without the sea view?" Ted Buffalo asked.

"They are only 4 million baht," Hermann replied, but they get higher priced when you go up towards the 7th floor.   That's the beginning price on floor number two."   Once again Hermann was lying.   He was giving the American the final gross sales price and not the low-ball introductory offer.   Later on once the building was completed he would be selling such units for 4 million baht, but that would be after the risk was no longer factored in as part of the deal.   By then construction would be complete and most of the units would already have been sold.   But at this early stage of the game with only the first two floors even being erected, whether or not most of the condos would actually be sold would be anyone's guess.

Especially in Thailand, whether or not a condo building would finally be completed amounted to a huge gamble.   Hermann normally discounted all his units by at least 600,000 baht, a practice that was normal in Thailand's real estate market.   But he also discounted them at least another half a million baht in order to lure the right kind of buyers into the community he was planning--the ideal community he had already visualized.

Ted Buffalo was the exact opposite of Hermann's definition of ideal.

Save me from this idiot, Hermann told himself. *I need to keep him out and everybody like him at all costs.*

"That's a little high," Ted Buffalo replied. And it's not at all what I have in mind. Thank you so much Hermann for your time but I need to get going." Ted Buffalo left the office without saying another word.

Ted Buffalo buys his condo

The American who had come into his office the day before was livid. "What do you mean to even suggest you don't have any of those larger units left for sale?" Ted Buffalo asked.

"I don't understand," Hermann lied.

"When I went back to my lodging, I immediately went on the Internet and found your company web site under Google. And there on your web site I found out that you haven't sold much of anything yet, which means almost all your units are still available. I also found out you are discounting your prices by around six-hundred thousand baht as your special introductory offer."

"We have not updated our web site for a long time," Hermann lied once again.

"I already checked that on the internet. Although your web site does not specify when you last updated it, I noticed that you have changed your web site since I last saw it. If you remember I told you when we first met each other that I found your condo building on the internet."

"Yes."

"And I wrote down that you still had forty-five units unsold. When I went back to my lodging, I checked your web site and I found that there are now forty-three units unsold which suggests that you have had your web designer change your web site in the past week."

"So what do you want to do about it?" Hermann asked coldly.

"What do I want to do about it? Well I am going to buy one of those 143 square meter units from you on the sixth floor, and you are going to give me your special six-hundred thousand baht discount that you are offering on your large sixth floor units."

"I don't know if I can do that without checking with my German partners," Hermann once again lied knowing all too well that he didn't have any German partners and that he was a sole operator.

"Look. I have 50,000 baht ready for a deposit. I will come in tomorrow with my lawyer to make a deposit on one of your 143 square meter units. And if you aren't prepared to do business tomorrow then you can just expect to find yourself in court." Ted Buffalo abruptly left the office leaving Hermann sitting alone in his chair with his mouth gaping.

I'm going to have to let him in, whether I like it or not, thought Hermann. *He will land me in the courts and even if they are not effective here in Thailand a lot of bad publicity is going to come out of all of this.* Then he smiled to himself when he suddenly remembered how Ted Buffalo had just demanded a six-hundred baht discount for buying early, on plan, before the project ever materialized. Hermann chuckled, as he spoke to an imaginary audience, "With so many projects never getting finished I'm not giving up anything. That's just the normal incentive given to nearly all early purchasers for taking on the risk. At least I won't be giving him the additional preferred owner's discount the others will all be getting."

Saint Peter

Hermann couldn't help noticing the man wearing the obnoxious flowered shirt holding court at the Emerald Bar as he passed it to have a few beers at the next bar. The Buffalo Bar had a band playing a wide assortment of music, most of it American and English golden oldies. The three men in the band were Thai, and every one of them, especially the band leader, was gifted. They had it all down instrumentally being far better than all but the most highly paid bands in America. Each man could sing, but most of the singing was done by the band leader who wore his hair long, and who from first glance looked like an American hippy from the sixties. But no matter how hard they tried, their vocalization didn't come out right, and it didn't matter which one of them was doing the singing as there was simply no way for a Thai to emulate a Mick Jagger or a Jimmy Hendrix. A German was singing with the band, a German Hermann had met a number of times before. The German had gotten a college teaching job in the U.S. and had wound up living there for twenty-three years, which was almost exactly the same amount of time he had lived as a German in his homeland. He had recently gotten his U.S. citizenship without renouncing his German citizenship. Anton could sing in Thai, German and English and he relished showing off in front of the crowd, most of which was German. But as impressive as Anton was, Hermann couldn't help noticing the large man sitting in front of the bar he had just passed. He decided to double back to the Emerald Bar and to come back to the Buffalo Bar another time.

The Emerald Bar was an open air beer bar facing a large parking lot that connected all of the surrounding bars. The large man was sitting at a table just outside the bar entrance facing the parking lot. Surrounded by half a dozen bar girls, he was the only male at the table. In front of him was a half-finished bottle of Chang beer, but the man had forgotten that he had only half finished it, and had already started a new bottle one of the bar girls had brought him.

Hermann approached the little group asking, "Is this seat taken?"

"It is taken," the man replied. "I have two more girls coming to take that seat. I never can have too many women." Then he laughed and replied, "Go ahead. I am just joking with you. I need some good company and all the girls here love me only for my money. They really care less about me."

Hermann took a seat opposite the man as one of the girls jumped up to offer him her chair. "I'm Hermann," he said to his new companion as he extended his hand across the table.

"Peter. Although most of the girls here call me, Mr. Baht.", the man replied as he shook Hermann's hand.

"No, No, We all love you too much, Peter," one of the girls replied as she put her arms around his neck.

"Where are you from?" Hermann asked.

"The U.S. of A. It's a dirty job but someone has to come here to keep all these girls happy so the CIA sent me to dispense foreign aid to the needy."

"And you keep them happy?

"Why sure I do. I come here practically every night, and I buy them all beer or Thai whiskey and when I'm good and ready, I will take one of them home with me."

"So what happens to all the others? The ones you have not chosen?"

"They just have to go back home to their rooms where they stay three and four to the room which they have to share together. But on some other night, I will choose them too."

"So they all take turns having to sleep with you?"

Peter laughed so hard that his enormous belly started heaving up and down. "Yep. It's a fate worse than death, and sooner or later all of them will wind up sleeping with me."

"What about the ugly ones? Don't you hate taking them home with you?"

"Ugly ones? By that time I will be too drunk to care. I won't even notice the difference."

Both men noticed the tall slender woman standing behind the bar. Peter instantly got a hard on. He had just noticed the new woman, who immediately caught his eye and smiled back at him. Transfixed, his eyes moved up and down her body, ogling her shamelessly. A few moments later she came up behind the group unnoticed and put her arms around his neck.

"Well who are you"? Peter asked the new girl.

"Name me Lon," the girl replied in a low throaty voice. "I new girl bar. Where you come from?"

"Me American," Peter replied. "I live here now" which wasn't quite the truth because Peter was renting by the month living each month as it came. He had set up a real estate company in Pattaya hoping he could make a go out of selling and renting condos. He didn't have a lot of money in the bank and his business had been fluctuating wildly which meant that he never knew how long it would be before he would be forced to move back to selling real estate in the U.S. He had been into real estate almost his entire life, and had gotten a large number of the right contacts through the years, while getting to know the American market thoroughly. He could hardly miss if he ever had to return home, which is one of the reasons he had gotten so bored living there. Peter thrived on challenges–especially when challenge came in the form of rescuing vulnerable bar girls from predatory unscrupulous falangs.

"I lie you too much," the girl replied which was the same thing practically every Thai girl Peter had ever met without a single exception kept saying to him. Like all the others she was stuck on using the phrase too much instead of saying what she really meant to say which was "a lot."

"Well, I like you too Sweetie," the American replied then added, "You make me Hung Yai"-- which meant big dick.

At first the girl appeared embarrassed. Then she reached down and thrust her hand between Peter's legs as she grinned and asked him. "You make hung yai for me?"

Hermann couldn't keep his eyes off the woman. Most of the girls in the bar were short and dumpy with not much to choose from between them. Not one of them even began to match his standards. He had learned a long time ago that he could comb two streets filled with bar girls, with Sois 7 and 8 being prime examples, and not find a single girl who attracted him. Often he'd return home empty. But on other nights he could find several or more girls that he'd gladly take home with him without a second thought. That was the thing about the beer bars he had decided. It was the thrill of the chase that counted along with the uncertainty of what, if anything, he'd finally come up with.

It was so different in the go-go bars. The girls were all scantily dressed in the go-go's and oftentimes completely nude so a man could see right off what he was buying. If there were any stretch marks he could see them before committing himself to taking a girl. The same applied to go-go girls with saggy breasts, small breasts, or breasts no larger than a man's. It was like going to the supermarket where one could choose whatever he wanted. In the go-go's the girls always wore numbers, so if a man liked number 22 while watching her perform on the stage, all he had to do was to tell the Mamasan or waitress, "Send number 22 over." He'd then buy number 22 a drink and if all went well he'd wind up bar-fining her for 500 or 600 baht, sometimes even more depending on whether or not she was one of the dancers performing a show.

He would then typically give the girl 1000 to 1500 baht to have sex with him in his hotel room for an hour or two, and if he wanted her to stay with him all night he'd give her 2000 baht.

On Walking Street alone there must be at least 40 go-go bars along with a large number of beer bars and still another large group of bars surrounding a Thai boxing ring. Here one could watch Thai boxers beating the hell out of each other in matches that were pawned off to an unsuspecting audience of tourists as the real deal. The matches were all faked like professional TV wrestling-- therefore not real--but the girls were. At the Thai boxing arena there were over twenty small bars alone with more than 100 girls for sale there. On Walking Street a man couldn't miss-- especially in the Go-Go bars, where a large number of Pattaya's real stunners could be found. But Hermann had too often found that the women, who had agreed to spend the entire night with him, would more often than not start asking him at 2 or 3 a.m. if they could go home. "My children need me" they would often tell him, which he knew was a complete lie because most of the women working in the bars and go go's had left their children with their mothers off in a village somewhere up-country and were living in Pattaya for only one reason only-- so that they could send large amounts of money back home to Mama and Papa. Such "large sums of money" might not be all that much by Western standards, but in Thailand, especially up north, to a family of farmers a little money went a long way. So when a go-go dancer told him she wanted to go back to her room to look after her kids, she might actually mean she wanted to go back to her Thai boyfriend, who was probably working as a motorbike taxi driver making two hundred baht a day if he was lucky, a go-go club doorman or someone working inside the club doing as little as possible. Still another possibility was that she wanted to leave his bed at 2.a.m. just so that she could go to Lucifers, Insomnia, Tony's or another disco where she could freelance and catch another customer who she would then spend the rest of the night with. The most disgusting possibility Hermann could think of was the girl charging her customer 2000 baht long time after which she'd run off to a Thai karaoke club where she'd find a good looking Thai guy who she would pay to have sex with. Hermann knew of at least 20 Thai karaoke bars catering to Thai female sex workers who were getting too much from their clueless Western customers. Still another possibility was the girl simply wanted to run off to be with her Thai girlfriends, but whatever the reason, Hermann had decided a long time ago that go-go dancers far more often than beer bar girls tended to take their customers for granted, charged them twice as much money and took far less care of their needs than girls a man might meet practically anywhere else.

More often than not, the go-go girls considered themselves to be better than all the other prostitutes. They charged more-- therefore they were simply better, they reasoned. And a beer bar, if it offered its girls a salary at all, that salary would be about 2500 baht a month, whereas a go-go bar gave each girl 10,000 baht and up. Since much of Thai society values money and wealth as the absolute pinnacle any human being can attain, never mind that a person is a total incompetent jerk who is incapable of accomplishing anything worthwhile, simply working in a go-go bar makes such girls feel they are better than other women making less regardless of education or skills. Hermann had long ago realized that this was an oversimplification and that go-go girls came in all stripes and shades of black and white just like human beings everywhere, but such oversimplifications had served him well. For him go-go bars were foul territory. If a man looked hard enough he could find equally attractive women in the beer bars and he'd only have to pay a 200 baht bar fine and 1000 baht for long time.

The girl nuzzling on Peter's ear both intrigued and puzzled Hermann. Hermann wished she were going home with him which was out of the question since he already had a girlfriend waiting for him there. But her voice had been just a little off. It was not the high pitched voice most ladyboys have, but it wasn't quite the same most Thai women have either. There was a slight huskiness to it. The woman's very presence seemed to permeate the entire area. *She would be like a second skin enveloping any man having sex with her*, Hermann decided, *and my member would feel caught inside as if it were coated with glue. Well maybe, then again maybe not—nevertheless it is an enticing thought.*

Suddenly Peter blurted out: "Honey, you are too good looking to be bar lady. Are you sure you not ladyboy?" Peter considered the possibility for a moment, then commanded: "Open your legs, baby. I want to slide my hand inside your shorts to make sure you are not ladyboy."

Hermann watched the American pry open the woman's legs while forcing one of his hands down the top of her shorts below her belly. Peter grimaced as his hands suddenly encountered resistance.

"Damn, those shorts of yours sure are tight. I can hardly get my hand into your pants. I just want to be sure you don't have a dick down here."

"Peter, Hermann said impatiently, "She's a lady. I think so. She's the best looking woman here, and if you cannot believe that, then I will just bar-fine her myself." Hermann already knew that out of the thousands of bar girls and free lancers walking around Pattaya's busy streets, 20 % of them were men. The scary part is that in more than half the beer bars the flashiest, most sensational women aren't women. Then it starts to get even more scary when a tourist goes to a restaurant, has a lady wait on him only to find out the lady is a man, and then has the ladyman correct him when he calls her, "he". This doesn't faze expats who've lived in Thailand for very long who start calling a he a she and refer to the guy's purse as her purse. But what gets really scary is when so many expats start pointing out at an attractive ladyboy to their friends while exclaiming, "Damn, look at the body on her." So it's hardly surprising that so many newcomers to Pattaya are so easily seduced by a ladyman's looks because of inexperience, too much alcohol or the mind draining effects of jet lag only to find out the new love of his life has a penis after taking "her" up to his hotel room. Usually it's the high pitched voices that give the ladymen away, or a prominent Adams apple, behavior that is much more aggressive than the deportment exhibited by most bar girls, or exaggerated feminine mannerisms such as a pronounced swaying of the hips when they walk. *That's just one more reason this country is often called "Amazing Thailand",* Herman almost said aloud, *especially when so many ladymen get breast implantations or have their Adams' apples removed and even get sex change operations.* Hermann had once been to one of Bangkok's busy plastic surgery clinics where he had seen the Ladyboys line up for their breast implants. It's one thing to calmly dismiss the thought of having sex or not having sex with someone who once had a dick back in Germany, Herman decided, *but it's quite another thing to dismiss the same thought upon coming face to face with someone who is so obviously attractive that a man has to keep reminding himself, "No good. That's a man. I know it's a man. I won't even consider having sex with a man."* Herman's thoughts went back to a conversation he had recently had with an Englishman who had just put down a 50,000 baht deposit on a condo at the Bahthaus. The Englishman was staying at the Plumeria where Herman was staying while waiting for the construction of the Bahthaus to be completed. Herman had started to notice all the tall slender women the Englishman kept taking back to his room. Finally he had asked the Englishman to have a beer with him in the hotel's restaurant. Although Herman wasn't particularly fond of homosexuals he had nonetheless offered the man a condo after finding out that he liked the man a lot. He found the man's logic and his honesty to be unshakable which made it nearly impossible to dislike the man. But the one thing Herman placed perhaps the greatest value upon was the quality of a person's intellect, after reasoning that a dog can be honest, loyal, and strong, but the animal was still a dog after it was all said and done. It was the quality of a man's intellect that usually set him apart from all others, Herman reasoned, and the points this Englishman keeps making are nearly impossible to argue with.

Conversation with the "errant Englishman

"Back in England when was it that you finally determined that you were a homosexual?" Herman had asked the man.

"I never was a homosexual. Back in England? No never. Having sex with a man? That is horrible and disgusting."

"You mean to tell me that during your entire life in England a man never gave you a hard on?"

"No. Never."

"But you get a hard on here with all these ladymen?"

"Yes. Absolutely. But they aren't the same at all."

"But they are still guys."

"No they aren't. Try it just once Herman. You won't regret it. Then you come back and tell me they are guys."

Herman's thoughts returned to the attractive woman when he noticed her smiling back at him as she patiently waited for Peter to finish groping her.

"I have to find out for myself," Peter said loudly enough for the whole bar to overhear as his hand fidgeted underneath the girl's shorts searching for a penis.

"I need another beer," said Hermann.

"Me too," Peter replied. Then loudly enough for the entire bar to overhear him, he cried out, "Nope. I can't find a cock in these shorts."

He's colorful enough, Hermann thought. Then he pulled out his card, and offered it to the American. "Where are you staying, Peter?"

"I've rented a room at a hotel just off Naklua Road," Peter replied, "which I'm paying by the month. It's not bad. It has a swimming pool and it's just a couple of blocks from most of the bars I go to."

"Have you ever thought about getting something a little bigger and more permanent?" Hermann asked.

"Sure, I've thought about it, but most of the condos around here are way too expensive."

"I've got something you might want to consider."

"What are you offering?

"I'm having a building built right on the ocean. It's a low rise so you won't even have to wait for an elevator but there will be one in any case. We will have our own swimming pool. Internet access will be made available to every unit, and the units will be quite large. I'm German so you can be sure that everything will be of the highest quality. I will also include nice balconies with every unit because we Germans like to sit outside where we can drink our coffee in the mornings and our beer at night."

"That sounds very promising. About how much will your units be selling for?" Peter asked.

"About three million baht and up depending on a unit's size and location, but if you are financially secure enough, some special discounts might be arranged."

"Sounds like a winner," Peter announced as he took Hermann's card and stood up to face the bar. Then he called out, "Check bin", which meant he was ready to pay his bill.

One of the bar girls behind the bar came over immediately as Peter fumbled with his wallet. Then he said to her, "Two hundred baht bar fine. Just add it to my bin. I'm bar fining this lady."

After the woman returned with his change, Peter took the girl behind the bar and shoved her abruptly against a pole while telling her, "I want to check again to see that you are no ladyboy."

"I no ladyman," the woman protested.

"I want to be sure," Peter replied, as he thrust his hands deeply into her shorts and pressed his fingers between her legs.

Hermann watched from a distance in silence--for the first time mortified at the prospect of selling the American a condo.

Finally satisfied that his love of the evening was not a man, Peter steered her up the street to look for his car.

"I forgot where I put it," Peter said to the girl.

He took the girl several blocks up the Soi, then a side street or two. Finally, not able to remember where he had parked his rental car; he hailed a motorbike taxi which took them both back to his hotel for sixty baht.

"Oh well," he ended up telling the girl. "It will be there for me tomorrow afternoon. I will just have to look for it then." Then he said aloud to no one in particular: "I must be a Saint. My friends back in the U.S. have no idea of the things I have to put up with.   Saint Peter, that's me."

"What you say? The girl asked. "I must call you Sane?"

Saint Peter buys a condo

"How did things go the other night?" Hermann asked the American.

"To tell you the truth, I don't remember much of it," Peter replied.

"What do you remember?"

"I took the girl back to my room and as soon as I got there she was all over me. She nearly raped me. I remember her getting my clothes off and falling into bed with me and then she started kissing me all over. Eventually she started sucking my dick and after that she rolled over on top of me and stuck my dick right up her ass."

"Was she a girl or a man?"

"To tell you the truth, Hermann, I really don't remember."

"Are you going to be seeing her again?"

"Uh. No."

"Then let's start talking about what condo you want to buy," said Hermann.

The two men walked up the street to the Bahthaus which was now three stories high. Fifteen or twenty men and women were crawling all over it, trying to get it done on time. Peter noticed that the men appeared to be much shorter than most Thai men. But he still didn't know that most of them were illegal workers brought in from Cambodia and Burma. Neither did Hermann for that matter. He had contracted with S & D Construction to build the Bahthaus which employed workers from Cambodia and Burma to do the actual work and several managers to rip everyone else off. This included the illegals who had no recourse to Thai Law and were much more pliable, which made them willing to work for a great deal less than Thais. Herman noticed three new cars in the parking lot, all bought by the three managers, but by the time he had noticed, it was too late.

Hermann took Peter up a wide flight of concrete stairs to the display units on the 2nd floor. Then he took the American into the smaller of the two units which he had completely furnished with a large leather couch and matching leather recliner, a kitchen and two bathrooms complete with showers, toilets and vanity.

After seeing the master bedroom, Peter fell in love at first sight. There was a twelve foot long wardrobe that took up almost an entire side where he could put all his clothing and other personal belongings. The wardrobe had three sliding doors upon which mirrors had been attached and a number of drawers built into its lower section. Bordering the mirrors were straw colored rectangles fashioned from bamboo that had been cut into thin long strips which had then been twined together by hand into a weave patterned fabric. Inset into each drawer the same material had been inserted. Alongside one wall was a king sized bed adorned with the same straw colored material. Both the bed and the matching dresser were teak and so were the two end tables on either side of the bed. Peter couldn't keep his eyes off the three foot long sailing ship model on top of the dresser. Made entirely out of wood, the attention to detail paid by whoever had made it, must have cost hundreds of hours of work.

"Where did you get all this stuff?" Peter asked Hermann.

"Everywhere," Hermann replied--"Most of it from Chiang Mai well to the North of here. As you already know, Chiang Mai is Thailand's 2nd largest city although Pattaya's catching up to it fast. But here in Pattaya nearly everyone's after the quick buck whereas Chiang Mai is well known for its handicrafts. It's most definitely the place to buy all of your furniture because you will save fifty percent by going up there when it comes time to furnish your place."

"What about the ship? Peter asked.

"That came from Vietnam. There's a shop selling all kinds of ships about like it here on Walking Street but one that size costs $1000 American. I got it in Vietnam for $60.00."

"How about those two lamps near the bed?"

"Also from Vietnam. But you can get some good ones here even in Pattaya if you know where to go. Then again, you are much better off in Chiang Mai."

Peter liked the view of the trees from the master bedroom window. A long balcony stretched from the bedroom all the way out to the far end of the living room overlooking the smaller plants growing thickly among the trees which rose above the 2nd floor level.

"How much?" Peter asked.

"We can get to that later," Hermann replied. "You haven't even seen the second display unit."

"How big is this one?"

"One hundred and eighteen square meters."

"How big is it in English? We don't use square meters in the United States."

"It's nearly 1300 square feet but that includes the balcony. "Come Peter. Let me show you my other display unit. You might like it even better."

The 2nd display unit was even larger. Its living room alone measured 25 by 22 feet although Peter didn't know that at the time. It's total area was nearly 1600 square feet. "Too big for me," Peter decided.

"I want to talk about one of the smaller units," Peter told Hermann decisively.

"Have a seat, Peter, so we can go over some figures."

Going back to the smaller unit, the two men sat down on the leather couch together. Hermann picked up a leather bound notebook in which he kept a number of pages that included a sample contract, a number of pictures of the display units, an artist's drawing of the final building and a price sheet.

"My pricing is simple. But first I must ask you. Do you want a condo with a sea view or town view?"

"What is the difference?" asked Peter.

"For one thing there is a big difference in price. The town view units cost quite a bit less. They are on the street so they are going to be noisier. However, if you get the double glazed windows and doors they will still be quiet inside. Out on the balcony is another thing. And no matter where you live a sea view will always cost more because nearly everybody wants a view of the ocean."

"I want the sea view," Peter replied firmly.

"Then it's very simple. First of all, you really cannot see the ocean unless you are at least on the 4th floor. You have noticed all the trees which are in the way even though you will be living just thirty meters from the beach. This display unit's on the 2nd floor. Its normal price is 3,200,000 baht. Each floor you go above it costs another 600,000 baht. This is for two reasons. First, because of the sea view and second, the higher up you go the quieter the units become."

"Say, I want a unit on the 5th floor?"

"Let me find it," said Hermann as he pulled the price list up. "That will be 5,600,000 baht which is four times 600,000 plus this unit's price of 3,200,000 baht."

"It gets a little high doesn't it?"

"That's before any of the discounts."

"Come again."

"First off the prices I'm giving you are not my final asking prices. These prices are effective after the building is completed, if there are any units left by then. Now when you buy any condo here or anywhere else you really don't know what the place will really be like or even if it's going to be completed. For this reason I'm taking 600,000 baht off. We are planning on this building being finished in nine months, so you will have to wait at least that long before you can move in. So that brings your price down to 5 million baht."

"That's getting to be more reasonable."

"But if you qualify, I am going to give you an additional discount of eight hundred thousand baht which then reduces your final price to only 4,200,000 baht."

"What do you mean qualify?" Peter asked, his mind churning with excitement as his mind grasped that 4.200,000 baht was just $105,000, an unheard of sum for such a large place offering a sea view that was certain to be of high German quality.

"Well, I don't allow just anyone to move in here. You have already passed my first test."

"What's that?"

"You seem to be the kind of person I want to have living here. You see, I'm going to be living here myself so I want people around me who I can get along with. My second test is you must pass certain financial requirements."

"Which are?"

"I want a copy of your last two tax returns so I can be sure you have enough income to be able to afford to make all the payments."

"What is your payment schedule?

"First, you must make a deposit of 50,000 baht. Then I will give you a contract to look over. You can have a lawyer look over it if you want and then I will give you two weeks to check out the contract and to suggest any changes to it. After that we sign the contract you must give me 20 % of the price of the condo less your 50,000 baht deposit."

"And then what?"

"Each month you pay 5 % of the total price of the condo. So if it is complete in 9 months, you will have paid 45 % of the price, as well as the 20 % leaving you with 35 % to pay when the building is finished or just before you move in."

"Okay, you have a deal," Peter replied. "I'll come in tomorrow to give you 50,000 baht, and then we will decide on what unit I'm buying, what I am getting and so on."

Spicy girl and the Chinese

When the condo was nearly finished, Hermann told Frank he could move in within the week, so there was no real reason for him to move out of his Central Pattaya hotel room other than his wanting to start getting to know his new neighborhood in Naklua. But after convincing himself that he needed to take advantage of its 50 meter long swimming pool and free buffet breakfasts, he had reserved a room at the Plumeria for a week.

Frank found Naklua to be vastly different from Central Pattaya where he had been spending the past year waiting for the Bahthaus to be built. Naklua's back streets which he would soon be making his home were much less heavily trafficked and far quieter than the noisy, raucous, beer bar lined 2nd and Beach Roads and the little short streets such as Soi 6, 7 and 8 that intersected them where several thousand beer bar girls plied their trade. Although Frank had immensely enjoyed himself over the past year in bustling Pattaya, the dark side of the beer bars had started to get the better of him. They were just too addictive and not just for him, but also for Spicy, who loved to drink and socialize. Several times, Frank, unable to sleep, had gone just outside his hotel to a beer bar within thirty yards of his hotel front door where Spicy, unwilling or unable to restrain herself, padded down to join him ten minutes later in her bathrobe.

On their way back to the Plumeria from having dinner at the Korean restaurant that was just up the street from the condo, Frank had forgotten to put his motorbike helmet on so he had replaced it with a light cotton hat and accelerated down Soi Wongamat past the Diamond Star Hotel. As the bike picked up speed, a gust of wind off the sea blew the hat off his head. Frank saw the hat in the middle of the street twenty meters behind his Air Blade and braked instantly. Fearful that a car might run over the hat, as soon as he came to a complete stop, Frank shouted: "Spicy, run back and get hat for me!"

As Spicy was running back to retrieve his hat, Frank noticed a small group of Asian women walking down the opposite side of the street. Obviously walking back to one of the opulent hotels close-by, the women were looking across the street at Frank, laughing at the incongruous sight of an older man getting his hat blown off his head while driving a motorcycle with his thirty year old girlfriend sitting behind him. Anyone would have laughed at the scene, especially after hearing the much older man order the Thai girl, "Spicy, run and get my hat for me." (Because I'm too lazy to do it). But when Spicy ran back to the motorbike with Frank's hat, she was fuming.

"Fuck you!" Spicy screamed loudly at the Asian girls who were still tittering among themselves as they continued to point at Frank and Spicy.

"What you say?" One of the Asian women called back to her.

"You China. Me Thai. Me Spicy. Fuck you!" Spicy hollered back at the small group of young Chinese women.

Surprised at Spicy's sudden outburst Frank looked back at her still standing behind the bike pointing animatedly at the Chinese girls. "Oh come on. "I am too funny. Falang ting tong to ladies. They laugh. Anybody laugh."

"I no care," Spicy replied. "China lady no good. Lady see you and think you old man. You buffalo and you lose hat. They see me, young lady, and they think old man and young lady no good. They no understand. Fuck them. Fuck China."

"That does it," said Frank. "I need a beer."

"Me too," Spicy spat back at him. "I want forget China. Chinese lady do not even shower before boom-boom. Not same same Thai lady. China lady smell very bad. No good for boom-boom."

At seven p.m. Spicy and Frank were the only guests in Plumeria's swimming pool. More than a hotel, Plumeria offered serviced apartments, hoping to draw in customers wanting more than just one or two weeks' accommodations as tourists, but who required one month's or even as much as a year's housing while they looked for something more permanent. Each unit had its own small separate kitchen with a refrigerator, microwave and other amenities, an in room safe and a small balcony overlooking one of Plumeria's two swimming pools. Near both swimming pools was a small waterfall behind a small lily pond. Even the smallest units were larger than a typical hotel room and much more fully furnished. A man could easily live a year in these smaller units which were designed to be very space efficient. Just off Soi Wongamat was a Family Mart and behind that was a small parking lot. Plumeria's lobby and restaurant were behind the parking lot with most of the serviced apartments situated still further from the road. Because it was set so far from the road, Plumeria was very quiet–so quiet that Frank felt he was staying at an idyllic Thai resort far removed from noisy boisterous Sin City. Yet some of Sin City's liveliest, most ill-famed bars were not much more than half a mile away and Soi Six with its many bars and prostitutes purveying short time sex in short time rooms above the bars, was a mere ten minutes from Plumeria by motorbike.

Spicy reached into the small Styrofoam cooler resting on the side of the large Jacuzzi they were sitting in and pulled out two Heineken bottles. Ignoring the bottle opener that Frank had put in the cooler when he had packed it with beer and ice from their little apartment, Spicy brought the first bottle up to her mouth, grinned and pulled the cap off with her teeth. Handing the bottle to Frank, she proceeded to bite the cap off the second bottle.

"Spicy, damn it, you've got to stop doing that. Teeth you, go kaput," Frank said in broken English. He spoke very slowly to make sure that Spicy understood.

Completely unperturbed, Spicy sat next to him, as her eyes crinkled into lazy slant eyes and smiled. "Me Spicy. Me hot lady," she laughed back at him.

"Yeah, and I don't want to be paying all your future dental bills either," Frank replied knowing she didn't understand one word of what he was telling her. "Not to mention even thinking of what that's got to be doing to your pretty face." He shuddered while thinking about all the enamel that would be cracking in his own mouth if he attempted being the human bottle opener Spicy relished being.

The Jacuzzi they were sitting in must have been nearly twelve feet long and have been built to accommodate up to fifteen people at a time. Two hundred yards away loomed the Sky Beach condo skyscraper, which towered forty-two stories over everything around it. Sky Beach like its two sister developments, Park Beach and Silver Beach, was painted a bright white. Just behind all three was the Gulf of Thailand which could not be seen from inside Plumeria. Other than Sky Beach, which was perfectly framed against the orange setting sun, nothing could be seen outside the inner world of Plumeria. Frank heard Plumeria's resident peacock crowing nearby, breaking the silence. He rarely saw the Peacock but heard it often, especially at night.

"Sodi Kapp," Spicy said to him, as she proceeded to drink straight from her bottle.

"Sodi Kapp. Life just doesn't get any better than this," Frank replied as he contemplated the palm trees and many tropical plants all around him while studying the high rise in the distance. Frank concluded that it was a symbol of Wongamat Beach's being the most glamorous, coming area in the region. As he drank deep from his bottle and felt the water from the Jacuzzi's jets massage his aching back muscles, he thought about the first time Spicy and he had met.

He had met her in a bar where she had been the cashier, had bar-fined her out of the place and brought her into the room he was renting while waiting for his condo to be finished. After staying with him for several nights, Spicy had popped the big one on him. "Do you want me for long long time?" she had asked. "You give me 10,000 baht one month, I stay, cook for you, clean and boom-boom. Good for you and good for me."

Never having had a live in Thai girlfriend, he decided "why not?" And she had been with him ever since.

He felt the jagged edge of a tile bite into his back which brought his thoughts back to the present. *In less than a week, I'll be moving into my new condo.*

Welcome to the Fun House

Frank saw the tall burly blue eyed Westerner climbing off his motorbike in front of the Bahthaus while on his way back from picking up a T.V. dinner at the Family Mart down the street. Frank instantly realized that the man was, like him, one of the new condo owners. The man broke into a smile when he saw Frank coming out of the condo entrance.

"Well hello, hello. You must be a condo owner like me. My name is Mickel," the tall man called out cheerfully to Frank.

"Yes. I now live up on the sixth floor. Right over there," Frank said while pointing at his new condo's outside balcony overlooking the sea."

"I see you have a corner unit. So do I," Mickel replied. "I live right below you in a sea view unit also but I'm on the fifth floor."

"I'm Frank and I'm from the U.S. Where are you from?" Frank asked.

"I'm from Norway, but it's good to be here. Very good. Do you like to drink beer? Maybe we have one together. We have many beers together."

"Let's do that," Frank replied.   "But first, I must get something to eat."

"I have already eaten, but go ahead. I wait for you."

"We can go somewhere. Just give me a few minutes. I just need to buy one of those Thai TV dinners and go up into my condo, microwave it and then I can meet you. How does half an hour sound?"

"Half an hour? Okay, I wait for you. Just come up to the fifth floor after you have eaten," said Mickel. "I know just the place where we can go."

The Hospital

Stretching out his legs lazily while watching the 50 inch television in his hospital room, Fast Eddy eagerly anticipated the arrival of the next nurse the hospital would soon be sending to his suite. He studied three menus while making his most important decision of the day–which was what to have for lunch. Fast Eddy knew something most Americans were completely ignorant about—that Bangkok Pattaya Hospital delivered a level of medical care, ambience and comfort most Americans would never experience–starting with modestly priced meals from two restaurants in the hospital and that didn't even include the hospital's own kitchen. He'd have to pay extra if he ordered off the menu of one of the two restaurants, but Fast Eddy figured, *Why not? I'm already paying a fortune to be here and I don't even have to be here.*

There wasn't anything wrong with Fast Eddy. He had come to the hospital just for the women, but he never told anyone at hospital admissions that. He entered the hospital complaining that he was experiencing shortness of breath and chest pains and that there just had to be something wrong with his heart. The hospital put him through a battery of tests on his first day and found nothing wrong with him. When Fast Eddy's doctor wanted to discharge him, Fast Eddy told him, "Doc, staying here for several more days will do me good because something just might show up on the electrocardiogram after a little time has passed." When his doctor still wanted to send him home, Fast Eddy retorted, "Never mind the cost. That's my problem and it's all up to me. I want to stay here. This place is better than a five star hotel."

Too young for a retirement Visa at 48, Fast Eddy was already receiving a lifetime pension from the U.S. military. He had put in his twenty years in the Marine Corps, ending up as a Master Sergeant and was now collecting over $2000 a month pension before deciding he could live much cheaper and better in Thailand than he could in the U.S. He had acquired his nickname Fast Eddie in the Marines and the name stuck. No one called him Eddie or Ed from then on. At 50 he could get a retirement Visa from Thai immigration. In the meantime he'd have to keep making his border runs to Cambodia once a month to keep his tourist Visa current. He'd already lived in Pattaya for four years and finally decided that bar girls were not for him.

An automatic 30 day visa is stamped into the passports of newly arrived visitors in Thailand. If someone wants to stay longer he can apply for a three month tourist visa or even go for the 1 year retirement visa if he's over 50. Those who wish to stay longer than 30 or 90 days can extend their visas by going out of the country after which they can reenter the kingdom and get a new 30 day or 90 day Visa. Many residents without retirement visas will take a bus ride to Cambodia have their passports stamped there, cross the border and go back into Thailand to get a new visa—which is a 1 day proposition.

He had argued the point with Frank who was hot on Nana, a go-go dancer he was seeing while Spicy was off visiting her parents, and he remembered Frank's words, "It really won't matter where you are going to find her, Fast Eddy. The girl is going to want your money, so she can send it to mamma and papa and I don't care if she's working in a bar, an office or even a bank. Unless her family is rich her first and most important mission is going to do everything she can to make sure her parents are well cared for. So I'm going to just stick it out with the professionals. That way I won't get too close to any one of them and won't get caught in that trap so many idiots fall into by thinking that this one is different. But Spicy had caught him nonetheless.

Fast Eddy had gone the bar girl route too many times and had usually found the girls were not qualified to do anything more demanding than working in a bar. Most of them had not even learned that it was important to show up on time or that it was essential to see a task to completion once they had started it. They had no concept of the value of money and so long as they had it now, had no concern for the future. Most of the girls he had met in the bars came from Issan, the poorest region of Thailand and had come from rural areas where they were lucky to have received even an eighth grade education.

Fast Eddy had concluded that those girls who had high School educations and even most college educated girls were incapable of logical thinking. Several times Fast Eddy had gone with girls who had regular jobs and a couple of them did have college degrees, but it always amounted to the same thing. Every single girl Fast Eddy had ever been with was incapable of thinking ahead. A prime example of this was when he was taking a girl out to a restaurant for dinner. Even if the girl knew she would be sitting down to a restaurant meal at 6:00, if given the chance she would more likely than not buy food from a sidewalk vendor at 5:00, which left her with no appetite by the time they got to the restaurant. He had also seen girls who would order six or seven courses that would cost over thirty dollars and wind up eating just 25 % of all the food they had ordered after watching their dates order only a single item from the menu. And although trying his best to put such incidents behind him, he kept muttering under his breath: "Morons". Then he'd wind up thinking, *At least they all aren't that bad."*

Then there was that insurance broker who had collected a 6000 baht premium from him for insurance on his condo. He had nice furniture in his place and if his pipes broke and leaked water down into the condo below him, he'd be liable to the man living below him for water damages. He had paid the female agent the premium and then waited for her to deliver his policy for over two months before finding out that she had never handed his premium money over to the insurance company which had left him completely uninsured. He never found out exactly what had happened, but he was sure that she had some financial pressures, perhaps even a Thai husband wanting his beer money, and that she had figured on paying for his policy after the emergency passed. It had never dawned on the woman that the money should have been earmarked to pay for his policy, and for no other purpose, and that only after she had turned in the money and paperwork to the insurance company was she entitled to a commission. She had wound up losing her insurance license for embezzlement.

For the most part he had found that nearly all the women he met in Pattaya lacked the most basic values. But the worse thing was that all of them whether they worked in a bar or had regular jobs, and even girls with college degrees, were products of Thai culture and Fast Eddy had decided that the culture that had influenced them since childhood was completely incompatible with his own. For one thing, Thailand is one of the most nationalistic countries on earth. In a nutshell nearly all Thais Fast Eddy had been meeting in Pattaya truly believed that Thailand was the number one country on the planet. It had never dawned on such Thais that their schools were greatly inferior to those of most Western countries.   Rote learning was the norm where students accepted things as being fact simply because someone in authority said they were. It continued to amaze Fast Eddy that no matter how many times the authority figures were proven wrong, people continued to believe in them.

And it didn't matter what you could do. What counted was what family you came from, how much money your family had and what color you were. And white skin's in whereas dark skin's out because having dark skin meant you had probably lived on a farm and that you therefore had to do hard labor for your money. To wealthier Thais doing hard labor is doing a buffalo's work. Worse of all was the concept of face. Face meant that you could not criticize anyone for doing a poor job or even an inadequate job at anything because by doing so you'd cost the person face. The reality is that because the other person could not be criticized without losing face, you would have to continue to accept the poor performance level of that person who would from then on have no hope for improvement without such criticism. And because most Thais considered Thailand as the number one country in the world, most Thais felt they had little to gain from Westerners beyond the cash they could get from them, which amounted to their being almost completely unwilling to learn from any Westerner.

Fast Eddy's mind drifted back to the brighter side of living in a place that had no values, specifically back to his good times with the cigarette girl.

He had been touring several of Pattaya's go-go bars with two of his friends. Iron Man was the third bar the threesome visited. Straight off Fast Eddy was put off by the bar's dimly lit interior. As he went back to the fifth stage while passing the first four which were lined up in a row, he felt as if he were walking deep into a fog where no one had a face and no one would care too much one way or the other about who did what or what kinds of things took place.

The stage had enough room for eight men to sit around it ogling a pair of girls performing in front of their noses. One of the girls was wearing a harness. The affair looked like a trapeze, but actually wasn't much more than a couple of handles attached to a pair of cables one of the girls grasped as she glided through the air in front of them.

Fast Eddy waited for the waitress to bring him his beer. Then he checked his bill just to see what his beer was running him. After looking at his ticket on which 90 baht had been written he noticed that the girl, who had suspended herself above the stage, was smoking a cigarette from her vagina. Completely fascinated, Fast Eddy couldn't look away as he watched a cigarette protruding out of the trapeze girl's love channel. The other girl kneeled over her monitoring the smoke coming out of her pussy while she watched the cigarette's glowing tip to make sure that it didn't go out. The 2nd girl functioned as a bellows by pushing down her companion's abdomen to force more air into the human air chamber. For a second several inches of the cigarette bobbed out of her sweet spot, and then most of it disappeared until only a stud remained, emitting smoke. Fast Eddy was entranced as he watched the cigarette alternately getting swallowed up into the girl and popping out like a narrow inverted penis.

He got a hard on and asked himself why since usually he remained unaffected by all the attractive women he kept coming into contact with. The girl noticed his erection and motioned down at her cigarette inviting him to pull it out of her and smoke it. She smiled at him, took his hand and guided it down to the cigarette. But as soon as he had nearly grasped it, she jerked to one side. His hand missed the cigarette and landed just an inch away from where it had been. She beckoned at him to try once more. Only this time he got his fingers around the butt and pulled it out of her. The girl then put two fingers against her lips, pretending to smoke a cigarette, beckoning him to smoke from the moistened butt he had between his fingers. He almost did it, but laid the still smoking butt in the ashtray instead.

Next came the Coco Cola trick. She took a bottle of one liter bottle of Coke Lite and held it between her legs. And then she stuck it inside of her. Fast Eddy watched half the coca cola disappear from the bottle. Then she pulled the bottle out of her vagina which expelled the air that was trapped inside her. Coca Cola gushed out of her, shooting a foot into the air while splattering a Russian sitting next to him.

The bar fine was 1000 baht, the room upstairs was another 300 baht and he still had to pay her 1000 baht for short time. But it had been worth it.

*****

Pattaya could have had a wonderful beach. Its coastline was lined with gorgeous rock formations meandering first to the North before disappearing abruptly to the East before turning North again, not once but three times before a man could finish a two mile walk. Such a coastline was never boring but each year it was becoming more and more polluted. Both Frank and Fast Eddy had long ago decided that things would never improve. The mayor and the city hall ruling Pattaya were first off not the brightest candles to graduate from their respective colleges and universities. Their parents were some of the wealthiest people in Thailand. The politicians who wound up in charge were sons who had used their parent's money and position to advance their careers. Then once in power, they had no interest in producing a beautiful beach that could attract tourists from all over the globe. Having to redo the narrow beach on the West side of Beach Road every year should have been an embarrassment to the stalwart politicians in charge of all the public works projects. The concrete walkways had many low points that formed large pools of water every time it rained because it had not dawned on anyone to put the whole thing on a grade or to even use a single level while building them. No one bothered to put drains in so whenever there was a heavy downpour the water would simply collect in large pools wherever there was a low spot. Fast Eddy had been sure he had seen construction crews of illegals from Burma and Cambodia doing all the work since most of the men seemed significantly shorter than most Thai males, but oh well, the money kept rolling in and that's all that mattered to the proud college graduates who had become Pattaya's power elite.

What turned out to be one of Pattaya's most embarrassing examples of poor urban planning was a long strip alongside Beach Road where the work crews had completely re-graded much of the area between Beach Road and the shoreline by putting in attractive new walkways and grass. But once they had planted all that nice green grass they never thought about having it watered. There was not a single sprinkler in sight. Then to insure that all the grass would die, the politicians had instructed their work crews to put tables and chairs out in the middle of all the grassy areas which would cause thousands of people to tromp the grass down as they made their way to the tables and chairs. The result was all the nice grassy areas soon got compacted into large earthen foot paths where nothing could grow. *Which was utterly brilliant,* Fast Eddy mumbled to himself, *because that means the work crews can come back in a year or two so the whole thing can be done over again so the politicians can keep lining their pockets.*

Fast Eddy never had any problems with the police--None whatsoever. They had always treated him with decency and respect so long as he paid his fines and smiled. He remembered the time he had taken a pretty 22 year old out of a beer bar and been pulled over at a road block a kilometer down the street. The closest policeman said, "No have helmet." Fast Eddy smiled at the policeman while pointing at the helmet he was wearing as he pulled out his Thai driver's license. The policeman then pointed at the girl sitting behind him and said, "She no have." Fast Eddy then looked at the girl behind him for the first time since he had handed her a helmet as he pulled away from the beer bar and noticed that she was still holding the helmet in her hand, not wanting to mess up her hair. He had to pay 400 baht to the policeman even though it was perfectly clear that he had complied with the law. One month later, while sitting at the same beer bar, Fast Eddy watched a pretty girl get on the back of a motorbike behind a policeman who then accelerated the wrong way down the street. The girl was not wearing a helmet.

What irked him is they let all the morons who kept breaking Thailand's traffic laws get away with everything and by not making them pay for their idiocy, they made Pattaya's streets a very dangerous place for him to be driving his motorcycle. It was all very simple, Fast Eddy had reasoned. All they had to do was to enforce the existing traffic laws which he was sure were nearly identical to those in the U.S. and start fining everyone they saw who was breaking them. But again, it was the inability or refusal to accept responsibility that was the root of the problem starting with the city's elected Civil servants who were not making the police do what police departments all over the world are supposed to do, and that is to serve and protect.

All it would take would be 500 baht fines on the spot with no exceptions," Fast Eddy concluded. And if you don't have the money, it's off to the monkey house where you'd remain in your cell until a family member or a friend came over to pay your fine for you. Drive North down a South bound traffic lane against the flow of traffic and boom–500 baht. Run a red light–500 baht. Drive recklessly by pulling in front of someone–500 baht. Drive on the sidewalk–500 baht. Now why can't they do such a simple thing? And besides, every time a fine was collected the police could put it in the city coffers to be later used the same way taxes were used. It was all so utterly simple. As it is these people don't have to pay any consequences for their acting like complete fools. Put a price on their acting like idiots and they are going to shape up real fast.

But it would never happen. Not when one or two policemen would be out on the street directing traffic when the school up the street from his condo was letting out and all the school kids were coming out of the school on their motorbikes, driving without helmets, sometimes up to four children on a single motorbike. So it was not okay for adults to ride without helmets, but it was just fine for their children to drive out of the school not wearing them just as it was okay for twelve year olds to drive who were obviously too young to have driver's licenses or four kids to be on the same bike.

Nothing about the place made any sense to Fast Eddy whatsoever and that's exactly what brought him to the hospital in the first place. Thailand and the people in it did not make sense and because of it he was willing to part with $6,000 of his hard to come by pension money.

The Pursuit of Excellence

He was looking for a place where the pursuit of excellence was paramount because he was afraid that if he didn't find it, he'd go insane. And he wanted a woman who could actually think. So there was something wrong with him after all.   He quite simply did not fit in. He could still do fifty pushups and run two miles faster than most thirty year olds. The Marine Corps had instilled in him the habit of getting up early. So in spite of his moving to the most thrilling party destination for night owls on earth, Fast Eddy usually got up by 6 a.m., and had already run four or five miles before the heat of the day started in at 10:00. Nearly fifty now, Fast Eddy was far more trim and fit than most twenty year olds. But he was here for reasons other than his health.

Whereas the police and those who give the police their walking orders fail to protect the people, hospitals do the opposite. And that's just one of many reasons Thailand is so often referred to as "Amazing Thailand" because the truth is, whereas hospitals in the U.S. are doing a very bad job of protecting those who need their services for the most part, Thai hospitals far outperform their U.S. counterparts. Thailand just happens to be one of the super achievers in Asia when it comes to delivering top notch medical care, while proving so successful at it, that Thailand is rapidly becoming a Mecca for those wanting the best medical care possible at far lower costs than the U.S. and many other Western countries are providing.

Pattaya has a number of hospitals. On the lower end is Banglamung, a large public hospital where most Thais go. A better hospital's at Siracha forty minutes away. There's a very reasonably priced hospital that is reputedly excellent, Queen Sirikit, in Sattahip but again, it takes forty minutes to get there. A navy hospital, Sirikit will admit everyone and its discount prices are far lower than the two top end Pattaya hospitals, International and Bangkok Pattaya. Memorial in Central Pattaya's not bad while not far away International Hospital gears itself for Westerners. Here the staff speaks good English and although its prices are high by Thai standards, they are very low compared to what one pays in the West. But the top hospital of the food chain is Bangkok Pattaya. Unlike International Hospital which is quite small in comparison, Bangkok Pattaya has all the most expensive state of the art equipment, such as an MRI machine while boasting over sixty specialists.   But unlike U.S. hospitals Pattaya Bangkok's excellent team of specialists are available within minutes of one's arrival to the hospital.

Even if one doesn't go to a hospital at all, Pattaya is full of inexpensive clinics where one can see a general practitioner while getting taken care of on the spot with little or no wait at all, oftentimes for as little as five or ten bucks. Obviously

> Thailand takes its health care seriously while employing substantial numbers of highly qualified people throughout the country. There is nothing second rate about the training its doctors receives, and its nurses, hospital technicians, etc. still have to meet the same rigorous standards their counterparts have to meet in the most advanced countries in the world.

The sort of woman Fast Eddy had decided that he'd better be meeting was a woman who had to struggle to become educated, to learn a well-paying skill and to have to pass a rigorous battery of tests to insure that she can deliver the goods. Pure logic had told him that he was likely to meet such a woman only in the Medical profession.

Cornhole

Thailand does not allow Westerners to be condo managers. If it did, Hermann would be managing the Bahthaus as any good German dictator would, effectively, while providing the widest range of good quality services and exceptional maintenance, at reasonable cost. And if anyone should disagree with him on the way things should be run, he'd simply say, "This is the way we are doing it. End of subject. We are wasting time." The problem was that Thailand has a policy of protecting the jobs of all Thais from falang who can probably do them better.

> The term falang refers to any Caucasian foreigner. In general the rules are different for falangs and Thais. For example a falang bar owner cannot work in his own bar without having to pay for a special work permit and even at that, the work permit must apply to a special duty such as manager or bartender. Without having a work permit a falang can be deported from the Kingdom. I know an American bar owner who the police took to the police station for just talking to a customer until his Thai girlfriend interceded. Falang are prohibited from owning land. The Western owner of a small hotel or bar must hire so many employees who he has to pay insurance on whereas a Thai owner doesn't. Also when there is a national or religious holiday and all bars are officially closed, one finds all the falang bars closed whereas many Thai bar owners will simply turn off the music and dim their lights while continuing to serve their customers.

The exceptions were for those Westerners who have a skill that no Thai could perform–such as teaching English or making atomic bombs. So finally it came time for Hermann to pick a Thai manager. He picked one and he hated himself for having to do it. He had to. Hiring anyone who was not Thai clearly violated the rules and regulations of Thailand's Condominium Act.

The first manager in Bahthaus history was unveiled during the first condo co-owners' meeting in the condo lobby where the owners had finished voting for the five committee members who'd represent them on running the condominium's operations. The committee's primary functions were to oversee the manager, approve staff salaries, hire and fire employees and facilitate the smooth functioning of the

Bahthaus.   It would be the manager's duty to direct the Thai staff and to run the office, since it was believed that a Thai could best work with other Thais, to avoid a lot of misunderstandings.

Hermann had just brought a frail looking crafty faced Thai in front of the thirty owners who were able to show up for the meeting while a half dozen reprobates lay somewhere in their beds upstairs, still asleep from their previous evening's drunken escapades, obvious to the fact that they would not have another chance to attend a condo owners' meeting until the next year.

"Khun Felonius is going to be our manager," Hermann announced to the condo owners—"Provided that you owners go along with my selection. So allow me to introduce him. Khun Felonius was recommended to me by a business associate of mine."

"Which means Hermann's girlfriend recommended her brother to Hermann," Lawrence, who had just been voted onto the committee, whispered to Fast Eddy who had also been selected to serve on the committee.

"And I'll bet his job experience was working as a motorbike taxi driver except he doesn't look strong beefy enough to hold up the motorbike," Fast Eddy whispered back at Lawrence.

"He's been working as manager of a well-known condominium community," Hermann continued, "so his credentials are just what we need here at the Bahthaus."

"And I'll bet Hermann found this little prick in the bottom of a Cracker Jack box," said Lawrence.

"Looks to be the part," Fast Eddy replied—"a real prize."

"Okay. Now we must be quiet if only for a few moments," said Hermann.   "We have just met Khun Felonius, so now we vote on this.   Is there anyone who does not want him as our manager?"

There was dead silence in the room, as half the owners looked around to see if any hands went up.   A few seconds elapsed before Hermann continued: "I see no one objects to our new manager, so it is looking like we shall have him for one year at least."

"Yeah, as if anyone is going to say they don't want Khun Felonius without knowing anything about him.   That would be one helluva way to start with our condo office," Fast Eddy whispered to Lawrence. "And get a load of that name. What's this Khun Felonius crap? This guy's gotta be a complete idiot. Felonius is obviously not a Thai name so this little prick must have come up with this Anglicized name just to make it easy for us to pronounce it. Obviously he's not done his homework however. Clearly he is clueless about how Westerners such as ourselves are going to react to it. I smell corruption here, don't you?"

"I think he's a real cunt," Lawrence replied, "but don't ask me to say that aloud. Time will tell."

There's a Cornholer in the Mirror

Khun Felonius quickly developed a reputation as the Invisible man at the Bahthuas. One should have called him the resident mascot because like a hibernating bear he was never to be seen unless one of the residents came into the office. Normally a manager might be expected to go up to each floor to check on how the condo cleaners were doing, to go out to the swimming pool to check what outside lights needed replacing or to see if whether or not the swimming pool was over chlorinated. Or he might even decide that some of his duties included training the security guards or to check on them to see if they were sleeping on the job, if they were wearing their uniforms or if they were being helpful to the condo residents. Unfortunately Khun Felonius never considered any of this to be very important. What was important was that he look and act like a manager. Immediately upon his arrival for work, Khun Felonius would go directly into the little bathroom in the condo office where he'd wet down his face and hair after which he'd give himself a little pep talk while peering into the mirror. He'd always recite the same mantra as he kept repeating the words to himself, "I am the manager. This is what managers look like. I manage by sitting inside the office looking the way a manager should look."

He wore a short sleeved dress shirt which he had opened at the collar, a pair of khaki or black cotton slacks which he wore with a belt, and dress shoes. Khun Felonius had decided a long time ago that shorts and t shirts were unbecoming of a manager. Aside from that his modus-operandi was to sit down at his desk and turn on his computer. He'd then glance over at Nang, greet her with a clipped "swadi kapp, Nang" and then he'd start to towel down his face as he scrunched up his eyes and whispered to himself. "I am the manager. It is necessary for me to look and behave as a manager."

His first great initiative was to introduce an annual building inspection. It took him two afternoons to see five prospects in their offices whose names and telephone numbers he had gotten from his brother in law.

The first man had his office down on Sukamvit Road which he shared with an insurance broker. The man looked up at him as Khun Felonius entered a little room that faced out onto the main area through a one and a half- meter wide glass window.

"You must be King Felonius, the new manager over at the Bahthaus," the man said to him. "What can I do for you?"

"We need to have an annual building inspection," Khun Felonius replied with a crafty smile. Our condo is only seven stories high and we have seventy-five residents. And I'd like whatever contract we draw up to guarantee both of us repeat business."

"Do you want an agreement where the larger fee is paid the first year with a smaller fee to be paid each year thereafter? By the way, I'm Tika," the man added. "But first things first—we need to come up with a reason why the building needs to be inspected every year. I think we can accomplish that by claiming the building is too high to be classified as a low rise. If we can accomplish that, we can claim your building needs an annual inspection instead of just once every five years that are required of low rises."

"So what do you think we should charge for the inspection?" Khun Felonius asked.

"I think we can make it about 90,000 baht," Tika replied.

"How much commission does that leave me?" Khun Felonius asked.

"That leaves you with 15,000 baht. Which still gives me and my company 75,000 baht," said Tika.

"Can we make it a little higher? I have a few gambling debts to pay."

"How about 100,000 baht then? We can make it 100,000 baht the first year and 90,000 baht every year thereafter."

"That's much better. That provides me with 25,000 baht the first year and 15,000 baht every year afterwards, Khun Felonius replied as his mouth watered over his now being able to afford the down payment on a new car with the commissions he could generate as the manager of the Bahthaus.

"That's right. The Bahthaus is going to need to be inspected for all its fire equipment, its smoke alarms, the positioning of all its staircases, its signs for fire evacuation routes and so on, Tika replied with a wolf like grin. And all this needs to be done every year to keep all of us happy."

******

Khun Felonius had three bids on his desk in a large manila envelope which he showed to all the condo committee members. The first bid was for 125,000 baht for the first year with 100,000 baht to be paid every year thereafter for the repeat inspections. The second bid was for 115,000 the first year with 90,000 baht for every year thereafter. The last bid was for 100,000 baht followed by 95,000 baht to be paid in the subsequent years. The manager's thoughts had already turned to new projects he could introduce to the condominium community.

Hermann laid the ground rules. "Unfortunately for us our building is exactly 33 meters tall. We'd be okay if it was just 32 meters. But since we are 33 meters high we are now a class two commercial high rise and that means a building inspection each year."

"What happens if we don't have any building inspections?" asked Fast Eddy.

"Nothing perhaps. It just depends upon how lucky we are," Hermann replied. "But if anyone comes out here from City Hall and finds out we are not doing our building inspections, we will be charged substantial penalties. For example, 8,000 baht for each day we operate this condo past the deadline for the building inspection, which is due one month from now. And that's not all. City Hall can also fine each committee member 1000 to 5000 baht a day also. I don't know what we should do. What do you think, Fast Eddy?"

"It looks like we must have it then. But those bids are way too high. I think Khun Felonius needs to go out and get us a much lower bid. I mean the most rot gut, bullshit, cheap ass company he can come up with because we all know this is a bunch of horseshit that is dreamed up by City Hall so that a bunch of Thais can make a lot of money off of us."

Fast Eddy looked over at Khun Felonius who appeared to be on the verge of crying. It was clear that the insult against city hall and any potential scam artists had registered on him and produced the exact impression Fast Eddy was hoping for."

When Fast Eddy left the committee meeting he was whispering to himself, "that good for nothing manager of ours has dreamed this whole thing up. From now on I'm referring to him as Cornhole since he's only interested in screwing all of us. I can already tell we will be getting it in the ass from now on."

The greedy Lawyer

"In my opinion, yes, your manager is getting things done that are unnecessary for The Bahthaus," Pontathorn said as he continued to leaf through the documents Fast Eddy and Lawrence had brought him.

"In other words, we never needed the building inspection in the first place?" Fast Eddy asked.

"Maybe yes. Maybe no. Building inspection in my opinion yes. It is necessary," said the lawyer. "But maybe in two more years. And for fire inspection only. Should be cheaper too. Maybe he charge too much."

Why can't I get a straight answer to this? Fast Eddy asked himself. *I know that much. Otherwise I wouldn't even have come here. Maybe two more years? Cheaper? How much cheaper? One tenth as much? Half as much? And why won't this lawyer simply come out with it—that this turd brained manager of ours is a crook?"*

"How much cheaper, do you think?" Lawrence asked.

Lawrence had come along just to help out although it had been Fast Eddy's idea to hire the lawyer. Lawrence had offered to pay Fast Eddy back half the lawyer's legal expenses. Fast Eddy did not think they should be asking the condo office to reimburse either of them for the lawyer's expense. After all, he, Hermann and the other committee members had all agreed on the fourth bid for the proposed building inspection, this final bid coming in at 80,000 baht the first year and 70,000 baht for each year after the initial inspection had been completed. The bid had come from a fourth company which the condo committee had to nearly force Khun Felonius into discovering several weeks after the committee had discussed the first three bids.

"I'm not sure," said the lawyer. "Let me check into it and I'll get back to you later."

"Then let me ask you this," asked Fast Eddy. "Do you think our manager has come up with a bullshit inspection and that he's getting commissions off the company that will actually be doing the inspections?"

"Not sure," the lawyer replied. "But in Thailand this is very possible. But he charges you too much, I think."

Damn right our manager's charging us too much, Fast Eddy thought. *He's probably getting $1000 commission for each* *year while the actual inspection is just costing $200 and this means the man he's dealing with who actually gets the inspection done is probably getting a couple thousand dollars and the whole thing does not amount to a single day's work.*

Suddenly Lawrence looked at his watch. "We've already been here for 2 hours, Fast Eddy. I think we'd better be getting back to the condo."

"You are right Lawrence." Then Fast Eddy turned to the lawyer. "How much do we owe you for these two hours?" he asked.

We get 5000 baht for the initial consultation and after that we get 4000 baht an hour so that's 9000 baht. But I still need to get for you answer for how much this inspection should be costing you, so you will then know how much more you are paying than is normal. So pay me 11000 baht or 2000 baht more. I will talk to my colleagues in Bangkok and then I will call you or e-mail you an answer," said the lawyer.

Between them Lawrence and Fast Eddy put 11,000 baht on the lawyer's desk. Then they left the building and walked over to where they had parked their motorbikes.

"Can you believe this prat? 11,000 baht for just a little opinion! Why that's more than solicitors charge in England," said Lawrence.

"And at least what they charge in the U.S. The difference is in the U.S. at least we'd have more of an idea of where we are at. Such as, Cornhole's buttfucking us by 60,000 baht and the inspection is supposed to be only 20,000 baht or we definitely don't need an inspection yet considering our building is less than one year old and it had to pass city hall's inspection before Hermann could get it registered. Hey wait a minute, Lawrence---that's it. We had to pass a building inspection to get registered in the first place. We are getting our assholes reamed without even getting them lubricated with Vaseline."

"Speaking of Hermann, what do you think he's up to about how?" asked Lawrence.

"Probably out racing his go-kart," Fast Eddy replied with a knowing smile. "You know Hermann. He's absolutely nuts about go-karts, big motorcycles and just about anything that goes faster than the scooters most of us drive around here."

Go Kart Racing

If Hermann could he'd have a Ferrari just because he felt it was the most beautiful highest performance machine of its kind. But spending half a million dollars just for a car didn't make sense to him even if he had it in his checking account ready to spend. But it wasn't just the money. He despised having to pay twice as much for a car in Thailand as he'd have to pay in Europe or the United States simply because the Thai government levied a 200 % import tax on foreign cars And although he would have loved driving one on Germany's autobahns or on one of America's interstates out West where the speed limits were much higher than on the East Coast and the police didn't seem to care if even those were exceeded, he couldn't see going much faster than 70 miles an hour in Thailand due to all the idiots he had to share the road with. This frustrated Hermann so much that he bought a high powered go kart that he could race.

Many Hondas, Toyotas, and even Chevrolets are assembled in Thailand although many of their parts come from Japan and the United States. A Mazda 3 that is assembled in Thailand might cost a man 30 % more to purchase in Thailand than it would in the US whereas a Mazda MX-5 sports car is going to cost him roughly $50,000 in Thailand while the same car would cost him just $25000 in the U.S. The key is all Mazda MX-5's are assembled in Japan. Since all BMW's, Porsches, Mercedes and Ferraris are assembled in Germany and Italy the man purchasing one of these high dollar cars will have to pay twice as much as he would in their countries of origin. I've found that many Germans who can easily afford even such outrageously marked up prices will buy much more inexpensive cars coming off Thai production lines. For example, a German casino owner friend who has both a 200 mile per hour Mercedes and a Ferrari back in Germany purchased a Honda City in Pattaya, claiming "it's all I need" and "I can get it serviced anywhere in Thailand."

The go kart weighed only 150 pounds or half the weight of a small 250 c.c. motorcycle which gave it a significant power to weight ratio considering that it was propelled by twin 30 horsepower Rotax 2 stroke water cooled engines. The hair on Hermann's arms stood on end when he flew down the straight away of a fast track at over 100 miles an hour with his ass just

3 inches off the pavement. The thing would turn on a dime. Hermann could just imagine what it must have felt like being a World War I fighter pilot firing at the enemy from an open cockpit or doing barrel rolls and split esses to escape his enemy's machine guns--and with no parachute. Although the danger level wasn't even close there was still nothing like squeezing through a crowded pack of karts piloted by drivers who were equally committed to winning. But although not even close to the mortality rate of World War I when air combat cut a pilot's expected life span to less than two weeks, there was still enough danger to more than get the adrenaline up.

Hermann admired the low slung body of his little racing machine. Barely over 2 feet high, the little kart was designed to turn inside anything on four wheels. He'd have to wear ear plugs to keep the engine noise from destroying his hearing. He had come to the track to inspect everything on his kart and to make sure everything was just right in his normal thoroughgoing German manner. He grinned with inner satisfaction over how he had it painted British racing green to honor Jimmy Clark and Jackie Stewart, two of the finest British champions to ever drive a formula one, who he had admired since boyhood.

The Bahthaus was far from his thoughts now. As it would be tomorrow while he competed against over twenty other drivers. And no matter how the race would turn out, the next night would see him celebrating with his buddies without a single thought about the condo building. The truth was, he had burnt himself out pushing a recalcitrant Thai work force to getting the Bahthaus completed just three months behind schedule. Getting the whole thing done just three months late was a miracle considering most projects wound up getting completed over a year behind schedule while others became bankrupt before they could be finished.

Racing in Little Germany

Hermann's hero was Erick Hartman, Germany's top World War II ace, who had been credited with shooting down 352 Allied aircraft. But now he felt more like Adolf Galland gunning down his nearest adversary in his Rotax twin engine Go Kart as he pretended to be at the controls of the fastest machine in sight. The difference was, skilled as he was, Hartman normally piloted a Me-109 fighter plane whereas Adolf Galland got to fly jets at the end of the war, and everyone knows the Messerschmitt 262 could fly nearly 100 miles an hour faster than any propeller piston engine fighter planes in the sky including Me-109's.

"I got him in my sights now" Hermann said to himself as he accelerated out of the tight curve. Boring down on the yellow kart in front of him, Hermann peered over the top of his steering wheel at the little machine that until now had been the leader. But like Galland and other jet fighter aces of the Luftwaffe, Hermann felt he had power on his side. The unholy racket of the twin two stroke engines would have deafened him had it not been for the balls of wax he had stuck in his ears over which he mounted his full coverage helmet which was there not only for his own protection but also to keep himself from going deaf. Hermann tromped the accelerator into the floor and felt the kart surge forward from the sudden rush of power as the little machine started to gain decisively over his enemy. Inexorably it started to overtake the slower machine.

"Aha," Hermann shouted from inside his helmet. "Germany win, Allies lose. And I owe it all to my having the power. And I am one of Germany's finest.   I should have been driving a race car at Indianapolis-- or in the Grand Prix."

The truth was that Hermann could easily afford to have Rotax's latest and greatest engines and that didn't even count his having Frederick as his ace mechanic. Frederick had moved to Pattaya from Germany where he had worked as a head mechanic for a large dealership that sold Mercedes and Porsche sports cars. Now he sold condos to Europeans. But this did not erase the hunger he felt while fine tuning an engine to get the most performance from it.

So in addition to his having the finest equipment money could buy, Hermann also had one of Germany's best mechanics, whose unrelenting search for perfection would squeeze the last one tenth of a horsepower out of any engine. Hermann watched the go kart behind him fade out of sight. "So long sucker," Hermann shouted above the wail of two stroke engines screaming at over 12,000 rpm's.

After crossing the finish line before all the other contestants, Hermann studied his little crotch rocket. *No. That British racing green color has gots to go, he said to himself. That color is just not me. British racing green is nice, but it's just too British. And the British are just too, (Hermann thought a moment for the right words) and then he said out loud--* "inept." *Except for Jimmy Clark and Jackie Stewart, of course, he conceded. But I think bright red should be my color.   I will be just like Von Richtoffen, with his red Fokker Triplane when he shot down 80 enemy planes making him World War I's top ranking ace.*

Thailand's Third Sex

"Now what possessed you to drag me to this bar?" Fast Eddy asked Lawrence. "The place is too loud."

"What do you mean? The music is terrific," said Lawrence and "what is most important, they serve draft beer here."

"Who cares whether they are serving draft beer or not. As long as it's cold, I could care less. But this place is despicable. I can hardly hear you talk."

"You can have those other places that don't serve draft beer, but I suppose it's good enough for you Americans. You never did have much culture."

"Draft beer is only for wimpy tea drinking Englishmen," Fast Eddy replied.

Only two girls were dancing on the little stage behind the bar. One was average in height, the other taller, both of them in their early twenties. But a much older woman who had just walked behind the bar joined the bar girls. The bar owner had practically forced the shorter of the two bar to get up on the stage in front of the crowd. So it took all of five seconds for the girl to offer her place in the limelight to the newcomer, especially when several of the other bar-girls were nearly shoving the older woman onto the stage.

The newcomer was in her middle forties and English. Whether she was short, tall or just average in height was a point that would have been lost on any crowd. What didn't was her weighing over seventy kilos which might have been typical for an Englishwoman or an American but which stood out like a turd in a punch bowl in a Pattaya beer bar. Aside from the girl on stage next to her, the tallest girl in the bar was a dainty 160 centimeters (five foot three). The grossest most overweight lard ass Thai girl in the place weighed fifty-two kilos.

Such comparisons were well beyond the scope of the Englishwoman, who danced confidently next to the attractive Thai woman, with her head somewhere in the nethosphere of her old prom days and the half dozen cocktails she had already consumed.

"See that falang lady dancing?" Lawrence asked Fast Eddy while rolling up his eyes.

"I was trying not to look."

"Okay then. I want to ask you a question. Who would you rather bang, her or Em? Em is the girl dancing next to the Englishwoman."

"Why I'd bang Em in a heartbeat," Fast Eddy replied.

"Suppose I said Em is a ladyman?"

"No. You mean the gal dancing next to the old goat? That's a woman, I tell you," Fast Eddy retorted.

"No way. Em's a guy. She's got a dick."

"Tell me it's not so, Lawrence."

"I'm telling you, Fast Eddy. Em's a ladyman. So getting back to my question now that you know Em's got a dick, who would you rather bang?"

"I wouldn't bang either," Fast Eddy replied.

"Let me put it this way. If you didn't bang either, you'd be killed so to save your skin, you must bang either Em or the old bag."

"If you put it that way, I suppose I'd have to bang Em."

"So would I," Lawrence agreed.

Lawrence could scarcely believe he had popped the question on Fast Eddy. What had gotten into him? Had he told anyone he would have preferred to bang a man over a woman back in his favorite English pub, he would have been branded a homosexual and the label would have stuck forever. But Pattaya had changed him. It had changed his attitude about a lot of things, especially sex.

The first time such blurring of the sexes had jolted him to a full red alert was when he had wandered alone into several Soi Six Bars. He had gone to the first bar where he had one beer before he was propositioned by a girl snuggling up next to him who had gotten a firm hold on his cock as he sat on his bar stool drinking his Heineken.

He took one look at her and asked himself, "Do I really want to put my dick in her?" Everything about the girl was wrong. She was overweight for his tastes, not fat, but not trim either. There were plenty like her everywhere on the planet, he decided. Her manners were brusque. There was nothing shy about her, no holding back, no reserve. Lawrence knew she had been through the mill, and that she had probably had sex with more men than he'd care to even think about. But he had been through all of that many times before, having met women who managed to keep the magnitude of their sexual activity in the background, out of sight and out of mind.

Deciding it was time to try out another bar, Lawrence paid his bin and went back out onto the street where he immediately encountered Mickel ambling about, looking for his next bar.

"Well Lawrence, how are you my good friend? I see you coming out of that bar. Is it any good?"

"It's just okay. Nothing special. I want to try out another bar."

"Lead on. I will follow you."

There were two good looking bar girls standing in front of the Red Point. The slenderer of the two grabbed Lawrence by his arm before he could manage to slide by her.

"Hey sexy man, one drink please?" the girl asked.

Lawrence considered asking the girl to join him inside the Red Point where he'd soon be drinking his draft beer next to Mickel, deciding the company would be excellent and the presence of the shapely girl to be the icing on the cake.

"Yes. Let's go in together, Mickel said loudly, then taking the other girl by the arm said, "I want you to give me back massage."

The two men sat on couches at opposite sides of a table just inside the bar, monopolizing the two couches until the girls came up and snuggled up closely to them. A waitress came up to their table and asked them what they wanted to drink, but when Lawrence announced that he wanted a draft beer she told him, "My me draft" which meant "No have."

"I'm sorry, Mickel, but I just have to have draft beer. We must go somewhere else."

"And leave these two beautiful ladies alone here by themselves? Well, they will just have to do without us then." Suddenly Mickel, irked by Lawrence's insistence on draft beer, came up with an idea. He knew just the place.

The place was Roxy's. In front of the bar a number of sharp eyed ladymen had gathered looking for customers. Before Mickel went in, Lawrence took him by the arm. "This is a ladyboy bar, Mickel. Do we really want to go in there?"

"Why sure we do, Lawrence. They have draft beers inside and that's what you drink, and there are a couple of ladies too-- good looking ladies."

Inside Lawrence found Mickel to be true to his word. They sat at the bar, alone for the first several minutes before a ladyboy came up to Lawrence and asked him to buy him a beer. At the other end of the bar a very attractive girl beckoned at him as soon as it was obvious that Lawrence was not buying the ladyman a beer. "I buy that lady over there a drink,"

Lawrence told the ladyman," which was, he hoped, a polite way of telling the ladyman to take a hike.

The woman at the other end of the bar came over to him as soon as the ladyman left. About five foot five, she was taller than most Thai girls, but the real attention getter were her ample mouthwatering breasts.

"Sawadhi Ka. Me Anne," the girl said to Lawrence as she gently grasped his hand.

"I'm Lawrence. Can I buy you a drink?"

"Kap khun kap. Buy for me Bailey's Creme? Is okay?"

"Whatever you want, Anne."

"Where you come from?" Anne asked.

"I'm English," Lawrence replied. My papa come from Foodland but my mama come from Disneyland. And you my dear Anne, where do you come from?"

"I come from Udon. You like Udon lady?"

Lawrence was surprised at the question, expecting Anne to ask the next standard bar girl question–"How long do you stay in Thailand." He knew from too much experience that most bar girls learned to ask three questions even if they couldn't speak much English. "Where do you come from?" would be the first. The second would invariably be, "How long you in Pattaya?" The third would most likely be "Do you have girlfriend?" An additional question might be "Where do you stay?" All were leading fact finding questions. The first query was to ascertain what country the customer was from, even if the girl hadn't the slightest idea where the country was in the first place. For the average bar girl England was a very big powerful country simply because there were so many Englishmen coming to the bars. The U.S. was not so big or powerful due to the declining numbers of Americans coming to Thailand while Germany was roughly equal to England due to the fact that there seemed to be about as many Germans around as Englishmen. It had been passed around that Japanese men were big spenders, so a girl would want to know whether he was Japanese, Chinese or Korean or from still another country whose people had Asiatic features. Englishmen were considered to be tight wads; Germans were known to be bigger spenders while Americans were considered to be without question the easiest Westerners to get money out of. The second question, "how long do you stay in Pattaya" was asked to determine what kind of strategy she might use in order to squeeze the maximum amount of money from the customer. If he told her he was staying a month, she might decide if things went well to try to lock him in for a one month contract, but if he told her four nights, she'd ask him for as much money as she thought she could get out of him for a single night or two. The third question–did the man have a girlfriend–was to determine if the man was a better short time or long time prospect since if he had a girlfriend staying at his place she most likely wouldn't be spending the night with him.

As to whether or not Lawrence liked Udon ladies, not being sure of how he really felt about it, he gave her an answer that he felt would please her: "Yes. They have very beautiful skin."

"They have dark skin," the girl interjected. "I think white skin more beautiful."

"I like darker skin. Ladies where I come from have light skin and they look like frogs because their skin is not so nice and smooth as yours," Lawrence replied as he started to stroke the girl's arm.

"Do you have lady Ingland?"

"No. I not have English lady for long time."

"No unnerstand. You handsome too much."

"I don't like English ladies and they don't like me much either."

"What is wrong with English lady?"

"They are too fat for one thing. And they only like men who have lots of money."

"I do too," the girl replied mischievously. "Man who don't have money is no good. He cannot feed me, he cannot buy me clothing, he cannot give me money so I can give money to momma and papa. What good is he?"

She's got a point there, Lawrence thought. *When you come to think about it, a man who cannot help provide for a woman or for his family is pretty useless. This does not mean he's a bad person. And he might be down on his luck through no fault of his own, but at the end of the day, he really doesn't provide a useful function to the woman. They can talk all they want about love and moral support for one's partner, but that doesn't put food on the table when people are hungry and all that moral support and what passes for love can easily be provided by someone else.*

"You like lady Thai ?" the girl asked.

"Of course, I love Thai ladies."

"I think maybe you no like Thai lady too much."

"Why do you think that?" Lawrence asked.

Anne grinned and replied. "Because Thai woman like money you too much."

"Are you telling me, Anne, that you would like me only for my money?"

"Yes. I want all your money."

"Well, what are you going to do?" Mickel suddenly interrupted. "Are you going to have deep philosophical discussions or are you going to take her upstairs?"

The short-time room was on the third floor, which they reached by a staircase that led from the back of the bar near the restroom. Unlike most hotel rooms this one didn't have its own toilet facilities. Lawrence had been with a few Soi Six girls before and found the rooms to be about evenly divided between those having a small bathroom in the room and the other half which used one or two small bathrooms out in the hallway. Anne directed Lawrence to the small toilet which was two rooms past theirs after giving him one of the two towels that had been placed on the bed. Then she left and went back to the room to wait for him.

He had been in the shower only for a minute or two before he heard the door being opened, then closed. Suddenly he felt Anne's body pressed up against him. What was odd was her ass touching him rather than her breasts or belly. He felt two hands closing around his penis. And then he felt Anne snuggle around him so that she faced the wall. Lawrence marveled at how firm and sharply defined her buttocks were. His penis was now fully erect. She had known exactly how to touch him and even though she had stopped holding his penis while adjusting her body so she'd be facing the wall with her ass aimed directly at him, he was still feeling the effects of her touch.

He had left his condom back in the room. "She probably didn't bring one with her either," he almost said aloud. Then he decided, "to hell with it--I'm going for it anyway." He pushed his groin up against her and started to rub himself up and down her backside.

"It feel so good. Fuck me now," Anne screamed.

Lawrence rubbed a finger up and down the crack of her ass as she reared up tightly against him and then he felt something that shouldn't have been there. As his fingers groped around the crack of her ass and back into her vagina, he felt what first seemed to be an overly large clitoris. But the protruding organ was a little too stiff and far too large to be a clitoris.

"Anne, are you a guy?"

"No. Me katoey."

"That is your banana I'm feeling down here?"

"Yes. You no understand I katoey?"

"No!" Lawrence's mind suddenly started racing as he searched for a new game plan. *I can't go through with it,* he decided. *But it's not really Anne's fault. I should have known better. Here I am in a katoey bar. I should have asked.*

"I'm sorry, Anne, but I just can't do it. I like girls. It's not your fault."

"You no like I?" Anne asked, visibly hurt.

"I like you very much," Lawrence replied. "It is just, I never go with Katoey before."

"Katoey same same lady. I smoke you good. Better. You must try."

Studying her carefully he noted the rejection in her eyes, then the petulant curl of her lips and saw, not a man, but a beautiful woman. Everything about her was just right--except for her having a dick. But his mind couldn't register this last little detail. Lawrence said loud enough for Anne to hear, "But you have a dick." But even after saying it, it still didn't register.

"I have dick?" Anne asked while turning her face up in puzzlement. "What is it?"

Lawrence couldn't help himself from almost breaking into tears of laughter. Everything about Anne was feminine. Even her voice. He had known ladyboys who had been utterly gorgeous until they had opened their mouths. It had been the voice that had betrayed them. Lawrence had remembered times sitting around beer bars completely relaxed and at ease with the world from drinking more than a half dozen beers, when he had been almost driven to bar-fining a stunning lady-boy until she had opened her mouth.   Until then one could have told him countless times—"She's really a guy," but his brain wouldn't let him believe the words, and then the lady-boy's voice suddenly intruded to vanish forever any thoughts of his taking the startlingly attractive person home with him.

He suddenly started to change his mind.   There was no ladyman voice to bring him back to reality.   And Anne had a pair of the most sumptuous breasts he had ever seen.   And there was no one around to watch him bar-fine her who might later laugh at him and to tell others that he was a homosexual. As for Mickel, it had been Mickel who had brought him to this place as a joke, so afterwards he'd simply deny the whole thing.   And even if Mickel wouldn't believe his denial, he'd simply make him an accessory and claim that Mickel must be bisexual for even taking him to such a place.

Anne seemed to have sensed his mood suddenly start to change. Gently touching his balls, she lightly started to glide her hand across his testicles and up his shaft. For a moment Lawrence closed his eyes as he waited to see what would happen. Expecting his appendage to grow limp, surprisingly he felt a huge erection coming on.

"Why not?" he asked himself. "I've never done anything like this before. No one is going to know. It's not like I'm taking someone up to my condo and the security guard sees it's a ladyboy and so the guard tells the rest of the condo Thai employees what I've done and from that point on I'm forever labeled. This has to be the most sensuous person I've ever been close to and if I don't do it I just might forever hate myself.

Lawrence firmly pushed Anne down into the bed and pried her legs open with his hands. She had a cock, yet it wasn't like a cock. Or at least not like one he had ever seen. It was much smaller and when he bent his head down to lick it he found that it didn't taste much different from his licking a girl between her legs.

He came twice, and then he looked at his watch and noticed that he had been in the room for over an hour. Lawrence decided to have one more beer, once he and Anne got dressed and went back downstairs. He bought one for Anne and one for himself. Suddenly Mickel perked up and challenged him.

"You are buying one for me too, aren't you?"

"Not on your life. You knew this was a katoey bar and you never warned me. You aren't getting shit from me."

"Then what have you been doing up there all this time. You have been up there for over an hour."

"I was angry when I found out that Anne here was a katoey. Then we started arguing what I should be paying her. Eventually we arrived at 250 baht as being fair. Then Anne and I just started to laugh about the whole thing and we started drinking and laughing it up and one beer turned into the second one, and here I am."

"Ha, ha, ha, Lawrence. Don't let it worry you. Don't worry about a thing. This is Pattaya, and here we can do anything. Anything. As for the beer, I buy you the next beer and then we go to another bar where we will get two katoeys for each of us."

*****

Yes. He'd bang Em over the fat Western woman any day. Lawrence thought about his friends in England and what they'd think about that. Since moving to Pattaya he had become much more tolerant about homosexuality and ladymen. *But because a man might fuck a ladyman, did this mean he was a homosexual?* Lawrence asked himself. He had found Anne to seem far more interested in him than he had found most ladies in either England or Thailand. Remembering his experience with Anne in the shower, and how he had gotten a terrific hard on while she was thrusting her shapely ass up against his dick, he still had a lot of questions concerning the role of the sexes. English girls had gotten to be as fat as cows. He found the thought of having sex with one of them to be disgusting. He thought about that for a moment and about how they would probably find him to be equally disgusting now that he had become an old fart. But suppose he was no longer living in Thailand and that's all he had to choose from. He'd become celibate, he decided. *But suppose Thailand exported all its ladymen to England and they were all getting breast jobs, wearing makeup and going to beauty salons. What then?* Then he thought about how life must have been over a hundred years ago in England when most people were still living on farms and women didn't go around getting their hair done and wearing makeup and how plain they must have all looked when one was around them day in and day out. There was no doubt about it, he decided. *If ladymen are looking this good, as good as Em and Anne, if I could bang either them or the fat cows English women had become, I'll take the ladymen any day.*

The Live in Girlfriend

Katrina, how many times have we met for lunch now?" Fast Eddy asked the doe eyed young woman sitting across from him.

"Not sure. Five times. Six. I like eating with you, Fast Eddy. It makes me forget hospital."

"But you keep refusing me when I ask you to have dinner with me. Why?"

"You are old enough to be my father," Katrina replied. "People who work with me would not like that."

"Why not? Why should you be ashamed?"

"I not lady bar. But people who see you with me will think I'm prostitute. People who work in hospital see me have lunch with you, I tell them I see you in restaurant and you invite me to your table, so how can I refuse?" Katrina giggled. "But not same at night. People wonder what I do out alone. I am with you, what do they think then?"

"I will never forget that day I left the hospital," Fast Eddy replied, his mind now fully made up to go for all the marbles or to crash down in flames trying. "I remember your taking me down to the cashier's office so I wouldn't leave the hospital before paying my bill. And when I looked at you and saw your pretty face, and the way you smiled back at me, I knew right then and there that you were the most beautiful girl I had ever seen. And will never forget your voice, the way you laughed when I told you that you didn't look at all like the woman in the picture on your hospital ID you wore pinned to your white gown. And then you asked me, "Why not?" And I said, "in the picture you are wearing your hair short and you look so much older in it than you look in real life with your hair so long and sexy. But it's when I told you to fire your photographer that I fell in love with your laugh."

"In love with my laugh?"

"Well sure. I asked for your phone number right before I went up to the cashier's counter, didn't I?"

"Yes. You did. But I never said we could see each other at night."

"Why not?"

"Because I am not Pattaya woman. I come from Udon Thani. My family good family. Send me to school in Bangkok. I get nursing degree. They pay too much so I can be RN. When people see me with you they think I'm same same lady who work in bar"

"I can understand how you feel," Fast Eddy replied, using one of the favorite lines many salesmen use to make their prospects feel they truly commiserate with them and understand their needs. "I'll tell you what. No one has to know--at least not at first. The first time you get a day off I want you to tell your roommates that you are going home to see your mother or your sister, but instead you are going to come to my condo. I have two bedrooms. I will let you sleep in one bedroom by yourself and I'll sleep in my other bedroom. And I promise not to touch you. We can drink some wine together and we can talk and you won't have to be afraid of anyone seeing us together."

"Why should I do that if I think it is bad idea for me to go with falang?

"Because I am betting that once you visit me that it's not going to be the last time."

"You good guy, Fast Eddy. But I think it's a bad idea."

"I think you are scared."

"I not scared."

"Then prove it. Come spend the night with me and show me and what is even more important, show yourself that you are not scared."

"Okay, Katrina replied hesitantly. I think about it and I call you if I think you have good idea."

******

Fast Eddy's heart raced when he got her call two weeks later. She had one day off, she told him. Two hours later, she was walking into his condo, making no secret of the fact that she was obviously impressed by what she saw. He had a fifth floor view overlooking the Gulf of Thailand to the West, and he had two bedrooms just as he had promised her and two bathrooms, one of them large enough to accommodate a spacious Jacuzzi. His living room was huge with a bookshelf dominating the room that went all the way from his floor to the ceiling.

True to his word, he insisted that she sleep alone in the 2nd bedroom. On her next day off she came to his place a second time. It wasn't long before her visits became a habit. She enjoyed sitting with him out on his balcony facing the ocean drinking wine, as her mind drifted light years away from having to deal with the demands of the hospital, the patients and two difficult roommates.   But her chief motivation for moving in with Fast Eddy was his offer to give her 20,000 baht a month. And when she still expressed her doubts about the arrangement because she didn't want to be seen with him, he offered her a proposition that she could not refuse, which was his promise that he wouldn't be taking her out on the town, and that at night they'd eat inside his condo, having restaurant carry outs brought to his door, or that they'd cook their meals in his spacious well equipped kitchen thus offering her the best of two worlds--the security of staying in a nice place with a steady flow of cash coming to her each month without having to suffer from the stigma of being a falang's girlfriend and whore.

The arrangement suited Fast Eddy as well. Katrina had a body to die for, with light pearly skin, ample mouth-watering breasts, a tight waist line and long shapely legs. She could speak English better than most bar girls, and she seemed to enjoy English speaking movies and television, which put her well ahead of most women he had bar-fined who seemed only interested in Thai soap operas, game shows and local news covering only Thailand. Her working at the hospital gave him a lot of space away from her, which gave him the freedom to do his own thing without having to indulge the whims of a woman.

The situation seemed nearly ideal, except for that little nagging voice in the back of his mind telling him–*If it were not for your nice condo, Fast Eddy, and the money you give her each month she probably would prefer a Thai man.* He resolved to give her the benefit of the doubt, but if he ever found out there was a Thai man in her life, he promised himself to be quick to throw her to the curb.

The Crazy Irishman

"Why did Socrates come to our office, nude?" Hermann asked Fast Eddy and Lawrence at the committee meeting.

"He did what?" Fast Eddy asked incredulously.

"You didn't know?" Hermann asked the small group with outstretched hands.

"No."

"He came down to the condo office. He must have been drinking all afternoon or longer because our staff tells me he drinks from the time he gets up in the morning until he goes to bed. They also tell me he uses our condo grocery cart to bring beer, whiskey and other alcohol up into his condo--a whole grocery cart full! Can you believe it? So, he came down to pay his bill for the utilities, his internet, telephone and television and Nang here still can't forget about what he did. He actually came down to our office without anything on."

Nang looked down at her desk trying to avert all eye contact, but she was unable to hide the huge grin on her face. Every month she sent all condo residents a bill for their utilities. She was also responsible for billing the semi-annual condo maintenance fees while accounting for everything in a well-known American accounting program she had to learn. The committee had provided her with an instruction manual in English which she had somehow managed to learn. Nang attended all committee meetings. So did Khun Felonius who sat next to her at the second desk in the condo office.

The manager took this latest news in with his usual sheepish smile. He had been in the office when Socrates had wandered in wearing only his sandals. Truth was, he was terrified of Socrates.

"What can we do about it then?" asked Lawrence.

Hermann turned to Fast Eddy and asked, "Can you have a little word with Socrates not to do it again? I never got along with him, so this would be better for you to do."

"I'll do it," said Fast Eddy, "but I'm not making any promises.

Socrates

"We can stay here and drink a little longer, Fast Eddy, but mind you, I have to go back to England early in the mornin."

"What time do you have to catch the plane, Socrates?"

"I have a taxi coming for me at 6 a.m. so I think I shouldn't stay in the bars past 10."

The two men were drinking in a German bar on Naklua Road which Fast Eddy liked because of the quality of the service, the fact that the music was held down to tolerable levels and above all because the bar girls were much cuter than practically anywhere else in Naklua. This was due to the efforts of a Thai woman the Germans had hired to manage the place, a woman around forty, who Fast Eddy and his friends always called Mamasan-- her real name unknown to them. Mamasan lived on Soi Loi Land, a street that wandered just off Naklua Road one block past the bar. But so did seventy-five percent of the girls working in her bar. Soi Loi Land was a favorite area for many of Pattaya's bar girls to live because of its relatively low rent and due to its proximity to Naklua Road which was the main baht bus route into Pattaya itself.

This meant that Mamasan had lots of opportunity not just to live around the bar girls working in her bar but also to meet a large number of other bar girls who she was constantly running into at the little neighborhood shops and street vendors' stalls where they were constantly stopping for their food.

Fast Eddy knew that Mamasan always recruited the prettiest girls because she had once asked him, "If you see any pretty bar girls, tell them to see me. I pay them 2500 baht (a month) salary and I think they like bar very much."

Although salaries of 2000-2500 baht a month were standard for bar girls while Go-go girls typically earned 7500 to 10000 baht, it had gotten to the point that many bars didn't pay any salary at all. Figuring that the average Naklua bar has ten bar girls, each bar owner has to pay out up to 25000 baht each month in salaries alone. This required each bar girl to coax a lot of beers out of the bar's customers for the bar owner to be able to recoup these salaries. In addition to that she was expected to do a lot of short and long times for which the bar owner charged 300 baht to each customer to take a girl out of his bar. And out of each bar fine the girl normally got 100 baht. Although Pattaya has a huge supply of beautiful women, the average beer bar girl is butt ugly, which often makes it difficult for her to get men to pay both her and the bar money for sex. This means that no more than half of all beer bar girls getting a salary are actually worth their keep. So it had gotten to the point, particularly in Naklua, that most bar owners stopped paying salaries except to their staff. This resulted in large numbers of bar girls working only for tips and their share of the bar fines from going out with customers plus a percentage of all the lady drinks and the alcoholic beverages consumed by customers.

If a girl was good looking whether she made a salary or not should make little difference. With the going rate for a short time, which technically speaking was anything less than spending the entire night with a customer, at 500 baht and with a typical long time earning her 1000 baht she'd make far more than her salary on these tips alone. The bar would offset her salary of 2000-2500 baht with her share of the bar fines and her earnings from all drink sales. The bottom line is if a girl was attractive and in demand, she was likely to make enough freelancing at a bar (while collecting no salary) and off her share of drink sales and bar-fines to more than make up what she would have made in salary.

Mamasan was the German bar's most effective secret weapon. At this German bar customers were allowed to buy bottles of cheap Thai whisky at the Family Mart for the girls, which was a lot cheaper than having to buy girls drinks at beer bar prices. And oftentimes the girls pooled their own money to buy bottles of whiskey for themselves. Most of the time there was at least one bottle of Thai whisky on the tables that immediately adjoined the sidewalk, which was terrific for business, because although the German bar owners were missing out on a lot of drink sales to the nearby Family Mart, on the other hand, its girls were some of the happiest campers in all of Naklua. More often than not they'd be dancing on the bar tables, on the floor or even in the street which brought in customers who would have otherwise gone to a neighboring bar. And Mamasan's personality was contagious. Back in her apartment on Soi Loi Land she often had parties and at these parties she not only invited her own bar girls but anyone she found attractive enough to be a good prospect for her bar. But when she had to be, she was as tough as nails.

"I think I'll have one more, and then we move to the next bar," said Socrates.

"Did you just tell me that you had bar fined a girl and brought her back to your condo already"? Fast Eddy asked the Irishman.

"And so I did. What's there to say about that, mind you?"

"I mean what are you doing with her?"

"Oh that. Well, she will be fine. She will be there when I get back. I gave her some money, so if she wants to go out and get cigarettes or anything else she doesn't have to need me."

"How long has she been at your condo?"

Socrates looked at his watch, and scrutinized the dial, bleary from the alcohol. "I think around four hours now. She will be alright though."

"When did you meet her?"

"This afternoon. I met her at the Seven Eleven and I asked her if she cared to come to my condo."

"She might steal from you then," Fast Eddy replied. "You don't know her at all then."

"I'm not too worried about that. If she steals, she steals. Besides, security will probably catch her if she does."

"Don't bet on it. Our security is non-existent."

An hour later, they left for still another bar, which was another German Bar just off Naklua Soi 18 in a small bar complex. They had three beers together when Fast Eddy offered to take Socrates back to the condo building. It was already past four a.m., and Socrates had his plane to catch which would be allowing him less than two hours of sleep if he left the bar immediately. Fast Eddy had more than enough beer for the evening. It was time to go home.

"I'm leaving for the Bahthaus, Socrates. You need to come with me. Remember—you have less than two hours to catch the taxi that's taking you to the airport. It's up to you, but I sure wouldn't want to miss my flight."

"Go ahead. I will come later," Socrates slurred his words in reply.

It was less than one mile to the Bahthaus. Certain that Socrates could walk it easily, even in his drunken state or at least catch a motorbike taxi, Fast Eddy drove away on his motorbike. The next day the Bahthaus staff told him that Socrates was fast asleep upstairs, and that he had come in after six a.m. Meanwhile the girl he had brought to his condo had gotten bored, wandered out of the condo, then she had walked up and down the street before returning to the Bahthaus before she became bored a second time and left the condo for the last time. Socrates couldn't get another flight to England for three days.

The Lazy Cleaning Woman

To say the cleaning of the Bahthaus building was not up to German standards was the understatement of the year. In the beginning, three women had been responsible for cleaning the building, the pool area, and the parking lot. The three women earned slightly less than $200 American a month and all were salaried employees. But after Fast Eddy and Lawrence brought it to Hermann's attention that at least two of the women spent too much time talking together on the condo front steps, the committee had decided to fire two of the women and replace them with a company that promised to supply two cleaning women every day along with all cleaning supplies for 19,000 baht (around $500 a month). Everything had gone well for the first several months until Fast Eddy noticed how one of the new cleaning women the Bahthaus had just inherited never went past the second floor. Then he noticed how the woman, who was twenty kilos overweight, was spending half her cleaning time on the first level cleaning the same metal slats in the wide window between the condo lobby and the parking lot.

When a cute young cleaner started working at the Bahthaus it seemed to Fast Eddy that half the time she was never to be found. Since the fat woman had already been working for the Bahthaus for several months, Fast Eddy decided that the younger woman looked up to her, but seeing how lazy the heavy set woman was, she had no doubt viewed her as her mentor and decided that she could also get by with doing as little work as possible. But where she was spending most of her time, Fast Eddy couldn't fathom.

Once, the old security guard said to him in broken English: "Young girl good. Good for you. You like? I can do."

Fast Eddy didn't know quite what to make of that one—whether the young cleaning girl had spoken to the old man to see if Fast Eddy might be interested in her or whether the old man knew something he didn't know and was offering her services to Fast Eddy. Fifty-fifty either way, Fast Eddy decided. That is, I give it fifty percent she's already doing at least one other resident. Perhaps that's what she's up to, and that might explain her disappearing act. But I'll give it 99 % she will bang me, if I go for her.

In the end he resolved to keep away from her deciding it was not good to be getting mixed up with the help--especially for a committee member. *But even if I weren't on the committee, banging her would wind up being one huge mistake. She's already in the building which means she would have instant access to my condo.*

Fast Eddy and Lawrence had been noticing that the cleaning of the condo had declined dramatically. The carpeted floor in the elevator had become very dirty. Garbage piled up in the ash trays next to the elevator on every floor. The hallways on the higher floors appeared unswept. Fast Eddy minced no words at the committee meeting.

"King Felonius needs to send that fat cleaning lady back to the company and he needs to tell this company to stop sending us their rejects."

"King, what's this king business?" asked Hermann.

"Sorry. It's my American accent," Fast Eddy replied. I meant Khun Felonius.

"What do you mean when you say, rejects"? Hermann asked.

"Look. This fat woman has now been with us for over three months. This woman on her best day moves like a turtle. She's so fat, lazy and slow that even if she's working at the fastest speed she is capable of going; she still can't get anything done at this condo. I will suggest that no other condo building would keep her, so they keep sending her back to the company and ask for a replacement who can actually get some work done. Then they send us a second cleaning woman, and since she's new, she looks at this fat woman as an example of what our condo expects from its cleaners. After all, the fat woman has now been here for a long time so whatever she's doing is good enough for us–at least that's what the younger girl must be thinking. Now I've talked to Khun Felonius about this several times, but he keeps telling me that he can't send this woman back."

"Is this correct, Khun Felonius?"

"This cleaner--she improve. She get better," Khun Felonius replied in broken English. "I speak to her about it.""

"So what! So what if you speak to her about it. Why haven't you spoken to her about it before?" Fast Eddy asked contemptuously. "That's your job as manager. It's not my job to be finding out how shitty a job the cleaners are doing. Besides, even if this woman tries to improve, she still is so fat, she can't possibly be doing enough work around here. This is not to mention that the second cleaner is not going to work any harder than she does."

"Okay. Watch her more carefully, Khun Felonius," Hermann replied, and "tell her she needs to work harder."

One week after the committee meeting, Fast Eddy couldn't find either cleaning woman. The third woman, the only one, who remained on the Bahthaus direct payroll, was inside someone's condo doing private cleaning for the owner, who'd be charged 500 baht per cleaning by the Bahthaus office each time he had his condo cleaned. This money was to be put in the condo checking account that was owned by all the owners. In any case, this woman was not Fast Eddy's problem since her job description did not specify her having to work alongside the two cleaning women who received their pay checks from the company the Bahthaus had contracted with. By this time Fast Eddy was cutting sheets of paper into small pieces which he scotch taped onto the tiled surface at several spots on each floor to see if the cleaning girls were cleaning the floors or not. He had also started putting cigarette ashes on the carpeted elevator floor in order to determine how often it was cleaned.

He finally found the fat woman dead asleep on the back stairway landing while figuring the young cleaner was probably inside one of the condos porking its owner. Quietly slipping downstairs Fast Eddy went promptly to the condo office where he found Khun Felonius playing computer games.

"That fat cleaning lady is asleep. Come with me," Fast Eddy told the manager.

Khun Felonius followed Fast Eddy to the 3rd floor on the elevator. Then the two quietly slipped down to the 1st floor level on the back stair case. When Khun Felonius saw the fat cleaning woman lying sprawled out on her back on the landing, he gently shook the woman while speaking softly into her ear. The woman suddenly opened her eyes and stood up.

The next day Fast Eddy went into the office to speak to Khun Felonius.

"Are you going to fire her now?"

"No. I give her one more chance," Khun Felonius replied.

"Imbecile," Fast Eddy replied angrily as he turned on his heel and walked out of the office.

"Imbecile," Khun Felonius said to himself. "What does that mean? Why Fast Eddy angry?"

One week later, Fast Eddy noticed that the young cleaner had gone and that she had been replaced by a woman he had never seen before. He also noticed that the new woman had started cleaning at 8 a.m. and that by 9 a.m. he had still not seen the fat cleaning woman. He asked the old man, the daytime condo security guard, "Pu ying oo-an, utinai kapp?" Which meant--"Where is the fat woman?" The old guard solemnly shook his head and replied—Pu ying oo-an no good. She no come."

Bells must have been ringing in someone's head because at that very instant Fast Eddy saw the fat woman coming into the condo front entrance, one hour late for work. Almost losing his composure on the spot, Fast Eddy got his cell phone and called Hermann.

"Hermann, do you remember that fat cleaning woman? Well last week we caught her fast asleep on the staircase. And today she came to work one hour late."

"Does Khun Felonius know about it?" Hermann asked.

"Of course he does. I was the one who caught her sleeping. Do you really think Cornhole caught her sleeping? Why that useless manager of ours doesn't even step out of his office to check if anyone's cleaning or not. The place is a mess, Hermann, and it's all because of that lazy manager of ours."

"Now don't blame it all on Khun Felonius, Fast Eddy," said the voice on the other end. "I know you two don't like each other. But what about the cleaning woman? Say that again."

"I didn't find her anywhere so I looked for her and caught her sleeping on the first floor landing of the back staircase. I went straight to the office and got Cornhole to go up there. He had to wake her up. Once again I asked him to send her back to the company and to demand they give us a real cleaning woman, but he replied to me, "I want to give her one more chance.""

"Okay, said Hermann. "I will tell him to get rid of her then."

Unsecure Condo

For Fast Eddy, there were no half way measures toward achieving good security. The Marine Corp had taught him that, and it wasn't just the iron discipline the Marine Corps instilled in all Marines. What the Marine Corps training did not teach him, combat in Vietnam did. Fast Eddy still got up nearly every morning at 6 a.m. and figured that if he could get up that early as a retiree, then condo security could at least do its job right. Security meant security with no compromises. This meant that anytime someone came into the building, the security guard had better be checking to see who that person is. And if the visitor was a bar girl, ladyboy or even looked like a sex worker, that person's ID not only needed to be checked, it needed to be confiscated until the condo resident accompanied his visitor back to the security desk to ask the guard to relinquish the person's ID.

Fast Eddy's approach to security was simple. If the front line was secure, no one could get into the rear area to create havoc. At the Bahthaus Fast Eddy considered the front line to be the condo front entrance, the condo parking lot and the rear entrance from the parking lot that led straight to the elevator and lobby. Fast Eddy felt that the security guard needed to be at his post where he could easily survey the parking lot, the elevator entrance and the main condo entrance immediately in front of him. Since the guard had a television monitor on which he could watch what the security cameras picked up on each floor of the condo, Fast Eddy felt it was not only completely unnecessary for the guard to walk up to each floor for his periodic checks, it was also completely undesirable since this left the front line completely unguarded.

First...if someone wanted to steal a motorcycle or anything left in a car or motorbike in the parking lot, there would be no security guard on the ground floor to stop him. Second, if the guard was theoretically going from floor to floor to check the condo corridors, what was to stop him from sleeping in the little office behind the security desk, or goofing off outside the building? If anyone saw that there was no guard at the security desk, he would assume the guard was wandering up and down the floors doing his job.

The outside toilet in the parking lot had already been trashed. Someone had slipped by condo security, gone inside, and broken the toilet stool, wash basin and the mirror above the wash basin. This was hardly any surprise to Fast Eddy given the fact that the daytime security guard routinely let any Thai wanting to use the toilet facilities inside the parking lot gate.

As for the night shift guard who came in at 7 p.m. the man was rarely to be found after 11 p.m.

Fast Eddy knew that at least one of the residents had already been robbed. The condo owner had gone down Beach Road on his motor bike where he found an attractive Thai woman trying to start her motorbike near the police station on Soi 9. The condo owner had stopped and offered to help her, but when neither one of them was able to start the motorbike they had pushed it into the police station parking lot. He had then taken the woman back to his condo, brought out two beers from the fridge, left one on the coffee table for himself while handing her the other one and headed to the shower. When he came out of the shower he had noticed that his beer tasted a little odd, but he drank it anyway. When he woke up a few hours later, he found that the woman had disappeared with two cell phones and his camera. Obviously the woman had put something into his beer. But there was also no shadow of doubt that if the security guard had confiscated the woman's ID, she would never have even tried stealing anything from the building.

Spicy had struck up a friendship with the old man responsible for handling daytime security. The old man despised the much younger man who relieved him at 7 p.m. The young man oftentimes didn't even bother to show up for work which meant that the old man had to work both shifts. And on many occasions the old man had found a blanket in the security office, which proved that the young man oftentimes slept through much of his shift out of sight of any resident passing the desk, who not seeing the guard there, would immediately assume that the guard was busy checking the hallways upstairs. When Spicy told Frank about it, Frank had confided to Fast Eddy that he thought the young night security guard had a second job during the day, which would have explained his sleeping half his shift away.

Several times Fast Eddy had told Hermann that he felt security needed to be checking IDs and that he believed King Felonius needed to set the law down for the two condo security guards. "They need to be tough as nails," Fast Eddy told Hermann. "They both need to be in full uniform at all times so they look like they mean business. This is bullshit, Hermann, this young guard thinking he doesn't have to be in uniform. He's slovenly. He looks like the janitor for Christ's sake because he's wearing a t-shirt instead of a uniform and he's not wearing a hat. The old daytime guard's in uniform and he's wearing a hat like security guards are supposed to be wearing. That younger guard needs to look like an authority figure, like a policeman so that he will command respect."

"I don't think it makes any difference how the guards look so long as they are doing their jobs properly," Hermann replied.

"Well they aren't. Neither of them are. And the night guard is as useless as tits on a boar. Just what the hell do we need a manager for, anyway? Cornhole isn't instructing the cleaning girls on what needs to be done, so they aren't getting jack shit done and he lets the two security guards do whatever pleases them."

"Give the man a chance," said Hermann. "I know you don't like him. Just try and get along better with him."

"Like hell I will. We need to tighten things up around here. I think the night time security guard is using his time around here to get a good night's sleep and when he isn't sleeping he's out in the parking lot talking to his Thai friends who come in from the outside."

"So what's wrong with that?" Hermann asked.

"Two things," Fast Eddy replied. First, if he's out in the parking lot talking to his friends, this means he's not at the front desk, where he needs to be checking who comes in the front door or helping the residents out when they have a problem. And he's not checking ID's either. The second thing is the Bahthaus is getting a reputation with the Thais for being a real push over. This means that anyone who thinks he can steal something here, either from a resident's condo or from the vehicles outside in the parking lot, knows this is just about the easiest place to hit in the entire Wongamat Beach area. If we take care of the little things, the big things will take care of themselves."

"You need to know this, Fast Eddy. Many of the residents here do not want to have their girlfriends' ID's checked. They don't want to be treated like children by our security guards. I know this completely. Also some of our residents like to bring ladyboys up to their condos and the last thing they want is to become embarrassed by our guards checking their partners' IDs and have other residents see and hear all that commotion as they suddenly realize their fellow co-owner is having sex with ladyboys. So they would rather quietly slip their ladyboy sex partners through the condo back door."

"Well, I don't care what some of the owners think," Fast Eddy replied. Most hotels insist on ID checking and so do a lot of other condo communities. There's two ways of doing things. The right way, in this case my way, or the highway, and as long as I'm on this committee I'm going to do everything I can to see that things are done the right way. And as for their not wanting to be treated like children, I have just one word for my answer."

"What's that?"

"Socrates."

Ted Buffaloed

As soon as he walked out of his condo and saw the Thai couple in the hallway looking out across the parking lot, Frank knew that something wasn't right. First off, the couple was Thai. Secondly they were too young to fit the Bahthaus co-owner profile which was primarily European, American, and Australian, with a smattering of Russians and New Zealanders thrown into the mix. Most Thais, especially this young, don't have the financial resources to have what it takes to join this crowd, Frank decided, and those who do, would prefer not living with this mob of Western misfits. He suddenly felt the urge to throw both of them off the balcony out of some perfectly normal feeling of prejudice that he felt was completely justified. Spicy came out of the condo door right behind him and started to whisper, "Lady have boyfriend, Falang. She stay in condo. Tilak go bye bye. Thai man boom-boom lady."

He wasn't sure who Spicy was referring to. If it were the couple in front of him, everything seemed to fit. As he walked past them, he looked over at the pair hoping one of them would catch his eye. This would give him the excuse to say something to them such as "What the hell are you doing here-- visiting someone?" But both of them averted their eyes. The Thai man pretended to be looking at something out in the parking lot while the girl's expression was completely vacant.

"Well, treat me like a non-person, will you? Frank grumbled angrily to himself. "We will have to see about that because I'm going to be taking your pictures right now, whether you like it or not." Frank started to walk back toward his condo to get his Nikon DX 3, a completely professional camera with its 300 mm heavy zoom lens looking every bit the part. *It's about as intimidating as an elephant gun,* Frank thought, *because anyone looking at it cannot doubt that it's a very expensive professional rig that is only used for serious purposes, such as magazine publication, high dollar portrait work or artistic masterpieces of one kind or another.* These two do not belong here. They are up to no good so I'm going to make them sweat their balls off.

But Spicy stopped him. "Where you go?" she asked.

"To get my camera to take their picture."

"Man and lady no like," said Spicy.

"Well I don't care if they like it or not. Fuck them!" Frank spat out. He was angry because Spicy actually thought they belonged there more than he did. He was angry because

Spicy felt they could do no wrong because they were Thai. He was furious because she felt he had no right to ask them what they were up to because they were Thai and he wasn't. But what made him really want to blow his stack, was on top of it all she knew they were up to no good. Frank remembered reading in "Fool in Paradise" Neil Hutchison's writing how money was number one to Thai women with Western boyfriends, how family came in number two, number three was friends, number four any Thai person down to the lowliest street beggar, number five the family buffalo, then the fly on the buffalo's behind and finally the Western boyfriend. This was a perfect example of the extreme nationalism Hutchison was describing that lurked deep in the heart of most Thais. And it wasn't just Spicy. Frank decided that any Thai woman he was likely to hook up with would see the non-resident Thai man as having more right to be there than any Western condo owner did and who was he, a mere Westerner, to be asking any Thai what they were doing here?

Then someone around the corner of the hallway, where it turned sharply to the right, approached them to get on the elevator. He heard a voice asking, "Who's moving out of the Bahthaus?"

The other voice replied," It's that German guy down the hall and his Thai girlfriend."

Then he remembered a conversation he had with the Thai woman who lived down the hall from him. She had mentioned having a German boyfriend and their moving out of the building to live in a cheaper place in the area. He thought she had mentioned they were moving this week.

That stopped him in his tracks from going back to get his camera. The couple was probably the woman's relatives-- perhaps even her sister and brother in law which would have explained why they looked so out of place there. They were there to help the woman move.

When he took the elevator downstairs, the sight of four or five workmen filling up two small pickup trucks with furniture confirmed that the Thai girlfriend and her German boyfriend were helping the woman move. And that was it in a nutshell. Frank continued to watch as the old security guard stood next to one of the pickups as he laughed and joked around with the men loading the truck.

*****

Several days later, Lawrence found Frank downstairs in the condo lobby where he informed him, "Ted Buffalo got robbed a few days ago."

"You mean my fellow American?" Frank asked.

"That's exactly who I meant--Your idiot friend from the United States."

"Well, he's no friend of mine. What happened?"

"His girlfriend ran out on him and took most of his furniture out the door with her."

"You're kidding me."

"No, I'm not. I've heard he lost 300,000 baht worth of furniture which is around $7000 to $8000 U.S, isn't it?"

"Yes. How did that happen? Didn't security stop her?" Frank asked. Then he remembered the Thai couple he had nearly photographed in the hallway and the pickup trucks in the parking lot and how the security guard had joked around with the movers.

"Hermann told me that Ted Buffalo had allowed his Thai girlfriend to stay in his condo while he was back in the U.S," Lawrence replied "and not only that—it turns out that his girlfriend had been a real pain in the ass with our condo office, asking and demanding special favors such as extra key cards and remotes--free mind you, can you believe that, even though the rest of us must pay 600 baht for an extra key card? And Ted, that stupid prat, had told the office to give his girlfriend everything she wanted and that she could have anyone stay with her while he was back in Falang Land. Apparently his girlfriend had asked him if her sister could stay with her because she was afraid of staying alone in the condo. But once he went back to America, she not only had her sister move in with her, she also had the sister's boyfriend stay with her. She might have even had her boyfriend staying with her as well."

"I saw the Thai boyfriend with her right in our hallway, Lawrence."

Frank told Lawrence the whole story about how he found the couple looking out at the parking lot and how the Thai boyfriend had averted his eyes when Frank had approached them and that if it hadn't been for him overhearing two men down the hallway talking about someone moving he would have gotten right in the guy's face with his camera, and there would have been a fight that would have ended with the boyfriend running off. And then the Thai workmen loading the pickup trucks would have been busted.

"Hermann even told me that Ted had told the Thai staff to back off of his girlfriend."

"So what did Hermann make of the whole thing?" asked Frank.

"He felt that Ted got what he deserved, that the man's a complete idiot and that he's an arrogant prick for telling our staff to indulge his girlfriend."

"I've only seen Ted a couple of times," said Frank. "He'd say hello to me in the hallway or elevator. That's it. That's where he really screwed up by never introducing his Thai girlfriend to me and he should have made a point of telling me all about himself and he should have gone out of his way to introduce all his neighbors to his girlfriend. That way as soon as anyone saw her with any Thai men around, they could have blown the whistle on them, either to Ted had he left a telephone number back in the U.S., or to our staff. I know I would have. Hell, Lawrence, you and I have even exchanged keys with each other so that either of us can go into the other's condo if there seems to be something wrong."

"Wouldn't that have been hilarious, Frank, if Ted Buffalo had given one of us a set of keys and instructed us to make inspections of his unit anytime we felt like it. We would have caught that girl friend with two Thai guys in Ted's condo, and. I would love to have seen the looks on all their faces."

"That was plain stupid of Ted not to make it a point to get to know his neighbors. The man's a complete moron. But you are the one on the committee, Lawrence, and I keep telling you that I still think you guys need to get real tough around here with our security. We need to have every live in Thai girlfriend register her ID with our office and we need to have our condo security guards check the ID's of all overnight visitors. Another great idea would be that anytime furniture gets moved out of the condo building, our manager needs to take careful notes about who's moving the furniture out, which condo the furniture is coming out of, who's doing the moving, the license plates of any vehicles transporting the furniture and so on."

"Fat chance," said Lawrence. "We'd be lucky to get our manager to come out of his office just to get himself a Coca Cola from the Seven Eleven up the street." Besides, Hermann's against it. He thinks all of us condo owners are grownups, who can take care of ourselves and that it's up to us not to be stupid. He's also mentioned that if we go around checking ID's that most of the condo owners will get really pissed off at our committee for infringing on their privacy."

"Well most condo owners around here are very stupid. They are like children if you ask me," said Frank.

Ted Buffalo's list

The next day, Frank saw Ted Buffalo scurrying over to the elevator. *No wonder he got robbed*, Lawrence thought. *He's like the Lone Ranger wearing his mask because he doesn't want to be seen. He doesn't want to get to know other people in the building.*

"Your name's Ted Buffalo, isn't it?"

"That's right."

"You got robbed by your girlfriend, I've heard," said Frank.

"You might call it that. Where did you hear that from?"

"I saw you getting robbed. And people on the committee have been talking about it."

"Well, she's going to be in serious trouble."

"You have reported her to the police then?"

"Well, of course I have and they've already caught her."

"Is she in jail?"

"No. I haven't pressed charges yet."

"So what have you done?"

"I've talked to my lawyer about it. And he recommended that I don't press charges. I didn't need some of that furniture anyway so I had my lawyer draw up a list and then he gave it to her. I said she could have the furniture in the first column on that list and then I had my lawyer tell her I wanted the furniture I put in the other column back, But the trouble is, she and her boyfriend had two moving companies take the furniture to South Thailand. Well, no one at the two companies knew it was being stolen from me. And now all the furniture has disappeared."

"And she has no money, right?" Frank asked.

"That's what she's told my lawyer."

"And what is your lawyer saying now?"

He's advising me not to press charges. He's telling me that if I press charges that I'm not going to get any of my furniture back."

"How much was the furniture worth?"

"350,000 baht is what I paid for it."

"So you really believe that you are going to see some of your furniture back or that you will recoup a part of your money from this girl?"

"Sure I am. Because if I don't she's going to be in a lot of trouble."

"A lot of trouble all caused by the fact that you haven't pressed charges?"

"But I will if I don't get the furniture back I put on that list that I still want."

"I am really surprised at you, Ted."

"Why's that?"

"Because I just told you that I saw your furniture getting stolen. And that you still haven't asked me a single question about that. I would have thought that would be of some interest to you."

"So what did you see?"

"I saw a girl I don't remember ever having seen before, standing on that balcony over there looking out on the parking lot standing next to a young Thai guy . I knew something was wrong with that whole picture because for one thing they clearly did not belong in our condo building. Then my girlfriend, Spicy, said something about a Thai guy fucking a falang condo owner's girlfriend. I didn't understand if she meant in the owner's condo or outside our building in the Thai guy's room. Spicy's English still isn't that good."

"Then why didn't you go down to the office?"

"For one thing another Thai woman who was living with her German boyfriend was telling me they were planning on moving out of the building in the next week, so I figured those two pickups were moving their stuff, not yours. Then, just as I was about to go back to my condo to get my camera and take a picture of the Thai couple, someone in our hallway said that this woman was moving along with her German boyfriend. I figured then that the couple were relatives of the German's girlfriend. But–before anyone said anything about that, I went right up to the Thai guy and your girlfriend and looked right into the man's eyes. He kept looking down into the parking lot, hoping to avert my eyes."

"So you think it was my girlfriend and her Thai boyfriend?"

"Well who else could it be? Turned out the German and his girlfriend were not moving that day, so it was all your furniture I saw getting loaded into those two pickup trucks."

"Why didn't you tell me?"

"I already told you why. And Ted, did you ever give me your phone number back in the U.S., an email address or anything? Hell, I don't even know what state you are from. And you should have introduced your girlfriend to me and all your neighbors as well."

"And just what would that have accomplished?"

Frank couldn't believe the stupidity of the man. "Because we would have caught them in the act, that's why!" Frank blurted out angrily. I would have known it was your girlfriend I was looking at, and that she was obviously with her Thai boyfriend. I would have challenged them, and then they would have tried to run or fight. As it turned out the security guard was downstairs acting as though he was supervising the loading of those two pickup trucks with all your stuff and our maintenance man and Thai engineer were down there with him. Had you just told us you were going to be in the U.S., all three of them would have had no other choice than to stop your girlfriend and her boyfriend. And if that prick had as much as smarted off to me, I would have knocked his head clean off his shoulders."

"Fat chance on that. The man's a Muay Thai boxer and he's quite a bit younger than you."

"I don't care. He would have folded on my first punch."

"I doubt that."

"Take my word on it. He would have had no chance," said Frank as he reflected on all his boxing experiences as a much younger man in the U.S. He had put in a lot of time on both the speed bag and heavy bag and been sparring just for fun since he was ten years old. Only once or twice was anyone able to stand in the ring with him. Back then he had lightning reflexes and a punch with either hand that could take a man down in seconds. He had four or five bar fights and each time the other man had not lasted more than six seconds.

"I'd bet on the Thai."

"He would have gone down like the sack of shit he is. Look, Ted, doesn't it bother you that this Thai guy slept in your bed and that he fucked your girlfriend in your condo? I'd kill a man for doing that to me."

"And just what could I do about it?"

"You could press charges against both of them for one thing. And I could identify both of them. I saw them watching those two pickup trucks being loaded up from our balcony. If it were me I'd even pay a fair amount of money for bribes to have both of them put in the monkey house for a long time."

"My lawyer advised against that."

"Well I'd get another lawyer then. Because I sure wouldn't have some Thai guy disrespecting me by taking over my condo and fucking my woman in my bed."

"Look. I'm busy right now. I have things to do," Ted Buffalo said as he walked over to the elevator and pushed the down button.

The condo wives bar

The condo wives group started with two Thai women who stayed with their Western boyfriends at the Bahthaus, but it expanded as more and more girlfriends of the condo owners joined them as the months went by. Their meeting place was the Sow bar, which had started life as a very small convenience store in one of the condo shops on the ground floor of the building facing the street. The culprit was Sow, a Thai woman in her early thirties who stocked her shop with beer, soft drinks, a small selection of whisky, Vodka, wine and other alcohol, cigarettes, candy bars and other snacks, phone cards, local newspapers in English and many other items that were also carried by the local 7-11's and Family Marts. Since the shop was close to the condo front entrance and Sow had put two tables and chairs out for her customers, it had gradually taken on a new life as a drinking establishment for some of the condo residents and several of their friends who lived in condos close-by.

Fast Eddy was the first to sarcastically call the growing group of Thai women frequenting the Sow Bar the condo wives. The creation of a Bahthaus condo wife started as soon as one of the residents contracted with one of Pattaya's female sex workers for a monthly fee that usually went from 10,000 to 20,000 baht when he moved her into his condo. More often than not the new condo wife soon became a permanent fixture at the Bahthaus as the monthly contract became an on- going financial arrangement. Most of the condo wives came from Pattaya's bars where they had been sex workers, but not all of them. A new condo wife at first approached her new existence reticently, preferring to hole up in her sponsor's condo where she cleaned and cooked, watched television and slept. But after staying a few months, she'd start to go down the street to buy things both for herself and the condo at the nearby 7-11's and Family Marts. Then she'd start to borrow her "boyfriend's" motorbike for errands, ranging from going to the grocery store, to having her hair done, getting down to the market and sometimes even visiting her friends.

But when her boyfriend started to drink beer with his friends just outside Sow's little shop, she'd start to meet some of the women who had joined their boyfriends at one of the tables Sow had put out on her patio for customers. It wasn't long before a group of Thai women living in the condo got in the habit of sitting together at one of the tables and after a month passed the women could be found at the Sow Bar more often than their boyfriends.

One of the newest condo wives was Marylee. A Chinese girl from the Mainland, Marylee was staying at the Bahthaus for one reason and that reason was Saint Peter who had purchased her plane ticket after deciding to let her stay at his condo for at first a month, but then the month had become a second month, then a third until Marylee had become just one more permanent Bahthaus fixture. Marylee had immediately been befriended by Win, a Thai woman whose English was far better than most of the Thai girlfriends. Win had a Danish boyfriend, who often went back to Denmark to visit his family. The Dane would often leave for a month or more at a time and when he left he gave Win the run of his condo. Becoming increasingly bored since her boyfriend's departure to Denmark, Win found new meaning in life mentoring Marylee. The two always conversed in English because Win couldn't speak one word of Chinese while Marylee spoke very little Thai.

All of this suited Saint Peter just fine who found his Nirvana in the bottom of a bottle. Saint Peter's mornings often started out with a short walk to the Family Mart or Sow's shop where he'd purchase a six pack of beer. From there he'd walk over to the condo swimming pool where he'd drink the entire six-pack before Noon. His next stop found him putting in a little time–sometimes a lot of time at the Sow bar where he'd polish off a few more beers. Sometimes he'd take a break and head up to his seventh floor condo for a siesta after which he'd reappear like a bear out of hibernation for his second wind. This often took him to his favorite bar where he'd hold court to all his female admirers who would gather around him at the Saint Peter throne room.

Having Win around as Marylee's constant companion fit in well with Saint Peter's plans because this gave him the opportunity to never hold back from anything he really wanted to do, which involved activities that always involved drinking a lot of alcohol. He simply would never worry about her and only because of two reasons, 1. He was always drunk, and 2. Win was nearly always present to keep Marylee entertained.

Spicy never liked any of the women who hung around the Sow Bar. While Frank was drinking beers with other condo owners, she had often sat at the other table with some of the Bahthaus condo wives.   There she had gotten an earful from the other girls, all of whom mistakenly thought she was loyal to Thailand, all things Thai and that like them she had no respect for Westerners.

"My tilak send me to school," Spicy heard one of them say. "So I go to school over on Soi 25 where I pay tip of 10 baht every day to the school for class. I get great idea. I decide take private English lessons and they cost 3000 baht every month. I tell tilak I need to go to school for two hours every day for private lessons, but I don't go to school and I keep money for myself."

"What do you do when he thinks you are in school?" one of the other girls asked her.

"I do what I want. Sometimes I go eat pok pok with other Thai people. Sometimes other boyfriend calls me from England to say he come to Pattaya. He want to see me when he come. I tell him I can stay with him only short time and he tell me he can pay 1000 baht. So when he come I go to hotel England man, boom-boom and get money. Good for me. Good for him."

"Do you ever go long time with falang, not your tilak?" the other woman asked.

"That is when I tell tilak I see family. I go back Udon Thani I tell him. Then I boom-boom other falang and get 2000 or 3000 baht. Sometimes I see new man on street, maybe Seven Eleven and he want me short time. I go to hotel. My tilak think I still in school. Maybe I tell my tilak I go see mama and papa after and new falang take me to hotel for 2 maybe 3 days. Maybe I get 4000, 5000 baht and then I come back to condo from Udon-Pattaya."

All the girls broke out into laughter as they thought about their Bahthaus condo wife companion getting 10,000 or even 20,000 baht a month from her unsuspecting condo owner sponsor, while she got another 3000 baht to go to a school she never attended and still managed to get at least another 5000 baht a month from her other customers."

"How much tilak you, give you?" one of the other girls asked who, like most Pattaya girls, was clueless about Pronoun-ology.

"He give me 18000 baht each month. And he give me motorbike too. Later I get him to buy car so I can go Udon Thani more often. Stay longer. Make more boom-boom. Make more money."

Once after Spicy and Frank joined four of the condo wives at the condo wives' table, one of the women asked Frank, "What happen condo you when you die? You give Spicy?" Spicy noticed how Frank winced with distaste before he replied to the woman: "Spicy no want my condo. She want me. But since you like my condo so much, I give to you when I die. I make paper tomorrow so you can have."

The faces of all four women sitting at the table turned to stone, then their faces became animated again as they continued their conversation in Thai. One of the girls bragged to the others in Thai, "My falang, he make house for me in Korat next year. House cost 1 million baht. Have three bedrooms. He die, I have house early. When house finished he buy car me also. Maybe I finish him then. Move to Korat. I have Thai boyfriend then who speak Thai very good. Make me laugh too much and make me very happy."

The other wives started to laugh. Another woman not to be outdone replied, "My tilak, Bill, have big big condo here. 220 square meters. It is biggest condo in Bahthaus. Have three toilets, big big balcony--very big living room and Samsung t.v.--60 inch. Same same like movie in shopping mall. I want condo him. He say to me, he give condo me when he die. I no want live in Issan. I stay in Pattaya when he die. I have big money then, but maybe I buy bar and be mamasan." Then she looked at the others craftily, smiled, and added, "I give you ladies job then. Work for me. Make boom-boom many times."

Outwardly Spicy remained calm. But inside she seethed, wanting to break all of their necks. She decided to never sit with the Thai wives ever again. And as for Frank, from that moment on, he vowed to call the Sow Bar the Pig Pen.

Spicy's Papa

Spicy was only sixteen when she first came to Pattaya. Her father had brought her, and then he took her to Soi Six, gave her 500 baht, after which he told her, "I want you to send me and mama 5000 baht every month. I old man. No one take care of me now. Big money here. Many falang give you money because you pretty girl."

Spicy had just had a baby with her Thai boyfriend from the village who had impregnated her when she was fifteen. The boyfriend had knocked her too many times so she had left him while her baby stayed with her parents when her father dumped her onto Soi Six where she spent the next four years doing tricks in Soi Six's short time rooms. Then she moved onto the beer bars after getting tired of the everyday grind of Soi Six. She had hooked up with a German for a few months; a relationship that ended abruptly right after her father came to visit her and her sister in Pattaya.

Her father had urged her to tell her German boyfriend that her son had an enlarged heart, and if the little boy didn't get 5000 baht for medicine every month that he'd die. The trouble was her father was clueless about how the German mind or, for that matter, many Western minds worked. The German didn't believe a word of it from the beginning, and then he asked himself, "Why did Spicy for the first time bring up the fact that her boy would die if he didn't receive 5000 baht of medication?" Then he asked himself the second question: "What is new in Spicy's life and answered his own question, "Papa's in town."

The concluding piece to the puzzle came when he remembered how Spicy had bought herself a little gold bracelet several days before she started telling him her little boy would die, and then he concluded that no woman would buy gold if her son was about to die and she had the means of saving him.

And so the relationship ended, with the German raising his voice, calling Spicy a liar, after which he told her that he thought her father had put her up to it. Stubbornly she refused to admit to the German that she had lied to him, and he wound up kicking her out of his condo.

Until then the German had been very fair with her, paying her 10,000 baht each month while paying for all her food and drinks. When her father insisted that she lie to the German she told him, "Tilak not stupid, Papa. He not believe me."

But her papa had replied. "He falang and all falang have big money. All falang big buffalo. Believe anything. You tell him you need 5000 baht more each month."

Spicy had been right. And then she started to think, "What has papa ever done for me?" She thought about how both her parents had given favorable treatment to her younger brother who they were about to send to college but they had only managed to send her sister to the sixth grade. Spicy had done even worse, having never gotten past the fourth grade, and now she could hardly read Thai, let alone English.

The more she thought about it the more she recognized that almost every bar girl she had ever known told pretty much the same story. Very few of them had ever gotten through High School. And in nearly every single case, the family had been either unwilling or unable to pay for their books or tuition. Meanwhile Spicy had observed how the family members' eyes lit up when their daughters had reached the age where they could make a good living working in the bars. The expectation was always there for an income each month the parents could live on, but such expectations continued to mount. It was not enough that Mama and papa wanted a new house and that they expected the falang boyfriend or boyfriends to pay for the new house, the bar girl's younger brothers also expected new motorbikes and beer money. The demands never seemed to end, and Spicy had seen over and over again how frustrated the Western boyfriends got if they didn't wind up broke first, and how nearly all of these long term relationships came to an end because of the constant lying for more money.

Spicy had long ago decided that if it had just been up to the bar girls many of their long term relationships with their Western boyfriends would have lasted far longer than they did. The problem started once a committee was formed to determine how much the Western boyfriend should have to pay in order to keep his girlfriend. The hub of the committee was nearly always the girl's parents with the committee extending to the aunts and uncles until there were at least four people and usually a lot more deciding what trick the girl should play next to separate the boyfriend from his money. Since the gravy train extended to the aunts and uncles as well as to the brothers and sisters of the bar girl, there was no limit on how much the family would ultimately demand from the guy, which often resulted in the boyfriend telling them all to just fuck off and leave him alone. The end result of this being, Spicy decided, that the bar girl would wind up getting old in the bar well past her prime, which was no concern to her family, which would soon lose interest in her once her shelf life had started to run out.

Finally, Spicy wound up blurting out, "What good are they?"

"Who?" Surprised at her outburst, one of the other girls, asked her—"Who are you talking about, Spicy?"

"Your mama and papa. My papa, my mama. What good do they ever do you or me?"

"They took care of me as a baby," the other girl replied. "They fed me and clothed me, so now it is up to me to pay them back for giving me life and taking care of me when I was a baby."

Spicy remained silent, knowing the other woman was completely unable to think for herself. Spicy held back the words she wanted to say: *You moron! Since birth you have been programmed by your family and practically everyone around you to accept the line of B.S. that it is the woman's lot in life to take care of her parents and even her brothers, and that if she is born with good looks, mama and papa will rejoice, not because they are proud of having such an attractive child, but only because they are already counting the baht the little girl can bring them when she grows up.*

"They took care of you alright," Spicy wanted to tell the other girl, "Until you were about twelve years old and after that they never even paid for your schooling. They probably never even paid anything for you once you hit 13 or 14 when they saw you develop little nubbins for breasts and watched them get larger until their eyes got wide from trying to guess how much money you could bring them from boom-booming falang. They never cared about you--or me. All they want is money so they can strut around the village telling everyone how rich they have become."

"So what's wrong with that, Spicy? It's good to be rich", Spicy imagined the other girl telling her.

"Yes. But what did your mama and papa ever do to earn it? Did they work all that hard? No. It's you that's doing all the work having to entertain falang and let them stick their big dicks in you. And all that time your mama and papa sat around in the village doing absolutely nothing. My mama and papa didn't even bother to teach me how to read. Do you ever watch falang movies? Falang always try to send their children to school and falang children go to school until they are 18 at least."

"Spicy could almost hear the girl reply, "Maybe you are right, and maybe you are wrong. You always have home with mama and papa."

Spicy wanted to blurt out in the middle of the imagined conversation, "Ka-- I have home--right in the middle of their dirt floor. Same same as you would give me if I asked you to let me stay with you. The only difference is you aren't asking me for 5000 baht every month. You'd do it to help me. They would do it only while they were thinking how much more money they can get out of me once I return to Pattaya or Bangkok."

Spicy knew the difference between how well American parents treated their children and how the parents in her village treated theirs. She had watched enough Western movies to see how much parents would sacrifice and save to send their children to college in American movies. But not in her village or in any other village she had ever heard of--at least not very often. Mama and papa were paying for her younger brother's college tuition out of the money Spicy and her sister were sending them. Whereas other Thai women would have been proud of helping to send their little brothers to school, Spicy hated both her parents and her brother for it, seeing him only as "that selfish little lazy pig." *But not all parents and little brothers were like this,* she kept telling herself. *Some of them are hard-working and smart. Not all are stupid, lazy and selfish. But most of them are. I hate my family.*

Saint Peter loses Marylee

The night before New Year's Eve Fast Eddy heard his doorbell ring and found Marylee patiently waiting outside when he opened the door wondering who on earth could be ringing his doorbell at 11 p.m.

"I cannot find my Peter," Marylee told him.

"What do you mean?"

"Do not know. We go Mike's Shopping Mall together. I want go shopping. Peter tell me to find him one half hour but I late and not come. I come one hour later and I not see him. I look everywhere for him and I not find. You have phone number Peter?"

"Why sure I have, Marylee. Let me get my cell phone and find it for you."

Fast Eddy took his cell phone off his desk, retrieved Saint Peter's number, then he wrote it down on a scrap of paper and handed it to Marylee."

"Oh thank you very big," said Marylee. "I go now, and call him."

Planning to get to bed early so he could make a big night out of New Year's Eve, Fast Eddy was just about to go to bed when he heard his door bell ring again. It was just past midnight when he opened his door, only to find Marylee there for a second time.

I call Peter and he tell me to come to bar," said Marylee, "but when I come to bar he get angry with me. He tell me to go away, so I come to you now."

Now that Fast Eddy had Katrina living with him, he had decided that he had a real honest hard working Thai girlfriend, not just one of those sleazy bar girl prostitutes most of his friends had for girlfriends.

But she had gone home to see her family up in Udon Thani for the New Year. As soon as he had let Marylee into his condo the second time, Fast Eddy realized that if any Thai saw Marylee coming to his door at 11 p.m., Katrina would be sure to hear about it through the Thai gossip vine. It would be the talk of the Thai wives for one thing, and even though Katrina didn't have the time to hang out with them, she still encountered most of the girls at one time or the other in the elevator, the condo lobby, at the swimming pool or the Family Mart just down the street. There was a chance the security guard might be making his rounds and he'd see Marylee coming to his door. There were also the condo security cameras in the hallways which the security guard might be watching. Even if the guard was watching television instead of doing his job monitoring the television screen across from the security desk, it was possible that the condo engineer and the maintenance man would be reviewing the week's video which the cameras' computer was recording. Fast Eddy was well aware of how nationalistic nearly all Thais were, how they were all brothers and sisters and how they'd all be sure to tell Katrina if anyone of them saw Marylee coming to his door.

"Uh. What's the problem now, Marylee?" Fast Eddy asked.

"Can I come in?" Marylee asked as she walked into his condo.

"Oh no. I shouldn't have let her in, Fast Eddy said to himself. I shouldn't have even answered the door."

"I call Peter, but he not answer. Then I go back to bar. He sit with other lady and I get angry with him. I tell him I angry. But he not come back to condo with me. Here I am. Alone."

"Why did you come to my door, Marylee?"

"I tell you. I worried. I afraid Peter have new lady and he no like me. I worry also he not use condom."

"What?" Fast Eddy asked, surprised at how personal the conversation was getting, and Marylee had just started.

"Can tell me, Fast Eddy, Peter can do condom with lady Thai?"

"I don't know. I never asked him."

"He no use condom me. I afraid maybe he have HIV, and then I have HIV. He have many many ladies I think."

"He gets drunk a lot, and when he gets drunk there is no telling what he's going to do and who he's going to have over at his condo. But most of the time I think he doesn't even know if he has a lady or not. I think he just goes to sleep."

His cell phone started to ring at 1:30 a.m. It was Peter.

"Is Marylee there, Fast Eddy?"

"Yes and she's talking my ear off. Can you come get her?"

"I don't want to spoil your fun Fast Eddy. Is she a good fuck? You should have her smoke you because she's very good at that."

"I'm not fucking her, Peter. There's no way I'd do that with any of your girls."

"You can have her now. I don't want her," said Peter.

"Look. She is your responsibility. She's come to my door twice now and she's talking my ear off. Katrina's out of town back in her village and if she finds out about this, she's going to be really pissed."

"She's your problem now," Peter replied as he hung up.

Marylee didn't leave until 6 a.m. when Fast Eddy finally kicked her out, but only after he answered a hundred questions such as "Do you think Saint Peter might have HIV, how many girls has he had back in his condo, why does he treat me like this, do you think his drinking all the time is a big problem?"--Fast Eddy managed to get only two hours of sleep before he woke up at 8:30 a.m. Unlike most of the other condo owners he was an early riser who usually got up at 5 to 6 a.m., a habit that had been instilled in him by the Marine Corps.

New Year's Eve

Fast Eddy saw the two women make a bee-line right at him before he could get his first drink down at the bar complex on Naklua Soi 18. Frank was there with Spicy and so was Mickel, who had come alone, after leaving his live in girlfriend back in the condo.

"Oh shit. Here they come," Fast Eddy said to Mickel who was already on his sixth beer.

"Do not worry about it," said Mickel. "Do not worry about anything. This is Pattaya and tonight is New Year's Eve."

"Here you are," Marylee said to Fast Eddy as she came over with Win. "I look you everywhere."

I wish you hadn't, thought Fast Eddy. "Where's Saint Peter, Marylee? I haven't seen him anywhere. Usually he's at the bar next to this one."

"I don't know," said Marylee. "I not see him today. Now I sleep with Win."

Neither girl had a drink and no one was stepping up to buy. Normally Fast Eddy would have offered to buy both girls a drink, but he had decided not to encourage them. From what he had seen, neither of the girls was a drinker and from what he had seen of Chinese girls in general, those who didn't do a lot of drinking couldn't hold their alcohol. Chances are Marylee would start hanging all over him and then Katrina would be sure to find out.

"Whatever you do, don't buy these girls a drink," Fast Eddy whispered to Mickel.

"Why not?" Mickel asked.

"Because then we will never get rid of them."

"So what's wrong with that? Both are good looking ladies."

"And that's exactly the thing that worries me," Fast Eddy replied. "Everyone will be telling Katrina that we have been going out with these two girls."

His cell phone started to ring. It was Katrina telling him she had just gotten on a bus at Udon Thani and that she'd be at the condo the next morning.

"Who was that?" Mickel asked.

"Katrina. She said she just got on a bus from Udon Thani and she'd get here before noon."

"You don't believe that, do you?" Mickel asked.

The truth was, Fast Eddy didn't. An odd feeling had started to come over him that Katrina had never gone to Udon Thani. Her wanting to take a bus on New Year's Eve just hadn't been making any sense to him. He wasn't sure, but he had thought that New Year's Eve wasn't a big holiday for Thais in the first place. Or at least not as big as many other Thai holidays such as Songkran and Loi Krathong. Songkran came in April while Loi Krathong was celebrated in November. During Loi Krathong Thais would go out and buy Krathongs which were little boats made out of Styrofoam and banana leaves. They'd then take their Krathongs out to a nearby river or to the beach if they lived anywhere near Pattaya, light a candle that had been fixed to the little boat, and launch it out into the water for good luck and as for Songkran, more than half a million Thais came into Pattaya on the last day of Songkran to throw water all over anyone who came into range. In Pattaya Songkran lasted more than a week during which nothing ever got done and many businesses closed their doors. Songkran was complete insanity with automobiles and pickup trucks clogging the streets slowing traffic down to a crawl. Large drums filled with water would be placed randomly up and down the streets with every bar making sure it was well supplied with its own water barrel while each pickup truck carried its own 60 gallon drum. People would squirt everyone in sight including the drivers of motorbikes, thus killing over four hundred people in motor bike related accidents during that week throughout Thailand. This went on even in periods of extreme drought with huge quantities of water literally going down the drain to the considerable amusement of hundreds of thousands of participants.

"Fast Eddy, Fast Eddy, I left my girlfriend in the condo tonight," Mickel continued. "So you know that our New Year's Eve is not very important to her. Do you really think your Katrina really went home to see her family on New Year's Eve? Think Fast Eddy, think. Because if it's that important to be seeing them on New Years, then why is she spending New Year's Eve coming here in a bus? This would mean she's not with her family and she's not with you either."

"How long does it take to get here from Udon"? Mickel continued.

"About 11 hours."

"Just as I thought. So she'd rather be spending 11 hours of her precious New Year's Eve on the bus than to be celebrating it here or with her family?"

"You are right, Mickel. Damn, you are so so right, Fast Eddy repeated as he suddenly realized for the first time with 100 percent certainty that Katrina was lying to him and that she was probably in Pattaya or somewhere close to Pattaya with another man. Then he turned to Marylee and Win and asked them, "Can I buy you girls a drink?"

Suddenly he realized what he had already suspected for some time--that Katrina had also been lying to him the last time she had gone to Udon Thani the night that her daughter had been in a school bus accident. He started to envy Frank for having Spicy. She was with him for one thing. In fact she was almost always with him. She might be uneducated and be unable to even read Thai, but she was loyal, which is one thing he couldn't say for most Thai women and certainly not for Katrina.

*****

Several months earlier, Katrina had gotten a phone call from her parents, which started her crying, and then she told him that her eight year old daughter had just been in a school bus accident just north of Udon Thani. It was still unclear how many of the children were injured or killed–only that another bus had hit the school bus while it was trying to pass. One hour later, Katrina got another phone call, learning only that the status of her daughter was still unknown. Fast Eddy immediately volunteered to buy Katrina an airline ticket to Udon Thani and within two hours, Katrina was gone. She came back late the next afternoon and told him her daughter had not been injured. But the whole incident didn't make sense to Fast Eddy. Katrina had been gone for less than twenty-four hours, and since she had not seen her daughter in nearly a year, he found it hard to believe that she'd cut her visit to less than twenty-four hours. He also found it hard to fathom how Katrina could make the 2 hour taxi ride to the Bangkok Airport, buy a ticket, catch the next flight to Udon Thani, land and still manage a bus ride or taxi to some little town over 20 kilometers north of Udon Thani, visit with her family, get a bus back to the airport, get on the next flight to Bangkok, grab a taxi from the Bangkok airport and wait still another two hours in the taxi getting back to the condo. He simply believed it couldn't be done and even if it could, a mother wouldn't go to all that trouble without remaining longer with a daughter she had not seen for a year, especially one who had just been in an accident.

"Do you have a receipt for the ticket you purchased from Air Asia?" he had asked Katrina.

"No. I threw it away," Katrina had replied.

"Do you have a boarding pass?" he asked. Then he added so there would be no room for misunderstanding, "a boarding pass is a paper with seat number on it."

"They never gave me one," she replied.

Fast Eddy couldn't remember ever having gotten on an airplane when they hadn't given him a boarding pass. But he vaguely remembered an Air Asia flight he had once been on when the airline had not given him an assigned seat. But he still thought Katrina was lying to him.

He had gone to Soi Six that night where he had over half a dozen beers before coming home at 2 a.m. Katrina was gone and so were all her clothes and other belongings. His condo seemed so empty once he realized she was not coming back, and that even if she was, he couldn't tolerate her lying. She was the price of an airline ticket richer. Completely convinced that she had pocketed his money, he didn't dwell on where she had gone or who she might have been with as he tried to snatch a few hours of sleep.

The next day he was still completely convinced that the school bus accident had never happened and that Katrina had never gone to Udon Thani. He was sitting in a restaurant having coffee with a friend when Katrina called him on his cell phone. She wanted to come back to his condo, she told him. "Do you still want me for girlfriend?" she asked him.

His friend was a hard bitten Australian who had lived in Thailand for over ten years, who had seen it all before, who had been cheated on and who had been lied to by past girlfriends. Fast Eddy was about to tell Katrina to go find another place to live when his friend blurted out, "You two have been together for a long time now so it's not like you just met last week. I think you really should go see her and find out what she has to say."

So he met her at a German restaurant where she convinced him that she could have made it to Udon Thani and back to the condo in less than twenty-four hours and that she had been telling him the truth about the bus accident. He still never had forgotten the incident, and every now and then this little voice would keep telling him that Katrina was about as honest and loyal as a three dollar bill.

*****

By this time the waitress had brought Marylee and Win the drinks Fast Eddy had just bought them as Marylee started edging closer to him. He suddenly came back to his senses when he heard Mickel's voice above the music in the bar, "She never went home, Fast Eddy, and she's not on any bus coming from Udon Thani to Pattaya."

For the first time Katrina's entire web of lies she had started to unravel. Katrina had told him that her mother was living in Udon Thani overseeing the family orange farm while her papa was working in Sattahip as a policeman. The story went that her daughter had been going to school close to Udon Thani and although Katrina had often gone to Sattahip to visit her father or to have her hair done-- as often as several times a month-- she had never gone to Udon to visit her daughter. Only once in the past two years had her daughter come to visit her, he remembered Katrina telling him.

"Katrina's spending the New Year over in Sattahip," he suddenly blurted out to Mickel. She never went to Udon Thani. She's not on an all-night bus and the daughter never went to school near Udon Thani. The entire family is over in Sattahip, and Katrina's got a Thai husband or boyfriend there and that explains why she wants to go to Sattahip so often. And that bus accident never happened, and Katrina never bought that Air Asia ticket and she pocketed all the money I gave her instead."

"You are right. I knew it. I just knew it," Mickel shouted.

"Mickel, we are going to Soi Six right now. Will you go with me?"

"Of course we go now. Let me just finish this beer. It will take me only five minutes," Mickel replied.

Soi Six

Lawrence parked his motorbike next to Mickel and Fast Eddy on Soi Six,. One long city block in length, there were over fifty bars lining both sides of the soi with over a half dozen girls working in each bar. Almost all of the bars were air-conditioned and unlike beer bars where the seating was outdoors, the customers sat indoors away from the prying eyes of outsiders. It was the perfect place for the man who already had a Thai girlfriend who wanted to keep his extracurricular activities a secret. Nearly all the bars had short time rooms upstairs. Some of the rooms were equipped with small bathrooms while others had one or two bathrooms down the hallway. The bars charged 300 baht for the room while the girls charged whatever was agreed upon between them and their customers which was typically 500 to 800 baht for their tips. Most experienced customers who knew the ins and outs of Soi Six never paid more than 500 baht. It was nearly always the newbies who wound up getting cajoled into paying more.

"Welcome to the promised land," Mickel announced jubilantly to Fast Eddy and Lawrence.

"Look, there's the Butterfly Bar," said Lawrence. "Let's have our first beer there."

"Do you want lady?" one of the girls said to Fast Eddy as she followed him inside.

"Perhaps," Fast Eddy replied. "I want massage."

The female bartender brought them their beers immediately after they sat at the bar while the girl who followed Fast Eddy inside, stood behind him, massaging the back of his neck. Two other women, who had already been inside the bar, went up to Lawrence and Mickel, hoping to score quick short times. Several other women remained outside where they kept a sharp eye out for prospective customers walking up the street.

The girl standing closest to Mickel, a short slightly plump woman in her mid-twenties, asked him, "Buy drink for lady?"

"But of course you can have drink, but you must drink beer."

"Me no like beer," the woman replied. "Me like coca cola."

"You have one beer with me," said Mickel. "If you want drink, I buy drink for you, but it must be beer."

"I no like beer," the girl replied.

"Okay, I don't buy you anything then," Mickel replied in an "I don't give a shit" tone of dismissal. Then turning to his two companions said, "Alcohol screws with their brains. They can only drink so much and they won't want to go to the next customer. They prefer making big boom-boom, so they can quickly move onto the next customer without getting slowed up from drinking too much."

When Fast Eddy finished getting his massage, he gave the girl forty baht, asked for his check bin, and announced to his two friends, "It's time to go to the next place."

> In Thailand the customer in a bar or restaurant has his bill placed next to him in a little container which is referred to as his bin. Prior to leaving the establishment he asks for his bin or check bin and then he settles his bill (bin).

Which was fine with Mickel and Lawrence neither one of whom was thrilled by the two dumpy looking girls, who had attached themselves to them like two hawks falling on their prey.

The next bar was The Red Point. Larger than the Butterfly Bar it also had twice as many girls working there. The three men were able to successfully get to a booth inside the bar without having any vultures descend on them. But by the time they ordered their beers from a waitress, a woman in her mid-thirties came over to Fast Eddy and asked if she could sit next to him.

"My Krap, Kapp Khun Krap," Fast Eddy replied using the polite Thai phrase for "No thank you."

The three men managed to finish off their first bottles of beer without having any new girls approach them until they were half finished with their second bottles, when Fast Eddy felt a woman's hands around his neck. He turned around and saw that the girl was pretty and young, no more than twenty, with a trim little waist, without trace of a belly. She was just what he was hoping for.

Smiling at him, she asked, "Buy drink for me?"

"Sure, I can buy you a drink," Fast Eddy replied. "You want lady drink?"

"Ka. Lady drink is okay."

"Where you come from?" Fast Eddy asked.

"Me come from Buriyan."

"You come from Paul Bunyan Land?" Mickel asked her in a loud voice. "I hear men big and strong in Paul Bunyan Land and the women have big pussy."

"Ka. Buriyan."

"But you too little to be from Paul Bunyan Land," Mickel replied.

Another girl suddenly appeared and sat next to Lawrence without asking while the girl who had been sitting next to Fast Eddy's snuggled next to him, put one arm around his neck and jammed her right hand between his legs.   Initially startled, Fast Eddy relaxed as he felt the girl's hand slither gently into his shorts. His eyes filmed over as he lay back into the couch savoring the exquisite sense of her touch, as she caressed the the underside of his balls.

"I think we finally went to heaven," said Fast Eddy. "I'm in love with this girl's hand."

"My han?" the girl asked.

"Yes. Keep doing what you are doing. Whatever you do, do not stop. I take you upstairs, short time, how much?" Fast Eddy asked her. "500 baht okay?"

"No. No okay. I want 700 baht."

"I give 500 baht. Okay?" Fast Eddy asked a second time.

"600 baht," the girl replied.

"500", Fast Eddy persisted. "If I like you I come see you again. Take you with me to condo long time. Maybe, but only if you good lady for me."

"500 baht okay. We go now?"

"Yes. I take beer upstairs with me."

"Are you going to do a short time now?" Lawrence suddenly asked Fast Eddy.

"Why not? Soi Six is going to close only one hour from now so that leaves us with very little time."

Lawrence winced as he looked at his watch. "It's still only 12 o'clock which is still early, but you are right, the bars on Soi Six close much earlier than anywhere else. It looks like I've better make up my mind."

"Bar-fine her," Mickel replied loudly. "Do not wait. We come here for ladies--not to use the toilet. You take her upstairs and I will find me a lady too. Believe me--I will find a lady right now, a very good lady."

Lawrence scrutinized the girl sitting next to him. She was probably the best looker in the whole place and this included the girls standing outside the bar. He could almost see her bare nipples pushing firmly against her blouse. Feeling his eyes on them, she smiled and pulled it open to give him a better look at sharply defined pointy breasts appearing full of milk. Lawrence had not seen her, or Fast Eddy's girl when they had first come in and concluded that both of them had been with customers upstairs and that they had later taken showers, freshened up and seeing new customers at the table, decided to vie for one more short time before the bar closed.

"She's a beautiful girl", Lawrence said to his two friends. "This will be sloppy seconds and I hate sloppy seconds. I never do them, but this girl's got the most incredible breasts which is making my dick about a foot long now." Lawrence watched the girl with a faint smile looking for a reaction.

"You want boom-boom me?" the girl asked him.

"I pay you 500 baht. Same same friend me, Fast Eddy," Lawrence said with finality.

"Okay. We make boom-boom now," said the girl. "Bar close too much."

Fast Eddy and his girl stood up from the table and went over to the bartender.

"You pay bar 300 baht," said the girl.

After he paid the bartender Fast Eddy followed his girl up the stairs into a small hotel room that had a single small window overlooking Soi Six, which was still busy. Fast Eddy looked through the window to observe a smorgasbord of activity below him–of Ladyboys yelling "Sexy Man" at Westerners walking down the Soi and bar girls going out to the carts of food vendors selling fried grasshoppers, moths, insect larvae, fruit, slices of pizza, rice dishes and kebabs. The food carts were mounted side car fashion onto small one cylinder motorbikes. He started to drink his unfinished beer from the bottle he had put on a small table next to the room's solitary bed and heard the girl say, "Shower."

She took him down the hall where there were three other small short time rooms to a small enclosed shower, handed him a towel and then she went back to the room having already showered after her last customer.

Lawrence was luckier than Fast Eddy, having scored a small room that had its own little bathroom with its own small hot water heater, shower and wash basin next to the toilet. After showering he noticed the large mirror on the ceiling directly above the double bed. "I can easily spend the night here," he said to the girl, knowing that she probably didn't understand a word he said. The room was more than he expected–being larger, cleaner and better appointed than he could have imagined from a whorehouse.

The girl shoved him gently down into the bed, pried his legs apart with her hands and went down on him, as her lips moved rapidly up and down his penis. She was a real pro, making him feel like he was 16 again, as he felt the first signs of premature ejaculation welling up, which would be very bad news because that would have resulted in his not getting his money's worth. Lawrence grabbed the girl by both shoulders and shook her hard enough to pull her hungry mouth away. He let a few seconds go while he collected himself. Then he got up from the bed to reposition his body and pushed his head between her legs, going down on her gingerly at first as he played his tongue around the outskirts of her vaginal lips.

Who's been here before me?" he asked himself. And did she take a shower afterwards? Did she take a good shower? Did she douche? But he was so turned on from her going down on him and her figure was so perfect that he no longer cared. But after thinking about the other guys he pulled away and brought his mouth up to her breasts. He felt her breast expand into his mouth as her nipple suddenly hardened between his lips. Imagining himself to be a baby glutting itself from its mother's milk he pressed his face into her bosom for a full ten minutes as he ran both breasts between his lips, mouthing each nipple gently before biting down just hard enough to cause her to cry out in pain. Then he lowered his face between her legs, no longer thinking about who had been there before him.

Several times he nearly exploded into her mouth. But each time he suddenly jerked away. He wanted her, now. Not asking for a condom, he pulled away one last time, and then he pressed himself into her and inserted his penis halfway in.

HIV! He thought about it for a second and then decided that it didn't exist and if it did, he was so physically strong that it wouldn't affect him.

He stayed in the room with her for an hour, even sending her downstairs for two beers, one for her and one for himself. He came easily the first time. Afterwards he lay next to her while she stroked his belly while gazing into the large mirror above the bed. He came once again before taking her downstairs after which he gave her the 500 baht they had agreed upon plus another hundred for a tip since he had cum twice.

Fast Eddy was already at the table waiting for him.

"Well, it sure took you long enough," Fast Eddy said irritably.

"Where's Mickel?" Lawrence asked.

"He went upstairs right after you and I went," said Fast Eddy. "But like you he's sure taken long enough."

"Your friend he upstairs," the bartender said. "He take lady. Buy room for all night. He go morning."

"He what!" Fast Eddy exclaimed loudly.

"He say he like lady too much. Take her long long time. I close bar now. Soi Six close very very soon."

Fast Eddy turned to Lawrence and said, "This woman's gotta be shitting us. Surely Mickel has not booked a room and a girl for the rest of the night. What's his girlfriend going to say?"

Mickel's girlfriend

Fast Eddy was almost certain Katrina was cheating on him. Otherwise he wouldn't have gone with Mickel and Lawrence to Soi Six, so when he came down from the Soi Six short time room after having sex he felt good about it. He felt good that he had banged the girl and even better than good because he knew he'd be back. But Katrina had told him she was on an all-night bus back to Pattaya, and even though Fast Eddy knew this didn't make sense, and that Katrina was probably staying in or near Pattaya, he still wasn't 100 percent sure. There would be an excellent chance she'd show up by mid or late morning, however. So the loud sound of his doorbell ringing at 2 a.m. came as a totally unwelcome shock. He'd already had little sleep the night before thanks to Marylee talking his ear off until 6 o'clock in the morning, and thanks to all the drinking he'd done he'd be sure of a hangover the next day.

He tried to shake off the rude sound of the doorbell and go back to sleep, but the ringing just wouldn't stop. Whoever was there was determined on rousting him from his bed. His mind in a total fog, Fast Eddy rose from his bed, snatched a towel from one of the bathrooms, pulled it around his waist and stumbled over to his door. Then he looked out the peep hole to see who was there.

It was Na, Mickel's girlfriend, who had to be just about the most unwelcome sight he could imagine. First, if he let her in, someone might see her enter his condo, starting with the security guard if he were watching the security cameras' monitor. He'd be in the same position he found himself the night before with Marylee. Even worse, he didn't have any idea of what to tell her. Mickel was by now fast asleep in a Soi Six short time room, oblivious to all of the world's problems. Fast Eddy decided, *There's no way I can explain Mickel's absence to Na. Even if I can come up with a good story by the time Mickel's gotten back to his condo and Na asks me my version of what kept him out all night, Mickel's story is going to be completely different from mine. And that's if I'm on top of my game.*

Fast Eddy felt his mind was about as sharp as a bowl full of porridge. He'd certainly have to answer a barrage of questions that would be unleashed on him in angry broken English. *I don't deserve any more of this crap,* he said to himself. *I only want to sleep. Mickel got himself into this so he will have*

to get himself out of it because no matter what I do I can only make things worse. Fast Eddy did the most intelligent thing he could possibly do which was to quietly retreat from the door and go back to bed without letting onto Na that she had succeeded in awakening him.

Mickel's Alibi

Mickel staggered into his condo at 2 p.m., after getting up at noon and eating breakfast alone on Soi Six. After having a half dozen cups of coffee he still didn't feel human.

"Where have you been? You forget me?" Na asked angrily.

"I've been out drinking with Olaf," Mickel replied. "And let me tell you this. We get very drunk. In fact we get so drunk we have to take a taxi to Olaf's room."

"Why you not come here back to condo?" Na asked. "I very angry with you."

"Do not be angry with me. Olaf and I cannot help ourselves. We get so drunk that I start to wonder, why you not come and get me and why you not call me.   I don't think you love me."

"I try to call you many times.   You not answer telephone."

"You call me many times?   Well, maybe I turn telephone off accidentally. Who knows. We get very drunk—I can tell you that for sure."

"Where you sleep?"

"On Olaf's floor. His floor is very hard, but it doesn't matter because I get very drunk and I'm so glad of it."

"You boom-boom other lady?"

"Let me think. Did I boom-boom other lady?   Come to think of it, I don't remember. Maybe I did and maybe I didn't. But I do not think so. We get so drunk that I don't think I boom-boom anyone. At least I do not think so."

Na fought back the urge to tear Mickel's face off with her fingernails, but then she decided, "He'll never change, and even if he make boom-boom with lady not I, at least he is giving me money. 20,000 baht a month which is three times what I can make working a regular job. And when he goes back to Norway, he is giving me thirty thousand baht a month, which is enough to keep mama and papa happy and I still have enough to give Thai husband 10,000 baht so he can buy car.

Socrates meets the Sidewalk

Socrates saw the woman driving down the sidewalk towards him on her motorbike just as he was turning left to enter the travel agency. He glared at her, standing his ground, as he thrust his arm out to intercept her head, expecting her to turn at the last second. But she either didn't see him or was in such a bad mood that she simply didn't care. The motorbike hit his torso at the same moment that his hand connected with her face, knocking him down. Then he heard the loud clattering of the motorbike scraping the concrete as it slid to a stop on top of its driver.

He heard people all around him. Two men picked the small motorbike off the prostrate woman. For a minute or two Socrates lay on the sidewalk groggily trying to regain his senses. He felt numbness in his right arm from his hand striking her face and noticed that his knees had been rubbed raw from the fall. Other than that he felt perfectly capable of getting off the concrete, and did--on wobbly legs.

The woman lay on the sidewalk groaning in pain, her motorbike shattered from striking the concrete hard and sliding on its side. For five minutes he heard the crowd milling around him jabbering excitedly away in Thai, each person giving his or her version of the accident. Then the police came.

The woman still lay on her back on the sidewalk as a policeman kneeled next to the woman's head to get her version of what had caused the accident. Socrates could hear her voice getting louder and louder, to a white hot pitch of anger, as she told the policeman what had happened. A Thai man and woman approached a second policeman as they stood over the woman and the officer kneeling next to her, as both of them spoke excitedly at the same time while pointing at him. Socrates couldn't understand a word they were saying. But there wasn't a doubt in his mind that they were siding with the motorcyclist.

Another policeman approached Socrates and asked in halting English, "What you do? Tell me what happen?"

"She was driving on the sidewalk while I was going into the shop," Socrates explained to the policeman as he pointed to the travel agency. "I see her driving right at me. Right at me, mind you, the stupid lady. Then she run me over."

"Lady not stupid," the policeman replied. "You hurt the lady and her motorbike finished. Somebody must pay. You have friend you can call?"

"No. Why should I call anybody? You should put this woman in jail where she belongs."

"If anybody in jail, you be."

"Oh no, not me", Socrates replied angrily. "You need to put this woman in a cage like an animal. People are not supposed to be driving on the sidewalk."

"Can do," the policeman replied.

"Not in England they can't."

"This Thailand--not Ingland. You need call some one. Woman need money for motorbike. She hurt too much. Need more money. You have big money? Have ATM? Have friend you can call?"

"No. I don't have my atm on me," Socrates replied. "And this woman-- she isn't getting any of my money."

"Then you no call your friend?"

"No. I will not!" Socrates replied angrily.

"Then you must come with us. You go monkey-house until friend come."

*****

There must have been ten men in the cell with Socrates. The vague numbness in his arm had become a sharp distinct pain, which Socrates recognized as a sure fire sign of at least one fracture. The thought of having to pay for the medical injuries of the woman who had run him down on her motorbike enraged him. He had heard of such incidents before in which the Westerner was always in the wrong. He had known of Thais running into the backs of Foreign driven motorbikes, and although the Thais were obviously completely at fault, the Western drivers wound up having to pay for new motorbikes for the Thais. The operating rule in these cases was that whenever property damages occur in an accident and/or medical injuries are sustained, someone has to pay for such damages, and since most Thai people are overwhelmingly poor compared to Westerners, the Westerner ends up paying all claims no matter how outrageously at fault the Thai culprit had been.

Of course the police have to get their cut too, so whenever a Westerner winds up forking over money either at the scene of an accident he had been involved in or at the police station afterwards, Socrates figured the Westerner is being overcharged at least ten percent and oftentimes more than 100 % over the actual cost to repair the bike and medical damages to the injured Thai driver.

Socrates dialed a number on his cell phone. When Frank answered, Socrates spat out, "Bad news, Frank. I hate to bother you, but I'm in jail."

"You what?" Frank asked.

"I'm in jail, Frank, and I need to have someone lend me some money to get me out. This Thai woman just ran me down on the sidewalk and the police want me to pay for her medical bills and for a new motorbike."

*****

Frank couldn't get Socrates out of jail until the next morning after the banks opened. The paperwork at the police station was minimal. Frank was amazed to find himself getting ahead of several Thais who were waiting in line. *Must be the smell of money,* he almost said aloud. *They know me here from yesterday and can't wait to get their grubby little hands on this little gift I've brought them.*

Ten minutes later, one of the police officers led Socrates into the police station's reception room which always seemed to be filled with people, most of them there to reclaim motorbikes that the police had temporarily confiscated for illegal parking. Frank had been there once or twice before to get his own motorbike back. He had found the entire setup to be a lucrative business for the police and their business associate who was called in to haul illegally parked motorbikes into a lot at the far end of town. Oftentimes the non-parking areas were poorly marked resulting in not one but oftentimes as many as a half a dozen motorbike owners parking their motorbikes next to all the others. The first time that had happened to Frank, he had parked across from the computer IT building on Pattaya Tai only to find his bike missing an hour later. At first he had thought someone had stolen it until a Thai woman tending a small shop next to where he had parked his bike, said to him: "Police take motorbike." In order to reclaim his motorbike, Frank had to go all the way back to his condo to get his green book (proof of ownership book) out of his safe. Then he had to go back to the police station with his green book and pay his fine after which he got a receipt that he had paid his fine. After all that he still had to get a motorbike taxi to take him to the motorbike towing yard where he showed his receipt and then had to walk around looking over the hundreds of bikes waiting for their owners to collect them in order to find his little Nouvo MX. Frank had found the attendant to be too lazy to help him find his bike.

"That sure was expensive, Socrates. I couldn't even get enough money out of my ATM for your bail," said Frank as the two men walked out of the police station together. So I had to let you spend the night in your cell because the banks didn't reopen until this morning."

"How much was it?"

"Sixty-five-thousand baht."

"Jesus Christ. I'll have to go to my bank tomorrow to pay you back, Frank."

"I figure it this way. You just bought that woman a new motorbike in order to reward her for breaking the law when she drove down the sidewalk. That leaves two or three thousand baht for minor medical injuries if she even bothered to go to the hospital at all for minor bruises and abrasions she might have gotten from sliding across the concrete. That leaves 20,000 to 30,000 baht for the police bribe."

"I should have gotten insurance."

"Why didn't you?"

I had it once, but when it came to my renewal I decided to look at what the policy actually said. So I went down to the insurance office. There were three employees in the insurance office but not one of them spoke English. So I came back to the condo here and I had our secretary tell me what my old policy actually said."

"And?"

"It only allowed 100,000 baht for medical injuries or 100,000 baht for accidental death if the other person happened to be killed."

"That sure isn't much. That's only about three thousand dollars.

"It might not be much but one thing is for sure. The insurance company would not have wanted to pay it. I would not have had to go to jail. And if the woman wanted to collect she'd have to get it from the insurance company and not from big money pockets rich falang like us. And the police would never have fucked with the insurance company. It sure is a shitty corrupt system they are running over here, and the biggest mafia of them all is the police. I now understand what happened to the United States in Vietnam and what's happening to the U.S. in Afghanistan and Iraq. This whole thing about nation building is a total crock. South Vietnam was corrupt to the core and anyone with the slightest sense of moral decency knew that. We Westerners can have no affect whatsoever on any of these people and that goes for all over the world. So we all ought to just let them try and solve their own problems and stay out. Hearts and minds--my ass. They are all out of their minds."

The Russian Invasion

The Bay Area Resort next door to the Bahthaus was packed with Russians. Although the hotel had gotten its name from the San Francisco Bay area, very few Americans ever stayed there. In fact, very few Americans were now staying in Pattaya at all, having been replaced by the Brits, Germans and a smattering of Scandinavians, Dutch, Swiss, and Australians, New Zealanders, Indians, Arabs, etc. As for the Bay Area Resort, although 65 % of its guests were Russian, 20 % Korean and only 5 % were Thai, the hotel for reasons that only Buddha understood offered its guests an overwhelming majority of Thai stations through Banglamung cable TV. Management apparently decided this was good enough and had not provided satellite TV service that provide CNN, the History channel, HBO and other movie channels along with the most popular European sports channels apparently because it did not want to pay for the increased cost of catering to hotel customers requiring Western channels.

> As of October 15, 2011 there were 4 Russian television stations offered in condominiums close to this hotel, 33 stations in Thai, and 19 in English through Banglamung cable and True Visions satellite with a handful of other stations in German, French, Italian Chinese, Korean, and Japanese.

As for the Russians, they don't know any better, the monkey concluded as he relaxed underneath two palm trees watching a heavy bellied Russian wash his shoes in the swimming pool. Blood rushed to the monkey's head as anger replaced the inner peace he had sought from enjoying his lush tropical surroundings.

"Stop that right now! You can't wash your shoes in our swimming pool!" the monkey screamed at the Russian. But the Russian continued to wash his shoes, oblivious of everything around him.

"You. Stupid Russian. Stop that right now. This is a swimming pool, not a public toilet" the monkey yelled across the pool at the Russian.

Finally hearing the monkey, the Russian stopped washing his shoes and glared angrily at the much smaller man lying in the beach chair across the pool from him.

"Fuck you," the Russian yelled back.

"Is that all they can teach you in Russia?" the monkey yelled back at the man. "You people are complete barbarians."

"Fuck you," the Russian shouted across the pool.

The monkey smiled to himself with the inner satisfaction that he had at least stopped the Russian from any further cleaning of his shoes. He'd complain to the Bay Area manager later. And then finally, maybe just maybe, the Bay Area Resort would finally do something about the Russians.

But Pattaya wasn't. The Russians had taken the place over. On the streets close to the Bahthaus, there were more signs in Russian than English. With the explosion of Russian tourism into Pattaya, increasing numbers of Russians, most of them couples, started crowding into the Seven Eleven and Family Mart convenience stores, either too proud or too stupid to speak as much as a single word in Thai or English, as they created log jams of confusion with employees, who were unable to understand what the Russians wanted or to make them understand what things cost.

"So here you are, Ling Noi," said Fast Eddy, as he slumped into the beach chair next to the Swiss. "I see you are once again trying to discipline the Russians." Fast Eddy often called his Swiss neighbor Little Monkey, which in Thai is Ling Noi because, *well, one just has to know the guy*, Fast Eddy shrugged as he thanked God for giving him such a wonderful neighbor.

"Don't you just love these barbarians, Fast Eddy? They all come from a pigsty. You Americans might be pretty stupid, but at least you are not complete morons like these Russians."

"As usual, you are once again showing you are a Swiss cheese, all full of holes," Fast Eddy retorted. "But you are right. Most Americans have become pretty stupid."

"I still wish we had more of your countrymen here," the monkey replied. Most of them are pretty nice. Not like the English who are always starting trouble."

"You have a point there."

"Or the Russians. Just look at them. But I can see why they come. They have too much money now and they have nowhere else to go. You Americans have a lot of beaches back in the U.S., and you have Mexico and the Caribbean so close to you. What do the Russians have--the Black Sea? They shit in it, I tell you. They are so stupid they shit in their own resorts."

"I don't know what hole all these Russians came out of," Fast Eddy replied. "But I do know this. They could never have defeated Germany in World War II, never have beaten us Americans in outer space by launching Sputnik and they would never have done so well in the Olympics all these years. I was in Russia over twenty years ago when it was the Soviet Union, and it seemed to me that the Russian people were very interested in talking with me. They were not at all like these people we have lumbering around here, who seem interested only in their own insufferable arrogance."

"The Russians have such terrible manners," the monkey continued. "I can't even swim my laps in this pool without them constantly getting in my way or running into me. It has to be obvious to everyone that I'm taking a line down the length of this pool as I swim back and forth. And these Russians will get out into the middle of the pool and just stand there talking so then I have to swim around them. So I cannot even swim straight and I have to swim almost in a complete circle just to avoid all these Ruskies."

"I have a theory," said Fast Eddy. "I read this article in "Newsweek" about Russia's new Feudalism. It all starts with Putin at the top of this pyramid. Just underneath him are something like ten top Russians who are policemen, ex KGB, bureaucrats or heads of organized crime. Anyway, KGB, the police, gangsters, it all amounts to the same because Russia has become a gangster state. Then beneath these top ten guys the control of the police and the country's economy spreads out. Now, say you own a shop and it's doing well, and if someone wants your shop he might ask you to sell it to him for say 100 American dollars. So you refuse because it's doing well. But if he is connected--If he is a member of the police or is friends with someone in authority, he can do anything to you. You will be beaten up, your place bombed or your car is set on fire. You can even be killed. Faked documents are arranged by the people in the bureaucracy and it's as if you never owned the place at all. So here's what I think. Unless you are a top engineer or a Scientist, a gifted athlete, or somebody special with huge natural talent, you aren't going to get ahead in Russia, so you will never have enough money to get into a hotel such as this. For that matter, you probably can't even afford the airfare to Thailand. So what we have here at the Bay View Resort are a bunch of gangsters. Back in Russia they think they can get away with anything and they do. And their women are the worse kind of women for marrying these monsters in the first place. So they come here and they refuse to even say thank you or say hello to the

Thais. They won't even bother to learn two phrases in Thai, "Hello" and "thank you". And if they've learned any English, they refuse to speak it because they want everyone to bow down to them. And then they parade up and down these streets in their little groups expecting motorcyclists and cars to have to stop for them."

"They are going to wind up controlling this country, I tell you. I've never known Russians to go anywhere in the world without trying to set up their networks of organized crime which has replaced the KGB," the monkey replied.

"But back to my theory. Many people who can afford to stay at this hotel are these Russian mafia types whereas decent Russians stay at home because they can't make enough money to travel. So most of these Russians we see around here are the very ones squeezing their countrymen out of everything and they feel nothing for anyone. And you know what. You hardly see any of these people in Vietnam. So what was that war all about? We Americans killed over one million Vietnamese to save them from Communism while we dropped three times as many tons of bombs on that little country as we dropped on Germany and Japan in World War II. We were afraid back then that the Russians would overrun the entire planet and we used Thailand for most of our airbases which we bombed Vietnam from. So now you and I are living in the middle of it–a Russian invasion of Thailand while Vietnam is doing 36 billion of trade with the U.S. alone and that is increasing by leaps and bounds each year. All I see is Vietnamese, English and French plastered all over signs throughout Vietnam without a single word of Russian to be seen anywhere."

"You Americans really lost that war, didn't you?" The monkey laughed out loud. "Next thing we know is the U.S. and Vietnam will become great allies against China. And we are going to wind up having to move to Vietnam just to get away from the Ruskies."

"Fucking Communists. If that's what they are in Vietnam, then we need a lot more of them here because then they might just force the Russians to take down all those offensive signs they've put up and down our street advertising all the condos they are selling and we can't get Pattaya City Hall to do anything about it."

> On December 6, 2011, 20 owners of a Naklua condo signed a police report against a Russian Restaurant playing loud music that reverberated throughout their building. Residents and the condo manager also complained to City Hall. Two weeks later the restaurant was playing its music louder than ever.

Snakes in the Bahthaus

"We must do something about all the pets in this condo!" Hermann thundered out loud to the other committee members as he opened the monthly Bahthaus Committee meeting.

"So what's the problem?" asked Lawrence.

"That damn Irishman, Socrates, has a snake in his condo. If we let him keep it, what's next--a man-eating crocodile? Perhaps we let tigers in next."

"You gotta be shitting me, said Fast Eddy. "Socrates has got a snake? I hope it's bigger than his dick."

"How do you know he's got a snake?" asked Lawrence.

"Our maintenance guys found it on the floor of Socrates condo while they were checking his water meter. They tell me it's a Burmese Python."

"Was it pretty big?" Fast Eddy asked.

"It was more than three meters long," they tell me," Hermann replied.

"What? We have snake in condo?" Khun Felonius suddenly asked, as slow on the uptake as usual. "What must we do about snake?"

"Good question," said Hermann. "Do you want to leave Socrates a note asking him to come down to the office to discuss it with you?"

"What do I tell him?" Khun Felonius asked.

Obviously annoyed by the Thai manager's question, Hermann asked "What do you think you should tell him? That you recommend Purina snake food to him and that our office is going to pay for it?"

"Purina snake food. I don't know that name," the manager replied.

"All you need to do is to call Socrates on the phone and ask him to come down to the office. Then show him the condo rules and regulations where it says, "No pets allowed." Once you have done that simply tell him he must get rid of the snake."

"When should he get rid of the snake?"

"Just tell him next year is just fine with you and all the condo residents," Hermann replied irritably.

"Okay. Next year is okay? I think I wait until next year to have meeting with him then."

"No Khun Felonius. Right now. Tell him he must get rid of the snake right away. Do it today," Hermann ordered.

*****

One week later, the committee had a short meeting to discuss the pet situation at the Bahthaus.

"Is the snake still around?" Hermann asked Khun Felonius.

"The snake? He around still," the manager replied.

"Why? I told you to get rid of it."

"Socrates. He not want to make the snake leave."

"He what?" Hermann roared. "What are you trying to tell me, Khun Felonius? That it is up to Socrates whether or not he can keep a snake here?"

"He show me the Condo Rules and condo rules say, "No condo resident can feed pets in condo that are causing problem or harm to other residents."

"So what? Socrates is in violation of our condo rules. I told you that."

"But Socrates say English in rules very bad. He say, he not feed pet snake in condo. He say he feed it outside condo and he say snake not attack or cause harm to other owner."

"Socrates does have a point," said Lawrence, obviously pleased at the German's discomfort with someone pointing out that his English was faulty. "The condo rules should specify, "No pets are allowed in the condo."

"The meaning is very clear," Hermann replied angrily. "There are to be no pets."   Then turning to face Khun Felonius, he asked the manager directly. "So what did you do after that?"

"I told Socrates I would tell you and the committee what he said."

"Khun Felonius, just what are we paying you for? You are supposed to be our manager. That means when I or this committee tells you to do something, you do it. Am I clear on this? And you don't have a condo resident tell you what he's going to do."

"Okay. So what do I tell him now?"

"I don't know. You figure that out for yourself. You are the manager. Now manage."

****

A few days later, a dog was heard barking in a condo a Korean family was renting from one of the owners. When Hermann heard about it, he once again called a short committee meeting.

"Is the snake out of Socrate's condo yet?" Hermann asked.

"I don't think so," Khun Felonius replied.

"No--Why not, then?" Hermann asked.

"I tell Socrates snake must go, but he tell me snake is going to stay because condo rules do not say he cannot have snake."

"Well now, there is a dog here too and people hear it barking. And someone just told me one of our Australian owners brought in a second dog and that when the owner took the dog out of his condo to take it outside so the dog could go the toilet, the dog pissed all over the cleaning woman while she was cleaning the elevator doors."

"I not know about the dogs," Khun Felonius replied.

"It seems that you don't know much about anything that goes on here at this condo," said Fast Eddy. "Let me ask you something, Khun Felonius. Except for when you get into your car to go home, when is the last time you ever went outside your condo office to check on anything? And by anything I mean how our security is doing, or whether or not our cleaning women are cleaning correctly, or do any of our swimming pools light bulbs need changing, are we having too much chlorine put in the pool and so forth.

"Leave my office? I don't know. Is the manager supposed to come out of the office? I thought that condo staff do everything."

"Khun Felonius, I tell you what. You just sit in the office and keep looking at yourself in the mirror telling yourself you are the manager and then I'll go out, look around the condo, see what needs to be done and then I'll have someone take care of it. But I want to get your salary while you get nothing except for 2 baht a day for mirror time," Fast Eddy said vehemently.

The Elevator Detective

The carpet covering the Bahthaus elevator floor had not been cleaned in over two weeks. The reason Fast Eddy knew this was that even though he didn't normally smoke, he had gone to the local Seven Eleven to buy a pack of Marlboros for testing purposes. Taking a few drags off a cigarette, Fast Eddy dumped a few ashes into his hand and sprinkled them across the elevator floor. After two weeks the ashes were still there.

Fast Eddy had also gone to each floor in the condo building with a spool of scotch tape, a scissors and several sheets of notebook paper. Cutting the paper into thin strips he then cut off pieces of tape which he coiled into little circles with the adhesive sides of each little circlet facing outwards. Finally he fastened the little scotch tape bracelets onto each scrap of paper and stuck three scraps to each floor, so that he wound up with one marker in the center of each main hallway and one at each end. The paper strips were just small enough to escape notice from anyone who wasn't looking for them. The tape made the bits of paper stick to the floor regardless of how hard the wind was blowing down the hallways. However, if a cleaning woman scraped her broom or mop across a taped strip the force of the broom would have either dislodged it or the cleaning woman would have noticed and removed the strip. In two weeks not one of the paper strips had been removed from the 5th, sixth or seventh floors whereas all the paper strips he had taped to the floors on levels 1, 2, 3, and 4 had disappeared.

"The damned cleaning women are only cleaning the bottom floors," Fast Eddy later told Lawrence. "And that shitty little Cornhole doesn't even know the difference."

When he found out the top floors were not getting cleaned, Fast Eddy exploded. Common sense told him to bring the subject up to his fellow committee members out of the hearing of the manager.

Instead, he went back to his condo and took his digital camera out, marched up to the 7th floor and started taking pictures of the three paper strips he had scotch taped to the floor. He then went into the elevator and took pictures of the ashes he had scattered across the floor. Finally he went inside the condo office to confront Khun Felonius. Not saying a word, Fast Eddy sat across the desk from the manager, took a cigarette from his pocket and calmly lit it. Then he exhaled a cloud of smoke while watching the manager's eyes for a reaction.

After playing an image back on the camera's digital readout of the ashes on the elevator floor Fast Eddy took a piece of notebook paper he still had in his pocket, laid it on the desk in front of the manager and dumped ashes from his cigarette onto the scrap of paper. He then handed the camera to the manager with the picture of the elevator ashes clearly visible on its display.

"Know what this means?" Fast Eddy asked.

"I no understand. You cannot smoke in office. You must put cigarette out."

Instead of putting the cigarette out, Fast Eddy inhaled slowly before offering it to the manager who refused to take it. "You see, Cornhole, I don't smoke normally, but I bought these cigarettes so that I could dump cigarette ashes out onto the elevator floor. They are still there after two weeks. Do you understand?"

"No. No understand. But put cigarette out, please."

"What this means is no one clean the elevator in two weeks. Haven't you noticed how dirty the elevator floor has gotten, Cornhole?"

"No."

"Then you don't notice anything around here," Fast Eddy replied angrily.

Fast Eddy jerked the camera out of the manager's hands and brought up the next image which he showed the manager. "See these little strips of paper. In two weeks they are still on the floors of levels 5, 6 and 7 of our building. Let me show you." Fast Eddy then took a little strip of paper out, attached a roll of scotch tape to it and stuck it to the manager's desk. Finally he took a pen off the manager's desk and used it to write "Not cleaned" in full view of the manager.

"Do you understand now, Cornhole? I put these pieces of paper on each floor and I also put the ashes on the elevator floor just to prove that you have been allowing our cleaning staff to do a real shitty job of cleaning. They have not been cleaning the elevator floor or levels 5, 6 and 7 of our building for at least two weeks. There are insects in the ceiling lights in the hallways. I don't think they've been cleaned in months and there is trash overflowing in the elevator ashtrays on the upper floors. Do you have the cleaning women do anything up there?"

"They are require to clean everything. Every floor."

"Do you ever go up there to check?"

"Sometimes."

"Do you know that I check all the floors every day and I don't even work here?" Fast Eddy asked.

"You check? Why you check?"

"Because you are not checking, that's why. Do you remember at our last meeting I said I'd go do your job for you, but you had to give up your salary to me?"

"Yes."

"Now you see. I find out this condo is not being cleaned correctly. I find this out--you didn't and that is your job. I'm retired., but from now on I'll have our committee instruct our office to pay me your salary, so you can have all the time in the world to play computer games."

"You cannot do job."

"Why not? I just did and I found out your cleaning girls are doing a terrible job, so it is now time for us to replace them."

"Not your job. You cannot do."

"Why not?"

"Me Thai. Manager must be Thai. Falang cannot manage. Thai laws say so."

"If all Thai people manage the way you do, then I say Thai people cannot manage but Falang very good managers."

"You no have work permit to work in Thailand. You cannot work—not even for free. Immigration deport falang who work in Thailand. Maybe Immigration deport you."

"Cornhole, Let me be clear about one thing. If you even try to report me to immigration I will cut your throat," said Fast Eddy as he drew his hand across his throat in a perfect pantomime of a knife cutting through a man's windpipe and carotid artery.

"Not true. I busy now. Please go away."

"Damn right I will. By the way, have you noticed that I've started calling you, Cornhole? Just in case you are wondering why, Cornhole means to fuck someone in the ass. And that's exactly what you have been doing to us condo owners. You keep taking your salary and yet you aren't checking anything around here. Our security guards are doing a miserable job. Our cleaning women aren't cleaning the top three floors. You are the most piss poor excuse for a manager I've ever seen. Believe me, Cornhole, you will be hearing more at the next committee meeting."

Skydiving at the Bahthaus

The security guard's voice was insistent. "Come now," he shouted into the house phone from the security desk in the lobby.

"What?" Hermann asked. "You want me now? Downstairs?"

"Come. Come Leo Leo." was his answer.

The man cannot speak English, Hermann said to himself. *But at least I know that leo leo means: Come quickly. Something must have happened.*

By the time he got downstairs, four or five Thais had already gathered in the condo parking lot that lay directly beneath Ted Buffalo's sixth floor condo. The body sprawled out onto the concrete was Ted Buffalo's.

"Falang kaput," one of the Thais jabbered in broken English to Hermann. "Die."

"You call police?" Hermann asked the security guard.

"My Cochai," the guard answered.

"Okay. You no understand," Hermann repeated. "Follow me," he said to the guard as he took him by his arm and guided him back to the security desk.

Hermann said sternly to the guard. "Telephone. Call police."

Even though he understood very little English, to the guard the command must have meant only one thing. All over the world it was common knowledge that when someone was killed in mysterious circumstances the police must be called. Ted Buffalo was obviously dead so Hermann could not possibly be asking him to call a hospital. The guard acted swiftly, calling out on the house phone immediately. He let the phone ring a few times before getting an answer--then he spoke to the person on the other end in Thai. After several minutes he hung up, looked at Hermann and said, "Leo Leo. Police come now."

The police arrived ten minutes later. Hermann followed them out into the parking lot while trying to reach the condo manager on his cell phone. There was no answer.

Ted Buffalo's body was lying on its back, its head crushed in from impacting the concrete as a six foot diameter pool of blood congealed around it. When Herman noticed the scratches on Ted's upper arms, he quickly knelt over the body. To the police officers it might have appeared that Herman was about to perform mouth to mouth resuscitation. But Herman had something else in mind. One look had told him Ted was dead. Almost brushing his lips against Ted's mouth was only a ruse to camouflage his inhaling deeply from his nostrils to detect the smell of alcohol. There was none. Two facts rang through Herman's mind: *No alcohol and scratches on the body equals sure signs of a struggle.*

One of the police officers grabbed the body's legs to straighten them in an effort to make Ted appear in a more relaxed position.

"No No, stop that," Hermann yelled out at the policeman. "Do not move him."

"I move him now. He not look good. Not comfortable," said the policeman.

"What does his being comfortable have to do with it?" Hermann asked the policeman. "You move the body. Maybe you destroy evidence."

"He okay now," the policeman said to Hermann. "He much more relaxed. Before legs no good. Look very very bad."

You fucking idiot, thought Hermann. Ted's legs were twisted around each other, one practically coiled around the other. *That might mean something. Perhaps at the last moment he was so terrified that he involuntarily tried to protect himself in some manner. Or possibly he was thrown off his balcony and he was trying to resist his assailants if there were any. But it's too late. The position of the body doesn't mean anything now.*

The police took the elevator up to Ted's condo, as Hermann tried to overtake them by using the stairs. Upon ringing the doorbell, they were met by a young Thai woman opening the door. Her face full of tears, she was still crying.

"What is your name?" one of the policemen asked her.

"Neon Wannate. Ted, my boyfriend me. I know not what to do," she said in Thai.

They went outside to the balcony overlooking the parking lot where Hermann noticed that the table and three out of four deck chairs were overturned next to the railing. Two of the police officers started to pick the table and chairs up in order to restore them to their original positions.

"Stop that!" Hermann screamed out in complete disbelief.

"No stop. Look no good," one of the policemen replied, obviously letting on that it was more important to tidy up the homicide scene than it was to keep everything intact, so the event could be studied closely and perhaps even reenacted.

It was obvious to Hermann that either Ted Buffalo had gotten very drunk before killing himself or that a struggle had taken place. If he had stood out on the table before hurling himself down onto the parking lot, it is more than likely that he would have done it resolutely and that only a single chair or the table would have been overturned instead of the table and three chairs altogether. If Ted had gotten completely drunk then it would have all made a little sense. He might have then clumsily thrust out with both legs as he made his fatal plunge. Even so, the table and chairs had been positioned a couple of feet in front of the railing. If Ted had jettisoned himself from either the table or a chair he would have risked falling head first against the railing instead of making a clean plunge down onto the concrete pavement. In all likelihood there would have been blood on the railing. Now all of this wouldn't matter because the evidence had been destroyed once the police had repositioned the table and chairs.

Hermann's logical German mind kept churning out the possibilities. *Were the police really this stupid or were they doing this on purpose as just another routine cover-up of Pattaya's rotten underbelly?*

Spicy's Revelations

Spicy ran out onto Frank's balcony when she heard the commotion downstairs in the parking lot from Thais shouting and the police arriving on their motorbikes. Below her she saw Ted Buffalo's motionless body, blood still pooling around it.

"Die. Falang die. Sure," she said loud enough for Frank to hear her.

Joining her on the balcony, he asked her: "What is going on down there?"

"Going on? Falang die. Kill himself. Falang fall down from up there." Spicy pointed at the condos above him. "Number six. Sure."

"How do you know he fall from floor number six?" Frank asked his girlfriend.

"Not sure. But I think he from number six," Spicy replied.

In some respects Thai women have the memories of an elephant and eyes that take in everything. A man's facial features, his physique, and his mode of dressing never fail to attract the scrutiny of most Thai women, especially sex workers, which Spicy certainly had been. Which is odd given the fact that the same women often appear to be blind when it comes to so much else such as while cleaning, a woman fails to see the grime and dirt in the corner of the room she is mopping or that the kitchen windows have become almost opaque from six month's accumulation of dust.

Spicy thought the body was Ted Buffalo's as soon as she noticed the loud, flamboyant touristy patterned shirt he had been wearing. It was the kind of tastelessly colored rag she had seen him wearing several times before that she had found to be almost as repulsive as his personality. She had also felt he was heading for a big fall as early as three months before, when she had learned from the condo Thai gossip grapevine that he had drawn up a will that would gift his condo over to his new girlfriend upon his death. As she gazed out at his body lying in the parking lot, it immediately dawned on her that Ted Buffalo's condo now belonged to his Thai girlfriend.

"He rich man--very stupid man," Spicy said to Frank.

"Damn right he's stupid," Frank replied. "It takes rare intellect to be able to fall off the balcony of one's own condo." Then thinking about what he just said, Frank thought to himself, *but why would any man want to kill himself by jumping off a* building? There is just too much of that happening in Pattaya and I don't believe that most of these deaths are suicides. For one thing, a person is not assured of dying. The jumper might land wrong and only wind up getting crippled. Or suppose the jumper is killed but he doesn't fall on his head so the death isn't instantaneous? The suicide might wind up dying of ruptured internal organs. No. It is too uncertain as to death being one's planned result and how much pain and horror will have to be endured.

"I no like him anyway," said Spicy. "He no talk to me when I see him. He have big head and little brain." She started to think what Ted Buffalo's girlfriend must have thought of him. *She have little little money. Her family from Issan. Very poor. Mama sick. Maybe die one year, two year. No one to take care. Doctor cost too much money. Now she not die. Maybe daughter able to take care. Send to hospital. She boom-boom falang and get big money. Very good. Good for her. Good for family. Now she have money for house, for mama, papa. Maybe she help Buffalo fall and kill him. Maybe have Thai boyfriend help her.*

She thought again about her own father and how much she hated him for making her prostitute herself on Soi Six when she was sixteen and how greedy he had been when he kept pressuring her to lie to her ex German boyfriend about her son having an enlarged heart so that he'd feel sorry for her and the boy and how he'd cough up even more money each month for expensive medicine the boy did not need nor ever take, money that she and her father could pocket. *Papa stupid and too greedy*, she reminded herself. *Boyfriend me before. German man. He very smart. He find out the truth, then he leave me so he can find new lady. But Buffalo here, now very stupid. Before he let old Thai girlfriend stay in his condo and have anyone she want stay with him. So she let Thai boyfriend stay with her and boom boom her. They steal from Buffalo and Buffalo do nothing. He very stupid. He think he have good brain. Maybe girlfriend he have now have many problems. Mama sick, Papa sick. Other ladies talk to me she have problems too much. So this okay. Buffalo die so Mama and Papa live.*

Khun Felonius in the Frying Pan

"As you know we just had an unfortunate accident here," Hermann said to his fellow committee members in the condo office. "We had someone get killed. Does anyone think we might have helped avoid that?"

"I only know that Ted Buffalo fell off his balcony from the sixth floor and was killed," said Lawrence. "Does anyone know whether Ted had a drinking problem or not?"

"No one seems to know much about him," said Fast Eddy. "If you saw him in the lobby or the elevator," he'd say hi and that's about it."

"There have been no reports about him drinking too much or misbehaving from our staff or security," Hermann added. "So this would seem to rule out his getting so drunk that he fell out of his balcony. That is not for sure, but I think so, which leaves open the possibility of suicide."

"That's possible," said Fast Eddy. "But if you ask me, most of these suicides around here are murders meant to look like suicides."

"Murder?" Khun Felonius asked sleepily. "Why murder?"

"For one thing, didn't he have a Thai woman living with him?" Fast Eddy asked the manager contemptuously.

"He did. But Thai lady not kill Ted Buffalo. I not think so," Khun Felonius replied.

"Come on, Khun Felonius. Maybe she think she get big money. Maybe condo, if boyfriend suddenly die," Lawrence replied angrily, dumfounded at the manager's professed naivety.

"Enough," Hermann announced to the little group, obviously annoyed. "It is too late for Mr. Buffalo. And we will never know whether he took his own life or someone came in to help give him a little push. The important thing is this. Should we learn from this? Should we be doing something different so that something like this does not happen again?"

"I say we need to be doing something different," said Fast Eddy. "Our security is non-existent."

"What do you mean?" asked Hermann.

"Well, I know for a fact that the security guard at night is in the little security office sleeping. Nearly every time I come in late at night, there's no one at the security desk and he's not at the door either or outside standing around the parking lot gates. I've even checked the floors and walked up to each floor looking for him. There's only one place he can be and that's inside sleeping."

"What do you think, Khun Felonius?" Hermann asked.

"Maybe he sleep. Maybe he no sleep. I don't know because I not work job at night."

"So when do you work job?" asked Lawrence. "Every time I see you, you are in the office. I never see you checking our building, and the cleaning in this place has gotten to be god awful."

"I used to be in security in the U.S. Marine Corps," Fast Eddy added. "In your case, you should be training our security guards on how they must do their jobs. This means you must come in on some evenings to see if they are here and what they are doing. Good God, Khun Felonius. You only work four hours a day anyway and every time I see you, you are always in the office playing computer games. It seems no one has ever caught you doing a lick of work."

"You say I should come see security guards at night?" the manager asked. "I live far away, have wife. have family."

"Sorry Charlie, but if you can't check to even see if your security guard is at the desk working, then you shouldn't be manager in this place. We have two guards, one who works days and one who works nights. The one who works nights is very rude to all the residents here. He's not at the desk. He's not in uniform and he's sleeping while we pay him a salary. It is your job to find out what he is doing. And it is your job to teach him what his job is," said Fast Eddy.

"What is he doing wrong?"

"Well, for one thing, nearly every night there's about three Thai guys hanging around in our parking lot. The guard goes out in the lot to talk with them. And when he's out there gabbing away he's not at the desk to help any of the residents. He's not at the desk to see what overnight visitors come into our building and he's not able to check their ID's either."

"We not require guard to check ID's," Khun Felonius replied.

"That's because you are not telling the guard to check ID's," Fast Eddy replied angrily.

"Condo owner, he get angry at guard who try to tell him to check ID's," Khun Felonius replied.

"Don't you get it, Cornhole. Don't you fucking get it? We got a man dead. He's probably been murdered by his girlfriend, although I don't want to say, because I can't prove it one way or the other. Meanwhile we got a security guard who is either gabbing away with his buddies on our baht or who's asleep in the security office. If Ted Buffalo's girlfriend slipped a Thai boyfriend or motorbike taxi driver upstairs to help her shove Ted Buffalo off the balcony, one thing is for sure, the security guard never saw him come in. And if this woman was responsible for Ted's death, you are responsible, because you didn't insist that our security guards do their jobs properly."

"You say I killed Ted Buffalo?" the manager asked tearfully.

"No, I did not say that. What I am saying is you are not doing your job as the manager. I had to go around and check to see if the floors were getting cleaned by our cleaning girls. I put little rolls of paper on each floor and found they were not scraping them up with their brooms and mops. I put cigarette ashes on the elevator floor only to find that the elevator had not been cleaned in over two weeks. What do you have our cleaners doing?" Fast Eddy asked. "Make boom-boom in room with our residents?"

"You say our cleaners make boom-boom?" Khun Felonius asked.

"No. I not say that. I make joke. But I am deadly serious when I tell you that I find you aren't doing anything to show you are worth even one thousand baht a month as manager," said Fast Eddy.

"That's enough now, Fast Eddy," said Hermann. Then turning to the manager he added, "Fast Eddy very angry now because his girlfriend boom-boom other man. He not mean what he say to you."

"My girlfriend boom-boom other man? Now that is complete bullshit!" Fast Eddy replied heatedly.

"Enough," Hermann shouted at Fast Eddy. "Not one more word. We will talk about this later in private, Fast Eddy."

Fast Eddy and Hermann

Fast Eddy entered Hermann's condo a few minutes after the meeting, still steaming about the manager.

"What is this crap about my girlfriend screwing some other guy?"

"I lied. You went too far with Knun Felonius," the German replied.

"I went too far? We went too far to have hired him in the first place. I tell you, Hermann, in my whole life I have never met a more worthless, lazy, good for nothing son of a bitch."

"Listen to me, Fast Eddy. If he quits, we must pay him severance pay equal to three months salary. And if he thinks we have insulted him and that's why he quits, the rest of the staff is going to find out about it and then I am afraid they are going to run away."

"You mean quit?"

"That could happen, I'm telling you, Fast Eddy. That's why I lied about your girlfriend boom booming other man."

"I don't understand."

"Well, if your girlfriend is boom booming another man, this makes you look foolish. Since you have already made so many derogative comments to our manager, things that make him appear to be worthless, I was afraid he was going to quit. So if I suggest your girlfriend has made you angry by going with other man, then our manager might think this is why you say so many terrible things about him. He still loses face, but you lose even more face, so now he feels better."

"I'll never apologize to that worthless bum."

"I know Fast Eddy, and that is why I said what I said. I'm sorry if it makes you look a little bad. I will explain this to the other committee members and that should make you feel better."

"You really think our staff would quit if Cornhole resigned in disgrace?"

"Yes I do. He's Thai and they are Thai and Thai stick together, no matter what. In their eyes we stupid falang have no right to fire a Thai because they feel superior to us. Unfortunately we need a Thai manager. It's the law, so we will probably have a bad one. You should see, Fast Eddy, the kind of managers the other condos have around here. I'd rather have a lazy Thai manager who follows orders and who doesn't steal from us than the alternative."

"I think I want to throw up."

The other Thai Lawyer

Hermann did a lot of business over the years with the Thai lawyer. There were all the land contracts, starting with the first one when Hermann bought the land the Bahthaus was built on. Then there were all the permits he had to get from City Hall. There were all the contracts he had to make with the Thai construction company which built the Bahthaus, then there were all the purchase contracts he had to make with each individual owner not to mention all the shell Thai companies the lawyer helped him set up for owners, who were not able to buy a condo through their own names due to Thai law requiring that at least fifty-one percent of all units sold must be sold to Thais. There was the registration of all the property deeds, and even that did not end the ongoing need for a lawyer. The portly middle aged Thai man sitting across from him had never disappointed him.

"You have many of our condo owners using you for legal work," Hermann said to the lawyer.

"Yes. Thanks to you Khun Hermann. Most of them have me do wills for them."

"Did you ever do work for Ted Buffalo?"

"Yes. I did. He had a problem with his girlfriend who stole his furniture."

"That's Ted Buffalo. He had big problem with her."

"I gave him advice on what to do. She had a Thai boyfriend who was a Muay Tai fighter. I most strongly suggested to Ted that he not press charges against the woman."

"Why did you do that?"

"I advised him that the authorities would never do anything to her. They would say there were no pictures of the boyfriend in the condo building, and that he did not appear on the security video. They do not want to have problem with a Thai, any Thai, especially a Thai who has a boyfriend who is a Thai boxer because he has friends. Maybe they make problem for policeman because policeman make problem for her."

"I think the Thai police don't want a problem because this problem doesn't make them any money," Hermann replied. "Do not make me laugh. Thai police scared of a young Thai boxer? I do not believe it."

"Okay, you are right, Hermann. The police here do not want to do anything that does not help themselves. We both understand that."

"Did you do anything else for Ted Buffalo?" Hermann asked.

"Yes. I made a will for him."

"And according to his will, who gets his money?"

"I cannot say. I am a lawyer for Ted Buffalo. I cannot divulge my customer's business to other people."

"Ted Buffalo is dead. He fell out of his condo balcony on the sixth floor," said Hermann. "Now, are you sure you want to be quiet about this?"

"Oh my God, I am sorry to hear that. Okay. In Buffalo's will, he gave his condo and all his money in his Thai bank account to his new girlfriend."

"Who killed him no doubt?"

"We cannot prove."

"Let me ask you something else. Do you think Ted Buffalo told his girlfriend she would get his condo if he died?"

"Yes, I think Buffalo did. He believes Thai lady every time. Maybe she asked him to give her more money and he told her she will get his condo if he dies."

"Can you give me Ted Buffalo's girlfriend's name?" asked Hermann. "Also her address, phone number, parents' names and anything else you know about her? The police are not going to give it to me. One thing for sure-- the police aren't going to help me or Ted at all."

"No problem, Khun Hermann." The lawyer went over to a filing cabinet, which he opened with a key. Finding the folder he wanted, he returned to his desk where he leafed through the folder and found the will.

"Her name is Neon Wannabe. I have several addresses for her. They include the address of her sister." The lawyer pulled out a spiral bound notebook on which he carefully wrote Neon's phone numbers, addresses, and other contact information. Then he tore off the page, and handed it to Hermann.

Hermann walked out of his lawyer's office with Ted Buffalo's girlfriend's name, her address, the bar she used to work at, the names and addresses of her parents, their phone numbers and all because Ted wanted to be one hundred percent sure she'd never have to work again if anything should ever happen to him. Hermann was certain she'd wind up very well off by Thai standards, and that knowledge made him sick.

The Thai Boxer

A pretty Thai woman in her late twenties met Rion at the door of her South Pattaya room and deciding he looked respectable enough, greeted him with a friendly "Sadadi Krap".

The woman smiled when he cheerfully told her in Thai, "Lady win free cell phone. I come to give her the free cell phone."

"Who is the lady?" the woman asked.

Rion pulled a document with a woman's name and address on it from his pocket, studied the text and read out loud to her, "Joy Phanita."

"No have woman here named Joy," the woman replied.

"I have address here, Soi 41, number 1103," Rion told the woman.

"That's our address."

"I am sure I come to the right place," said Rion. "Who live here with you?"

"There are three of us. One of them live with falang at Condo Bahthaus. The other woman is her younger sister. Her name is Nim."

"There must be a mistake then. Maybe our office got the woman's name wrong. I check again. Do you know where I can find the woman who lives at the Bahthaus?"

"She often go to bar. Bar is in Thai boxing place when you first come to Walking Street. Name of lady, Neon."

"How often does she go there?" Rion asked.

"Now? Very often. Her boyfriend die."

"What happened to him?"

"He fall off condo balcony. Neon now very rich lady."

"Why is she rich lady now?"

"She get condo of rich falang now. She very happy and tell us everything. Falang drink too much. Every night he drink Vodka too much and beer."

"Why does she go to this bar so often?"

"She also have Thai boyfriend. He boxing all the time in Thai boxing ring."

"I go find her soon. Maybe she win cell phone. If she not win, maybe she knows Joy and Joy might have given us this address because she stay somewhere else for short time."

"What kind of cell phone did the lady win?" the woman asked.

Rion took a small box out of his front pocket and showed her a slim cell phone. "See, it's small but you can play lots of music from it. Very good phone."

"I wish I had that phone."

"Maybe you will. If we have the wrong name and the address is correct, you might be the winner. Our company has special promotion. It gets names from supermarkets and other stores, the electric company and other sources. I will let you know if you are the winner."

Rion worked as head of the safe department at the Pakabit store on Thressprassit Road. Pakavit sold furniture, kitchens, lighting, vacuum cleaners, bedspreads, towels, sheets, silverware, plates, microwaves and almost everything else that a condo needed to become completely habitable. An owner of a new condo could furnish it with everything he needed, except for a television set or stereo system, without ever having to leave Pakavit. He had once hoped to be a policeman before deciding that police work was not for him. And although he would have been very good at it, he had been put off by the corruption that ran rife throughout the entire police force. He had sold Hermann the German his first safe, and when Hermann discovered that Rion sold just about any kind of safe a man could possibly want, he recommended Rion highly to several of his German friends.

Hermann hadn't been in Pattaya for very long before discovering that his International Driver's license was legally good only for tourists and that long term residents such as himself needed to get a Thai driver's license. But being the busy man he was while building the Bahthaus and selling condos, he asked Rion to get a Thai driver's license for him. Rion charged him only 1000 baht; then he went to the driver's license center over on route 36 where he bribed one of the employees 500 baht to produce a valid driver's license for Hermann. He had then brought the license over to Hermann's office. Hermann was ecstatic over what he had accomplished with so little effort for a mere 1000 baht.

But if Hermann was ecstatic, Rion was eternally grateful to Hermann who wound up buying a very large selection of beds, refrigerators and even entire kitchens from Pakavit with Rion getting a nice cut from the action. The relationship prospered between the two men. Rion was always on time, while never failing to deliver on anything he promised Hermann.

Considering that Hermann's request for a little undercover detective work wasn't unusual and the long boring hours he spent working at the Pakavit Shopping Center, an excuse to go to a few bars so that he could prod a few women for the answers to his questions was an assignment made in heaven.

The Bahthaus Digital Film

There was something very wrong with the footage from the Bahthaus security cameras. For over two hours camera number eleven had displayed absolutely nothing except for a dark background. The odd thing was that it displayed a digital counter that had been running for the entire period. Camera number eleven was positioned directly in front of Ted Buffalo's condo. Herman knew that camera number twelve had been working correctly because it had been displaying the hallway extending from the condos on Ted Buffalo's side of the building all the way down to the back stairway. Over the two hour period that camera number eleven was shooting a black background, camera twelve had showed several residents walking down the hallway to their condos. The thing that was completely wrong with the total picture was that for two hours not only had camera number eleven failed to record anyone using the elevator, it had completely failed to display the elevator at all. That could mean only one thing. If someone used the elevator to visit Ted Buffalo's condo, he wouldn't have been picked up by the camera, Hermann reasoned.

And since security was practically nonexistent in the building, thanks to our worthless Thai manager, this means that either our night time security guard would not have seen the culprit due to his hiding or sleeping in the security office or he wouldn't have been paying much attention to who was coming in or out of the building. Hermann decided that even though he couldn't prove it, someone had thrown a garment, towel or piece of cloth over the security camera, which would have rendered it completely blind while the murder was being committed.

The Thai Boxing Arena

The whole thing was a hoax.   Rion knew the score even if most of the tourists didn't. Over twenty bars surrounded the boxing ring with each bar being serviced by a half dozen girls, which meant over a hundred sex workers to choose from. The girls played the role of junior bartenders running off to get drinks for their customers, which was almost always beer, with Heineken, Tiger, Chang and Singha to choose from. Half a dozen Thai boxers were either standing in the ring or sitting on a bench just outside the ring getting ready for their next fight. The heaviest of the boxers weighed about 165 pounds which made him the largest fighter there, since the other contestants were little guys only five foot six or so who weighed no more than one hundred and forty pounds at best. The arena was where Beach Road became Walking Street right before the turn into Pattaya Tai (Road). At the first bar he came to, Rion asked the bar girls, "Where is the Princess Bar?"

The Princess Bar was next to the ring, making it the perfect spot for one of the Thai boxers and his girlfriend to hang out, although the boxer would still be spending most of his time inside the ring. A Thai woman in her forties presided over the bar who Rion assumed was Princess. Rion was already sitting at the bar when one of the bar girls asked him, "Khun Tai, my ka" which meant, "Are you Thai?"

"No. I Vietnam," Rion replied knowing only too well that Thai men were not welcome in the bars there.   They were for tourists and so were the girls even though most of them had Thai boyfriends when their Western sponsors weren't paying attention. Well aware that having the Thai boyfriend hanging around the bar was bad for business, the Princess enforced the unwritten rule with an iron hand.

Rion drank four beers at the bar before he saw the pretty Thai woman taking a seat across from him just a few feet from several Thai boxers sitting at the narrow bench just outside the ropes. It didn't take long for Rion to notice that she was very familiar with most of the bar girls working there. After the largest of the Thai boxers finished his fight it was just as obvious that he was the newcomer's boyfriend.

The boyfriend won his bout by knocking out a much smaller opponent. In the meantime he had gone down twice himself, the first time lying on the canvas for three seconds before getting up, the second time taking a full eight seconds before recovering and finally getting up with what appeared to be his last remaining strength to finish the fight with a hard kick to his opponent's jaw.

To anyone who knew anything at all about fighting, the whole thing had obviously been faked. The Thai boyfriend hadn't gone down immediately after taking two punches from his opponent, so there had been a delay of one or two seconds between the cause of either knockdown and the effect. Rion also noticed that although the Thai boyfriend appeared to have the speed necessary to avoid them, he seemed reluctant to evade either of the two punches and had actually waded right into one of them as if he were welcoming an old friend. Even though he had not worked out in a gym for years, Rion felt he could have easily avoided either punch.

After what really amounted to an exhibition bout, both boxers circulated among the twenty bars looking for tips from tourists who didn't know better. When the Thai boyfriend arrived at the Princess Bar, it became even more obvious to Rion that the pair was together. There was the air of familiarity between them not to mention a little smirk on the Thai boxer's face and a certain arrogance he displayed toward the woman that suggested that he had been with her sexually far more often than once. On her face he saw the hint of adulation for the man of the hour. Paying close attention to his surroundings while acting a lot more tipsy than he actually was, he noticed that she slipped the boyfriend a little parcel with the twenty baht tip she handed him. Rion couldn't be sure, but he guessed it to be drugs–Yabba most likely. Even if he were mistaken, it wouldn't matter because what did matter is she had passed the Thai boxer something that was more than a tip, and that single act alone etched into stone the fact that Neon was the boxer's girlfriend.

Eager to meet the man, Rion jumped off his bar stool when he saw the girl hand the Thai boxer the little packet . "Good fight," he said to the man in English. Then he asked, "Your girlfriend?", as he slipped the fighter twenty baht.

"We know each other little bit," the woman replied. For a moment the boxer appeared confused because of the language barrier, then he replied, "Kap Khun Kapp (Thank you)".

"You fight good," Rion said to the fighter. "You number one."

"Kap, Kap," the fighter replied.

It was good that Hermann hadn't come here," Rion decided. The girl would have almost certainly recognized him from the condo and might have even known it was Hermann who had built the condo and that he was the head of the committee running the place. That might have caused her to stop coming to the bar and she would have certainly warned her Thai boxer-boyfriend, who from that point on would have had his guard up. So far everything had gone perfectly.

The Security Expert

"What's on your mind, Hermann?" Fast Eddy asked as Hermann let him into his condo.

"Take a seat," Hermann suggested while pointing to the recliner across from the sofa. "Can I get you a beer?"

"A beer will be fine," Fast Eddy replied.

As the pair sat across from each other drinking the two beers Hermann's Thai girlfriend had brought them, Hermann got right down to business.

"I won't beat—beat around the bush. Is that what you Americans call it?"

"Something like that," said Fast Eddy. "It means getting to the point."

"Well, I come to the point then. It is very possible Ted Buffalo's been murdered by his Thai girlfriend with the help of her Thai boyfriend, who is a fighter down at the Thai boxing arena."

"Well that's coming to the point alright," Fast Eddy replied. "Didn't Ted Buffalo get robbed by his previous Thai girlfriend, who also had a Thai boxer boyfriend?"

"Yes, he did."

"Doesn't that strike you as too much of a coincidence, Hermann?"

"What do you mean?"

"That Ted Buffalo just happened to have one girlfriend and she has a Thai boyfriend who's a Muay Thai boxer. They both steal all his furniture while he's back in the U.S., and then he finds a second girlfriend who's also got a Thai boxer boyfriend?"

"Perhaps Ted had a habit of going to Thai boxing places to find his girlfriends," Hermann suggested.

"Either that or possibly Ted already knew the 2nd girlfriend while he still had the first girlfriend living in his condo with him," Fast Eddy replied.

"That is very possible," said Hermann.

"The second girlfriend might have even been a good friend of the first girlfriend. Come to think of it, I'd say it's even likely."

"Why's that?"

"If you ask me, there's just too much coincidence here. Ted gets robbed by one woman who has the audacity to have her Thai boyfriend stay with her in Ted's condo, and now he is killed while a second Thai girlfriend is living with him. And both women have Thai boyfriends who are Thai boxers."

"I see what you mean."

"There's a lot of truth to the saying, "Birds of a feather flock together." Both of these Thai women are very bad ladies. Perhaps they were friends. Or they at least hung out at the same places--Thai boxing arenas for example. And Hermann, I just had another thought on that subject."

"What's that Fast Eddy?"

"I'm just guessing, but there are a lot of guys and even women for that matter who are attracted to the wrong people. Most normal people have this little voice in their heads that's warning them to stay away from certain types of people they meet, while others are attracted to individuals who are poisonous and dangerous, so that little voice becomes a mating call instead of a warning. There's a lot of masochism at play here. I have a hunch that Ted was that kind of guy, and that he was attracted to the same danger signals that must have been radiated by both women."

"That is all very interesting Fast Eddy. The truth behind all this is, one of our condo owners has probably been murdered and I need you to help me find out more."

"So how can I help you?" Hermann.

"I want you to help me get at the bottom of this, and after that we can discuss this in more detail, to see if we can do something." Then Hermann added. "I think you had a lot of experience with the American Marine Corps in Vietnam?"

"You might call it that."

"What kind of experience?"

"I was with Force Recon. It's the Marine Corps answer to the Green Berets. We went behind enemy lines to do all kinds of special operations."

"What kind of special operations?"

"I don't like to talk about it," said Fast Eddy. There's a lot I did that I shouldn't have, and besides, I have an obligation to the Corps not to disclose anything other than the fact that I was there, and that I had served my country."

Here's what I think, Fast Eddy. I cannot prove it, but I believe Ted Buffalo's girlfriend and her Thai boyfriend shoved him off his balcony."

"Do you know who the Thai boyfriend is?"

"Yes. His name is Suvanaporn. He's a Thai boxer at the arena just before you come to Walking Street."

"What is the name of the girlfriend?"

"Her name is Neon Wannate. She has been staying in his condo for eight months now, more or less. Now that Ted is dead, she's been going nearly every night to the Princess Bar next to the Thai boxing ring."

"So what do you want me to do?"

"First, I am almost sure those two killed Ted Buffalo. Our condo security is doing a lot of sleeping, so if the boyfriend went upstairs the guard was either asleep, not there or too stupid to notice. Second, when the police came here to investigate, they interfered with his body down in the parking lot, and when they came upstairs, they rearranged the furniture out on the balcony. The table outside and three chairs had been knocked down. They had been at least one meter from the balcony railing. Do you really see how Ted Buffalo could have jumped or fallen off alone and while doing it, knocked down so much furniture?"

Fast Eddy thought about it for a moment and then replied a few seconds later, "No. I really don't. Even if he had gotten very drunk and knocked all that furniture down, that sixth floor balcony railing is pretty high. He is likely to have propped himself up on at least one of the chairs or the table so he could climb up on it and throw himself over the railing. But if he had climbed up on the railing he would not have touched any of the chairs or the table when he jumped."

"I see a problem with that."

"What problem?'

"There was one chair that was still upright so he could have used it to get up on the balcony railing before he jumped."

"You have a point, Hermann. But can you see a man; no matter how drunk he's gotten, knocking down three out of four chairs and the table as well?"

"It is difficult to imagine," Hermann replied. "And that table is pretty heavy. I cannot imagine it being very easy to knock it down while drunk. However, in a struggle, if Ted Buffalo were fighting for his life, I can imagine all those chairs and the table falling down. Ted would have outweighed the boxer boyfriend, even though he was a big fat marsh mellow, so I can see him putting up quite a struggle. Also, the Thai girlfriend was there also. And who knows, perhaps there were two or three men pushing Ted off the balcony."

"I think you are right."

"Fast Eddy, I want you to take a look at our security cameras on the sixth floor. I believe that the Thai boyfriend or his girlfriend put something over one of them, so it could not take a picture of whoever was getting off the elevator on the sixth floor or getting back on it after killing Ted."

*****

At first the blemish on the security camera was barely noticeable to Fast Eddy's trained eye. But the more he looked the more certain he became that something had been glued or taped to the camera. He went to his own condo for a short step ladder he kept out on his deck that he used for changing light bulbs in his ceiling fixtures or for getting up high to drill holes on his walls to hang pictures and for doing other little projects. Taking two steps up the ladder, he was finally able to look directly at the camera. The unmistakable trace of glue remained on the security camera casing. He ran his finger down the rough surface that had been left by the glue, and then he ran it across the rest of the plastic casing. It was smooth. He looked at the rough part of the surface again.

Now why am I seeing a gluey sticky surface on the camera housing? Fast Eddy thought. That's impossible. There's a tiny bit of gluey residue here that's obviously been left by a piece of tape that adhered to it at one time. But that doesn't prove much. It could have been a price sticker that had been left on at the store which sold the camera.

Suddenly he came up with a clincher of an idea. Stepping off the short stepladder, Fast Eddy moved it down the hallway and placed it directly underneath security camera twelve that commanded the back stairway. Once more he checked for signs of a gluey residue on the security camera casing. He found it to be uniformly smooth to the touch.

Still not satisfied, Fast Eddy climbed up the back stairs to the seventh floor where he checked both security cameras. Finding them both to be smooth to the touch he concluded that someone must have put tape across the security camera on the sixth floor. The camera was very small; being approximately five inches across including its housing, so it wouldn't have required much tape to temporarily blind the camera.

There still remained one little problem. Since obviously no one had spotted a piece of paper or cloth that had been taped to the security camera while the crime had been committed, this would have meant that the culprits would have had to remove it and remain out of the resulting video while doing it. Fast Eddy was sure that the video during the camera's two hour period of blindness had showed absolutely nothing. So if Neon had gone out in the hallway from Ted Buffalo's condo to tear off the tape, the camera would have picked up on her even if it hadn't picked up on her Thai boyfriend while he was leaving prior to her removing the tape. The solution suddenly came to him. They must have inserted a piece of string to the tape, so that she could open the condo door a crack just wide enough to allow her to yank on the string, which would have pulled the tape off and then she would have pulled it back into the condo. A bit of monofilament fishing line would have been perfect, Fast Eddy decided. It would have been strong enough to do the job without a single chance of failure and it would at the same time have been almost invisible. And as for the tape, all that would have been necessary would have been to lay a 1.5 inch square piece of paper across the camera lens to completely disable it. So if someone should walk by the now blind camera it would have almost been a certainty that the person would not have noticed the 1.5 inch square piece of paper or the monofilament line.

The Mission

"What did you find out?" Hermann asked Fast Eddy.

"I found that someone definitely taped something across the security camera lens."

"Are you sure?"

"100 percent."

"So what is your conclusion about this whole thing, Fast Eddy?"

"First in any crime we have motive. Clearly the Thai girlfriend had the strongest possible motive to kill Ted Buffalo--Money. Second, she had the means to accomplish it--the Thai boyfriend who just happens to be a Thai boxer. Second, she could help get him into Ted's condo unobserved or at least unnoticed due to the miserable security guard we have on our night shift and because the security camera could have been easily disabled. Moreover, it's obvious that some sort of glue or adhesive had been placed near the lens of the security camera. The fact that this is the only security camera that has had an adhesive applied on both the sixth and seventh floors will support this conclusion. Lastly there's the body itself. The police obviously tampered with it and they tampered with the crime scene itself and that proves a lot to me."

"I don't understand," said Hermann.

"Practically no one kills himself by throwing himself off a building."

"I agree with you, Fast Eddy, but what brings you to this conclusion?"

"Ever read about the U.S. Marines taking Saipan during the Second World War?"

"No."

"Saipan is very close to the Japanese home islands. When we Americans stormed it, those Japanese troops who were not killed during the battle's first stages were able to convince hundreds of Japanese civilians to commit suicide. Some of them used hand grenades but most of them hurled themselves into the sea from cliffs."

"All that proves is that people like committing suicide by throwing themselves from tall heights. That disproves what you are trying to tell me, Fast Eddy."

"No way. In fact, it proves the opposite. Those cliffs of Saipan probably provide one of the best databases known to man about what really happens to people who kill themselves by jumping from high places."

"What happens?"

"For one thing a large number of them didn't die right away. There's even a lot of film footage of crushed human bodies practically impaled by the rocks below crying out in pain, sometimes for hours, before the person finally dies."

"So it's not the quick and painless death most people think it is?"

"No it's not. But most people don't really think of it as a quick and painless death. There's always the fear of the unknown–the unknown being exactly what will happen to a person once he steps out into the abyss. I think that deep down inside anyone who even thinks about such a death for even one minute, that something tells him that he might not die at all, that he might be only crippled or at the very least that it's going to be a very painful horrible death. And when you compare it to shooting yourself with a gun, you simply put the gun to your head, preferably into your mouth, then you pull the trigger and suddenly it's lights out. But if someone hurls himself from a building or other great height, there's the fall itself and the sensation of imminent doom. It's going to take a couple of seconds for the person to land and then, well—just imagine that for a second Hermann and tell me what you think."

"I think there can very easily be a lot of pain at first--unless one falls right on his head in the right way."

"Now just imagine, Hermann, that you jumped off this building. That's about sixty feet. And suppose you hit feet first. Landing on your feet is going to break your legs, but it is also going to break your fall. Your legs are going to crumple and then you are going to hit the concrete a second time. Suppose your ass is the next thing to make contact with the concrete. That's going to break your fall a little more. And finally you strike the concrete with your head. That's gotta hurt, but it might not even be fatal."

"You are right. Hardly anyone is going to want to kill themselves that way."

"And yet we are constantly hearing about all these suicides dropping out of buildings into parking lots. Most of these are not suicides. They are murders and the police are told to cover them up and to declare them all to be suicides. It's bad for tourism and it gives Thailand and especially the police department a bad name for not being able to solve all of these crimes But if you ask me, I think a lot of so called suicides all over the world weren't suicides at all."

"I get it now," said Hermann. "That's why the police rearranged Ted Buffalo's body which I initially saw with one leg pulled up as if he had been in a struggle and why the police pulled his chairs and table off the floor of his deck. They wanted no evidence of any possible foul play, and they had been taught to destroy any such evidence whenever there's one of these murders that is meant to look like a suicide."

"We are in complete agreement then," Fast Eddy added.

"I am having one problem with this theory, however."

"What's the problem?"

"I've read on the internet that throwing oneself off tall bridges and rocks into oceans and rivers is a pretty popular way of committing suicide."

"I've thought about that too," said Fast Eddy. "I think it's the water that is throwing people off. Deep down people know the fall is going to kill them, but another side of their brains tells them it will be a clean and painless death. Water invites. It lures. It's a bit like a laxative, but jumping out onto concrete or rocks is something altogether different. It's plain terrifying."

"I see what you mean," Hermann replied. "I'm with you. I think a lot of these suicides from falling out of buildings are murders, but the authorities pass them off as suicides, so they don't have to think about them very hard. And one more thing, Fast Eddy."

"What's that?"

"How do you feel about killing and fighting?" Hermann asked the American. "I think it's obvious to both of us that the Thai boyfriend helped Ted Buffalo's girlfriend kill Ted. Our little community here can't leave that unanswered."

"I've done enough of it while I was in the Marines and I want to forget about all of that."

"If you knew for sure that this Thai boxer was in your condo building, the place you call your home, and that he helped Ted Buffalo's girlfriend kill Ted and the police had decided to let them both go to give them a chance to kill another human being, would you be willing to stop them?"

"Sure I would. I hate those kind of Thai men and I hate the Thai women who take our money, just so they can give it to their Thai boyfriends."

"Do you think you are in a position to revenge Ted Buffalo and our little community by dealing with the Thai boyfriend?"

"That's what the Marines taught me to do. They put me through Special Forces Training, Ranger training, advanced martial arts, specialized Marine reconnaissance techniques and so on. This is what I was destined to do, so dealing with this Thai boyfriend would not be any problem for me. But what is it exactly that you want me to do?"

"I leave this one up to you, Fast Eddy. It is not my right to tell you what to do. You can get into a lot of trouble. If you beat the boyfriend up and a bunch of Thais come over to help him, you can get seriously injured or killed. If the police come, you might even get deported from the country. Just remember that you are considered a guest here, and that you have no rights whatsoever. But you are going to need a little help." Hermann paused for a moment deep in thought and then asked: "Who is the toughest, baddest guy in the condo?"

"That would be Mickel, hands down," Fast Eddy replied.

"Why Mickel?"

"Because when he's up North of the Arctic Circle working for the Norwegian Coast Guard intercepting vessels that are illegally fishing, smuggling drugs and illegally running guns, he's known as the Menace from the North."

"I suppose that means people on the other side of the law are terrified of him?"

"They are shitting their pants at the mere thought of running into him," said Fast Eddy. "If I were to have one man help me do a job like this one, Mickel's the one I want."

"Here's my idea, Fast Eddy. If you and Mickel are to carry this thing out, the two of you must go down to the Thai boxing ring and arrange a fight between one of you and the Thai boxer boyfriend."

"And?"

"Which one of you has the best chance of winning?"

"That would probably be Mickel. Although I am very skilled in Martial arts and hand to hand combat, Mickel is younger than me. And he's also got a quality that hardly any man alive possesses."

"And that's?"

"He has no fear whatsoever--of anything. If you pitted him against a tiger he'd simply attack the Tiger and the Tiger would be so scared that it would run off squealing. He is unstoppable. He's big and he's strong, he does not experience pain whatsoever and he's as quick as a cat."

Disguises

Fast Eddy stuck a piece of electricians tape across the security camera's lens as Mickel followed him into his condo.

"The Thai boxer and his girlfriend put a piece of paper or bit of cloth on the camera to cover the lens and they must have taped it on. I really don't think it's all that necessary for me to tape this on," Fast Eddy told Mickel. "I'm just making sure that the camera doesn't pick either of us up in our disguises."

"Do you really think that the Thai police will be checking the movies taken by our security cameras? No way. You will see, Fast Eddy. There will be no investigation."

"I don't think so either," Fast Eddy replied, while rummaging through a small suitcase he kept in his closet. "But I want to be thorough because one never knows."

Fast Eddy studied Mickel's face and then he pulled several items from his suitcase. "When I moved here from the U.S., I came fully equipped, as you can see," he told the Norwegian. "You have blue eyes which is typical of you Scandinavians. We will have to change that. Here, take these into the bathroom and put them into your eyes."

When Mickel came out of the bathroom, Fast Eddy smiled at the transfiguration. The brown contacts had most definitely made a profound change to Mickel's appearance.

"Now we will have to do something about your hair. It's brown with a noticeable amount of gray in it. Here's some hair dye that will turn it jet black until you wash your hair since it's only temporary. And here's a very special skin conditioner. I want you to rub it into your legs, arms, neck and face since you Norwegians are pretty light skinned. This stuff will give you a brown complexion wherever you rub it in, so you are going to wind up looking like you came from a Mideast country, like an Arab. They might even think you are a terrorist." Fast Eddy handed Mickel the bottle of hair dye along with a large bottle of the skin conditioner, a concoction he had made up himself.

Half an hour later, Mickel emerged from the bathroom looking like a completely new man. He could easily have passed for a bedouin coming out of the desert to join the carnival Pattaya had become.

"And what about you? You are going to disguise yourself also, aren't you?" Mickel asked.

"I'm easy to disguise," Fast Eddy replied. "You see--you have to fight whereas I don't, so I don't have to be as careful. A wig can fall off, especially if someone's hitting you in the face. I've become almost bald, so everyone expects me to be bald. Now, notice how much this wig completely changes me when I put it on."

Fast Eddy looked like a different man after he put the wig on. "Now excuse me while I go to the bathroom to add the final touch."

When Fast Eddy came out of the bathroom Mickel was impressed by how much two simple things had transformed his appearance. By using what was left of the hair dye on his moustache and eye brows while adding a little mascara, his face became the face of a much younger man.

"I think we are ready to roll, Mickel. It's time for us to have some fun."

Thai Boxing

Suvanaporn should have been the winner of every match Fast Eddy and Mickel watched, Fast Eddy decided. He was by far the largest Thai boxer at the arena. The second largest man was the referee, who took a turn entertaining the predominantly Western audience drinking in the bars throughout the outdoor arena, playing dice or Connect Four with the bar girls, or actually watching the exhibitions. Taller than all the other Thai boxers with the exception of Suvanaporn, the referee was underweight for his height which Fast Eddy estimated at five foot nine, give or take an inch. Fast Eddy put the referee's weight at around one hundred and forty pounds while estimating Suvanaporn's weight at one hundred-sixty-five, his height an inch taller than the referee's. Another fighter, who Fast Eddy thought to be no older than twenty, was a couple of inches shorter than Suvanaporn, but had the same general slight build of the referee. There were three other Thai boxers, ranging from five foot four to five six. One of the shorter men, an over the hill Thai in his middle thirties, had been paired off against the referee, who performed as a boxer when he was not refereeing the bouts.

As the referee calmly stood back against the ropes watching expressionlessly, the over the hill Thai boxer kneeled in the middle of the ring praying to Buddha and all the Thai boxing Gods. Thai boxing music filled the arena, whining dreadfully, practically indescribable except it vaguely resembled the awful din being played in Indian Cobra snake demonstrations in which the snake charmer plays a flute while pretending to hypnotize the hooded snake arching its head over two feet above the ground.

When he finished with his prayers, the much shorter boxer got off his knees as the referee now turned boxer walked out into the center of the ring to meet him. Suvanaporn, who had replaced the referee for this match, watched as the two boxers briefly touched each other's gloves, then he blew the whistle to announce that the match was on.

The shorter boxer was the aggressor, coming at the referee with a flurry of kicks. It was then that Fast Eddy realized one of the reasons Muay Tai is so popular in Thailand. *It's because short guys like this are built much closer to the ground than Western men, a physical fact of life that makes it so much easier for them to kick their feet out at another man's head,* Fast Eddy decided.

Nearly every kick landed squarely on the referee's face. He shook off first one, then the second, then two more kicks. Suddenly he went down onto the canvas. He rose to his feet as Suvanaporn stood over him giving him the four-count. The slender referee landed several punches to the other man's face, then he arched his right leg upwards driving his foot into his opponent's face. Appearing completely unfazed, the shorter man thrust his hands out at the referee, motioning them inward in the universal sign language that means "Come to me." while taunting the referee in Thai, "Come on. Is that all you got? Give me your best kick." Then he lowered his arms to both sides of his body, which left his face completely undefended as the referee delivered one kick after the other into his head. The boxer arched his eyes in mock pain each time one of the referee's kicks landed

"I like the way this guy pretends that he's really hurt," Fast Eddy told Mickel. "I'll give him this. He's a tough little bastard."

"It's a good thing the referee doesn't have much power though," Mickel replied.

Suddenly the smaller man went down after the referee hooked a foot behind one of the fighter's legs. The boxer got up quickly, but the referee, resurgent, pummeled him with three punches to his head. The referee shot a kick into the shorter man's head, who stood still defiant for a moment before finally falling onto his back.

"You see that, Fast Eddy. The boxer took a long time falling down after the referee kicked him. That kick did not knock him down. And just look at him lying in the middle of the ring, pretending that he's been knocked out. I've come here a few times before and every time the referee wins. I suppose they have to have someone be their number one fighter, but the referee has no power."

Five minutes later both boxers walked from bar to bar collecting their tips. Fast Eddy gave each man twenty baht.

"Good fight," Mickel called out to the loser. "I think if you didn't fix the fight you can beat the shit out of that skinny little referee. He fights like a ladyboy." The fighter, who did not understand one word, bowed slightly and smiled to thank Mickel for the compliment as Mickel handed the little man twenty baht.

Suvanaporn, standing close by, understood just four words. Shit, little, fights and ladyboy–which was just enough to make him instantly dislike the boisterous Norwegian. An hour passed before Suvanaporn took his turn in the ring. His opponent was a fighter who was short even by Thai standards.

"Watch this," Mickel told Fast Eddy, then turning to the Princess said, "I want to speak to the referee."

"What? No understand," the hard bitten woman in her forties replied.

"Tinon. Pom chop pud pachai kun Thai" (I want to talk to Thai man), Mickel explained in a bad Thai accent as he pointed at the referee. Showing her a thousand baht note, Mickel continued to point, first at Suvanaporn who was having boxing gloves put on his hands by one of the other boxers, then at Suvanaporn's opponent standing at the other side of the ring.

Gambling is illegal in Thailand. Although Mickel was aware that he might have to pay a stiff fine, he also knew that for most Thais, and especially the police, money talks. The Princess called the referee over to her little bar. As the Princess spoke to the referee in rapid fire Thai, the referee smiled back at Mickel.

"One thousand baht not enough," the referee told the Norwegian. "You must bet two thousand."

"What? Two thousand baht!" Mickel almost shouted at the referee. "Oh, I get it. You have arranged the fight already. You know who is going to win and now if I bet money you might have to change things. Okay, then, I bet three thousand baht. Puchai yai not win.. Puchai noi will beat the shit out of Puchai Yai. Puchai yai no good." (Big man not win. Little man beat the shit out of the big man).

"You think so. We will see about that," the referee said to Mickel. "Do not give me money. Give three thousand baht to Princess. Maybe police see too much. Princess keep money for us, no problem. I take money maybe big problem."

Back in the ring, the referee summoned the two fighters for last minute instructions. Suvanaporn glared over at Mickel while listening to the referee's instructions.

"I think the short little man is supposed to win and now I've spoiled things," Mickel explained to Fast Eddy. "I'm going to lose my three thousand baht-- you can be sure of that, but it will be worth it. Already, that little weasel, Stupid Porn, hates my guts. Soon he will really hate me."

"It's obvious to me that in a real fight the smaller man would have no chance," Fast Eddy replied. "The bigger man is also much younger. I think no one in this crowd thinks the small guy can beat the larger guy. So your betting against the obviously better fighter has got to be a slap in his face."

"Exactly. I make Stupid Porn lose face. That is the whole idea."

At first, the fight went to the smaller man. Suvanaporn threw first one, then a second halfhearted kick at his much shorter opponent, who adroitly danced backwards. After Suvanaporn's third attempted kick, the smaller fighter caught Suvanaporn off balance and delivered a hard right hand to Suvanaporn's face. Pretending to be hurt, Suvanaporn put his hands in front of his face while tucking his elbows against his sides as the small man continued to pummel him.

By the end of the round, Suvanaporn was obviously losing. The second round was a continuation of the first, with Suvanaporn covering up, then clinching by enveloping the smaller man's arms against his sides as he pretended to be helpless. The referee interceded by pushing the two men apart. The younger fighter seemed listless as he tried to connect with several punches to his opponent's head. The older man missed with a kick but landed the second kick in the middle of Suvanaporn's face. A second passed before Suvanaporn went down onto the canvas. The knockdown had obviously been faked when the bell rang with Suvanaporn vainly trying to rise on a six count.

The tide turned in the third round. A kick from the smaller fighter missed. No longer appearing to be exhausted, a resurgent Suvanaporn caught the smaller man with a left hand to the face. The smaller man recoiled from the force of the blow. As the older fighter tried to cover up, Suvanaporn delivered a non stop flurry of body shots to his opponent's stomach. The small man lowered his hands to shield his stomach from the unrelenting barrage, leaving his head unprotected.

Seething from Mickel's choosing the much weaker man, Suvanaporn's face contorted into a mask of rage. He threw a hard right to the smaller man's face forcing him backwards. The second punch snapped the small man's head back. The third punch dropped him. The referee counted the fighter out as he lay on his back.

"He's a killer alright," said Fast Eddy. "Did you see the look on his face?"

"Yes, but of course. I have this fool playing right into the palm of my hands," Mickel replied. We come back again--one, maybe two more times. One week, maybe two and then I show you a real fight."

Khukuri House

Khukuri House claims to supply the Nepalese Army with most of its Khukuris, the legendary curved edged weapon revered as the Gurkha soldier's most prized piece of equipment. Treasured even more than the soldier's rifle, the khukuri can roughly be compared to a World War II Japanese officer's Katana although comparing a khukuri to any knife or sword is inaccurate because although khukuris are made in short sword lengths that are used to decapitate buffalos in animal sacrificial ceremonies, most Khukuris have much shorter blades measuring 10 to 13 inches. During World War II ferocious Nepalese Gurkha troops fighting in the British Army were renowned for their skill at beheading their Japanese enemies when it was said that a Gurkha must never sheath his khukuri until it has tasted blood.

Gurkha boys are often given a Khukuri as early as their 6th birthday from which point on it becomes their most prized possession. A khukuri will perform like an axe for chopping down trees and perform the functions of a machete in the jungle, while being much more portable than a long sword such as a Japanese Katana yet it is able to whack off limbs and heads with equal ease.

Two characteristics of the true Khukuri make it so fearsome. The first is the blade's very pronounced curve. It is a well-known fact that curved blades have significantly greater cutting and tearing ability than straight edges of similar length. The second is, a real Nepalese Khukuri from Nepal is extremely heavy for its length. To put this in perspective, Cold Steel's 11.5 inch Bowie knife, the Natchez, weighs 20 ounces whereas the GI3 model made by Khukuri House to commemorate the exploits of World War II Gurkha soldiers, has a 13 inch blade and weighs 37 ounces, which is almost twice as much. .

Since he couldn't legally own a gun in Thailand, Fast Eddy wanted the most devastating weapon that he could legally buy. The Khukuri seemed to offer the outstanding lethality he was looking for in a package that was small enough to be easily hidden in a motorbike or backpack. Fast Eddy perused Khukuri House's online catalog for his ultimate edged weapon. He liked the idea of the World War II model since it had proved itself many times over during the Second World War, leaving no room for doubt that it could literally cut its way through just about anything from jungle vines and small trees to human torsos. But he was torn between it and a smaller model, the 11 inch Xtreme which had a special handle with a finger groove. Looking up several internet reviews he found that those who had bought the Xtreme raved about this handle design, claiming it to be vastly superior to other Khukuris in terms of overall comfort for the hand as well as its ability to impart a much greater degree of control and force.

Fast Eddy noticed that Khukuri House offered its customers the ability to custom design their own Khukuri. As if offering over thirty different models wasn't' enough, a customer could get a quote on just about anything he liked. He could choose between buffalo horn, several kinds of wood, brass or aluminum for a handle or he could request a customized Xtreme, and have it fitted with a 12 or 13 inch blade, while specifying the weapon's weight, as well as the width, thickness of the blade and other characteristics. He could have it hand engraved at extra cost or have just his name etched into it for free. Fast Eddy decided that the ultimate would be a World War II 13 inch blade combined with the Xtreme's handle design. He could go larger, to a 15 inch or even an 18 inch blade but this would have meant a weapon that was too heavy and cumbersome for his intended use.

What put him off was the delivery time. Although one month for a custom hand crafted weapon made to his own specifications and having it shipped from Nepal to Thailand might be considered excellent service, he wanted the delivery time to be two weeks or less. He composed an email to Khukuri House outlining his predicament.

Ideally I want two custom designed Xtreme model Khukuris specially made for me with a 13 inch blade weighing about 1.2 kilograms. I need my khukuris to be delivered to me here in Thailand within two weeks and I seriously doubt you can get this done in time. Apparently you already have an existing stock of Xtreme model khukuris with standard blades measuring 11 inches. So I have two questions. First, can you go through your present stock for me and select two Khukuris, each to be at least 1 centimeter thick so that my Khukuris are at their maximum weight for an 11 inch blade and second, can you guarantee a delivery time of 2 weeks or less to me?

His reply came 12 hours later.

Yes. As you probably are aware all of our Khukuris are made entirely by hand. Each one's blade is forged from truck springs which are made out of the highest quality steel. Our kamis make our khukuris entirely from scratch without any machine tools so no two khukuris will be exactly alike. Our Xtreme khukuris have a blade thickness ranging from 8 to 11 millimeters so yes, we can be sure to match your exacting specifications. If you submit your payment to us via PayPal within the next 24 hours we can guarantee getting your shipment out to you within two weeks.

Fast Eddy sent out one more email to Khukuri House before submitting his payment through Pay Pal. He got his reply three hours later.

We send out our Khukuris by courier and not by the normal post office. We mark all our packages as handicrafts, not as swords or knives to keep the import tax low, which we pay so you need not pay the tax. You will get a phone call from the courier and then he will deliver the package right to your front door.

Fast Eddy had bought a pair of Japanese replica swords from a U.S. dealer and while getting excellent service in a surprisingly short period of time, he still had to drive his motorbike to the Thai post office where he had to pay the import tax. His condo security office had given him a notice, which had been sent by the post office, on which it had written the exact amount of the import tax. At the post office he didn't have to wait more than five minutes before he was on his way home with the pair of swords. In spite of such excellent service, this time he didn't want any such paperwork haunting him so when Khukuri House assured him that it was bypassing the Post Office, he sent out his Pay Pal payment immediately.

The Challenge

Although Mickel and Fast Eddy had gone to the Thai boxing arena many times before in their disguises no one had ever recognized them sitting in the Princess Bar. They might just as well have been tourists from anywhere, like thousands of others, who might have come to Pattaya once and never returned, their faces long forgotten. Fast Eddy drank his Heineken slowly, as he smugly savored the moment. The disguises had been perfect. Although he had often felt that he had almost dropped off the far corner of the earth after moving to Thailand, thousands of miles from home, he still knew that someone from back home could easily just run into him. *The world is a lot smaller than most people think,* he kept reminding himself. But now, this was different. He had become a non-person. He watched Mickel surveying the situation, except it wasn't Mickel. The contact lenses had totally transformed Mickel's piercing blue eyes making him seem like an altogether different man. The black hair dye and the paste he Mickel had used to color his skin had completed the transfiguration. Fast Eddy was now looking at an Arab. Only his mind told him differently.

Mickel eyed the pretty Thai woman sitting across from him like the wolf watching Little Miss Red Riding Hood, noting that she had the sweetest little ass in the entire Thai Boxing arena as well as the most eye dropping delicious looking breasts he had seen in a long time.

"Princess", Mickel called out to the older woman running the bar as he pointed across the bar at the girl, "I want to buy that pretty lady over there a drink."

"You want to buy drink for Neon?" the Princess asked.

"Yes, Neon, Buy her drink for me."

"She no work bar here," the Princess replied.

"I don't care if lady work bar or if she not work bar. I don't care if she's the toilet lady. She's the most beautiful girl I've seen in a very long time. She can have anything she wants."

After speaking with the Princess for a few moments, Neon shouted across the bar at him, "Thank you very much. I want Black Russian. Is okay?"

"Honey, I am in a very good mood since I see you here tonight. You can have it and after that you can have another, then another. We get drunk together," Mickel yelled back.

Neon smiled back at him; then she came over and took the stool next to him. "Thank you too much. I so glad you come. Where you come from?"

"I come from Iceland. And you? Where do your mama and papa live?"

"They live in Korat."

"Do you have baby?"

"I have one baby. I have little girl."

"I want you to have many babies."

"You want? I? Many babies?"

"Yes. I want you to have first one baby--with me and then I want you to have many babies. We make number one boom boom together."

Suvanaporn, who was standing just outside the ropes of the ring, didn't like what he was seeing, and Mickel, who really didn't have too much to drink yet, noticed the Thai boxer's discomfort and gloated over it. Fast Eddy, sitting next to Mickel, broke out laughing, knowing only too well that Mickel was only starting the windup.

"You stay in Pattaya long time?" Neon asked.

"No, I stay in Jomtien," Mickel lied, "but just ask me to and I stay here forever. Yes. You and me, we stay together long long time and we will have children together and live happily ever after."

"You very ting tong," Neon replied.

"Yes. I am crazy. I crazy for you. What is your name may I ask?'

"Neon."

"Well, I'm Mickel. Neon, may I ask you something?"

"Maybe."

"Do you have Thai boyfriend?"

"I no have Thai boyfriend. Thai man no good," Neon shot back at him.

"I agree, Neon. Thai man no good. Thai man lazy and take money from Thai lady. You should not be with any Thai man. You should be with me", Mickel said loudly enough for Suvanaporn to hear.

One hour later, Neon had already had two black Russians and two shots of Tequila Mickel had bought for her. Suvanaporn had just fought and lost to a malnourished looking kid in his late teens--but that didn't stop him from making his rounds to collect his tips. When he came up to Mickel, Mickel eyed him up and down suspiciously.

"You take Yabba?" Mickel asked Suvanaporn.

"Me? No yabba. Not good for fighting," Suvanaporn replied as he stretched out his hand for his tip.

"I think you do yabba," said Mickel "because you lose fight to skinny little man. You must be on Yabba drug. I cannot believe you fight so badly," Mickel continued while raising his voice to emphasize his disdain for Suvanaporn's fighting ability.

Then Mickel turned to Fast Eddy and asked in an even louder voice, "Fast Eddy, can you believe this man not take drugs? Why he even look like a junkie." Then he turned to face Suvanaporn once again. "No, I not give you tip. You not fight any good. In Iceland, we do not think you are a man. Instead we use you for dog sled and hitch you up with the dogs. Then we say to you, "Mush and off you go pulling dog sled. Yes. That is all you are good for."

Suvanaporn only understood part of what Mickel had been saying to him, but he had heard enough to turn his face beet red. The part that really got to him was being called a dog.

"You think fight no good. You fight me Falang. You lose for sure."

"Now that is a great idea," Mickel replied. "The next time I come here or the time after that, I will fight you. I make Suki Yaki out of you and then the dogs can eat what is left of you."

By the time Suvanaporn finished collecting his tips he was shaking uncontrollably. He rejoined the other Thai boxers hanging out just outside the ring.

Neon

Neon was having the time of her life listening to Mickel cut her Thai boyfriend down to size. But when the question was put to her for the first time she felt a sliver of fear.

"Neon, we make boom boom together. I pay you one thousand baht to come to my hotel room with me."

Knowing that Suvanaporn hated Mickel for his insults that had caused him to lose face in front of the bar, Neon was certain he would beat her afterwards if she accepted only 1000 baht, and then spent the night with Mickel. But another side of her kept telling her to do it anyway and that she would experience the most profound pleasure in upsetting Suvanaporn, knowing that his place lying next to her was taken by a man who had done everything short of bitch slapping him in front of the entire Thai boxing crowd.

"I cannot. One-thousand baht not enough. I no work bar here."

"How much then?" Mickel asked.

"Three-thousand-five-hundred baht," she immediately replied knowing that if Mickel accepted and she spent the night with Mickel that Suvanaporn would still be tormented but at the same time he could hardly refuse getting to share the 3500 baht windfall. Even though he had lost big face to Mickel in the Thai boxing arena, some of that face would be restored because he would feel superior to this falang for making him pay such an exorbitant rate. Neon had enough experience with men to know that Suvanaporn would feel the same sense of superiority over Mickel some men get when they ejaculate into a woman's vagina, knowing that less than an hour afterwards another man, who didn't know any better, would be licking it with his tongue."

Such little considerations didn't bother Mickel in the least. He accepted Neon's offer without hesitation.

One hour later the pair arrived at the Jomtien hotel room Mickel had rented. Mickel poured a shot of Bailey's over ice for her, pulled a large bottle of Chang out of the refrigerator for himself and said to her, "Now we take shower together. We leave our drinks here for afterwards."

They took their clothes off together; then Neon got into the shower and started to wash herself. Mickel thought about the 3500 baht he would have to pay her the next morning, and deciding not to waste time, he opened the shower door and came up behind her, took a small bar of soap from the soap dish and started to run it up and down her ass. Neon quivered and tried to back up against his arm.

Mickel was astonished to see how trim her ass was. He had never encountered anyone like her since going with the dart girl from Sexy A-Go-Go who used to do two shows a night. One of the dart girl's featured acts was to insert a small plastic tube into her vagina out of which she'd blow darts at balloons the waitresses handed to the club's customers. The girl never missed and when she was finished with the balloons she'd smoke a cigarette from her vagina and blow smoke from it into the air. The go-go dancer never drank and obviously exercised regularly. She was a one of a kind who took her work seriously, who had a tight little body which made his skin tingle every time she pressed herself up against him.

Reaching up between Neon's legs with both hands, he stuck the bar of soap part way into her. Then he stood back, removed the bar of soap and used his other hand to wipe the soap out of her. Scooping her up in his arms he gently laid her on the tiled floor of the shower stall, propped her legs up against its walls and bore down on her. Mickel watched her nipples harden as she tried to anticipate what was coming next. He had never seen such beautiful nipples, which were long and colored a brilliant red from something she had painted on them. She didn't show a trace of fat on her waist, stomach or legs which were as firm and smoothly muscled as a swimmer's. Lowering himself onto the shower floor he bent his head down into her chest and snatched one of her lush nipples between his teeth.

Mickel bit down into her nipple; then he swept his tongue around her breast and salivated on it just enough to wet it all the way back into her tit. He felt both the tit and nipple harden; then he popped the nipple in and out of his mouth and sucked deeply from it like a baby.

He noticed that she had shaved all her pubic hair off which accentuated the lower part of her body, which was as nubile as a slender fifteen year Old's, which made him immediately doubt that he could get the entire length of his penis inside her. He fought off the urge to plunge his face deep inside her, taking her other nipple into his mouth instead.

As his face bore into her chest he kept thinking about how her tapered slender legs flowed into her beautifully formed vagina. A full ten minutes passed before he pulled his face out of her succulent breasts and shoved it firmly between her thighs.

At first he could only get the tip of his tongue inside her narrow opening. But as he flicked it back and forth, it started to open--but only a little since he still couldn't get even the tip of it in. Licking it gently and trying to force his tongue in, he was unable to get it even one inch inside of her. He felt only a little hole around the very tip of his tongue but his tongue kept going as if on automatic pilot as he continued to enjoy the taste of her. Slowly almost imperceptibly, her lips opened, allowing the tip of his tongue to enter.

Although he couldn't see her pretty face, it was etched indelibly into his memory. Her eyes had seemed gentle at first, deer eyes, innocent looking and pure. Then he had looked deeply into them and seen them change into a devilish glint. His tongue worked deeper, probing against nearly immovable walls. Slowly he was able to squeeze it into her opening.

He felt the water start to fill up the bottom of the shower rising until it ran over his chin and then his mouth. By the time it had gone over his nostrils he could no longer breathe, but the lure of the inner cavern of her vagina made his tongue want to continue to probe once he finally was able to suck a slight trickle of her juices out of her. He was almost willing to drown before he finally forced himself to pull away. Then he saw how the water had risen several inches from the shower's tiled floor because the drain had gotten covered up by her hand. She had done it on purpose to practically drown him just to see how far he would go and now she lay there laughing at him.

She giggled and said to him, "You funny man. I can kill you and you like it. You want me to."

"We will see about that", Mickel said to her. "Two can play this game."

He scooped her up and took her over to the bed, placed her firmly on her stomach and pulled her legs high up into the air; then he put a pillow underneath her firm buttocks. She was lighter complexioned than most Thais, having skin that was perfectly smooth and tight without the slightest hint of a wrinkle or blemish. He pressed his face into her and once again his tongue met firm resistance. Refusing to give up he patiently worked his tongue back and forth all along and through her crack that went all the way up into her ass, but he stopped each time he got to her second hole until a little fluid started to seep out onto his tongue. Then he started to insert part of his finger inside her ass as he continued to work his tongue into her vagina which finally started to respond as rivulets of cum seeped into his mouth. Working his finger in a little deeper, he felt her suddenly start to shudder and then, his tongue finally slid all the way in.

Fifteen minutes passed, then twenty. He kept working his tongue up inside her, at first shallowly, then as deep as he could get it inside. He found himself licking her all along the entire length of her private area while stopping his tongue just short of probing her asshole.   By this time she was writhing in ecstasy while screaming, "Fuck me. Fuck me. Fuck me."   But he wasn't finished just yet.

Thoughts of Neon

"He wants me," Neon said out loud talking to no one in particular. "He wants me more than anything." Then she nearly repeated herself, but this time she was talking directly to him.

"You really want me? You do anything for me--anything?"

"Anything," Mickel promised.

"I make you love me. Only me."

"Maybe my little whore, but we not finished yet."

He turned her over onto her side which forced his face away from her, but only for a moment. Then he once again tucked his face deeply between her legs while thrusting his pelvis up close to her face. She took his penis into her mouth, then spat it out and started to suck on his balls.

Mickel rubbed his face back and forth against the outside of her opening as he flicked his tongue deeply inside. She was soaking wet and still producing more juices. Then he stuck his tongue into her tight little ass, which still remained, unyielding. He tried to work it in and found that although it opened a little, he still couldn't get it in nearly deep enough.

I finish with his balls now, Neon thought to herself. I make him cum-- he not fuck me yet--I make him mine so he have no control. Then she sucked in his penis--just half of it at first. Working it back and forth in her mouth for a few seconds, she slowly started to work more and more of it inside her mouth and then she took it all down into her throat-- having learned how to avoid gagging a long time ago before she had passed her sixteenth birthday.

He cannot last much longer she gloated to herself with self-satisfaction as she pulled her legs up around and still deeper into his face. Then she thought about the money and how she would get 3500 baht the next morning. 3500 baht made her feel good. It was power that would allow her to buy anything that she wanted and power that she could use to get more of everything she wanted. *Falang like to pay more than they should* she told herself. *Although they know they don't have to be paying more than 1000 baht when they finally find a woman who makes them pay a lot more, falang get become obsessed. But this same woman must be able to provide great sex and think of things other women do not think of. Falang then become possessed and they cannot escape. They will end up giving Thai lady everything she asks for.*

Such thoughts were suddenly interrupted when he suddenly broke away from her. By this time she had her legs entwined completely around his head while he sucked furiously trying to get his tongue past her sphincter muscle.

"You not open your little door for me!" Mickel announced loudly. "We can see about that." Then he pulled her up from the bed, placed her back on her stomach, thrust her ass up high in the air again and put the pillow underneath her. His penis was ultra-hard from almost coming into her mouth.

Mickel stuck the tip of first his little finger and then his much larger middle finger up into her ass. It started to yield allowing him to work his finger more than an inch in. As he patiently worked his finger back and forth he finally managed to get it past its middle joint. Still unsatisfied, he kept probing until he felt the finger getting sucked all the way in as Neon's sphincter muscle finally gave out.

Neon was in agony. But as her sphincter gave out she felt his finger running into her like an unstoppable piston. Although the pain was unrelenting, she eagerly welcomed whatever would come next as goose bumps started to run up and down her body.

"Now take this my little slut," Mickel said to her as he pulled out his finger and jammed himself tightly up against her. "I own you now, bitch."

She felt one of his hands pressing into her stomach while he shoved her head violently into the mattress with his other hand, as the sheer weight of his body kept her legs pinned.

He came in huge spurts she didn't even feel. Afterwards they lay next to each other, neither of them talking. Half an hour later she broke the silence after having just come up with a fresh idea.

He win this time, thought Neon. *But he not know it, but Suvanaporn probably know where he live already. If this Mickel still make Suvanaporn angry Suvanaporn will steal his motorbike, beat him or have me help him rob him. Maybe this Mickel will die just like Ted Buffalo. So he not win for long. But I must make him never forget me, to always want me.*

"I give you massage. You want?" she asked.

"Now that idea is very very good," Mickel replied

"Okay. You have oil?"

"Yes. I have some in the toilet. Wait here while I get some for you."

"Lie down on your back," she told him after he returned from the bathroom with a bottle of baby oil. By the time he had stretched out comfortably on his back, Mickel was more than ready for the oil massage, as he tried to anticipate what it would be like to have 100 percent of Neon's complete attention. Instead, she started to go through his ward robe after telling him to wait a few moments which was a complete letdown until he saw her return to his bed with seven or eight t-shirts. Then he watched her knot them together in twos, so that she ended up with four pairs of t shirts with each pair being fastened together by a single knot.

"Just what are you doing?" Mickel asked.

"You will like very much. Relax now."

She tied the first pair to his headboard then she fastened the other end to his wrist. Mickel didn't move a muscle to stop her. Fascinated by what she would do next, he let go and allowed her to do whatever she wanted with him. After she had secured his arms and legs to the headboard and footboard of his bed, she started to loosen the knots fastening his wrists; then she pulled the make shift ropes taut and redid the knots. She repeated the procedure with the two pairs of t shirts securing his legs.

"You like?" she asked him.

"I don't know. But it's different."

"Okay I show you something now." She left him alone for a few moments, went out into his kitchen and returned with two trays of ice. She dumped the ice cubes up and down his chest then for good measure she took a good half dozen ice cubes and pressed them underneath his back.

"See, I can do everything. And you cannot."

Taking a few ice cubes off his chest she rearranged them so that they surrounded his balls. "How you feel?" she asked.

"It's cold down there. But it's exciting."

"I show you something more." She left him again--this time for five minutes before returning with a pair of scissors.

"I can cut you now and you cannot stop me," she said to him as she pushed the pair of scissors up next to his scrotum. Then she started to snip off a few clumps of his pubic hair and laughed, before moving her whole body closer to the headboard as she started to cut strands of hair from his head."

"See. I can do anything to you and you can do nothing. You cannot stop me."

"You think so?" Mickel asked.

"I can do anything and then I can just walk out your hotel room. Then I go home and leave you here. Security not stop me."

"Just go to the hotel room door and see if you can go out," Mickel replied.

She left and let an entire five minutes elapse before returning to his bed.

"Where did you put key?" she asked him.

"You see my small safe on the cabinet that is almost over the door?"

"No."

"Go out and look again. Look up above your head next to my door, then come back and tell me what you see."

She left him for a few short moments and coming back a few seconds later said: "You put safe near your door."

"That's where I put the hotel key, Neon. I do it every time I bring a woman into hotel. I do not trust in room safe these hotels have. It is easy for someone who knows how to break into them. So I go out and buy my own safe and I buy new lock. I change the lock of this room and put in the new lock which is very special because you need the key to open this lock even if you are inside my room. When I opened the door and we came into the room I already had the door to the safe open. You did not notice me throwing the key into the safe, then my closing the safe?"

"I cannot get out of the room?"

"Of course not, my little Neon to the world. Only I can let you out of this room so you had better be good to me," Mickel lied. He had been lying about buying a new safe and had merely moved the safe that had come with the hotel room, so that it was now repositioned high up on a small ward robe close to the door. However, he had equipped his condo over at the Bahthaus in the same manner he had described to her for the express purpose of trapping any girl inside who might have had any thoughts about robbing him once he had gone to sleep. As for the lock, he had bought a new lock at Home Pro and easily replaced the lock the hotel had put in with the new one which he could only lock or unlock with his key from both sides of the door.

"No more ice. Right now I want you to smoke me. I want number one blow job."

Then it dawned on him. It was their first night together and already she was practicing bondage on him. Clearly she was really into it for she had left no room for his doubting that she was trying to show him that she had complete control over him. He looked down at his feet and saw that he had the largest erection he ever remembered. *Had this also happened to Ted Buffalo? Possibly, just possibly she had played her little bondage scheme on him one last time and put something in his drink to make him drowsy before letting her boyfriend into the condo.*

"You want smoke. I make number one for you," Neon replied.

Neon lowered herself across Mickel's chest as she started to rub her tight nippled breasts across his chest, then his groin. After a few moments she repositioned the pillow by sliding it beneath him, as she lifted his buttocks off the bed to raise his groin rose higher into the air. Then she inserted his engorged penis between her breasts. Sliding her body along his cock while squeezing her breasts together, so that they firmly encased his penis, she felt once again in control and that she could do anything with him she liked. The thought of the door locked, so that she could not get out of the condo, faded into the recesses of her mind.

A few moments later, she slid lower down onto the bed, so that her mouth was even with his balls, took half a scrotal sack into her mouth and sucked hard. Mickel shuddered in pain, until she spat out his testicle and took his penis gently into her mouth. The pain went away, replaced by the exquisite sensation of her wet mouth working his penis deep inside her throat. She sensed when he was about to cum. Pulling away she lowered her mouth once more to his balls, engulfed one of them in her mouth and bit into it just deep enough to graze his skin. Once more she worked on his balls with her tongue and the tips of her teeth as she brought Mickel from ecstasy to agony then back again. Finally she took his shaft once more into her mouth. This time she was relentless until several minutes had passed and he started gushing thick riveting streams of cum down her throat.

"That was very good. Very good," Mickel said to her. I think we must do this more often."

The arrival of the Khukuris

The two Khukuris arrived in a single box. Fast Eddy had them delivered by courier from Nepal to a friend's place in Pattaya that was more than four kilometers from the Bahthaus. The friend was drunk most of the time, so when Fast Eddy had called him to ask him to hold onto a package for him, his friend didn't ask many questions. Fast Eddy's telling him he would be out of town for a couple of weeks and that his own condo building's security could not be trusted to make sure he'd get the package was good enough. The package had several labels on it. One had typed on it the delivery address, another had the sender's name and address neatly printed on it. and finally there was the one for Thai custom's use only, identifying the package's contents. Khukuri House had described the box's contents as "souvenirs". Whatever arrangements Khukuri House had made with the Thai government pertaining to import taxes, bribes or other financial details didn't concern Fast Eddy. What mattered was that he had covered his tracks well enough to virtually eliminate any future tracking of lethal weapons to him.

When he got back to his condo, he carefully opened the box containing the two khukuris, then he slit open the two plastic bags containing the two implements. The khukuris had been heavily greased to protect them from rust. Using a paper towel he wiped off most of the grease after which he carefully inspected their edges. Khukuri House had done a reasonably good job of making sure that both Khukuris had razor sharp edges. But when Fast Eddy ran each Khukuri's edge across one of his fingernails he found there were several spots on each edge that failed to bite into his nail which indicated the need for a little touch up work.

It took him two hours' work with his Lansky sharpener to get him the results he found necessary on both knives. When he finished he took a tape measure out of his tool box and measured the thickness of both blades. One measured 9 millimeters while the other measured a full centimeter, indicating that both khukuris were robust enough to perform the work of a small axe, capable of splitting logs or cutting down six inch diameter trees. He put one, then the other Khukuri on a little scale, a small cheap version of the ubiquitous scales one finds all over Thailand's markets, which vendors use to weigh fruit, vegetables and meat. One Khukuri weighed 34 ounces; the other one kilogram. That's a full 2.2 pounds, Fast Eddy whistled softly to himself. That's almost twice as much as a Cold Steel bowie knife and these blades measure only 11 inches which is about the same.

Suvanaporn and Neon

"You go with falang who I don't like!" Suvanaporn shouted nastily to Neon.

"But you tell me you need money and that I should boom-boom falang," Neon replied. "You don't make nearly enough on your boxing tips to pay the rent."

"I know I tell you that--but not this falang. He no good. He make me lose face, and now you make me the laughing stock of everyone."

"He give me big money so it's okay."

"Not okay." Suvanaporn raised his hand to slap her before her next words stopped him.

"He give me three thousand five hundred baht."

"He give you three thousand five hundred baht? Is he ting tong?"

"I think I'm worth it."

"No, you are not. But give me that money."

Suvanaporn snatched the money out of her hand as soon as she pulled it from her purse. Then he handed her back one thousand baht after taking out two thousand five hundred baht for himself."

"Okay, you go fuck him again," Suvanaporn hissed back at her. "I make sure everyone understand how stupid this falang is."

Back at Ringside

Full of himself, this time Mickel decided to really get Suvanaporn angry at him. He had just beaten one of the bar girls four times in a row at Connect Four, telling her each time he won, "You can beat me easily, but I think you want to boom-boom me so badly that you cannot concentrate."

Connect Four is a bar game that is played in nearly all Pattaya's beer bars. Winning is the same as in Tic Tack Toe except the winner must place four counters in a row. The game consists of a small plastic frame comprising seven columns and six rows. Along with dice and other bar games Connect Four is a useful tool beer bars use to help break the ice between their bar girls and their customers because it helps to overcome the language barrier.

He waived over one of the Thai boxers; then he pointed at Suvanaporn who was standing just outside the ring within earshot of the bar.

"I want to bet one more time against that man."

"You sure?" the boxer replied.

"Sure I'm sure. Suvanaporn is no good. He is a bum. My momma would kill him in the ring. My sister has more power than Suvanaporn."

Nudging him in the ribs, Fast Eddy whispered into Mickel's ear. "Excellent work, Mickel. Don't let up now. Make them all hate you."

"How much?" the boxer asked him.

"I think two thousand baht. Yes. I have two thousand baht that tells me Suvanaporn is one big pussy. I could beat him with one hand tied behind my back."

"He number one boxer here," the boxer retorted.

"That may be," Mickel replied. "But that's because not one of you can fight. You people remind me of my mother's momma and all her friends playing bridge."

By now Mickel was having a blast, feeling he had nothing to lose, while Fast Eddy felt far less vulnerable due to his taking the precaution of putting one of his khukuri's under the seat of his motorbike just in case Suvanaporn and his friends would decide to follow them home. He had brought it along for insurance after deciding, *if tonight is to be the night so be it. Luckily the khukuri fit under the seat, but just barely.* Fast Eddy would have felt better if he had bought the 13 inch World War II Khukuris, but his choice for the smaller model had been the right one due to its far greater portability.

Through slitted eyes Mickel watched Suvanaporn turn red in the face with rage. Although he knew that neither Suvanaporn nor the fighter taking his money to place his bet couldn't possibly understand fully the full force of his insults, he was certain they understood the gist of them. The rest was simply for Fast Eddy's and his own amusement.

"You say Thai man no can fight?" the boxer asked him.

"Stupid man, that is exactly what I am saying. But I don't care. I give you my money anyway because it makes me laugh."

The fighter scowled. This time it was all out in the open. Before, all the betting had been done clandestinely with Mickel putting his bet into the Princess's hands just in case there were any policemen present. Now the whole crowd saw Mickel's money change hands. And some of the people actually could hear some of Mickel's insults above the din of the arena.

Overcome by rage, it didn't take long for Suvanaporn to knock his opponent down, not once but three times in rapid succession. The referee told the other fighter to stay down and then he counted ten and the fight was over.

By the time Suvanaporn got around to the bar to collect his tips, his face showed that he knew he was the toughest man in the place. He smiled contemptuously at Mickel and said to him, "I want tip now. I show you I number one."

Mickel reached into his pocket for his wallet, pulled it out, and took out one hundred baht. Then he started to shake his head and replied, "I only have one hundred baht. That is too much and I no have Hah baht (5 baht) which is all you are worth. Sorry but I cannot tip you. You very bad fighter." Then he put the one hundred baht back into his pocket.

"Me no good!" Suvanaporn exclaimed. "Let me see you fight. You die here. Anyone can kill you."

"Oh you think so?" Mickel retorted. "Well I will make you very happy. Two nights from now. My Shy pruhmee dawn yen (Not tomorrow night). Wednesday. Prumee. Ti lang (tomorrow, later). I fight you. Di kap? (Okay?) My shy donee (Not yet). Prumee, prumee. (Tomorrow tomorrow)."

Although his Thai was horrendous, it was still good enough for Suvanaporn to understand that he was being challenged.

Mickel wanted to fight him. Not for tonight and not for tomorrow night, but later than that. Perhaps the night after?

"What do you mean?" the Princess asked Mickel. "You want to fight Suvanaporn but not tonight and not tomorrow?"

"That is exactly what I mean. I want to fight him right here in this ring the day after tomorrow."

"Day after? You sure?" the Princess asked wanting to be sure that she got the date straight.

"Yes. Wednesday. Today Monday. Tomorrow Tuesday. Not tomorrow. Day after," Mickel carefully explained.

Princess spoke to Suvanaporn in rapid Thai who nodded to show he understood that he was to fight Mickel on Wednesday night. Then he glared back at Mickel and snarled, "Falang, you die."

Mickel stayed another hour at the bar with Fast Eddy, until after it closed, buying shots of tequila for Neon, Fast Eddy and the Princess. By the time the pair left, both were obviously very drunk. What the Thais did not understand is that both men were very good at holding their alcohol.

There were two ways back to the Bahthaus. One was down a busy street. The other was down a road that was seldom used because it had too many curves and speed bumps. It was this road that Mickel and Fast Eddy took on their motorbikes, but by the time they got back to the Bahthaus they hadn't seen any signs of anyone following them.

"I expected that maybe they might try and follow us on their motorbikes," Fast Eddy explained to Mickel. "But I guess that Suvanaporn wants to humiliate you in the ring instead."

"You will soon see who humiliates who in that ring," said Mickel.

The Ring

"Here is your Khukuri," Fast Eddy told Mickel as they worked on their disguises.

Mickel pulled the Khukuri out of its sheath and fingered its edge, almost cutting himself. Then he waved it through the air several times, testing its heft. "That is one deadly weapon," Fast Eddy. "Where did you get them?"

"I got them from Khukuri House out of Nepal--ordered them both from the Internet."

"That edge is like a razor. Did it come that way, Fast Eddy?"

"Yes and no. I touched the edges up. They were pretty good to start with, but I want them to be 100 percent perfect in every way."

"Will they fit in our motorbikes?"

"Yes and no. Here, take this. They'll fit under my seat, but I am nearly sure your motorbike doesn't have enough storage down there. Here's another gift for you." Fast Eddy tossed a small gym bag to Mickel. "Since you are fighting tonight they will almost expect you to be carrying something like this, and a larger Khukuri will not fit in one of these. I won't be fighting so I have a special bag for medical supplies-- just in case you get hurt." Fast Eddy winked at Mickel confident that his friend would not be the one getting hurt.

Mickel put his khukuri into the little bag Fast Eddy had given him, carefully packing a pair of gym shorts and a fresh t-shirt on top of it. The two men were soon on their way to the Thai boxing arena on their motorbikes.

Neon was already at the Princess Bar when Fast Eddy and Mickel arrived. When one of the girls asked them what kind of beer they wanted, Fast Eddy replied that both of them wanted water instead.

Mickel drew Neon close to him, then he pulled a scrap of paper from his pocket on which he had printed—"After I win, we celebrate together at Marriot Hotel." Then he put a hotel key card into her hand. Neon's eyes brightened, especially when he told her he was giving her five thousand baht for the night.

"Do you understand, baby!" her said firmly to her as he cupped his hands around her ear and spoke between them to create a megaphone effect.

"Yes. I understand," she replied.

"I beat Suvanaporn's ass tonight. You will not want him anymore when I've finished with him. We celebrate. I pay you, 5000 baht but you must come to the Marriot. Then to make sure she understood, he added—"Marriot, next to Royal Garden Shopping".

"No problem. I come to you as soon as fight finished."

Then Mickel blurted out to everyone around him, "Tonight I only drink water because now I want to fight."

The Princess's face broke into a huge smile. "You want fight now?"

"Yes. I want to show you people how to fight. Tonight I show you a real fight," said Mickel.

Princess motioned at one of the men assisting the fighters in the ring who came over to the bar to see what she wanted. Princess pointed at Mickel and said, "He want to fight." Then she exchanged a few words in Thai with the man.

"Who do you want fight?" the man asked Mickel.

"I want him," Mickel replied as he pointed at Suvanaporn who was still in the ring talking to several of the other fighters.

"Okay. I get big boss now."

Moments later the referee joined Mickel and Fast Eddy at the bar. The referee had a few words with the Princess in Thai, then he turned to Fast Eddy and asked. "You sure friend you want fight Suvanaporn?"

"Yes. I want to show him how to fight," Mickel replied.

"Understand Suvanaporn no like you already," the referee explained. "Maybe he hurt you too much."

Breaking into a huge belly laugh, Mickel roared, "Suvanaporn hurt me? He will be lucky if I do not kill him." Then he added, "I hope you have good insurance because I think Suvanaporn will go to hospital for a long time."

"He good fighter. Are you sure?" the referee asked.

"I am sure that Suvanaporn is no good. He fight like ladyboy."

"Okay. You fight next fight," said the referee. Then he went back into the ring to have a few words with Suvanaporn, who kept glancing over at Mickel. The eyes of the two men did not meet due to Mickel's incessant banter as he joked nonstop with Fast Eddy and the bar girls. When one of the girls came up behind him and started massaging his neck and shoulders, Mickel cocked his right arm back and invited her to feel his biceps.

"Feel the power in these arms, baby," he crowed.

"Suvanaporn have no chance," Mickel boasted. "He little man. He have no power. When he meet me in the ring I will boom-boom him. You can be sure of that." Mickel glanced over his shoulder at Suvanaporn whose face had once again turned beet red with anger. For a brief moment the eyes of the two men met, then Mickel winked and yelled at the boxer, "Little man, you better leave now because I will make lady man out of you. When I finish with you, you won't have a dick."

Two boxers entertained the crowd as Suvanaporn and Mickel bided their time. When Suvanaporn came outside the ring to socialize in several bars with the mamasans and bar girls, clad only in boxing trunks, and shirtless, he was clearly agitated, moving from bar to bar spending only a few moments in each one. In the ring, a young kid appearing no more than eighteen went up against a short paunchy man in his mid-thirties. Rail thin, the kid looked too insubstantial to pose a threat unless someone handed him a gun. After several faked knockdowns the young man finally prevailed, as the bout ended with the older fighter prostate on his back in the middle of the ring, as he grasped both sides of his head between his hands grimacing in pain.

Then it was Mickel's turn. When the referee motioned at him to come into the center of the ring, Mickel swaggered towards him while shouting at the Thai boxers on the sidelines: "Enough of this bullshit. Now comes a real fight. If you do not believe me, just watch and I show you."

One of the ring handlers came over and laced the boxing gloves on him, while another man assisted Suvanaporn who had already put his gloves on and only had to have his laces tightened. Suvanaporn came out into the center of the ring, kneeled down on one knee and looked vacantly around the arena as if he were supplicating the Gods for the coming victory he'd soon dedicate his performance to. Thai boxing music accompanied the ritual, that god awful din, screechy crap created only to impart some form of erotic atmosphere to the performances–or at least that's the way Mickel saw it.

"Go on. Pray you moron. But God not help you when you meet me," Mickel shouted at Suvanaporn.

Until then the crowd had been quiet. Most of the customers were Western males, some of them accompanied by Thai women they had met at other bars. Most were newcomers to the Pattaya bar scene, who believed that the fights were real, whereas long-time real expats who had been living in the area, had long ago recognized that the ring performances were rigged, and that they had been put on only to provide a show that the tourists had never seen before. Most of the customers had been quietly watching the match, playing dice and connect four with the bar girls or chatting with their girlfriends, but Mickel's loud insults to his opponent and disparaging comments about the entire event was clearly waking the crowd up. Some of the customers loudly cheered the Norwegian. Others booed. But most were clearly on his side because Mickel was the upstart and probably untrained in Muay Thai, which meant that the advantage was probably with his opponent.

Upon the opening bell Mickel came out into the center of the ring looking like a stiff. Completely disrespecting his opponent, Suvanaporn immediately caught him with a swift left hand to his face, which he followed with a kick to Mickel's thigh. Mickel stood in place unwilling or unable to move, flat footed and bewildered, grimacing in pain. Suvanaporn followed with another swift kick to Mickel's head which shot back from the impact. Part of the crowd started to go wild with a dozen guys getting up onto their feet, cheering the Thai fighter. For a moment or two the fight seemed about all over for the Norwegian who took a right hand to his jaw and crumpled to one knee. Suddenly a malicious grin appeared on Mickel's face. He got up quickly and leered at the crowd--then he turned to face Suvanaporn.

"You think you hurt me little man? I just pretend you hurt me. Now, I give this to you."

Hard eyes bored into Suvanaporn's face--eyes of the Arctic wolf without remorse. For the first time Suvanaporn was afraid.

The Menace from the North feinted with a left jab to Suvanaporn's face which forced Suvanaporn to cover up with both of his hands leaving his belly wide open. Then Mickel threw a crushing right hand into Suvanaporn's gut. Suvanaporn doubled over in pain as the crowd rose to its feet. But Mickel backed away deciding not to go for the kill and stood a few feet out of range patiently waiting for Suvanaporn to recover.

"Come on little man. I wait for you. I give you a chance to come get me," the Norwegian taunted the smaller man.

Suvanaporn stood in the center of the ring hunched over trying to catch his breath. On wobbly legs somehow he managed to unleash a kick at Mickel's chest. But it was a different Mickel standing in front of him, a Mickel who was fully awake, with alert eyes picking up every one of the Thai boxer's moves. The big Norwegian caught Suvanaporn's foot in midair, and slowly lifted the Thai boxer's leg upwards. For an instant Suvanaporn stood in the ring with his body stretched to the breaking point and then Mickel gave a quick upward twist with his arm that forced Suvanaporn to stretch upwards with all of his weight on one foot until he fell backwards onto the mat. More embarrassed than hurt Suvanaporn jumped back onto his feet to face his antagonist.

Mickel shouted: "You too slow, little man. Muay Tai no good. I can destroy you whenever I want."

Seething with rage, Suvanaporn aimed a round house kick at Mickel's face, but Mickel saw it coming and side slipped his head forcing Suvanaporn to miss. But Mickel didn't, shooting a left hand straight into Suvanaporn's nose which he followed up with a thundering right to the same spot. Suvanaporn could hear a sickly crunch coming from his nose as the blood started to spurt out onto the ring.

Puddles of bright red started to pool onto the mat as Suvanaporn stood before the crowd sputtering like a sick cow.

"I can take you now and put you out of your misery, but this fight has not gone on long enough. The crowd feels cheated because of you. You fight like little girl you coward," Mickel shouted at Suvanaporn. "So I play with you like a little baby."

He shot one jab, then another, which he followed with more left hands at Suvanaporn's face. Then Mickel started to work on the Thai fighter's belly. Each time he attacked his opponent's belly, the crowd cheered him on, confident that just one more crashing punch would end the fight, but at the last moment Mickel deliberately pulled his punch so that his fist only grazed Suvanaporn's belly. He played with his now helpless opponent the way a boxer might spar with the heavy bag, with first his left arm flashing out, then his right. He could not miss, and still he continued to pull each punch so that it landed with no more force than a pillow landing on a bed.

"I am very bored," Mickel announced to the crowd. "I want to drink some beer. Suvanaporn is a chump and a weakling so I finish him now."

Tired of all the antics, Mickel went back to work, delivering several gut-wrenching punches to Suvanaporn's belly. Then he unleashed a straight left to Suvanaporn's nose which he followed with a devastating roundhouse with his right. The two blows knocked the Thai boxer backwards against one of the ring posts. Collapsing onto the floor in a pool of blood, Suvanaporn tried to get up on the count of ten, then he crumbled to the mat a second time as the referee counted him out.

But Mickel wasn't finished with him yet. Upon the count of ten, Mickel stomped the back of his prostate opponent's neck, then he rubbed Suvanaporn's face into the mat with his heel. Mickel was sure the insult would have maximum effect.

Considering that the foot is the lowest portion of the human body, Thais believe the mere act of pointing one's foot at a person to be an insult. Mickel grinned, confident that his degradation of his opponent was complete.

The Indian Flask

Fast Eddy had brought an ornate silver flash to the bar. Larger than the usual metal liquor flasks men often carry in their pockets, Fast Eddy had bought it in India.

"Let me pour you a drink of this finest Russian vodka I've gotten for you," Fast Eddy said to Mickel: "To your astounding victory."

"Well thanks," Fast Eddy," Mickel replied. "But it really wasn't much of a victory because Suvanaporn cannot fight. He same as lady."

Suvanaporn sat at a nearby bar licking his wounds. He would have preferred being at the Princess Bar, but he had lost so much face from putting on such a dismal show, that even the briefest appearance was out of the question. He felt the razor's edge of the most acute anger he had ever experienced in the pit of his stomach since it had become obvious to everyone in the arena that Mickel had been playing with him, even in the beginning when Suvanaporn had landed several telling blows. It irked him that Mickel's initially appearing to be mismatched and out of his league had been faked and that he had not even come close to hurting his opponent. Then he had been unable to get up after Mickel had floored him proving to the crowd that he had been a helpless dupe, who proved to be completely unable to defend himself. He couldn't forgive himself for that. Mickel's placing his foot on his neck was merely the final act in a show that featured maximum humiliation and contempt for himself, the martial art form of Muay Tai and for his country. He could not let the defeat and the insult go unanswered.

Several of his friends were now drinking with him, two of them fellow boxers. Their drink was Thai Whiskey, a concoction similar to Rum, which they drank with Coca Cola.

"Look at the falang, drinking like buffaloes at the water trough," Suvanaporn said to his friends. "Drink--just don't drink as much as they are. With luck, we can surprise them on their way home."

Fast Eddy had a special beverage in his flask–pure water, completely unadulterated by alcohol. He knew the Princess would have thrown Mickel and him out of the bar for bringing their own alcohol. So he had appeased her by buying her three straight shots of tequila. Meanwhile he kept pouring colorless liquid into two small bar glasses he had reserved for Mickel and himself from the silver flask. He offered Neon a shot of tequila which she politely refused. Then he offered her a Bacardi breezer, and then a beer before finally telling her, "I buy for you B-52 or wine or anything you want because we want you to celebrate with us."

Again and again, Neon politely refused his offers. Finally Fast Eddy bought several breezers for two of the bar girls. By this time, Mickel looked very drunk. As the bars in the Thai boxing arena started to close, the two men left the bar together. They were not alone.

As they approached their motorbikes, Fast Eddy ordered Mickel to partially unzip his gym bag before draping it over the hook that Yamaha had put on the bike for fastening grocery bags, women's handbags, laptop computers and other items. Several seconds later, both men were speeding down Pattaya Thai (South Pattaya Road).

After walking unsteadily to their motorcycles, Fast Eddy and Mickel drove erratically down 2nd Road from Pattaya Tai to confirm the impression that they were drunk, driving quickly to make it very difficult for anyone to pull up alongside them. Fast Eddy had been dead certain they'd be followed, but he wanted to make it almost impossible for anyone to pull up alongside of either of them and get off a shot just in case their pursuers were carrying firearms. Fast Eddy took the lead, oftentimes changing lanes abruptly. Mickel, who was completely unimpaired by the water he had been drinking, found it easy to follow him. Luckily they got the green light at Pattaya Klang. Not having to choose between stopping or running the light, the pair sped on to North Pattaya Road, around the Dolphin round about and on into Naklua. Fortunately traffic was light.

The Pursuit

Suvanaporn was astonished by the rapid pace set by the two Westerners. Since both men were very drunk by the time they had left the Thai boxing arena, he was surprised they were able to weave through traffic as well as they did. *But they had to be completely wasted*, he decided. *Otherwise they would have seen that they were being followed by four men.*

One of the men was a fellow Thai boxer he often trained with although the pair didn't box in the same arena. The other two were his brothers who had come to watch him destroy the impudent falang, but who had wound up not just disappointed but enraged and embarrassed by how things had turned out.

The four Thais followed a quarter mile behind Fast Eddy and Mickel, which was the maximum distance Suvanaporn felt they could maintain without being spotted and still be able to rapidly catch up with the two Westerners once they turned off the main road. Had traffic not been as light as it was, they would have had to follow much more closely. Suvanaporn watched first Fast Eddy, then Mickel make a left turn onto one of Naklua's sois leading down to the beach and grinned with satisfaction that it was a street that was not heavily trafficked during the day, so it was unlikely that it would have anyone on it at this early hour in the morning.

Still keeping a discrete distance from the two falang, Suvanaporn and his three accomplices followed them down the Soi for several hundred meters, then watched them take a right onto yet another street, this one even less traveled. This couldn't be more perfect, Suvanaporn decided as he turned into the street after them and accelerated to narrow the gap between them. He knew the street well as it had several abrupt curves in it and was for the most part devoid of street lights, both conditions perfect for what he had in store for the two hapless foreigners. The first turn was a long ninety degree bend. As Mickel and Fast Eddy rounded it and disappeared from sight, Suvanaporn twisted his bike's throttle wide open, which brought him up to within two hundred yards of his prey.

The road had become well-known as one that was best avoided, especially at night. Many Westerners had been robbed here while walking, they thought, just a short, therefore, safe distance to their condos or hotel rooms. In Thai motorbike taxi driver circles this particular stretch of road had become very well known as a picker upper for those in dire need. For the man short on cash who had little scruples about how he was going to get it, swooping down on a pedestrian or two on his motorcycle to quickly come down upon his unsuspecting victim was a recipe that seldom failed. Sometimes the weapon of choice was a gun. But more commonly the simple expedient of a club was enough.

Suvanaporn and Ajax carried twenty-four inch sections of heavy pipe while Suvanaporn's brothers, not as hardened yet to the idea of violence, were both weaponless.

There was a short straight section of road followed by another curve, this one shorter than the first, but even more abrupt, which would bring the two Westerners to an even slower pace. It was here that Suvanaporn and his three companions overtook Fast Eddy and Mickel, right after coming out of the winding S curve which first turned to the left, straightened for fifty meters or so, then turned once again, this time abruptly to the right. Suvanaporn flew past the two falang, followed by one of his brothers while his armed companion and his other brother approached closely to the rear. Once they had gotten a short distance past Fast Eddy and Mickel, Suvanaporn and his brother spun their bikes around to block off the road.

Looming in front of Fast Eddy and Mickel while keeping his piece of steel pipe out of the light at waist level, Suvanaporn approached Mickel who had just gotten off his motorbike. His younger brother followed him a couple of meters to his left. Fast Eddy seeing the two Thais approaching Mickel from the front, got off his motorbike, drew his khukuri from his half opened gym bag and quickly spun around to face any new threats to his rear. Swinging at the back of Fast Eddy's head with his steel pipe, Ajax narrowly missed and only because Fast Eddy had turned to face him just in time. But Fast Eddy didn't. Grasping the khukuri's sheath firmly in his left hand, his thumb found the finger groove in the Khukuri's handle as he pulled firmly back on the big knife. It took less than a second for him to clear the khukuri from its scabbard. Quickly raising the khukuri to just over shoulder height Fast Eddy brought the two pound weapon straight down upon Ajax's shoulder as he flicked his wrist sharply to give its blade even more momentum.

Had Fast Eddy struck Ajax's shoulder with only the blunt edge of the khukuri's blade he would have still broken the Thai boxer's shoulder. Hearing the sickening crack of Ajax's shoulder disintegrating from the force of the blow, Fast Eddy watched the khukuri's blade bite through the man's clavicle, as it knifed through over four inches of muscle, flesh and bone. Ajax stumbled from the immediate impact of the blow and went down on one knee as a fountain of blood spurted out of his body. Fast Eddy's second swing drove the khukuri's blade straight through Ajax's side. The blade broke several ribs as it bit six inches into Ajax's body, cutting him halfway in two.

Satisfied that Ajax wasn't getting up, Fast Eddy turned on one of Suvanaporn's younger brothers, the one who had hoped to attack him once Ajax had knocked him senseless with his steel pipe. His first blow took the brother's right arm clean off at the elbow. As its trunk spurted copious amounts of blood, Fast Eddy swung for the young Thai's face. The blade caught the man on his lower chin, lopping a large chunk of it straight off as it continued to bite deeply through his neck. Had it not been for the chin taking most of the force of the blow, the young Thai would have been decapitated. As it was the khukuri bit deep into the arteries of the neck, severing the spinal column. The man went down immediately and quickly bled to death as Fast Eddy rushed up to help Mickel. It had taken him less than ten seconds to dispose of both of his assailants.

Exultant when he saw how successful he had been at cornering the two Westerners, Suvanaporn expected to take his revenge out on Mickel, who was now helplessly trapped on a lonely road without hope of help. He had watched Mickel and then Fast Eddy, drink one Vodka after another before the pair wobbled over to their motorbikes. And although he had been thoroughly beaten in the ring, this was before the alcohol had completely taken its toll on the two falang. Fast Eddy and Mickel were also outnumbered two to one while both he and Ajax now carried two foot long pieces of heavy pipe that were capable of breaking bones and splitting heads. Mickel's sudden production of a long knife from his gym bag took him by complete surprise. Not expecting the drunken fool to move so fast, Mickel's transition from being empty handed to being fully armed almost shocked the bone marrow right out of him.

Suvanaporn froze in place as he watched Mickel raise his khukuri over his right shoulder. He had been caught off guard because he was still holding his chunk of steel pipe at waist level hoping to keep it out of sight. His mind went slow motion calculating how much time it would take him to inflict a crippling blow on Mickel as he tried to avoid the lethal blade. Swatting Mickel in the face with the pipe was out of the question, since it would leave him exposed to a fatal blow from the khukuri before he'd even be able to get the steel pipe in position. A head shot would be even worse because Mickel already had his khukuri raised and was nearly six inches taller, which meant the khukuri was likely to get him before he could bring his club down on Mickel's head. Doing nothing would have been worse of all. He took the head shot and was almost able to smash Mickel's face in before the khukuri found its target.

Mickel focused on a single point on Suvanaporn's neck as he whipped his khukuri downward. Suvanaporn was much too slow, having been caught flatfooted and mentally unprepared as he slashed his club upwards at Mickel's head one second too late. The Khukuri's blade intersected Suvanaporn's neck with surgical precision, biting right through his carotid artery and spinal column. Mickel had put most of his body weight behind the blow–just enough to separate Suvanaporn's head from his body--as Mickel felt the Khukuri's blade meet resistance from Suvanaporn's spinal column before severing heavily through. Suvanaporn's torso remained on its feet for several seconds as blood spurted from what was left of his neck before falling over; then Mickel turned to face Suvanaporn's brother cowering in front of him.

The youngest Thai was defenseless against the khukuri so he took the only option that made sense--which was to run. But Fast Eddy, who had just finished off both of his assailants, was now running him down from the left. Seeing Fast Eddy at the last moment, he turned around in a desperate effort to get away. But Mickel who was already moving forward was able to get one fatal step on him. The khukuri slashed deeply into his back knocking him to his knees. The second blow came from Fast Eddy as Mickel pulled his khukuri out of five inches of severed flesh. The heavy steel blade sunk deep into the young man's skull, killing him instantly. The third blow came from Mickel swiping down across the Thai's neck. The head came right off and rolled across the asphalted road before finally coming to a rest against the trunk of a tree.

Let's get out of here, Fast Eddy," shouted Mickel.

"Okay. But pull up just short of the next street."

With the gym bag still dangling from the bike's carrying hook in front of his knees, Fast Eddy followed Mickel to a dead stop. Taking a small towel out of the gym bag Fast Eddy threw it at Mickel.

"Take that, turn around and let me have a good look at you," said Fast Eddy.

Mickel nearly caught the towel dropping at his feet. He picked it up and turned to face Fast Eddy. "Now what?" the Norwegian asked.

"You have blood on your face," Fast Eddy replied. "Use your motorcycle's mirrors so you can see the blood and wipe if off with the towel. Then look at your hands and arms and wipe any blood off of them you see."

Mickel looked into the bike's right mirror and saw there was blood sprinkled on his face which he wiped off with the towel.

"What about my shirt? Do I have any on it?" he asked Fast Eddy.

"Sure you do, so don't even look," Fast Eddy replied. "Change into this," he added as he reached into his bag and tossed a fresh t-shirt at Mickel.

"You think of everything," said Mickel.

"I thought it would be wise to think each step through," Fast Eddy replied as he wiped his hands and arms down with a towel. Then satisfied that he had most of the blood off, he put on a short sleeved shirt he had stuffed into his gym bag.

"Let's get the hell out of here," Mickel said.

Fast Eddy had thought about simply driving back to the Bahthaus. The security guard was likely to be asleep, but he had decided they could not take the risk just in case he was awake, and that just this one time he might be paying attention to who was coming in and out of the condo building. Then there were the security cameras which would have shown them coming back into the building early in the morning. There were also the disguises he had to worry about. If the guard was on the ball he just might notice two strangers coming into the building using their keycards to get past the back entrance from the parking lot.

The pair doubled back to Naklua Road, which they took to Beach Road to the Holiday Inn. Fast Eddy and Mickel parked their motorbikes and walked into the front entrance as one of the desk clerks nodded in their direction when they headed for the elevator. With the exception of the desk clerk, no one saw them returning to their room. Fast Eddy opened the door to the room with his key card, walked straight over to the refrigerator and took out two Heinekens.

"Considering we haven't had any alcohol yet, I think we owe ourselves a couple, don't you, Mickel?" Fast Eddy said as he handed one of the beers to Mickel.

"I think we should have more than one," Mickel replied then he added, "No one will even know if we spent the night in our condos or stayed out all night. You paid cash for the room and neither you nor I ever came into this place. We are just two guys, who never existed thanks to our wonderful disguises."

Hacked to pieces

Mickel and Fast Eddy savored the large bottles of Chang beer as they watched the Pattaya news in Mickel's condo. Unlike American televised news which spares its viewers the blood and gore of the everyday mayhem from traffic deaths, suicides and murders out of respect for sensitive stomachs and human privacy, Thai television leaves nothing to the imagination. Mickel and Fast Eddy had both seen Western men dead on their toilets, bodies splattered all over the street from motorbike accidents, and long dead corpses that had decomposed in rooms so long that no one missed the deceased until the smell had gotten too rank to be ignored. The video footage of the four dead Thai men was some of the goriest they had ever seen. The video camera zoomed in on a decapitated head, then panned over to the body it had once belonged to. The camera didn't miss the pools of blood still on the road or the human intestines hanging out of one of the bodies.

A few days later, the story was picked up by most of the area's newspapers. There was speculation that the four homicides were the result of Thai gang warfare, which Naklua was infamous for. But there was also speculation that other elements were responsible for the deaths of the four men, and that the decapitating of heads, huge cuts into human torsos and the slicing off other bodily parts indicated that Naklua gangs had not been responsible for the killings, which more realistically bore the stamp of a Russian mafia style hit.

Fast Eddy was certain that the impending investigation would be short-lived. This would be a flash in the pan, making the news only once, then conveniently forgotten about. It was bad enough for tourism the way it was, so the entire event would conveniently be swept under the rug, while the police went on to indulge themselves in more profitable pursuits.

Neon Reconsiders Boyfriends

Neon left the boxing arena early, right after Mickel had knocked Suvanaporn out. His rage would be ungovernable, and she was terrified that he would take his humiliation out on her. In the ring against Mickel, Suvanaporn had lost too much face. "How can I even show up in the Arena again?" she kept asking herself, the impact of the words hitting her repeatedly like a jackhammer slamming into her brain. Being the girl- friend of the disgraced boxer had suddenly become incomprehensible.

Only two options presented themselves. 1. She could get as far away from Pattaya as possible by going back to the village she had grown up in. Even so, there was a good chance that Suvanaporn would eventually find her there. Then again, after enough time had passed he might never go there again out of embarrassment. The second choice was the easiest and the most profitable. Suvanaporn would never find her at the Marriot Hotel. As far as she knew Mickel had never stayed there. For a few hours, perhaps for as much as several days, she could vanish with Mickel. And then she could carefully weigh her options.

As she approached the hotel elevator, the security guard asked: "Are you a guest?" Without saying a word, Neon waived her room key card in the man's face. The guard smiled and extended his arm in the universal gesture that meant, continue on.

When she got up to the tenth floor she found the room, inserted her key card into the slot and watched the little light turn green as she heard an audible click indicating that the door was now open. But when she went inside, she immediately saw that she was not alone. Surprised to find someone else in the room with her, Neon said "So Sorry, must be mistake."

The other person smiled and replied, "No Neon. Mickel told me to wait here for you, and to get you a drink until he could get back from the Thai Boxing. Did he win?"

"Yes. He win. Very bad. I think he have big problem now.?

"What happened?"

Mickel, he very bad to Suvanaporn. Suvanaporn now very angry. I very scare of what Suvanaporn do now."

The other person was vaguely familiar. Neon had seen him before at the Bahthaus. Suddenly she remembered the man.

"I know you. You come to door of Buffalo. You very drunk. You come over and ask Buffalo to come drink beer with him."

"That's right. My name is Socrates," the man replied. "I used to drink too too much alcohol which would make me very lonely so I'd go from door to door ringing door bells looking for someone to drink with me."

"Sure. You very drunk. Now I remember. Buffalo he come to door and when he see you, you fall down in hallway."

"Yes. That would be me. I was so drunk I could never remember coming to people's doors. But now we must drink together and wait for Mickel. Come Neon. Let us drink together out onto the balcony. What can I get you? There is beer, and wine in the refrigerator. And Mickel bought some Bacardi Breezers for you at the Seven Eleven before he went to the Thai Boxing arena. There is Strawberry and Lemon."

"I want Lemon," Neon replied as she followed Socrates out to the balcony and took a seat at a small teak table.

Socrates disappeared for a few moments, reappearing with a bottle of San Miguel Light and a cocktail glass which he had filled with ice and Bacardi. Then he sprawled out in the chair across from her.

"You very funny man. I see you fall down in condo. Very drunk. You drink very much. Why you drink too much?" she asked.

"Well I suppose I can tell you why because it doesn't matter anymore. They say a dead man tells no tales so I suppose the same is true about a dead woman."

"What you mean?

"What I mean is I have a History."

"I don't understand."

"I drink to forget."

"Why you forget?"

"I forget because I do not want to remember. That is why I come to Pattaya—to drink and to forget. About all the people I have killed while I was in the IRA."

"I no understand."

"Neon, you are too beautiful and empty headed to understand. Come to think of it, I think you are too brain dead to understand anything."

"Brain dead. What you mean?"

"It means you do not have the ability to think. Consider this. You have a boyfriend, a Thai man named Suvanaporn. What do you get from him? And do you even know what the IRA was?

"No. Not understand IRA and what you mean Suvanaporn, he get me something?"

"That is the whole point, Neon. Suvanaporn is a bad man. He is evil and here you have him for a boyfriend."

"What you mean? Suvanaporn good man. He handsome. He have big power."

"How much money does he give you?"

For the first time Neon appeared confused as she searched for an answer.. "He give me nothing. He Thai. Not for him to give lady money. He big man. He Thai boxer."

"So here's my next question then. How much money do you give him?"

"I don't know."

"And how about Ted Buffalo? How much he give to you?

"He give me money mak mak."

"Okay then, who better? Man who give you big money or man you must give money to?"

"Suvanaporn better. Buffalo, he stupid man."

"You know what I think, Neon?"

"What you think?"

"I think Buffalo was good man. A very good man. He loved you and he trusted you. And not only I, but almost all falang think Suvanaporn is an animal. He is nothing but shit, excrement that is what he is. I know you don't know what excrement means so I will have to tell you. It means poo poo. So when I go poo poo on the ground that is Suvanaporn. He same same poo poo. Think about that, Neon.

"What you say? You call Suvanaporn same same as poo poo?" Neon replied angrily.

"That is what I am telling you. And Neon, you should not be angry. You are too loud. In fact, you should be very scared."

"Scare? Why scare? Scare of you? I not scare of anything."

"You should be very scared, Neon. Just remember that last time you and Ted were on the balcony together—at the Bahthaus. Who was there with you?"

"No one with me. Only Buffalo."

"I know differently. I know Suvanaporn was with you and Ted."

"No. I alone."

"Come on, Neon, we all know you and Surpaporn were with each other when Ted fell off his balcony. We also know that Ted not really fall. We know you and Suvanaporn push Ted off balcony. How does it feel to know that you killed a man, a good man and that you got his money so you could give to poo poo man, Surpraporn? Did it give you pleasure? Did you enjoy yourself? Did you think Suvanaporn smart man and Ted Buffalo was stupid?"

Neon's face suddenly turned beet red as two thoughts blotted out everything else in her mind. One was the certainty that Socrates, and who knows who else, knew that she had helped Suvanaporn kill Ted Buffalo; the other was—"Who was this foreigner to accuse her of anything? He had no right to." Glaring at the stupid foreigner, Neon bolted out of her chair. Then she felt a sharp slap in her face knocking her backwards.

Socrates had gauged her reaction perfectly, expecting that she'd rise from her chair to escape the trap he had carefully

254

laid for her. He had left the hotel room door unlocked deliberately in order to give her the confidence that she could leave at any time and that she should have nothing to fear from him. But, as soon as he saw the anger in her face while he was accusing her of killing Ted Buffalo, he rose to his feet to unleash a crushing blow that sent her reeling backwards. At first Neon seemed to sink back into her chair. Then she spun sideways onto the floor.

It would have been impossible for Socrates to have delivered a more coordinated or effective blow. His slap took her in the side of the head, away from her mouth where it would have drawn blood which might have later aroused suspicion. But he had delivered it from his full height so that it had enough force behind it to knock her off her feet. He watched her rolling around beneath him as she tried to regain her feet.

"I will wait for you to get up so that we can resume this conversation, Neon. But you must not be rude to me. Not ever again. And you must not try and leave this room because then I will really have to hurt you. When you are able you sit down in your chair again, you will listen to me and not speak until I tell you to."

Then he sat down and waited patiently for her to regain her senses. After a few moments Neon was able to get off the floor and regain her seat.

Socrates then took out a cell phone and started playing with it. He clicked a little switch which brought up the pictures he had stored into the cell phone's memory. "I have only two pictures on this cell phone, Neon. Look at them." He then pulled up one picture, then the next. One was of Ted Buffalo. The second was one of Suvanaporn someone had taken at the Thai boxing ring.

"Notice Neon, that this cell phone is pink. It is the kind of color a woman might want her cell phone to be. It is not the color a man wants for his cell phone so you can be sure I did not buy this phone for myself. I bought it for you. So from this moment on, this is your cell phone."

Neon glared back at him sullenly, unwilling to reply. But slowly she started to grasp what Socrates was up to.

"When they find you, Neon, they will also find this cell phone. And I can assure you, they will never find the man who rented this room. Such a man never existed. The police will then decide that you have had two boyfriends, Ted Buffalo and

Suvanaporn, and that for some reason your involvement with one or the other of them, perhaps both of them caused you to kill yourself. The police will never be sure. It might even dawn on them that you and Suvanaporn killed Ted and that you couldn't live with yourself afterwards. But, no matter. The police will be more than happy to decide that you killed yourself and that will be that." For the first time there was fear in Neon's eyes as she grasped the full impact of what he was telling her. That--he, they, had planned all of this meticulously, and their well thought out plans focused around her death. And there was nothing she could do about it. Neon weighed no more than ninety-five pounds making Socrates twice her weight. And she had already felt what kind of punishment he was capable of inflicting on her. One huge slap had knocked her onto the floor. Her stomach churned as she resigned herself to her fate.

"You bore me with your silence," Socrates said in a voice of contrived sadness. "You have such a beautiful body and you have a gorgeous face. What a shame. Such a terrible waste, but now I must say goodbye."

Suddenly he stood up and with the entire force of his body behind it he delivered a second blow to Neon's face. But this time it was a closed fist. Hoping that it had not knocked her unconscious, he stood back watching her. It would have been difficult to throw her off the balcony alone, even though she was only half his size because she would have fought for her life and put up too much of a struggle. So he had intended the blow to stun her just enough to take any remaining fight out of her. He kept watching her until he was certain that she was fully conscious and that she was absorbing what was happening to her. Then he pulled her from her chair and hurled her over the railing.

Escaping was a simple matter of taking the elevator downstairs and walking past the front desk out of the building. He smiled thinking to himself how simple his escape plan was. Once the police started to undergo their preliminary investigation they would decide Neon's death had been a suicide anyway, and even if they determined that she might have been murdered he wouldn't be on their list of suspects.

Cornhole Quits

Khun Felonius had watched the televised footage of the carnage that had taken place less than two kilometers from the Bahthaus and read the newspaper accounts of it. One of the members of the staff had told him that one of the slain men had been the Thai boxer boyfriend of Neon, who had been staying with Ted Buffalo until Ted had disappeared off his balcony. Khun Felonius had always suspected that Ted had been shoved off his balcony with Neon's help, but he had kept his mouth shut knowing nothing would ever come of it. But now he was sure of it. This couldn't all be coincidence, he had reasoned. Four men including the Thai boyfriend being hacked to pieces so close to the Bahthaus in such a dramatic show of blood with no witnesses left behind was just too professional and too complete to be the result of normal gang warfare. This had to be more than just a simple murder of gang members. This had to be a message to all those who knew a lot more than what the papers reported. Certainly anyone who was at all acquainted with the Thai boyfriend, would from now on be staying clear of anyone who had quarreled with him. His own staff was even rumoring that "people" living in the Bahthaus had killed the four men.

Fast Eddy came into the office a few minutes after the secretary left. "I want to pay my bill," Fast Eddy told the manager.

"Okay. You pay now. Not before?" Khun Felonius asked.

If only Fast Eddy had come in earlier so the secretary could deal with him, I wouldn't have to interrupt my video game now, the manager ruminated to himself. *Now I'm going to have to log into the condo's accounting system, make the journal entry for our office's receipt of payment, collect the cash and print out a receipt for Fast Eddy.*

"I pay now. You just give me the receipt," Fast Eddy replied testily.

"You not wish to wait for tomorrow when secretary here? It's better for everyone."

"No. I want to pay now. By the way, did you see the news about those four guys getting killed not far from here?"

"Yes."

"Interesting," Fast Eddy continued. "One of the men was the Thai boyfriend of the woman staying with Ted Buffalo. Wasn't her name Neon?"

"I don't know." the manager lied.

"I've heard some people say that the boyfriend was a Thai boxer and that he and Neon shoved Ted Buffalo off his balcony. What do you think?"

"I don't think it happen?"

"I do. I'm sure of it."

"You sure?"

"Yes I'm 100 percent sure. I think people in our building didn't like it when the Thai boyfriend came into the Bahthaus to boom-boom falang's girlfriend. Back where I come from they used to hang chocolate men who didn't know their place."

"Know their place? What you mean?"

"Chocolate men used to be slaves. White men thought they were inferior and not as good as white men. Whenever white men thought a chocolate man boom-boomed a white lady, they often hanged him."

"Hang?"

"Yes. Hanged--With rope--They killed the chocolate man." Fast Eddy made the sign of someone having his throat cut by dragging his left hand across his throat, then putting his hand back on his throat raised his right hand above his head parodying a rope being drawn up taut. "They called these killings lynching's in the old days. They were against the law, but no one ever did anything about it back then. Now things are different, but I think in this condo there are people who would simply take a Thai man out and kill him for having the same girlfriend one of our condo owners has staying with him. But here everyone believes this Thai man killed Ted Buffalo. I think some of our residents killed all those men to teach people a lesson."

"Why you tell me this?"

Fast Eddy looked directly into the manager's eyes and stopped talking for a few moments to make his point very clear before continuing. "I don't like you, Khun Felonius, but you already know that. But I worry about you and don't want to see anything happen to you. It's bad for the Bahthaus. So I tell you this. People in this building think you do very bad job as our manager and they think if you had been doing your job correctly Ted Buffalo would be alive today."

Khun Felonius's face turned white as the full impact of what Fast Eddy had been telling him registered.

"How do you mean it's my fault?"

"We have our night time security guard sleeping when he's supposed to be doing his job. No one's trained our security guards to do their jobs. They let people do anything they want around here. I think everyone believes they can do anything in this building. If they thought we had good security and our guards were doing their jobs, they might not be willing to do everything they do around here. Neon would have been too scared to even think about having Ted Buffalo thrown off his balcony. It was your job to train our security to do their jobs correctly and to insist they do their jobs correctly. So some of our owners think you helped kill Ted Buffalo."

"I think I do good job," Khun Felonius replied.

"It doesn't matter what you think," Fast Eddy replied angrily. "What matters is what the condo owners think. And they think you helped kill Ted Buffalo. I am telling you this because I don't want to see you having an accident and winding up dead."

"I don't think anyone try to kill me."

"You don't know what kind of people live here. Some of them are wanted by the police back home and come to Thailand to escape. Some of them are mafia."

"I don't see problem."

"I do. Here's what I owe for my utility bill." Fast Eddy handed the manager the exact amount that was on the invoice the condo office had put under his door.

The manager pulled a receipt book from out of his desk, wrote Fast Eddy's name, the date and the amount he had paid in it and handed Fast Eddy a copy. He did not log into the Bahthaus accounting system, thus failing to make the necessary journal entries, because he didn't have the slightest idea how to make them. He had also forgotten the password. He'd just let the secretary handle the accounting in the morning.

Fast Eddy hesitated for a moment before walking out the door. Then he told the manager, "Listen to what I just told you." Then he walked out.

******

The next day the secretary found a note on her desk when she reported for work. It read, "I find it impossible to stay as manager of the condo so I quit, effective immediately–Khun Felonius."

All is well at the Bahthaus

Hermann the German sat alone in his condo reflecting on Khun Felonius's sudden departure as manager. The prospect of the Bahthaus condo community having to do without a manager until a new one could be hired was the best news he had received for a long time. Hermann smiled and promised himself, I will manage this place by myself until we find Cornhole's replacement. But that will take some time and I'm going to make sure it takes as long a period of time as I can drag it out under Thai law. He then considered the events that had occurred since he had built the Bahthaus. He thought about Ted Buffalo's getting murdered and whether he, Mickel and Fast Eddy had done the right thing or not. He decided, yes, killing Suvanaporn and his accomplices was completely justified. Not because they owed Ted Buffalo or that Ted Buffalo deserved to be avenged. It had to be done. Hermann was certain of it–not for Ted but for them. He was sure his two friends would agree with him—that not one of them could ever feel he was really a man-- so long as he felt the locals felt they had power of life and death over him. He poured himself a glass of German beer from one of the bottles he had bought from a German restaurant and said aloud, "All is well here at the Bahthaus. Its residents are safe now with me in charge and my committee. We will have no more unfortunate incidents and everyone will be safe and happy in paradise."

www.ingramcontent.com/pod-product-compliance
Lightning Source LLC
Chambersburg PA
CBHW050459260626
47157CB00004B/1109